FORBIDDEN PLEASURES

Monica Burns

Erotic Historical Romance

New Concepts   Georgia

Be sure to check out our website for the very best in fiction at fantastic prices!

When you visit our webpage, you can:
* Read excerpts of currently available books
* View cover art of upcoming books and current releases
* Find out more about the talented artists who capture the magic of the writer's imagination on the covers
* Order books from our backlist
* Find out the latest NCP and author news--including any upcoming book signings by your favorite NCP author
* Read author bios and reviews of our books
* Get NCP submission guidelines
* And so much more!

We offer a 20% discount on all new Trade Paperback releases ordered from our website!

Be sure to visit our webpage to find the best deals in e-books and paperbacks! To find out about our new releases as soon as they are available, please be sure to sign up for our newsletter (http://www.newconceptspublishing.com/newsletter.htm) or join our reader group (http://groups.yahoo.com/group/new_concepts_pub/join)!

The newsletter is available by double opt in only and our customer information is *never* shared!

Visit our webpage at:
www.newconceptspublishing.com

Forbidden Pleasures is an original publication of NCP. This work has never before appeared in book form. This work is a novel. Any similarity to actual persons or events is purely coincidental.

New Concepts Publishing, Inc.
5202 Humphreys Rd.
Lake Park, GA 31636

ISBN 1-58608-734-7
2005 © Monica Burns
Cover art (c) copyright 2006 Eliza Black

NCP books are available at special quantity discounts for bulk purchases for sales promotions, premiums, fund raising, or educational use. For details, write, email, or phone New Concepts Publishing, Inc., 5202 Humphreys Rd., Lake Park, GA 31636; Ph. 229-257-0367, Fax 229-219-1097; orders@newconceptspublishing.com.

First NCP Trade Paperback Printing: February 2006

For Cathy Gosney, who at the age of 40 finally discovered what a romance book was. Thanks for being my first and biggest fan.

And with thanks to Charlotte Featherstone for pushing me to make Devlyn a true Alpha

Monica invites her readers to visit her website at www.monicaburns.com to vie for prizes, special events and upcoming releases

LOVE'S REVENGE

Chapter 1

"Fischer!" Quentin Blackwell, Earl of Devlyn, hollered for his butler as he strode through the front door of his country home. Behind him trailed two enormous wolfhounds. As Devlyn halted in the foyer, he peeled off his riding gloves and slammed his crop down on the long table braced against the wall.

The mirror overhanging the furniture flashed his reflection at him, and he grimaced at his appearance. He was a mess. The sleeve of his jacket was ripped at the shoulder and a smudge of dirt streaked its way across his browned cheek, emphasizing the scar that ran from his ear almost to his mouth. Shoving a hand through his tousled black hair, he turned and headed toward his study.

With each stride he took, his fury grew. If it were the last thing he did, he'd make Spencer Hamilton rue the day he'd picked a fight with the Devil of Devlyn's Keep. The insolent pup.

"Fischer," he roared. "Where the devil are *you*?"

The door to the study slammed backward against the wall as he stormed into the room. A moment later he was splashing a stiff shot of whiskey into a glass. Tossing the liquor down his throat, he relished the burning sensation. Where the hell did the boy get the idea that his sister was the injured party in their brief affair almost five years ago?

No doubt, Eleanor was responsible for the boy's misconceived notions as to his sister's innocence. The idea infuriated him. A sudden snap rent the air as the glass he held shattered under the weight of his grip.

"God damn it!" He grimaced as shards of glass bit into his hand. "Fischer! Get the hell in here!"

Whipping a handkerchief out of his pocket, he proceeded to clean the small cuts lacerating his palm. Behind him, he heard footsteps hurrying into the study.

"I'm sorry, my lord. There was a minor catastrophe in the kitchen and Cook required my assistance." The sparse looking man eyed Delyn's appearance with an arched eyebrow. "Another brawl, my lord?"

Devlyn glared at his butler, manservant and all around man of affairs. When one's finances were in such a miserable state as his, he was fortunate to have a loyal retainer like Fischer. But the man had the ability to make him feel like a chastened schoolboy at times. And today wasn't a good day for being chastened.

"I never brawl, Fischer."

He clenched his teeth at the skeptical look the man gave him. At least not anymore he didn't. Granted, the man had dressed his wounds from more than one brawl in the past. The last time had been when a sailor had sliced his cheek open two years ago. It had taught him to curb his temper and walk away from a fight. Now as Fischer studied him with an air of disappointment, he grimaced.

"If you must know, the baron's youngest offspring discovered I'd returned and tried to avenge his sister's supposed honor."

"I see."

"Damn it, Fischer. Even you think me guilty."

"Not at all, my lord. I know you too well to imagine you capable of betraying Miss Hamilton."

Devlyn turned away abruptly at the statement. No, he would never have betrayed Eleanor. He'd been in love with her. The day she'd broken his heart, he'd set out to earn himself the title, Devil of Devlyn's Keep. He'd explored every debauched sin and deed in the past five years with the sole purpose of obliterating her from his mind.

Until today, he'd been successful in doing so. Then Hamilton had accosted him at the pond this morning, ripping open the wound he'd thought scarred over completely. But it wasn't the wound he'd expected. For the first time today, he realized he didn't love Eleanor. Probably never had. No, what scarred him was the injustice of it all.

Shrugging out of his torn jacket, he tossed it to Fischer. "See that it's mended. I don't know when I'll have funds to purchase a new riding coat."

The humiliating statement made him twist his lips in a bitter grimace. Eleanor Hamilton had done her work well the day she'd betrayed him. Running to her father, Eleanor had convinced Baron Townsend to avenge her so-called honor. The man had made it his business to destroy what little of the Devlyn fortune still existed. The bastard had almost succeeded. If it hadn't been for his attorney's quick thinking to shift his investments, he'd be destitute.

As it was, he retained his townhouse in Mayfair, Devlyn's Keep here in Shellingham and a few small investments that provided him with enough to live on if he was frugal with his spending. At least until his American investments came to fruition, which he expected sometime in the very near future.

"Perhaps you might forgo my salary this month, my lord. I think it might afford you at least a new coat. This one is rather worn. I'm surprised the sleeve hasn't ripped before now."

The man's generous offer made Devlyn tighten his jaw. He often forgot how much Fischer truly was a part of his family. He was the last living Devlyn, and Fischer had been with him throughout his younger years. Forcing a smile to his mouth, he shook his head.

"I'm not that destitute, Fischer. You'll have your salary as always, and you can't say you don't earn every farthing."

"No, my lord. Indeed I can't." Folding the coat over his arm, the manservant nodded toward Devlyn's hand. "Shall I send Cook in to look at that hand?"

"No, I'll be all right. That will be all, Fischer."

"My lord." The manservant bowed and left Devlyn alone with his thoughts.

Eleanor. He wanted to wring the bitch's neck, slowly squeeze the life out of that dainty, golden-haired body of hers. No, that would be too easy a punishment for her. No. He wanted to humiliate her. Make her pay for the lies she'd told and the humiliation he'd suffered. And he wanted to make Townsend pay for trying to strip him of his fortune.

He'd been the innocent and gullible fool throughout the entire thing. Eleanor had simply used him to avoid the scandal her pregnancy would have wrought. When she'd declared him the father of her child little more than a month after he first bedded her, he should have known something was amiss.

Unwrapping his cut, he stared down at the miniature lacerations already puffy and red. He reached for the brandy and poured a small amount of the liquor over his palm. He grimaced. The stinging reminded him of Eleanor's betrayal. He'd been oblivious to every one of her faults.

Instead, he'd allowed love to let him believe her lies. He'd even come close to marrying the woman. Never again would he allow his heart to blind him in such a way. No doubt, she would have continued her whoring after they were married. But fortunately, he'd caught the bitch and her lover rutting like common beasts in one of the Townsend's horse stalls.

It had hardly been surprising to see Eleanor turn into a raving witch when he'd broken their engagement. Then when Townsend had confronted him over the matter, things had only gotten worse. Eleanor claimed the child was his and Townsend hadn't needed anything else to propel him into action.

In less than a week, the bastard had put him on the edge of financial ruin, while Eleanor had married some unsuspecting member of the peerage a few weeks later. Thoroughly disgusted, he'd traveled to America to rebuild his fortune. While there, he'd taken it upon himself to explore every debauchery he could find. In doing so, he'd achieved a modicum of success, not only in his sinful endeavors, but in his financial situation as well. Still it would take several more weeks before his ventures turned profitable.

He wrapped his cuts with the clean side of his handkerchief and moved to stand behind his desk. With his uninjured hand, he sifted through a thin pile of invitations. Word had already spread throughout the county that a Devlyn was once again entrenched in the keep. He smiled cynically. It seemed his neighbors were more than ready to overlook his past transgressions. Well, to hell with them. To hell with every one of them.

"My lord." Fischer's voice ended on a high-pitched note pulling Devlyn's gaze up with a jerk. Whatever had gotten his manservant into a state of apoplexy had to be important.

"What is it, Fischer?"

"It's a lady, my lord."

"A lady?"

"Yes, my lord. But ... well, I'm afraid...."

"Out with it, man!"

"It's Miss Hamilton."

His body snapped to attention, his limbs rigid with tension. Eleanor. No. She was married now. She wouldn't use her maiden name. Her sister most likely, hoping for a verbal duel with him as opposed to the physical one he'd endured with the youngest Hamilton. Her visit would no doubt be quite interesting. "Send her in, Fischer. Send her in."

"Very well, my lord."

A moment later, he watched a tall, lushly figured woman enter the study. Caesar and Beast immediately stood and approached the woman. Despite their size and fierce appearance, the wolfhounds were gentle creatures, but his visitor couldn't have known that. He waited for her to draw back in fear. Instead, she scratched Beast under the chin and tugged on Caesar's ear before straightening.

Dressed in a royal blue riding habit trimmed in black, there was a mysterious quality about her. Black netting covered her face and he couldn't distinguish her features. The woman made a slight curtsey then inhaled a deep breath. Behind her, Fischer closed the door to the study. She jumped at the quiet sound of the latch falling closed.

"Lord Devlyn. I hope you'll forgive my intrusion. I'm sure it's unexpected." The husky sound of her voice tickled his spine. It intrigued him.

He gestured toward the chairs in front of his desk and waited as she sat. There was a fluid grace to the way she moved. It reminded him of a sleek cat. The dogs trailed after her, and he scowled at the traitors before ordering them to return to their usual resting place. Sitting down, he leaned back in his chair and threw his feet up onto the desk. It was a rude gesture and he knew it. Her body stiffened in response, and he smiled with just a touch of derision. Had she really expected him to be a gentleman? He'd dispensed with gentlemanly behavior a long time ago. The Devil of Devlyn's Keep answered to no one and did as he pleased.

"So tell me, Miss Hamilton, to what do I owe this honor?"

"I ... I came here with a ... a proposition for you, my lord."

"A proposition." He arched an eyebrow at her. The woman had definitely piqued his interest. "Do go on."

"I'm here to offer you revenge."

The words made his limbs tighten with tension. What exactly was this hussy up to with her offer of revenge? Revenge for what? Despite her efforts to hide her trepidation, he saw her hands tremble, and the netting over her face quivered from her rapid breaths.

From the tremor that shook her, he knew his insouciant reaction intimidated her. He smiled slowly, the slight curl of his lip tilting upward on one side. Although he couldn't see his own features, he knew his smile emphasized the scar on his face. Women had told him it gave him a dangerous look.

"What an intriguing concept. Revenge on whom?"

"My sister, Eleanor."

He'd expected the words, but they surprised him nonetheless. So this was the mysterious Sophia Hamilton, Townsend's eldest brat. He'd never met Eleanor's only sister. She'd been away in Scotland while he was courting Eleanor.

"You're willing to betray your only sister?"

"Yes."

"Why?"

A shudder shook her body as he watched the netting covering her face stir with her accelerated breathing. The sight fascinated him for some reason. It reminded him of how fast a woman breathed when she was on the threshold of a climax during lovemaking.

"Because what my father and sister did to you was wrong. Eleanor ... Eleanor has always been spoiled. She's only ever cared for herself, and my father has simply catered to her every whim."

"This is all quite fascinating, but you'll forgive me for being just a tad skeptical as to your offer."

"Of course, I understand. But I assure you, my lord, I'm most serious about this. I have information that will allow you to recoup what my father stole from you, and at the same time, you'll have the opportunity to confront Eleanor with her lies and deceit."

"You've still not really answered the question of why. Why are you willing to betray your father and sister?"

Confusion and trepidation radiated out from her. She sprang to her feet, twisting her hands around the riding crop she carried. "I'm sorry. I shouldn't have come. Please ... please forgive my intrusion."

Not about to let her leave without learning more, he scrambled to his feet and pursued her to the door. Her hand was on the knob when he braced his palm against the wooden barrier, preventing her escape. She immediately took a step back and he followed. Her height amazed him. If he lifted her veil, she'd be almost eye to eye with him. And something made his hand itch to remove that netting, but he refrained for the moment. Instead, he trailed his forefinger along the edge of her jaw, the coarse netting hiding the softness he was certain lay beneath the veil. It aroused him.

"Surely you don't think I'm going to let you leave without discovering why you're willing to betray your family."

"Please, my lord. It was a mistake to come here."

"Perhaps, but nonetheless, I'll have an answer from you."

"Or what?" The sudden challenge in her voice amused him. At least she had backbone.

"Hmm, what could I do to persuade you to answer?" His fingers touched the snowy cravat tied around her neck. With a lazy movement, he gently tugged at one of the ties. Her cravat tumbled open to expose her creamy throat. God, she was a tempting wench. She gasped as he pressed his thumb against the hollow of her throat. Again, the netting fluttered wildly against her face.

"My lord, please."

"Please is a subjective word, Miss Hamilton. Are you asking me to do something wicked? Or are you begging to tell me your reasons for this interesting proposition of yours?"

"I ... I wish to ... oh bloody hell!"

Her abrupt response was so completely unexpected he jerked back in surprise. She began to pace the floor in front of him, and his eyes narrowed as he watched her prowling. Again she reminded him of a cat. After a moment of tense silence, she stopped and whirled to face him.

"My lord, I came here to offer you revenge on Eleanor and my father because I want revenge too. You weren't the only one they betrayed. They betrayed me as well."

"I see." He folded his arms across his chest and waited.

"When Eleanor became pregnant with her lover's child, she needed a husband. You suited her purpose, but when you refused to marry her, Father helped her steal my fiancée instead."

"You were engaged to that weakling, Shively?"

"Yes. He was ... he was my last hope."

"Last hope?"

"Yes. I'd already given up hope of ever marrying until I met Andrew. I was never the pretty one in the family."

He watched her take a deep breath as she slowly reached up toward the netting covering her face. As she revealed her features, he eyed her with curiosity. For someone who believed herself unattractive, she was quite the opposite.

Although she wasn't a beauty by any stretch of the imagination, her hazel eyes were large and echoed with warmth, while her complexion was smooth and creamy. Wisps of brown hair framed her heart-shaped face and her full mouth pouted in a manner that brought his cock to attention. The reaction startled him. Clearing his throat, he turned away from her.

"I think you underestimate yourself, Miss Hamilton. I'm sure there are plenty of men willing to offer for you."

"No, my lord you're wrong. Offers of marriage have been nonexistent for many years."

"Come now, I think you exaggerate."

"Do I?" With his back to her, he could almost see the small shrug of her rounded shoulders. "Perhaps. Well, my lord, you've received the answer to your question. Now if you don't mind, I should like to leave."

He didn't want her to leave. She intrigued him and something about her made him feel protective of her. Eleanor had hurt her too. He understood that pain.

"Before you go, why don't you tell me what you'd hoped to receive in exchange for this method of revenge you offer me?"

"Marriage."

Stunned, he spun around to stare at her. "Marriage? To me?"

"Yes."

"Good God, woman. Whatever made you think I'd make a suitable husband?"

"I didn't. In fact, I knew you would be far from the ideal husband."

"Then why settle for me? I'm sure there are any number of men willing to marry you."

She heaved a sigh of annoyance. "I'd heard you were intelligent, my lord; however, I'm beginning to have my doubts. I'm Eleanor's older sister. What man would want to marry me?"

"I can only guess at your age, but since Eleanor is younger than I am, I'd say you're about my age."

Her pink mouth formed a moue of astonishment before she burst out into laughter. It was a pleasant sound. "Oh my word. I must admit to being extremely flattered. But you see, my lord. I'm much older than your tender years."

Irritated by her amusement, he frowned. "I'd hardly refer to the age of thirty-two as my tender years."

"It's quite tender when I consider my own age of forty-one."

The comment made his jaw sag. How was it possible that this attractive woman could possibly be so much older than him? She hardly looked old enough to be his age, let alone having almost ten years on him. Impossible.

"You jest."

"No, my lord. Sadly enough I'm an old maid. Any hope of marrying vanished five years ago when Eleanor ran off with my intended."

"And yet you still want to marry?"

"Yes. I want to experience what it's like between a man and a woman." She blushed and it made her look like a fresh debutante. "I could pay for the experience I suppose, but I'm not quite that bold. Coming here was the boldest thing I've ever done."

The idea of teaching this woman about the pleasures of the body captured his imagination. An older woman who'd not yet been initiated into the art or power of lovemaking. An intriguing possibility. His cock stirred again. He stepped toward her and traced the curve of her mouth with his forefinger before his thumb pressed down on her lower lip. It was plump and tender.

He heard the sharp intake of her breath. It excited him. When was the last time he'd had the pleasure of initiating a novice? Years. The scent of lilacs drifted up into his nose as he lowered his head toward her.

"And you're willing to put yourself completely into my hands?"

"Ye-yes."

"Are you certain of that? I've not earned my title without a great deal of wickedness."

"Your sexual prowess has always been widely touted in social circles. I doubt you've acquired more deviant practices while in the colonies." The pulse at the side of her neck fluttered beneath her skin. He excited her. A smile tilted his mouth and he leaned forward until his lips were just a hairsbreadth away from her shell-shaped ear.

"I believe you'll find the social circles are only half accurate. I'm far more decadent than any rumors you may have heard."

"Oh," she breathed.

"So shall we strike a bargain then? My name and experience for the means to avenge myself."

Speechless she barely nodded. What the hell was he doing? A wife? He studied the woman in front of him closely. Perhaps it was time to try for an heir, and he could do much worse that this delectable creature. And if the woman didn't give him a child, then his cousin's brat could inherit for all he cared.

Another smile tugged at the corner of his mouth as he watched excitement and trepidation flash across her features. Her heart had to be pounding in her breast. He glanced down at the snug fit of her royal blue habit. And they were firm, plump looking breasts too. It was difficult to believe she was so much older than him. The anticipation of the decadent pleasures he wanted to introduce her to as his wife made him grow hard as a rock. His lips curled into a deeper smile as he pinned her with his gaze.

"Then we're agreed. Revenge and nights of pleasure. A decidedly decadent proposition."

Chapter 2

Sophie stared into the features of the man who'd just agreed to marry her. She was mad. Stark raving mad. Her tongue darted out to lick her dry lips, and Devlyn growled low in his throat. It was a predatory sound. She wasn't surprised at all when excitement skimmed its way through her blood.

She took a quick step back. Not because he intimidated her of course, but because.... Heavens! Of course the man intimidated her, not to mention disturbed her. Something about this man said his kisses would be potent and heady. Completely unlike the brief caresses she'd received in the past.

Devlyn's mouth tilted upward on one side in that dangerous smile of his. It emphasized his scar, making him every inch the wicked rogue people claimed he was. It also made him look quite capable of breaking her heart if she allowed him to do so. But she would ensure that wouldn't happen. This was strictly a means to escape her father's tyranny and experience the pleasures a man of Devlyn's reputation could offer her.

"Are you having second thoughts, my lady?"

"Most certainly not." She straightened her spine and tilted her head at a proud angle.

"You don't appear all that certain."

"And exactly how do I look?"

"Like you're afraid I'm going to take a bite out of you."

"You exaggerate, my lord."

The swiftness of his movement caught her by surprise as he reached out and pulled her against him. The scent of sandalwood teased her senses as her face came within inches of his. Even through her gown, she could feel the heat of him warming her body. What would his bare skin feel like against hers? His finger traced her lips, and she trembled at the intimate touch. Was he going to kiss her? The green eyes staring into hers took on a lazy gleam as he studied her.

"Exaggeration is for the timid, my dear Sophie, and I'm *far* from timid. But be assured of one thing. When I take a bite out of you, and I will." His lips brushed over hers in a feathery caress. "I promise you'll never forget my doing so."

Good Lord, if she didn't take care, this man would rule her heart with just the sound of his voice. She had to do something to restore the balance of power between them.

"And I'm sure you'll never forget my letting you, my lord."

"Touché. It seems you're as eager as I am. I suggest we dispense with the formalities of an engagement and marry three days from now."

"Three days! I don't think--"

"I have a feeling you think far too much. But I have just the thing to keep you from thinking."

His features blurred as he captured her mouth. The touch of his lips against hers was warm and sultry. No one had ever kissed her like this before. The heat of it spread its way into her body, igniting a fire inside her belly she didn't know how to quench. Weak at the knees, she fought to keep her senses from reeling.

Without thinking, she kissed him back. His tongue swept into her mouth, and she moaned with delight. Heat raced through her body, and she wanted to sink into him, melt into him until he did whatever he wanted with her.

This was something she hadn't anticipated. She'd never expected to feel so wanton, so eager for him to take her to his bed. Sweet Lord, this was beyond her wildest dreams. Restraint. She needed to come to her senses. Desperate to regain control of the situation, she turned her head away from him to break the kiss.

Immediately, he released her. Devoid of his heat, a chill swept over her. She didn't like the cold sensation. She wanted the warmth his touch gave her. He'd released her so abruptly. Still shocked by the wanton feelings he'd aroused in her, she kept her eyes averted.

Had he simply been playing with her, toying with her? She'd responded to his touch like a woman starved for love and affection. Well, she might crave love in her life, but pity was the last thing she wanted from anyone, least of all this man. She might be an old maid, but she still had her pride.

"My lord, I'm ... perhaps this is a mistake."

"No, Sophie, it's not a mistake to feel desire."

"I don't know what you're talking about."

"I think you do."

God in heaven, this man made her feel like an innocent, despite the fact that she was so much older. How could she marry a man so much younger than herself? Not only was it unheard of; it just wasn't done. She winced and forced herself to look at him. She expected amusement, but the assessment and curiosity brightening his green eyes surprised her.

"My lord, I made a terrible mistake in coming here today. I don't think I can do this."

"I see."

"I am sorry, but it's just that ... that I'm ... well I'm much too old for you. I'm certain you'll need an heir, and the possibility of me bearing children is questionable. Then of course, there's the age issue. I don't see, even if I could give you an heir, how I'd be a suitable mother. I'm sure you've plenty of younger women from whom you can select a bride. I just don't think this—"

"*Enough.*" The harshness of his voice scraped a chill down her spine. She would not want to cross this man. She didn't move or speak as he folded his arms and glared at her. "I can't abide prattling in anyone, least of all a woman."

"I was not prattling." He arched a stern eyebrow at her. She went silent.

"You have something I want, Sophie. You offered it in exchange for my name. I agreed to the arrangement. You might be having second thoughts, but I don't intend to let you or my chance for vengeance slip away."

"But you don't understand—"

"I understand perfectly. I excite you, and that frightens you."

"Now you're being arrogant."

"Simply because I'm younger than you, it doesn't make me a fool. You might be older, but I have experience beyond your tender education. Experience you covet."

She flinched at his confident tone. He was right. She was a frightened spinster who was terrified of what this devastating rogue might do to her heart. His reputation for breaking hearts was well known to her, and she had no desire to relive the pain she'd experienced when her sister had stolen Andrew from her.

More than that, she hated to admit he was right. She'd offered him something in exchange for his name. He'd agreed, and honor dictated she not renege on the offer. The calculating gleam in his green eyes was intimidating. It made her wonder if he could read her thoughts.

Well, she refused to let him intimidate her. All her life, she'd allowed her father to bully her. She refused to give her husband-to-be the same power. When she married, she would lead her own life and Devlyn would lead his. That's how all her friends' marriages worked. It would be no different for her. After all, wasn't she simply buying a husband with her offer of revenge? Determined to regain her footing on the slippery slope she was climbing, she sent him a forthright look.

"You're correct, my lord. I proposed a bargain to you, you accepted. It would be dishonorable of me to back out of the agreement."

"Then it's settled. Now then, I want to know what you're going to tell your father."

"My father?" She flinched. She didn't want to think about her father. Lord she'd been a fool to start down this disastrous path.

"Surely you didn't think he would just let you waltz down the aisle with me."

"No, but in all honesty, I didn't expect you to agree to my proposition." For the first time, she realized it was true, she really hadn't expected him to say yes to her proposal. A small smile twisted the corner of his mouth.

"Well, now that I've agreed, we need a plan."

"A plan?"

"Yes, a plan. Tomorrow, I'll procure a special license and we'll marry in three days. I believe my vicar is still in residence at the Devlyn parish. He can perform the ceremony. With regard to your father and sister, I believe surprise is the best tack to take."

"But--"

"Are you familiar with the trail that winds through the glen toward the old woodcutter's cottage?"

"Yes."

"Meet me there tomorrow at noon. I'll bring a lunch basket."

"I'm sorry, my lord, but I don't understand."

"How long have you known me, Sophie?"

The question stunned her. How long had she known him? Less than an hour if the mantel clock was accurate. "Not long, my lord."

"Precisely. The gossips will wag their tongues at our alliance, but if we spend time together before our marriage, we can honestly say we courted in secret. It will protect your reputation to some degree."

He was worried about her reputation? It was an honorable gesture, and it warmed her heart. She'd learned a long time ago not to believe anything her father or Eleanor said, but her friends had hardly been complimentary about this man, either. Her face must have signaled what she was thinking as his mouth twisted into a derisive smile.

"My reputation for debauchery doesn't mean I have no honor."

There was just a tinge of bitterness in his voice. It was deeply buried, but she sensed the pain and resentment. She shook her head.

"I try never to listen to gossip. Invariably, it proves false in the end."

"So, I'm to marry an innocent philosopher who craves excitement." The gentle teasing made her cheeks hot. She bowed her head, but a firm hand cupped her chin, forcing her to meet his gaze. "Remember, Sophie, desire is not shameful, but lying to one's self is."

"And you call me a philosopher?"

He laughed. It lightened his dark features and made him look like a youth far younger than his thirty-two years. "Just remember that I also hold the title of rake as well."

The wicked glint of humor in his eyes made her want to laugh, but she offered him a smile instead. She would need to guard her heart well. Despite what she'd heard about this man, he was far more enigmatic than she'd ever expected. Marriage to him might be more exciting than she'd ever dreamed possible.

* * * *

Sophie quietly entered the back door of Townsend Hall and hurried up the back stairs. Inside her room, she breathed a sigh of relief. Deceiving her father wasn't going to be an easy task. She'd never been very good at lying.

It didn't matter. She had to do this. She needed to escape this stifling environment, and if it meant righting the wrong Eleanor and Father had perpetrated against Devlyn, then all the better. No one deserved having their life and fortune destroyed on the whim of a spoilt woman.

And she wanted them to acknowledge her pain as well. But more than that, she wanted freedom--freedom to enjoy life and not rot away working as her father's bookkeeper. With a sigh, she quickly shed her riding habit.

As she tossed the garment on the four-poster bed, she caught a glimpse of herself in the full-length mirror. She paused and faced her reflection. The woman staring back at her didn't look forty-one. In fact, she looked much younger.

With an astute and critical eye, she scanned the mirror's offering. Brown hair that had a tendency to curl when wet. No facial wrinkles, a smooth complexion, firm breasts--even if they were a bit too large. Hips a bit too wide, but not overly so. Through her sheer chemise, she could see legs that were full and plump. She might have the body of a young woman of marriageable age, but it didn't help her forget her age.

With a final glare at her reflection, she turned away and retrieved a day dress from her wardrobe. The serviceable poplin reminded her of the tasks she still had to accomplish today. Father would be far from pleased. She would just have to beg his forgiveness. Although that was something he rarely gave her.

The grandfather clock in the main hall chimed its onerous announcement of the hour, and she darted from her room to race downstairs for lunch. As she reached the foot of the stairs, her brother Spencer strode out of the library. He was young and impetuous, but had a giving heart. The bond between them was not only strong, but quite special despite their twenty-year age difference.

As she caught a glimpse of his face, she gasped in horror at the black eye he sported, and the abrasions on his cheek. "Dear heaven, Spencer, what happened to you?"

"Now don't you start in on me too, Phe." Her brother sighed as he used the nickname he'd had for her since his childhood. "It's not as bad as it looks."

Stepping up to him, her fingers gently turned his face toward the light. "Have you had Mrs. Hobarth look at this?"

"Yes, it's just a few bumps and bruises. Nothing more."

"Has Father seen you?"

"Yes, and believe it or not, he actually said he was proud of me."

"Proud of you for brawling." She spat out her disgust. "Who did you fight, some mortal enemy of the Townsend clan?"

"Actually, yes. I found out Devlyn was back in residence at the keep. I sought him out this morning at the pond."

Dear Lord, it was a wonder the man had even received her this morning after what Spencer had done. No doubt, Eleanor had filled their only brother's head with falsehoods and pleas for justice. She needed to clarify things with him at the appropriate time. She wasn't about to have him and Devlyn employing their fists on a regular basis.

"Well, your eye looks like it's going to shine for at least a week, maybe more."

"I don't mind, Phe." He leaned toward her with a conspiratorial smile. "Don't tell Father, but the man was quite an excellent pugilist. He beat me fair and square."

"But a brawl, Spencer." She shook her head with reluctant amusement. Unwilling to chastise him any further, she entwined her arm with his and pulled him toward the dining room. "Promise me you'll not harass the earl anymore. I don't want to see you hurt."

"If it makes you feel better, I promise. But you need to stop mothering me. I'm quite capable of handling myself."

"I'm sure you are, but--"

"Damnation, woman, let the boy alone and let him get in here to eat." The bellow that echoed out of the dining room shattered the lighthearted atmosphere, and Sophie immediately pulled away from her brother.

As she took a seat opposite Spencer at the table, she clenched her teeth at the way her father ignored her. Well into his sixties, Lord Townsend looked every inch the merchant baron. He'd once been a handsome man, but now his paunch had spread from his stomach to his chin. The once lively eyes had become almost lost in layers of fat, and the thinning hair on his head showed several bald spots. His dissipation had finally caught up with him.

"Well, boy, it looks like I'll see you a man yet. Damn proud of you, I am, for defending your sister's honor against that wretch Devlyn."

Sophie ignored the blatant lie, as she unfurled her napkin and placed it in her lap. A platter of cold beef sat in front of her place setting, and she took a small helping before passing the platter to her father. He took the serving dish from her hands without a word of acknowledgement.

Across from her, Spencer frowned, and she gave him an imperceptible shake of her head. It was of little use trying to get Father to notice her. He'd never had time for her, and he had even less tolerance now for a spinster daughter. The only time she could expect his complete attention was when she was reviewing his ledger with him.

She ate her meal in silence, barely listening to the sound of her father's voice as he droned on about Devlyn's poor character. His hatred only seemed magnified, now that Devlyn was once more in residence at the keep. Heaven knew what he'd do if he discovered her plans to marry his enemy.

It had been a foolish thing to go see Devlyn this morning. She couldn't remember the last time she'd done something so imprudent or spontaneous. But he'd agreed to her proposition. She would be married and out of this godforsaken house in three days time. All in exchange for betraying her father. Was she really capable of doing this? It was so beastly. Could she really give Devlyn the information he needed to avenge himself? She had no choice now. She'd agreed.

"Damn it, woman, I asked you a question." Sophie jumped as her father's hand smacked the table and she jerked her gaze in his direction. "I asked you what took you so long this morning."

"So long?"

"You were gone riding for more than two hours."

"Oh ... I ... the morning was so beautiful, I lost track of time." She couldn't remember the last time her father had ever commented on the amount of time she spent riding. Dear God, was he watching her? Did he know where she'd been? The food she had just eaten threatened to rise in her throat.

"Well, I expected you to go over the accounts with me before lunch, now we'll have to do it before dinner. I have an appointment with the widow Waltham."

"Yes, Father." She ducked her head at the mention of Mrs. Waltham. The widow wasn't much older than she was. It pained her to think another woman almost the same age as her could have buried a husband and yet still receive suitors. Perhaps she should have accepted one of the offers of marriage she'd received her first Season.

But she hadn't. She'd been an ignorant fool hoping for a love match. Men didn't want love in their lives. It complicated things. She'd held out for a marriage of love, only to become a spinster in charge of her father's financial affairs.

The baron roughly shoved himself away from the table. "Damn it, Sophie. What's the matter with you today? I asked if you've finished tabulating those numbers off the Indian Princess' cargo."

She flinched. "I'm sorry, Father. Yes, they're completed. I'll show them to you later this afternoon."

The sight of his angry glare made her bite her lip nervously. He appeared ready to chastise her further, but instead he snorted with disgust and strode from the room. His departure made her release a breath of relief. Across from her, Spencer threw his napkin onto the table.

"The bastard," he cursed softly.

"It's all right, Spencer."

"No it's not, Phe. You don't deserve to be treated in such a way. You do everything he asks, and yet he doesn't even bother to acknowledge your presence."

"Father does as he sees fit. Neither one of us can change him."

"You're too kindhearted, Phe."

She stiffened at the statement. Her brother would soon be proven wrong. Giving Devlyn the means to destroy Father's financial affairs was far from a kindhearted act. But she was doing the right thing. She was restoring what had been stolen from Devlyn. It was the right thing to do, wasn't it? Confused, she rose from the table.

"Father's right, Phe. Something's wrong; you've hardly touched your meal."

Aware of her brother's ability to ferret information out of her, she forced a smile to her lips. "I'm fine. I'm just thinking about the Indian Princess. I can't believe I forgot to finish the figures."

"Finish the--but you told Father you'd finished them already."

She bit her lip. Blast! Oh what a tangled web she was weaving. She had finished the figures, and now she was lying to Spencer. Frowning, she shook her head.

"Did I, I suppose my dotage is showing." Spencer gave her an odd look, but didn't push the matter. Pasting another smile on her face, she circled the table and gave him a swift hug. "You worry too much, although I adore you for it."

Before he could say another word, she brushed his cheek with her lips and scurried from the dining room. She really would have to take care with her words. It would be bad enough to arouse Father's suspicions, but Spencer was far more observant where she was concerned. Moving swiftly down the hall, she entered her father's study. For the past fifteen years she'd been keeping track of her father's accounts. When his accountant had died unexpectedly, she'd offered to tally his accounts until he found someone to replace the man.

She could still remember his raucous laughter when he'd heard her offer and scoffed at her ability. Determined to prove him wrong, she'd crept down to his study in the middle of the night and straightened out the accounts. The following morning, she'd wearily shown her father what she'd done. At first, he'd been furious, but after reviewing the books, he'd even seemed pleased.

It had been one of the rare times in her life, when she'd earned his approval. From that point forward, she'd worked as her father's accountant. In the beginning, she'd thought it might bring them closer, but if anything, it set her apart from him. She was his employee, not his daughter. The pain never seemed to go away, and when her mother died giving birth to Spencer, she was assigned to his care as well. She still missed her mother, but even her mother's love had not made up for the lack of her father's affection.

Seating herself at the desk her father had told her to use so many years ago, she pulled out one of the books she kept stored on top of the desk. Flipping open the book, she ran her finger down one column. Her finger stopped on one entry. There it was; the first of so many entries that would help Devlyn regain his fortune.

Her father had never tried to hide his illicit business dealings from her. Perhaps he'd just assumed she'd never consider doing what she was about to do. Refusing to dwell on the subject, she retrieved the second set of books she'd been keeping for almost the past year.

She didn't remember ever coming to a sudden decision to track her father's illegal activities; she'd simply started doing so. If he knew about the second set of books and her offer to Devlyn, disowning her would be the gentlest of punishments he'd impart on her. It didn't matter. She'd been banished a long time ago from this family. If not in body, at least in spirit. She was through hiding her father's duplicitous ways. For once, she intended to see justice served while freeing herself of his tyranny.

Chapter 3

Devlyn stood on one edge of the glen, flanked by Caesar and Beast. The wolfhounds seemed to sense his irritation, and Beast used his large head to nudge at him. He absently patted the animal as his gaze scanned the tree line that separated his property from the Townsend land.

Since yesterday morning, a pair of hazel eyes and a heart-shaped face had persistently filled his thoughts. Sophie was by far the most intriguing woman he'd ever met. Soft one moment, feisty the next, she was an enigma, and he'd not been presented with a challenge like her in quite some time. He wasn't sure what to make of her. For all he knew she might have been sent by Lord Townsend in an attempt to wreak more havoc. It would be just like the bastard to use his daughter like that.

But he didn't think Townsend had sent her. Something about her convinced him she really was everything she said she was. It was refreshing actually. During his stay in New York, and in the few months he'd spent in London before returning to the keep, women had filled his nights. None of them, however, had fascinated him quite like Sophie did.

Their kiss yesterday had surprised him. It had made him want to carry her to his bed and keep her there until he spent himself of the desire she'd aroused him. His cock stirred to life in his trousers.

"God damn it. I had more control the first time I bedded a woman." Disgusted by his inability to control his body when it came to his thoughts about her, he frowned. He might have agreed to marry her, but that didn't mean he had to act like a hot-blooded youth anxious for his first lay.

He pulled his watch out of his pocket to check the time. Twelve-fifteen. She was late. No doubt, she'd had second thoughts and decided not to come. To hell with her. He turned around to survey the blanket and lunch he'd spread out on the glen's green carpet.

Once again played for a fool by a Townsend brat. He'd thought Sophie was different. What the hell did it matter? She was a spinster, hardly worth his time. Striding forward, he knelt to clear the lunch away. As he did so, he heard the sound of horse hooves cantering toward him. He turned his head, and a surge of relief lashed through him at the sight of Sophie riding in his direction.

He brushed aside the feeling. It was simply because he wanted to exact his revenge that he'd been worried. Nothing more. Standing up, he waited for her to come to a halt in front of him. She looked lovelier than yesterday with her flushed cheeks and sparkling eyes. His hand grasped the bridle of her mare, and he arched his eyebrow.

"Are you always so punctual, Miss Hamilton?"

The crimson in her cheeks darkened, but she held her head high. "I apologize, my lord. I had to take care leaving the house."

Irritation flashed in her eyes, and his mouth twisted with amusement. He'd not been mistaken. She might appear demure and reticent, but underneath that cool exterior was a fiery minx. Yes, he was going to enjoy taming Sophie Hamilton very much. He extended his free hand to her.

"Come, lunch is ready."

Although she hesitated, she released the reins and accepted his hand. With a lithe movement, she hopped off the horse to stand close to him. She radiated warmth, her sensuous curves making his fingers tingle with a need to explore every inch of her body. He knew immediately when she tensed. Already he was in the habit of noticing the way she bit her lip when she was nervous.

As he led her horse to a nearby shrub to tie the animal to a branch, he observed her bending over his dogs. She'd conquered them already. Beast was already on his back begging her to scratch his belly, while Caesar was trying to lick her face. Something about the scene pleased him.

"Beast. Caesar. Enough."

She smiled at him. "They're quite playful. Which one is which?"

"Beast is the gray one, Caesar is the sandy-colored one."

She gave both animals one last caress then turned and followed him to the picnic blanket. She waited just on the edge of the spread, her fingers clenching the riding gloves she'd removed. Not waiting on her, he sank down onto his knees and sat back on his heels, watching her quietly. She frowned and sat across from him on the checkered coverlet.

"Your manners are appalling, my lord."

"Are they? I hadn't noticed." He suppressed a grin at the way her mouth tightened with irritation. "Now then, what can I offer you? Cook prepared a cold chicken, a selection of cheeses, fresh vegetables, bread and apples for desert."

"Whatever you're having will be fine, my lord."

"What if said I intended to have you for lunch?"

She flushed, but didn't hesitate with her reply. "Then I fear you're apt to suffer from indigestion, my lord."

"Oh, I doubt that. In fact, I'm certain I'll find you a tasty morsel."

"I thought we were here to get to know each other. A speedy courtship as it were."

"You disapprove of my courtship? Would you prefer I anticipate the marriage bed?"

For a moment, she stared at him aghast. Then to his surprise, she laughed. It was a robust and musical sound, quite pleasant to his ears. She shook her head and smiled at him.

"You are a rogue. I think you're deliberately trying to shock me."

"I simply speak my mind. The thought of bedding you is one I've contemplated quite a bit since our kiss yesterday."

Although he was preoccupied with preparing a plate for her, he heard the telltale hiss of her sucking in a sharp breath. He bit back a smile. It seemed their kiss had caused her some contemplation as well. Today, he had every intention of giving her even more to think about. He handed her a food-laden plate before stretching out his long legs to recline back on one elbow.

"Tell me, Sophie, what do you intend to do once we're married?"

He watched her forehead furrow slightly. "I haven't given it much thought actually. I suppose I'd like to go to London."

"And what would you do in that sprawling town?"

"Well, I enjoy the theater and the opera."

"Good God! Don't think I'll agree to escort you to the opera."

"I'm sorry. I didn't mean to imply I expected you to serve as my escort. I'm quite content to go on my own. In fact, I assumed we would lead separate lives for the most part."

His gaze met hers as he picked up a piece of cheese and slowly bit into it. She darted her gaze away and proceeded to eat her meal in silence. Curious, he watched her eat. The way her white teeth bit into a piece of cold chicken. The precise manner in which she broke her cheese in half before placing it between her full pink lips.

"So you thought we'd live apart. What if I prefer to keep my wife in bed?"

She arched her eyebrow at him. "I find it hard to believe you'll be that enamored with me, my lord."

"Enamored or not, you indicated you wanted my experience. Did you lie to me?"

"Of course not!" A blush crested her smooth cheeks. "I do want to know what it ... how to... Blast! You know what I'm trying to say. But, I don't expect it to last for very long at all."

"Interesting."

"What is?"

"Your logical, fatalistic approach to the subject of our matrimony. Your view of it is quite startling."

"I don't see what's so startling about it. After all, marriage mainly serves the purpose of allowing a man to line his pockets with money from the woman he marries and the pursuit of an heir. Nothing more, nothing less."

"And what of love, Sophie? Do you not long for love?" The words were out of his mouth before he realized what was happening. Bloody hell! What the devil possessed him to ask her such a ridiculous question? Of course she longed for love. What woman didn't? Love wasn't something he was capable of giving. To do so required him to trust, and that he would never do again.

Her eyes were wide as she looked at him. Frowning, he cursed himself again as she smiled with a touch of irony. "Love is for the young, my lord. Something I no longer am."

"You enjoy pointing out your age to me. I wonder why?"

"Not at all, I'm simply a realist. Love is for idealists, and I've learned practicality is a far better companion than wishful thinking."

"So what do you expect from our marriage, aside from living apart from your husband?"

"I'm not sure what you mean. If you're concerned that I'll make demands on your time, I can assure you I'm quite self-sufficient."

"Of that I have no doubt." He grinned. She was more than capable of taking care of herself or she wouldn't have possessed the ballocks to disturb the devil in his keep. "It's unheard of for a beautiful woman to accost me in the keep with the intention of marrying me."

A bright red spotted her cheeks at his words, and she glared at him. "It seems you enjoying making fun of me, my lord."

"Good God, I'm not making fun of you, woman, I'm simply teasing you."

"Oh." She worried her lower lip. "I'm unaccustomed to such banter. The gentlemen I've known never did so with me."

"Ah, but I'm no gentleman, Sophie. In fact, I'm worse than any rake you might have heard of before."

She laughed again, and her face lit up with amusement. It made her lovelier still. Taking a sip of his burgundy wine, he wondered how the local male population had failed to see this woman for the beauty she was. Her laughter died away, although a smile remained on her lips.

"You shall have to work harder than that to appall me, my lord. I'm now convinced you say wicked things simply to shock me."

"Do you now? What if I were to say something wicked to you?"

"Whatever it is, I'm sure the initial embarrassment will dissipate quickly, leaving me better prepared for your next sinful expression."

Clutching his chest as though in great pain, he shook his head solemnly. "You wound me grievously, my dear. To think my wicked ways won't shock you is sad news indeed."

"I'm certain you shall recover quite nicely, my lord."

"Ah, but will you? After all, my sins are many, and I intend to teach them all to you."

Another blush crested her cheeks. "I can imagine you think me completely uneducated, but I do read, my lord. I shall not come to our marriage bed without some small idea of what happens between a man and woman."

The haughty reply took him aback a moment. Why the little minx thought to set him down, did she? He arched his eyebrows, watching her pink tongue dart out to wet her full lips. "So tell me, Sophie. What do you expect will happen between us on our wedding night?"

"Well, I ... I ... we'll share a bed ... and I...." Her voice trailed off into silence.

"Ah, so the bravado you exhibit in your speech is far removed from your actual understanding."

"That's unfair. You can hardly expect me to describe such an intimacy."

"Why not? Shall I tell you what I *know* will happen?"

He watched her spine stiffen and straighten as she glared at him. "I doubt you would provide me with any information I'm not familiar with already."

"A challenge." His mouth twisted into a smile. "Very well. On our wedding night, I'll slowly remove your clothing, allowing myself to enjoy the firmness of those delightful breasts I've yet to see fully revealed."

Her gasp encouraged him to continue as his eyes met her shocked gaze. "Once you're naked before me, I intend to explore every inch of you with my mouth and tongue. Especially your nipples. I have a fascination with nipples. They're one of the few places on a woman's body that remain as hard as my cock during lovemaking."

This time her gasp was more of a choking noise as she stared at him in appalled fascination. He arched one eyebrow, daring her to protest. She glared at him but remained silent. Fully aware of his ungentlemanly behavior, he continued.

"I intend to suck on your nipples, Sophie, until that delightful spot between your legs is hot and wet. I'm going to use my mouth to make you writhe in my arms, begging me for a release you've not yet experienced."

"My lord, I--"

"Then when I'm quite certain you're ready for me, I'm going to plunge my cock deep inside you over and over again until I spill my seed in you. And all the while, I'm going to enjoy hearing you cry out from the pleasure of it all."

Silence fell between them, and he noted the rapid rise and fall of her breasts. Far better she know now than later the man she was marrying. There was still time for her to change her mind. Reluctantly, he had to admit that he didn't want her to change her mind, and her relatively calm composure pleased him.

Most women of her background would be running from him in hysterics, but not Sophie Hamilton. Either she was made of sturdier stuff or she was completely enthralled with his vivid description. And he found himself hoping it was the latter.

She took a deep breath as the tip of her tongue darted out to dampen her lips. What would those luscious lips feel like surrounding his cock? He was going to teach this fascinating creature to do things no wife would ever expect from her husband. The idea made him grin as he bit into a tart apple.

"You seem well pleased with yourself, my lord."

"I am."

"I suppose you find me amusing." Her cool tone almost completely hid the pain and anger lying beneath her words.

"You think I'm laughing at you."

"Aren't you? Isn't that what this is all about? A bit of sport with the old maid?" This time the bitterness was more evident. He leaned toward her and grasped the hand that was twisting her napkin with extreme violence. With a gentleness that surprised him, he carried her hand to his lips.

"Sophie, I was not having sport with you. I'm not a gentleman, far from it. But I can assure you, what I just described will be one of the most pleasurable experiences of your life."

He deliberately stroked her forefinger with his tongue, before pulling it into his mouth. As he sucked on her finger, he watched her shocked expression give way to reluctant pleasure. Releasing her finger, he turned her hand over to kiss her wrist. The tremor shooting through her reverberated against his fingers. Instinct told him it wasn't fear, but excitement.

"Tell me, Sophie, what do you think about when I touch you?"

"I ... I don't ... know. I suppose I like how nice it feels."

"Nice." He arched an eyebrow at her. He'd not heard a woman use the word nice where he was concerned in years. It didn't do much for his pride. "I believe I need to help you with your definitions regarding pleasurable sensations."

Not waiting for her answer, he tugged her toward him so she lay prone across his lap. She stared at him with a look of shock. Her mouth pouted in a slight "O" of surprise, and his cock stiffened at the sight. With a slow stroke, he ran his thumb along her bottom lip and it quivered beneath his touch. He refused to wait any longer to taste her.

Cradling her chin in his hand, he took her lips in a hard kiss. The scent of honey and lilac washed over him, teasing his senses. The women he'd made love to in the past had always worn exotic scents, but Sophie smelled of fresh wind and meadows. His tongue plunged into her mouth in an imitation of the carnal act he intended to avail himself of with her.

Unlike yesterday, this time she tentatively swirled her tongue around his. It made him rock hard. He pulled away and gently nibbled on her lower lip before his mouth drifted down across her jaw to the side of her neck. The soft moan that escaped her lips made him smile against her throat.

Not content with this simple surrender, he wanted more. He wanted her to beg for his touch and whimper when he denied her pleas. Then when he'd teased her some more, he would enjoy hearing her cry out with pleasure as he slowly introduced her to the ways of the flesh.

His hand slid up to her neck, where he deftly undid the buttons of her riding jacket. When she murmured a protest, he kissed her again. His fingers splayed her jacket apart, exposing the soft chemise beneath.

Unable to help herself, she parted her lips to give him access and she entwined her arms around his neck. A moment later, she was stretched out on the blanket with his long, hard length covering her. Her brain was fuzzy as to how she'd arrived in this position, but she didn't care. His touch thrilled her and she didn't want him to stop. The sudden touch of his fingers undoing the laces of her chemise made her inhale a sharp breath. He stopped and raised his head to look down at her.

"Tell me what you're thinking," he commanded in a rough voice.

The sound thrilled her; she excited him. Sophie Hamilton, spinster, excited the Devil of Devlyn Keep.

"I ... I want more."

"More of what?"

"More of you kissing me ... tou-touching me."

"Then you shall have it."

His lips slanted over hers again in a deep, hot kiss. Sandalwood and spice mixed together to tantalize her nostrils, while she could taste the smooth burgundy he'd drunk with his cheese. It was a gloriously earthy sensation. She gasped against his mouth as his fingers slid beneath her chemise and across the top of her corset.

The ache in her breasts grew more tangible as her nipples hardened, straining against her underclothes. Oh God, she wanted him to touch her there. To somehow assuage the tension stirring inside her. Instinct made her force her breasts up higher in a silent plea for his touch. A moment later, his tongue slid between the valley of her breasts, and she uttered a soft cry of delight.

She craved the touch of his hand on her, everywhere, even in that most intimate place between her legs. Spiking her fingers through his hair, she shuddered beneath his caresses. Heat streamed its way through her limbs until fire encased her entire body. She'd never felt so deliciously wicked in her entire life.

Cool air caressed her skin, the fire doused almost immediately by his retreat. From where she laid on the blanket, she stared at him in puzzlement. He appeared angry. Had she done something wrong?

"Not like this, Sophie. I won't take you here in the meadow for someone to stumble upon us. We'll wait until our wedding night."

She didn't know what to make of him. Mere seconds ago, he was caressing her body into a raging inferno, and now--now he was irritated and seemed unaffected by the kisses they'd exchanged. Well, perhaps that wasn't an accurate statement. His breathing was harsh, and there was a smoldering flame in those beautiful green eyes of his, while his tightened jaw tugged his scar into a taut line.

Offering his hand to her, he pulled her to her feet. Close to him once more, she trembled against his heat. The fire in his gaze flared bright in his eyes before he released her and quickly stepped away. Disappointment squeezed at her. Heaven help her, she liked being in his arms. It excited her. If this was what it would be like between them, caution was necessary. She refused to lose her heart again only to find herself supplanted by a younger woman.

With trembling fingers, she fastened her clothing. She cast him a furtive glance, noting how the white line of his scar contrasted with his dark skin tone. He was dangerously handsome, and just the type of man who could easily break her heart. There was something about him that told her an altogether different man hid behind his devil-may-care attitude. She watched as he folded his arms and studied her with a rigid jaw.

"I think a walk is in order. Shall we?" He offered her his arm.

Bewildered by his brusque behavior, she accepted his arm and allowed him to guide her toward the path that trailed through the forest. She didn't know what to say, so she remained silent as they walked. They'd walked for several minutes when he came to a halt.

"Sophie, I want you to carefully consider what you're doing. Tonight, I want you to think about what will happen if you marry me day after tomorrow."

"I'm aware of the consequences, my lord."

"Tell me what you think they are."

"My family will disown me." She averted her eyes from his gaze.

"And?"

"I don't understand."

"The guilt, Sophie. Can you live with that?"

Could she live with the guilt? Did she really have a choice? Everything she knew about her father's dealings confirmed that Devlyn wasn't the only person her father had swindled.

"I can live with it," she said quietly.

"What else?"

"There is nothing else."

"What are the consequences of marrying the Devil of Devlyn's Keep?" The bleak look on his face made her want to ease the cynicism she saw in the depths of his green eyes.

"The only consequence I can foresee is that the Devil might have to answer to my brother."

"Are you referring to that young pup who assaulted me at the pond yesterday?" Just a glimmer of amusement brightened his eyes.

"He's not that much younger than you."

"Perhaps, but I'm more than capable of handling young Mr. Hamilton. What I was really referring to were the consequences of marrying a man who is a dissolute, unreformed rake."

He was warning her not to fall in love with him. Well, the man had nothing to fear from that quarter. Falling in love with a younger man wasn't part of her plan. She smiled. "I understand our bargain completely, my lord. You have something I want, and I have something you want. It's as simple as that."

"Then we understand each other. Come, you need to return home before someone questions where you've been." There was a disturbing gleam in his eyes, but it vanished before she could decipher the emotion.

Walking next to him, she wondered what it would be like to be the mistress of Devlyn Keep. She would at least have the opportunity to return to London. She'd always enjoyed the theater, but her father had refused to spend money on a daughter he said would never marry. Hopefully, Devlyn had enough funds to allow her some freedom. If not now, then when he recouped his monies from her father.

When they finally reached her horse, he helped her up into the saddle. His hand rested on her knee, the warmth of him sinking through the material of her dress to heat her skin. "I have business tomorrow midday. Meet me here at four, and I'd like to review the documents you have related to your father's business dealings."

"Oh, I forgot." She retrieved two ledgers from her saddlebag. "I meant to give these to you earlier. I thought you might want to see what you're paying for before you give your name away."

As he accepted her offering, a strange expression crossed his face. Biting her lip, Sophie studied him in silence. Something she couldn't account for had prompted her to bring him the ledgers. His long fingers ran over the green material before he accepted the books. He lifted her hand to his lips and brushed her fingertips with his warm mouth. Although he didn't say thank you, she read it in his manner. It was as if she'd given him a rare gift by trusting him.

"Until tomorrow then," he said.

With a smile, she wheeled her mare away from him then spurred the horse into a canter. As she rode away, Devlyn watched her, his fingers gripping the green books she'd given him. Beneath his fingertips was the weapon he needed to restore his honor and fortune. What had possessed her just to hand over this information before their wedding day?

Was she foolhardy or was this her way of saying she trusted him? Trust. Bitterness layered his soft laughter. Trust was for impetuous fools and starry-eyed maidens. God help him, but the last thing he needed was to have Sophie trusting him. She'd do far better thinking him the devil, rather than a man worthy of redemption. For something told him that's what she saw.

Perhaps the best thing to do would be to take the ledgers and forget he'd ever met her. No, that was impossible. Forgetting Sophie wasn't something he wanted to do, even if he could.

Chapter 4

Sophie breathed a sigh of relief as her father strode out of the study. For most of the afternoon, she'd been trying to explain to him the cargo manifests from the Cleopatra. Despite her best efforts, he'd been unwilling to accept the fact that one of his ships had taken a loss.

It reminded her of how he would react when Devlyn extracted his revenge. She was glad she wouldn't be here to see her father's rage. For it would be nothing less. Giving Devlyn the ledgers yesterday had been a foolish risk, but she wanted to know that she could trust him. She needed to know his honor was stronger than his lust for revenge.

Tomorrow they would be married. There was an honorable man beneath Devlyn's devil-may-care attitude. She believed that with all her heart. The why or how of that belief was beyond her. Devlyn had already made it clear that he wasn't a man she should fall in love with. Did he think she held some idealized view of him and matrimony?

She supposed to some degree she did. Perhaps he had more insight to her than she had to herself. She'd always tried to be honest with herself, and now she had to face the reality of what she was about to do. Marrying a younger man was scandalous enough, but to consider the idea of a relationship with him was preposterous.

Her gaze shifted to the clock, and she muttered a soft oath. She'd been dawdling and she'd be late again meeting Devlyn. Yesterday he'd made it quite clear how important punctuality was to him. Clearing her desk, she quickly left the study and hurried toward the rear of the house. There was no time to change into her riding habit, so her work clothes would have to suffice.

As she crossed the stable yard, she looked up at the ominous sky. Should she risk being caught out in the rain? No, she had to know if Devlyn had kept his word to meet her. Inside the stable, she ordered her mare saddled, despite a protest from the groomsman. Moments later, she rode off across the grassy plain at a fast gallop, her cape streaming out behind her.

She pushed her horse hard hoping to reach the woodcutter's cottage before the rain started. To her dismay, she was just at the edge of the forest when a heavy downpour unleashed its wrath over her head. By the time she reached the woe-begotten hut, she was soaked. Tumbling out of the saddle, she left her mare in the lean-to. The empty, makeshift stable made her heart sink. She'd been wrong. Devlyn hadn't come. He'd gotten what he wanted and left her to face her father's wrath. For once the financial upheaval started, her treachery and betrayal would be clearly evident.

Biting her lip, she stood in the cold, damp stall filled with uncertainty. A shiver went through her at the way her clothes were chilling her. She didn't want to contemplate the future at the moment. She simply wanted to be warm again.

Dashing through the steady rain, she hurried into the hut. Although the interior was relatively clean, it was dark and lonely. She quickly removed her clothing down to her damp chemise. Rubbing her hands up and down her arms, she tried to warm herself. She needed to start a fire.

The sight of a small stack of firewood and kindling next to the stone hearth made her sigh with relief. Now all she needed was a piece of flint. In the near darkness, she could barely make out the flint box resting on the mantle. About to reach for the starter, the hut door slammed open and she let out a scream of surprise as she wheeled around to face the newcomer.

"It's all right, Sophie. It's me."

Still shaken, she swallowed her fright as he closed the door behind him. Removing his overcoat, he shook it out then hung it on the rack beside the door. When he turned to face her, she could just make out the harsh lines of his face. He strode toward her and grasped her shivering shoulders.

"Why the devil didn't you stay at home? I would have thought you had more sense than to come out in this type of weather."

"It wasn't ... wasn't rain ... raining ... when I ... left home."

Her chattering response made him frown darkly. Whipping off his jacket, he covered her shoulders with it. The garment was relatively dry, and the warmth of it eased most of her discomfort immediately. She watched in silence as he busied himself getting a fire started.

One knee braced against the hearth, he arranged several pieces of wood in the fireplace. Her breath hitched at the way his linen shirt stretched taut against his back muscles. With each movement he made, his muscles rippled with a hypnotic power. The desire to run her hands over his back then slide her fingers through the wet layers of his dark hair was an ache inside her.

Her eyes drifted down to where his riding breeches hugged his firm buttocks. Fire burned her cheeks as she wondered what it would be like to see him naked. Would the muscles in his calves be as sinewy as they looked beneath his clothing? Her heart skipped a beat at the thought.

His shoulders flexed beneath his white shirt, as he stoked the smoking wood. He was the most virile man she'd ever seen. There was a suppressed strength about him that could be destructive or protective depending on his mood. The memory of his words yesterday returned, and she wondered if he would like her boldness if she touched him. What would he do?

Dear Lord, she was losing her mind. How could she be so attracted to a man so much younger than she was? Flames crackled in the hearth and the temperature in the hut slowly inched its way upward, but she wasn't sure whether it was her or the fire that was providing the warmth.

Apparently satisfied the fire wouldn't die out, Devlyn stood and turned to face her. The expression on his face was foreboding, and she narrowed her eyes at his fierce glare.

"You should have stayed home, Sophie. If I ever catch you doing anything so dull-witted again, I'll beat you within an inch of your life."

"Don't you dare threaten me, my lord. I'm not some doltish miss who doesn't know how to take care of herself."

"Is that so?" He growled as he slowly stepped toward her. "And what would you have done if some rake had come through that door?"

"You're the only rake in this county, and I'm certainly not afraid of you." She stepped back quickly as he drew near.

"Then I think it's time to show you exactly *why* you need to fear me."

Taking another step back, her leg encountered the edge of the cot that lined one wall of the hut. In her haste to avoid him, she tumbled backward and fell onto the narrow bed. Devlyn towered over her, the scar on his cheek highlighted by the bright flames crackling in the fireplace.

He pressed one knee onto the edge of the cot and braced his hands on either side of her shoulders. A strange fire glowed in his eyes as he stared down at her, and his clean, male scent washed over her. There was a dangerous edge to him she'd not seen before. It sent a shiver through her. To her surprise, it wasn't one of fear, but of excitement.

"Unlace your chemise." His lips tightened as she hesitated to obey the command. "Now, or I'll do it for you."

The roughness of his voice scraped her skin as her fingers fumbled with the laces holding the thin muslin together at the bodice. Her skin grew hot and she found herself dragging in short, rapid breaths as he watched her. Slowly she undid the laces, all too aware of his wicked eyes observing her every movement. His gaze moved to where she could feel her nipples rising to taut, hard peaks beneath the cotton undergarment. She flushed at the realization he could arouse her without even touching her. His mouth curled at one corner in the semblance of a smile.

"Open it up so I can see your breasts."

Her eyes widened at the command and she gave a slight shake of her head. She wasn't ready to expose herself so fully to him. She needed more time. His eyes narrowed at her hesitation.

"Afraid, Sophie?"

The mockery in his voice infuriated her but still she hesitated. An instant later, his large hand pulled the garment wide open in a sharp movement. She gasped as he did so, the cool air of the hut brushed over her skin. Her nipples hardened and the surrounding skin puckered up like goose flesh.

Devlyn sucked in his breath sharply, his green eyes darkening as he stared down at her. The desire in his face was raw and earthy. It made her heart race with a mixture of fear and excitement. He reached out one hand and cupped her, his thumb flicking over the stiff peak. She gasped at the sensation as her body trembled beneath his touch.

Oh God, she was far too old to be acting like a wanton with him. Is this what it was like between a man and woman? This yearning, this ache? His thumb continued to circle her nipple, and her mouth went dry at the sinfully delicious pleasure of it. Her eyes fluttered closed.

Yesterday he'd told her he was going to suck on her nipples. Would he do it now? He switched hands to attend to her other breast. She arched her back, wanting him to do as he'd promised. She moaned. God, if only he'd take her into his mouth and suckle her nipple like he'd described.

"Tell me what you want."

Her eyes opened to meet his piercing gaze. Hot color burned her cheeks. He knew. But how could he? She gasped as he gently tweaked her nipple.

"Tell me."

"I want ... I want you to ... to do what you described ... at lunch yesterday."

"Yesterday? Did I happen to say something specific?"

"You know you did." She inhaled a quick breath as his thumb circled her nipple.

"You'll have to refresh my memory."

His fingers continued to fondle her, and she arched toward him. God help her, but he was going to make her beg him for it. She tried to control the fire spreading through her body, but all she could focus on was how much she wanted him to suck on her breast.

"I want you ... oh God, Devlyn ... please take me in your mouth."

"With pleasure," he murmured.

An instant later his tongue flicked across a rigid nipple before he clamped it between his lips and sucked on her. The gratification was sharp and instantaneous. Triumph surged through him at the way she arched upward into his mouth. He nipped at her stiff peak and she cried out at the keenness of the gentle bite.

God, she tasted wonderful, felt wonderful. How in the hell could she possibly be forty-one? Her body was as firm and ripe as a woman half her age. He needed to remember this was about justice- -his name in exchange for the power to recover what had been stolen from him. But damn if she didn't make that difficult to do.

His hand slid over a supple, silky thigh. Bloody hell, he wanted to ram into her right now. Control, he needed to control the way she was affecting him, maintain his perspective. No, he needed to have her begging him. He wanted to hear her pleading with him to plunge into her.

He swallowed her sharp breath of surprise as he sought her lips. His tongue plunged into her mouth, mating with hers. She moaned softly and wrapped her arms around his neck, clinging to him as she matched the harsh intensity of his kiss. Sweet Jesus, she learned quickly. His blood surged throughout his body, and his cock tightened with the anticipation of assuaging its thirst for her hot, slick passage.

Breaking their kiss, he sought the side of her neck with his mouth. Beneath his lips, he tasted the fluttering beat of her racing pulse. He nibbled gently at her skin, then down to her shoulder. As he made his way down her arm, he brushed his thumb over the gooseflesh that encircled a hard pink pebble.

He continued to tease her nipple as he sat up and bent her leg. The cotton chemise fell down around her hips to reveal a rounded thigh and a triangle of hair that was already glistening with her hot cream. Her eyes flew open and she gasped at the way he'd exposed her.

Slowly, he trailed his fingers down her leg while keeping his gaze locked with hers. Erratic breaths puffed past her lips, and his mouth tilted upward in a small smile.

"Tell me what else I should do to you."

"I ... I don't ... don't under ... stand."

Using his tongue, he traced a small circle at the crease where her leg was bent, while his finger stroked through the curls to caress the hidden nub at her core. The touch made her buck her hips.

"Tell me."

"Oh God, yes." She moaned and her eyes closed. "Yes, please, touch me there."

Her words ended in a soft whimper as he caressed her swollen sex. The point was to drive her beyond caring for anything else but him. He wanted to obliterate every thought from her head so the only images consuming her were of him and his touch. Christ, he wanted to drive her so mad with desire that she'd never want anyone but him.

As he played with her, her hips pressed up against his hand in a silent plea for more. Her hand slid down his arm to cover his as he increased the pace of his strokes to her core. She was slick with heat, and he inserted one finger up her snug passage. A moment later, she arched her back as she climaxed and her steamy cream covered his fingers.

"It's time for me to drink from you, Sophie."

"Drink ... I ... oh dear God." She jerked slightly at his words, her eyes opening to meet his. As he started to lower his head, her eyes widened in shock, and she tried to close herself to him.

With a growl, he parted her damp curls and swirled his tongue around her hot nub. Her scent was musky with a slight bite to it. He nipped at her sex gently, and a guttural cry broke past her lips. First, he suckled and then he caressed her with his tongue, all the while taking pleasure in her whimpering moans of pleasure. As she bucked against his mouth, he drank the sweet cream gushing from her as she climaxed once again.

Ah, she was a sweet find indeed. She would ride his cock better than any tight grip he might use. And when she came like this, she'd grip him and squeeze him until he exploded inside her. Rising up, he stared down at her. Her hand was curled up by her mouth, her little finger resting against the edge of her lips as if she were about to suck on it as he'd just been sucking on her. The sight tightened his ballocks, and he wanted to plunge into her now, brand her as his. Her pose was that of a willing supplicant at the altar of wickedness. It aroused him all the more. She was more than ready for him and he refused to wait.

His thumb rubbed over her nipple, and she whimpered at the sensitivity of the stiff peak. Dear God, what he'd done to her was indescribable. It was the most decadent, wicked thing she'd ever experienced. She could still feel the shudders rippling between her legs. His touch was like a drug and she wanted more. She wanted him to touch her again. To ... dear God she was wicked, but she wanted his mouth down there on her again.

Satiated and relaxed from the experience, she barely registered his movements. Suddenly the tip of him was nestled in her curls. Hot and hard, he slid partway into her tight core and she gasped at the sensation. His tongue swirled around her nipple as he pushed deeper into her slick passage.

Heat emanated from him, and she trembled as his mouth continued to tease her. Each time he slid out of her, he returned to probe deeper. Beyond all thought, she clung to him, her hands moving beneath his shirttails to skim over his sinewy chest.

Her hips arched off the bed as her body tried to keep him inside her. Desire blotted out everything except her need to have him fill her with his blazing heat. Her hips rose to meet his as he withdrew once more only to plunge deeper into her. She cried out at the slight pinch, and then he was filling her, expanding her with his heat.

The sensation was glorious, and she met his every thrust with equal zeal. Fire built between them as he slammed mercilessly into her, and she didn't care. It was the most freeing thing she'd ever done or experienced as he thrust so fiercely into her over and over again. The friction raged through her as he rode her with an intensity that sent her emotions shattering into oblivion.

With a wild cry, she arched up into him, her body shuddering as thousands of intense waves of pleasure rolled over her. A moment later, he too cried out and throbbed inside her with a pulsating strength that triggered another round of pleasurable waves that crashed though her. As his climax finished, he lowered himself down on top of her. She accepted his weight with pleasure. Lying beneath him with her eyes closed, she sighed. If this were what she could expect on a regular basis, she would not mind being married at all.

The moment she sighed, he stiffened and his powerful forearms pushed him upward so he could stare down at her with blazing eyes.

"You see, Sophie, this is what a rake does. He takes an innocent simply for his own pleasure."

Stunned by the blunt statement, she could only stare up at him in horror. What was he saying? That he'd taken her simply to prove a point. Her mouth moved, but she heard nothing come out. With an abrupt movement, he retreated from her. Standing up, he adjusted his clothing and studied her with an unreadable expression on his face.

"Come, your dress should be dry by now."

As he turned away, she pushed herself up out of the bed. Ice flowed through her veins where only moments before fire had heated her limbs. "You bastard."

The quiet words were all the more strident in the small hut. She saw his back stiffen and he jerked his head around to glare at her over his shoulder. A derisive smile curled his mouth. "Rakes usually are, my dear. But you were the one to approach the devil in his keep. It's not as if I lured you here."

Sophie ignored the truth of his words and quickly tied the laces of her chemise. She wanted to clean the sticky area between her legs, wash away the evidence of his possession. But would she be able to wash away the way her body still cried out for his touch? She was a fool.

Fury warmed her as she wrapped her stays around her body and started to lace them. When he stepped forward to help her, she jerked away from him. As she finished her task, she glared at him.

"You're correct about one thing, my lord. I might have made a deal with the devil, but I don't have to keep it."

"What the hell's that supposed to mean?"

"You have the ledgers. Do with them as you will. But I'll not marry you."

"Don't be a fool. We both know your father will know you're the one who betrayed him. If there's one thing I know about Townsend, he has a filthy temper."

She knew he was right, but at the moment, she didn't care. All she wanted was to run as far away from him as she possibly could.

"I'll deal with my father when the time comes, but as for you--"

At that moment, the hut door flew open and she stared in horror at the sight of her brother standing in the doorway shaking off the rain from his clothes.

"Phe, what the devil were you thinking coming out in this downpour ... bloody Christ!"

In a long, drawn out moment, all of them stared at one another in varying states of horror, anger, trepidation and calm indifference. With a low cry of fury, Spencer stepped toward Devlyn. Without thinking, Sophie leaped forward to put herself between them, but Devlyn shoved her behind him.

"I'll kill you for this, Devlyn. You weren't satisfied with ruining Eleanor, now you have to prey on Sophie."

"Eleanor was beyond ruin when I met her, Hamilton. And if you must know, Sophie came to me."

Spencer drew up short and Sophie met the stunned expression of her brother over Devlyn's shoulder. Anger mixed with disbelief as he stared at her. "You're a liar, Devlyn. Sophie would never come to the man who ruined her sister."

The conviction in Spencer's voice snapped the tenuous thread in Sophie that connected her with the father and sister who had betrayed her so cruelly. Furious, she shook her head and tried to step around Devlyn. An oath escaped his lips as he blocked her path.

"Damn it, Sophie, you're not dressed decently."

"A bit late for proper behavior now, don't you think, Devlyn?" her brother sneered.

"Stop it, Spencer. Devlyn's done nothing wrong. I came here of my own free will."

"He's making you say that somehow." Hate filled Spencer's eyes as he glared at the man standing guard over her.

"No, Spencer." She shook her head again. "We've only anticipated our wedding night by a few short hours. We're to marry tomorrow."

"Good God! Have you lost your mind, Phe! This man isn't just a rake, he ruined our sister."

"*No!*" Sophie shouted the word with all the fury inside her. "Don't you ever say that again. Eleanor was whoring with one of the stable boys when she got pregnant and tried to convince Devlyn it was his child."

Spencer snorted loudly. "I suppose he told you that."

"No, I stumbled across Eleanor and her lover one morning before I went riding. She laughingly stated that she was going to marry Devlyn simply to give her child a name."

"But, Eleanor told me--"

"Eleanor lied to you. You weren't here, and I could hardly write about something like this. When Devlyn refused to marry Eleanor, Father went into a wild rage and swore to destroy him. When they couldn't find a way to force him to marry Eleanor, they convinced Andrew to marry her. Then Father stole nearly everything Devlyn had."

Spencer looked bewildered and she recognized the pain of

betrayal in his features. She wanted to go to him, but Devlyn's strong hands reached behind him and held her in place as if reading her thoughts.

"Hamilton, I suggest you step outside for a moment. Sophie needs to dress."

Dazed, her brother nodded and left the hut. As the door closed behind him, Devlyn turned to face her. His jaw was tight, emphasizing the jagged line across his cheek. She took a step back from him at the dark look on his face.

"So you changed your mind," he said softly. "A wise decision."

"The only reason I did so was to save Spencer."

"Another wise choice."

"Yes, it was. Otherwise he would have killed you." She spat out the furious words. "And as appealing as that thought is, I have no intention of seeing my brother imprisoned, or worse, simply for the demise of a despicable rogue."

His face was cold and unreadable as he studied her. "It seems you finally understand my true nature. Don't forget it."

Without giving her a chance throw another insult out, he stormed out of the hut.

Chapter 5

Devlyn glared at Spencer Hamilton as he slammed the cottage door closed behind him and stood on what could barely pass for a porch. He dared the impudent pup to even open his mouth. But the boy simply turned away from him to stare out at the fine drizzle that had replaced the earlier downpour.

"Do you love her?"

The quiet question made him start as he glanced in Hamilton's direction. The young man didn't turn his head. Something told him the boy would only appreciate honesty, just as Sophie would. He ignored the twinge of guilt at how bluntly honest he'd been with her.

"We have ... an agreement."

"Then you don't love her." Hamilton's voice had a hard edge as he turned to face him.

"I'll never lay a hand on her in violence and when my investments mature, I'll see to it that she wants for nothing."

"You're too young for her."

"Age is a state of mind. Your sister is in many ways younger than I am."

"Not from what I just witnessed," the young man replied grimly.

Devlyn shrugged and looked out at the wet landscape. What the hell was the matter with him? Why did he feel like the villain? Sophie had sought him out, not the other way around.

"If you hurt her, I'll make you pay dearly, Devlyn."

At the love and loyalty in the boy's voice, he turned his head to look at Sophie's brother. There was a calm determination in Hamilton's face, and he was quite certain the boy would indeed avenge any slight to his sister. He nodded.

"Understood."

The door behind them opened, and Sophie joined them under the rickety overhang. She scarcely afforded him a look before she touched her brother's arm.

"Spencer?"

For a moment, he wasn't sure the boy was going to answer her, and he tensed ready to call the lad to heel. As the young man turned, his eyes gave Devlyn a silent warning. He returned the look steadily. He might be a despicable rogue, but he still possessed the honor of his word.

"I don't suppose you've told Father of your plans."

The quiet statement made Sophie start, and Devlyn watched her bite her lip out of nervous habit. What was going through that complex brain of hers? She heaved a sigh and shook her head.

"You know what would happen if I did, Spencer."

When Hamilton didn't answer her, she turned away from her brother to face him. Her hazel eyes were still slightly glazed with pain at his verbal abuse, and a silent oath sliced through his head. Damnation. He should have taken more care with her. No. If she harbored illusions about him, better to destroy them now before the worst happened. He bit the inside of his cheek.

"I've arranged for the vicar to perform the wedding ceremony at eleven tomorrow morning."

"I'll be punctual, my lord."

She turned away, adjusted the hood of her cloak, and stepped out into the rain in the direction of the lean-to where the horses were. Hamilton made to follow her then stopped.

"I'd like to stand with Sophie tomorrow if you have no objection."

"None whatsoever."

"Tomorrow then." Hamilton nodded at him before following his sister out into the rain.

He didn't move from where he stood, simply watching as Sophie and her brother retrieved their mounts and rode off toward Townsend Manor. The fact that she didn't even cast him another glance irritated him. What the devil had the woman expected? She'd been aware of his reputation. *But she expected better of you, Devlyn.* The internal reproof infuriated him.

"God damn it!"

He threw the hut door open and reentered the small dwelling. As he yanked his overcoat off the wall hook, his gaze came to rest on the narrow cot. His body tensed as the memory of making love to Sophie his flooded his head. The sound of her excited cries still echoed in his ears, and he could still smell her tangy aroma. The memories were enough to tighten his mouth in a straight line. Beginning tomorrow, he'd take her over and over again until he wearied of her. Then he'd have her out of his head for good.

* * * *

Sophie shook the rain off her cloak as she stood in the back hallway. Beside her, Spencer's face wore a frown. She glanced over her shoulder to ensure no one was within earshot before she turned to him.

"You didn't say a word on the way home."

"What was I supposed to say, Phe?"

"That you understand."

"What am I supposed to understand? That you're about to marry a man you don't know? A man who's almost young enough to be your son?" The harsh disgust in his voice stung, and she stiffened.

"And yet it's quite appropriate for Father to be courting a woman younger than his eldest daughter."

He started and had the grace to blush with embarrassment. "Damn it, Phe, you know what I mean."

"No, Spencer, I don't. You seem to think I have no need for companionship or a home of my own. The only reason Father doesn't try to marry me off to one of his friends is because I'm useful to him. The man doesn't even love me, his own daughter."

She inhaled a deep breath as she spit out the words. Not about to explain herself any further, she stalked off to her room. Spencer's anger wasn't a surprise, but she'd expected him to be supportive once she explained about Eleanor. Instead, he'd only pointed out the age difference between her and Devlyn.

Inside her room, she went to her washstand and poured a substantial amount of water into the basin. Lifting her skirts, she tried to erase all trace of Devlyn's mark from her body. When she finished, she sank down at her dressing table to stare at her reflection. She didn't look any different, but she felt different.

She bore Devlyn's brand, and no amount of water could wash away the sensation. Burying her face in her hands, she shuddered as she remembered how he'd taken her, then just as easily pointed out how it meant nothing. He'd warned her, and she'd failed to listen. The man she was about to marry was a confirmed rake. A man who thought only of his own pleasure first. No. That at least she knew wasn't true.

Once again, she studied her reflection. Her gaze fell to her bodice as she remembered the way he'd commanded her to reveal her body to him. He'd been masterful and arrogant with her today, but he'd made certain to pleasure her to the fullest extent possible.

Only when she'd surrendered and begged for his skillful touch had he sought his own pleasure. And God help her, she wanted to experience his lovemaking again. The decadent, sinful nature of it was thrilling. The muscles between her legs tightened as she remembered the way his tongue had probed and teased her until her insides exploded with a fiery heat.

She closed her eyes against the figure watching her from the mirror. Was this what she had become? An old maid craving the touch of a younger man like a bitch in heat. She couldn't do it. She couldn't go through with the marriage. Springing to her feet, she prowled the floor.

How could she marry him? How could she bear his pity and his granting her his touch when the mood suited him? But did she have a choice? Staying here was no longer an option. Her father's tyranny was too oppressive and when he discovered her treachery, her life would be worth nothing.

A knock on the door interrupted her thoughts and she crossed the room. Opening the door, she frowned at Spencer's contrite expression.

"I'm sorry, Phe. I should have understood."

"Yes, you should have. You of all people know what it's like to live here, but at least you get to leave."

"I know. That's what I realized a few moments ago."

She heaved a sigh. "Then you'll help me tomorrow."

"Of course. What are little brothers for?" The beguiling grin on his face made her own face tug in response. A reluctant smile tilted her lips.

"I don't know why I put up with you."

"Because you love me, Phe. Admit it. I'm your best brother."

"You're my only brother."

"A minor point to be sure. Come, it's time for dinner. Your last as an unmarried woman."

The jocular comment startled her and she closed her bedroom door to walk with him down the hallway. He was right. It was her last night as Sophie Hamilton. Tomorrow, she would become Sophie Hamilton Blackwell, Countess of Devlyn. A title Eleanor had coveted. She was about to have something her sister never could. The thought should have pleased her greatly, but all she could think about was Devlyn's words. "You see, Sophie, this is what a rake does. He takes an innocent simply for his own pleasure."

* * * *

Devlyn stood quietly in the nave of the church, his hands clasped behind his back. The vicar remained quiet as well. He liked that about the man. Although he'd never been particularly fond of religion, he did understand the need of his tenants to have a place to come to on Sunday mornings. This new vicar seemed a decent sort, but more importantly, the man didn't fawn all over him or pontificate.

The wooden door of the church screeched open and his gaze flew to where a ray of light streamed down the church aisle before Sophie's shapely curves blocked it. Tension eased from his body, and he frowned. Why the devil had he been so uneasy about her coming? He didn't want to know the answer.

She wore a dove gray walking dress, and he was again struck by how young she looked. Young and quite lovely. Out of habit, he pulled out his pocket watch and glanced at the time as Sophie reached his side.

"I am quite punctual, my lord."

Her soft voice held a note of steel in it, and he clicked his timepiece closed. His eyes met hers, and he tightened his mouth at the reserved expression on her face. Spencer Townsend stood a short distance away, looking ill at ease. He didn't blame the boy; he was experiencing a similar sense of disquiet himself.

Extending his hand to Sophie, he watched her hesitate for a split second before the soft grey leather of her gloves warmed his palm. She was trembling in spite of her serene appearance. He gave her hand a gentle squeeze as he looked at the vicar.

"I believe we're ready to proceed, Reverend."

With a nod of his head, the vicar began to recite the marriage ceremony. Half listening to the words, Devlyn breathed in a quiet floral scent. Her scent. She was different today. Had his actions yesterday brought that about? There was a steely, determined air to her. It intrigued him. No, challenged him. Damn if the woman wasn't an enigma begging to be unraveled.

The vicar said his name pulling him back to the matter at hand.

"Do you Quentin Thornton Blackwell, earl of Devlyn, take Sophie Faith Townsend to be your lawfully wedded wife?"

"I will."

Sophie's hand trembled in his. Without thinking, he covered it with his other hand and she looked at him. He stared into her eyes as the vicar posed the marriage question to her. For a moment, he thought she might flee. Instinctively he tightened his hold on her not about to let her escape, but she simply dropped her gaze and responded firmly to the query.

The remainder of the ceremony passed swiftly. As the vicar pronounced them man and wife, satisfaction warmed him as he kissed her. The sensation startled him. He should be feeling resignation, not this triumph at making Sophie his bride. He took a quick step back from her and turned as Spencer Hamilton stepped forward to congratulate them.

"My congratulations," Sophie's brother said quietly.

There was a wary look in the man's face as he offered his hand to Devlyn. He understood it. Hamilton wasn't sure whether he was trustworthy or not, but the man also knew there was little he could do about his concerns.

"I'll keep her safe." Devlyn grasped Hamilton's hand in a strong, firm handshake. "And you'll always be welcome in our home."

The suspicion in the young man's face eased somewhat as he nodded and clasped his other hand over Devlyn's. Watching the two men exchange a firm handshake, Sophie trembled. She'd done it. She'd actually married the Devil of Devlyn's Keep. The rake who'd had his pleasure with her only yesterday. Today he seemed oddly gentle with her.

When he'd covered her hand with his during the ceremony, she'd been startled and confused by the gesture. Was he having regrets about his behavior? It didn't matter. She had no intention of succumbing to his wicked charms again. They'd had their wedding night. It didn't warrant repeating. He could find a mistress and leave her be for all she cared.

It was a lie. She did care. Whatever had made her imagine Devlyn might possibly be a man capable of reform? Yesterday had proven how incapable he was of changing. She flinched as his hand settled at the small of her back. Fire swept up her spine at the touch. Now the only family she'd ever truly known was about to leave her. Spencer took her hands in his and kissed her cheek.

"I'll call on you in a few days."

"Promise me you'll not tell Father you knew about this. I have no wish for him to punish you."

"I can take care of myself, Phe. Just be happy, something I know you weren't at home."

"Blast it, Spencer. *Promise* me." She gripped his hands tightly and glared at him.

"All right, I promise. Now for the love of Pete, will you stop trying to break my hands?"

Sophie immediately released her grip on her brother. With another bow toward Devlyn, Spencer turned and walked out of the church. As he walked away, she sensed her old life leaving with him. A light touch at her elbow caught her attention. Turning her head, her gaze met her husband's unreadable one.

"Come, we need to sign the registry and the license."

Nodding, she allowed him to guide her into the recesses of the

church to sign the formal paperwork. When they finished, Devlyn
escorted her out to a small curricle drawn by two chestnut horses.
He helped her into the vehicle, then circled round to the opposite
side and climbed in beside her.

As he slapped the hindquarters of the animals, he sent her a brief
glance. "I take it from the exchange with your brother that you
didn't tell your father about our matrimonial plans."

"No. I thought it best to simply leave. I sent my things to the keep
with a trusted servant, who I asked to come with me."

"And what will your father do when you turn up missing?"

"I left him a letter in my room."

He nodded his understanding as he drove the team around a sharp
turn in the road. Ahead of them, Devlyn Keep rose up to greet them.
Dark and forbidding, the massive stone structure had once served as
a mighty fortress against marauding knights. She bit her lip at the
realization that she was now mistress of this gloomy home.

The long drive leading up to the keep was lined with a smattering
of oak trees, their leaves just beginning to change color. It was a
reminder that fall would soon be here. As they pulled up to the front
of the grim-looking dwelling, the front door opened and three
servants emerged to greet them. When she was standing on the
ground, Devlyn drew her forward toward the small group.

"This is your new mistress, the Countess of Devlyn." He gestured
toward an older man. "This is Fischer. He's been with me since
before my father died. He runs the household, but I'm certain he'll
appreciate your guidance."

She nodded as the wiry man bowed toward her. An older woman
stepped forward whom Devlyn introduced as Cook, followed by a
young girl of about thirteen who was the housemaid. A very small
staff for such a large house. Her face must have revealed her dismay
because Devlyn frowned darkly. His large hand clenched around
her elbow and he pulled her into the house toward his study.

"It's a small household, my lady, since I've not had the resources
to expand. My staff members are loyal, hardworking people. I'll not
tolerate any contempt directed toward them."

His abrasive tone scraped down her spine as he roughly guided
her into his study. Narrowing her eyes at him, she glared at him.
"Do not mistake me for my father or sister, my lord. I might not
have your noble lineage, but I am far removed from any semblance
of a boorish social clod."

As they entered the masculine domain, the two giant wolfhounds
sprang to their feet. With a single flick of his wrist, the animals

immediately sank back down onto their rug. Devlyn turned his head and studied her for a long moment before he gave her a sharp nod. Wheeling away from her, he moved to stand behind his desk. From where she stood, she could see the green ledgers she'd given him two days ago. His manner abrupt, he flipped open one of the books.

"It says here your father owns two warehouses on Liliput Road near the Royal Victoria docks. What does he normally store there?"

"Whatever his ships bring into port."

"Does he own the warehouses free and clear?"

"No, a Mr. Mearn shares ownership in the building. What are you thinking?"

"That your father is about to lose an accommodating partner. I have several shipments coming into port in three weeks, and I've been looking for some storage space. This will give me the space I need, plus force your father to recompense me for space at a higher rate."

"How can you make him pay a higher rate if he already has ownership in the building?"

"Unlike Mr. Mearn, I don't intend to move my cargo to make space for your father's goods. He can pay me a much higher premium for me to move my goods, or he can go elsewhere. Either way he'll suffer a loss, whether from selling his cargo for a lower price just to get rid of it or by paying me a higher price simply for the privilege of storing it."

The simplicity of the plan made her appreciate his keen business acumen, and something told her it would not be long before Devlyn had her father on the brink of financial ruin. The thought of such a thing tugged at her. Guilt. He'd warned her about this, and she'd assured him she could handle it.

She reminded herself that her father's business dealings were far from legal in many cases. He would reap what he'd sown. At least she was beyond his reach. Still, the pain of his rejection would always be with her. Witnessing his downfall would not diminish those feelings. "If you think to stop me, Sophie, be warned I'm an unforgiving man." His flat voice made her start as her eyes searched his implacable features.

"I'm well acquainted with your less than charitable qualities, my lord."

"As long as we understand one another." His gaze narrowed on her.

"We do."

He studied her for a moment until he slowly rounded the desk.

She swallowed hard as he stopped in front of her, the distance between them less than a foot. God, how could she have such mixed feelings despite their encounter yesterday? Part of her wanted nothing more than to rail at him, condemn him for his behavior yesterday. While the other half of her wanted to fling herself into his arms and beg him to touch her again. She was older than he was. She should be able to control this infatuation that was growing inside her.

An arrogant smile tilted the corner of his mouth, and her heart pounded against her breast at the close proximity of him. The tantalizing scent of sandalwood caressed her senses, and she struggled not to retreat. He'd only see that as a sign of weakness. The heat of his fingers singed her cheek, and a familiar sensation spiraled through her belly. She didn't want to feel this way with him. Taking a quick step back, she frowned while attempting to control her erratic breathing.

"My lord, if you'll excuse me, this morning's events have been quite trying and I'd like to rest."

"Shall I show you to your room?" A frown replaced his smile, and his eyes darkened with something resembling concern. She dismissed the notion as she shook her head.

"That won't be necessary, I'm certain Fischer or the housemaid will be able to help me find my way."

He nodded, and she fled the room with as much undue haste as possible.

Chapter 6

Sophie awoke with a jerk. Sitting up in bed, she looked around at the room Fischer had shown her to when she'd fled Devlyn's study. The bedroom had once been quite lovely, but now the curtains, bedspread and carpets were all well past their prime. Her mouth twisted in an ironic grimace. Not unlike herself, she supposed.

Despite its aged appearance, there was a quaint charm about the room. It was clean and welcoming, even down to the fresh flowers in the vase beside her bed. Through the windows, she could tell the sun was setting, so she knew she'd slept most of the afternoon.

She'd not slept well last night, and her nap had been a welcome relief from the morning's stress. Sliding off the bed, she moved to the dressing table. Wincing at the bedraggled creature staring at her from the mirror, she undid her hair and set about repairing her appearance.

As she brushed her hair, she wondered if her father had found her letter yet. The only thing she expected from him was anger, but a small part of her still hoped he might harbor some feelings for her. Earlier when Devlyn had described his first plan of attack against her father's finances, her feelings of guilt had surprised her. She'd not expected to feel anything but bitterness and a desire for revenge.

Even more unexpected was her reaction to Devlyn. She still wanted him, in spite of his behavior yesterday. She should be ashamed of herself for craving his touch. He was a rake, full of wickedness and sin. It intensified his appeal. Of course, he was far too young for her. But he made her feel alive, sensuous and coveted. The one thing he'd not done was hide his desire. He'd made it blatantly clear that he meant to have her time and again.

She shuddered as she stared at her reflection in the mirror. No matter how much she might be attracted to Devlyn she couldn't allow herself to succumb to his touch again. It was too dangerous. The need for love in her life left her vulnerable. Eventually, it would be far too easy to mistake his lust for love if she continued to give herself to him. She refused to let that happen. Surrendering her soul to him only meant she'd have to pick up the pieces of her heart in the future. No. Yesterday would be her only taste of pleasure in Devlyn's arms. She couldn't risk her heart with another encounter.

* * * *

Devlyn frowned as his latest attempt to draw Sophie into a conversation failed. What the devil was wrong with her? He wanted tonight to be special for her. Yesterday had been a mistake where she was concerned. He'd allowed his emotions to control him, and when he'd regained control, Sophie had paid the price. But tonight he'd make up for his lack of control.

He studied her as she used her fork to push her meal around on her plate. Of course, she didn't seem in the mood to make things easy for him. Frowning again, he took a sip of his wine. As he did so, she suddenly laid her fork down with a deliberate movement and dropped her napkin onto the table.

"If you'll excuse me, my lord. I think I'll retire. It's been a long day."

Long day? Hell, she'd spent the entire afternoon in her bedroom. Well, at least she'd be well rested for their wedding night. He nodded and set his own napkin aside as she rose from her chair.

"As you wish, I'll join you later." His words made her freeze, and she sent him an icy look.

"We've had our wedding night, my lord. There'll not be another." She didn't wait for a response but walked stiffly toward the dining room door.

For a fleeting moment, he was speechless. Then anger took over. It had been a long time since a woman had cut him dead in his tracks. He'd be damned if he was going to let his wife get away with doing so. Shoving back his chair, he crossed the dining room floor in three strides catching up with her as she reached the door.

Blocking her way, he glared into her stormy eyes. Anger had turned them the loveliest shade of green. The moment he acknowledged the fact, he immediately pushed it aside. The last thing he needed was to be distracted from his purpose. With a quick twist of the key, he locked the door then tucked the key in his pocket. They were going to have this out before they retired to his bedchamber.

"There are a few things we need to clarify between us."

"And these *things*, my lord, are they rules or commands?" Her voice made each word sound like the bite of a crisp apple.

"You may label them whatever you choose as long as you heed them."

"Then please proceed, I'm all atwitter at your every word."

He gritted his teeth as her sarcasm fueled his anger even more. The wench was acting like a fishwife.

"First, I enjoy pleasant conversation during dinner. I'll not tolerate apathetic or morose behavior at my table."

"I see. Exactly what do you term apathetic or morose?"

Narrowing his eyes at her, he ignored her question and stepped toward her. She retreated in equal measure. "Second, while this is your home too, I, and I alone, rule here."

"Well, I find your sovereignty sadly lacking in more ways than one, but after all, you're a rake. Why should I be surprised?"

"So that's what this is all about."

"I don't know what you're talking about."

"You're still angry about yesterday."

"Why on earth shouldn't I be angry? You had your way with me simply to prove a point." She glared at him, her eyes a mossy green. Damn if she wasn't fetching in her anger.

"And do you know what the point was, Sophie?"

"To show me exactly what type of fool I am for having entered into a bargain with you."

"You missed the point of the entire exercise."

"Exercise!" She threw herself at him, her hand swiping at his face. "You're a bastard, Devlyn."

Catching her easily, he pinned her arms gently, but firmly behind her back and pulled her close. "Why? Because I gave you exactly what you wanted?"

"That's a lie."

"You think so? You're forgetting how you begged me to suck on you." A flush crept into her cheeks, but she refused to respond. He couldn't resist grazing her heated skin with his lips.

He shouldn't be surprised that her anger hadn't abated. So why had she married him? For that matter, why the hell had *he* married her? The answer to that question whispered through his head, and he ignored it.

"You've had your fun, now let me go."

There was a pained tightness to her voice and a thread of guilt tried to wind its way around his heart. He tore it to pieces. His gaze raked her face, and he noted the stubborn tilt of her chin with irritation. She was the one who'd wanted to experience what men and women did in the bedroom. And he knew damn well she'd enjoyed herself yesterday. Hell, she'd been more than eager for him to do whatever he wanted with her. And damn if he didn't want to experience her again.

"I'll let you go on one condition."

Her eyes narrowed like a suspicious cat as she met his gaze. "What condition?"

"You're to kiss me." One hand still binding her wrists together, he rested one finger on her lips as she sputtered with anger. "And not a simple brushing of the lips, Sophie. I want you to make me hot."

"Go to hell."

"Kiss me."

He watched the indecisiveness cross her heart-shaped face. Her tongue flicked out to wet her lips, and his cock tightened in his trousers. Before the night was through, he intended to prove to her how much she wanted him. Then he'd be able to purge himself of this desire that had been steadily building inside him since the first time he'd laid eyes on her.

Slowly she leaned into him, her mouth inching closer until she slanted her lips over his. The scent of lilacs wafted under his nose as she pressed her mouth firmly against his. Elated at having bent her to his will, he knew it was only a matter of time before she came to understand he was in charge at Devlyn Keep.

The sudden sensation of her tongue lacing over his lips shot a bolt of surprise through him. Good God, the woman was a temptress. He opened his mouth to welcome her exploration, and she swirled her tongue around his as she deepened their kiss. She tasted as tart as the baked apples they'd had for dinner.

His hands released her arms and slid to her waist to meld her to him as closely as he could. Her arms slowly wrapped around his neck, and their mouths continued to collide in a kiss that stirred his cock to a stiff point. A moment later, she shoved her way out of his arms.

"Are you hot enough now, my lord? After all, teasing is what a rake's wife does best."

Stunned he stared at her for a brief second, then grabbed her arms and pulled her against him. "Then tease me some more, madam wife, for I am not about to let you go until my need is satisfied."

"How typical of a rake, always taking."

"Oh no, Sophie, not tonight. Tonight you'll beg me just like you did yesterday. The only difference will be that I intend to make you beg throughout the night."

"You may try, my lord."

"Shall we wager how long before your first plea?"

He didn't wait for her answer and simply crushed her mouth beneath his in a harsh kiss. No, he was losing control. He needed to seduce her, not force her. But it had to be soon. It wasn't just his cock throbbing with desire. His entire body lusted after her with an ache beyond anything else he'd ever experienced before.

Easing the pressure of the kiss, he trailed his fingers along her neck in a featherlight caress. While he stoked her skin, his lips made their way along her jaw toward her earlobe. As he nibbled at her neck, he ran his forefinger along the bodice of her gown.

She quivered at the touch, despite her resolve to remain unmoved. Dear God, why did she respond to him so easily? He was right, and she knew it. She did want him, even if he was a rake. That was the agony of it. Despite knowing who and what he was, she wanted him, foibles and all. His finger slid under the edge of her bodice, probing until the tip of his finger brushed against her nipple. Before she could stop herself, a small gasp broke from her lips.

Swallowing the sound with his mouth, his tongue mated with hers in a heady dance. The excitement of it made her cling to him as she'd done before, her response willing and passionate. Heat engulfed her body, and her fingers sought the buttons of his shirt. She wanted to feel his hard skin beneath her fingertips again. Of all the men she'd known, why was he the only one who'd ever made her feel this raw need? His kiss tugged another moan from her as she answered his demanding caress with her own summons.

As the linen shirt gave way beneath her fingers, she slid her hands across his hard, muscular chest. Heat filled her palms as her hands skimmed over sinewy muscles. The warmth of him sent her blood singing exultantly through her veins as her tongue danced with great fervor in his mouth. Her thumbs circled his nipples, and when his muscles flexed at her touch, she knew he enjoyed the caress.

What would happen if she were to suckle him as he'd done her? She pulled her mouth away from his and left a trail of kisses to the side of his neck. Doing as he'd done, she nipped at his skin, pleased by his ragged breathing. Her mouth slid down across his chest until she found one nipple. She flicked out her tongue and circled the peak then clamped her teeth down gently and sucked. The low growl of pleasure echoing over her head told her how much she was pleasing him. He wanted her. The Devil of Devlyn's Keep desired her. It was a heady sensation.

"Sweet Jesus, but you're a wanton, Countess."

An instant later, he lifted her off her feet, carried her the short distance to the table and set her on top of it. His mouth covered hers again with heated urgency. She returned the kiss with a frantic need of her own. There was no time to think as his hands raced across her clothing until her bodice and stays fell away from her breasts. She struggled to remove her chemise until his warm hands gave it a sharp tug, renting the fabric and exposing her to his mouth.

The pleasure of his tongue swirling around her stiff nipple pulled a low cry from her lips. Dear Lord, but his touch made her willing to do whatever he asked. Even here, in a room far removed from the privacy of a bedchamber. She'd never been so totally out of control in her entire life. But she wanted his concession too.

Her hand slid down his chest and over the waistband of his trousers until she could feel the hard bulge straining for release. Uncertain as to whether her touch would affect him, she ran one fingernail down the rigid length of him. He jerked at her touch, his breaths deep and jagged as he lifted his head to stare into her eyes.

"Tell me what you want." His voice was low and harsh with desire.

"I want to hear you say you want me as much as I want you."

His green eyes darkened slightly as his large hands grasped her head. "It would seem that our desire is equal tonight, Countess. However, I won't wait any longer."

The moment his mouth captured hers, his hands lifted her skirts until her entire dress was scrunched together at her waist. Desire curled in her stomach until she ached with the need for his touch with a physical intensity. She barely registered the sound of him sweeping the table's place settings out of the way so he could press her down onto the table.

Spreading her legs apart, his fingers slid through the curls at her apex and stroked her as he'd done the day before. She jerked against his hand as wave after wave of heated sensation washed over her, engulfing her in a fiery blaze of desire.

As he caressed the sensitive spot between her legs, he leaned over her and sought the hardened peaks of her breasts. She uttered a sharp cry as he sucked on one nipple while playing with the other. Heaven help her, but she wanted him inside her. Nothing mattered at this moment, not their age difference, his reputation or the desire for revenge that had brought them together. The only thing that mattered was that he possess her, over and over again until they tired of one another.

"Oh God. Please, Devlyn."

Lifting his head, his eyes burned through her and his face was dark with a passion that thrilled her. He wanted her. She stretched out her hand to him, and with a sharp movement, he unfastened his trousers and drove into her.

A deep groan flew from his mouth as she cried out at the moment of his possession. He was hot, thick and powerful inside her. Her muscles flexed around him and she wanted to weep at the intense pleasure of it. He withdrew and drove into her again. She expanded and contracted around him.

The tightness of her muscles around his cock filled him with the need to keep her like this forever. He shuddered at the orgasmic spasms rippling over his hard length. Christ, she was so tight and hot. He couldn't remember the last time he was ready to come so quickly.

How could this time be even better than yesterday when he'd made her his? The silky fire of her passage exploded around his cock, pulling him along on waves of hot pleasure. With one final plunge into the depths of her, he released a jubilant cry as she bucked against him amidst her own release.

Shaken by the intensity of their joining, he tried to control his ragged breathing. Staring down at her, he inhaled sharply. She was a magnificent buffet of creamy skin and rose-colored nipples. Her eyes met his, and he watched as her fingers trailed lazily over one of her nipples. Bloody Christ, he wanted her again.

Jerking her up, he crushed her lips beneath his, but she didn't retreat. Instead, she kissed him back as if it were their last hour on earth. It was intoxicating, maddening and far too close for comfort. He brushed aside the thought.

His desire for her would be spent by the break of dawn, but until then he'd plunder her sweetness over and over again until they were both exhausted. Drawing back from her, he quickly adjusted his clothing. Out of the corner of his eye, he saw her begin to dress. Immediately he removed his coat and covered her breasts, then swept her up into his arms.

"No, Sophie. I'm not about to let you even think about dressing."

She smiled up at him. It was a womanly smile of surrender, and triumph surged through him. Walking toward the dining room door, he remembered the key was still in his coat pocket. To hell with the door. His boot crashed against the doorknob, and it gave way with a splitting screech. Pushing through the door with his wife in his arms, he headed upstairs. All the while, ignoring the fact that his wife's smile also held just a hint of satisfaction as well.

Chapter 7

The soft murmur of voices pierced Sophie's sleep. Stirring beneath the covers, she yawned sleepily. Last night had been the most incredible night of her life. With each intimate possession, Devlyn had marked her with his masterful brand of pleasure. She'd never felt so alive, so womanly. Her body ached from all the activity, but it was the most delicious ache she'd ever experienced.

A door closed with a quiet thud and a moment later a warm hand slid beneath the comforter to cup her breast. She opened her eyes and met Devlyn's green eyes, which were flashing with wicked amusement. Fully dressed, he exuded the air of a country gentleman not the rake she knew him to be.

"Is it your habit to sleep in each morning?" He grinned at her.

"I always rise early."

"Do you call the hour of eleven early?"

Startled, she sat upright in bed the covers falling to her waist. "Eleven! Why on earth didn't you wake me?"

"You were sleeping peacefully, and considering our athletics last night, I thought you needed your rest. Of course, it seems you're more than ready to continue our exercise program."

Warm color burned her cheeks, only to scorch her skin a second later. His thumb brushed over the hard nipple of her breast and she inhaled a quick breath. Heat stirred in her belly, quickly spreading itself downward. Somehow, she had to break this spell he was weaving around her. But she didn't know how. She wasn't even sure she wanted to quench this fire between them. Surely it would burn itself out soon enough. Why not enjoy it while it lasted?

Devlyn leaned into her, his mouth brushing across her shoulder as he pressed her back into the pillows. Bracing his arms on either side of her, he shifted his attention to her breasts. As his tongue teased first one nipple and then the other, a small moan escaped her lips. With a lithe movement, he stood and stared down at her, his eyes twinkling with a wicked gleam of amusement.

"You're a tempting package, Lady Devlyn, but work calls. I'll arrange for Fischer to show you around the keep, and I'll join you later for dinner."

Suddenly aware he'd had no intentions of bedding her and had simply meant to tease her, she grabbed one of the pillows by her head and swung it at him. Laughing, he dodged the plump missile. With a wag of his finger, he made a chastising sound as he walked across the bedroom floor. Infuriated, she flung the pillow at him, which hit the door as he closed it behind him and his laughter.

Flinging herself back into the pillows, she glared after him. The man was far too dangerous for her peace of mind. Her gaze flew upward and she stared into the mirrors hanging over the bed. His bedroom had the most sinful décor she'd ever seen. Her irritation evaporated as she recalled his lovemaking.

It had been exhilarating and erotic to watch as Devlyn lavished her body with caresses last night. He'd driven her to the brink and beyond several times throughout the night. And each time she'd forgotten everything, except for his touch and the way he made her feel. If she didn't take care, she'd find herself falling in love with him. He'd warned her of such folly, and she intended to take his warning seriously.

A knock sounded on the door, and she quickly covered herself before entreating the visitor to enter. Seconds later, Emmie walked through the door. Grateful to see a familiar face, she smiled. The young girl smiled in return and offered Sophie the robe she carried.

The knowing expression on the girl's face made her cheeks warm. She could only imagine what the rest of the household must think given the way Devlyn had broken down the dining room door last night to carry her upstairs. She accepted the robe as Emmie turned away and crossed the room to a side door.

Climbing out of bed, Sophie returned to her bedroom through the door adjoining Devlyn's chamber with hers. Once again, she found the room's aged furnishings in direct contrast to its well-kept appearance. She would have to ask Devlyn about monies for new furniture and other necessary ornamentations.

With Emmie's help, she dressed quickly and made her way downstairs where she found Fischer dusting the large mirror in the keep's main entrance. The high ceiling arches with their wood buttresses were vivid reminders that she was living in a centuries old fortress. The man greeted her warmly, and together they set out to explore her new home.

Everywhere she turned, there was something needing attention or remodeling. As the tour progressed, she realized what a monumental task she had before her. It would take years before the keep would be restored to its former glory. Did Devlyn have any idea what the true condition of his home was?

After several hours, Fischer ended his tour in the main salon, where Sophie gratefully sank down into a worn sofa. There was so much to do; she didn't even know how to begin. But begin she would. It was difficult not to be drawn to her new home. It was her husband's heritage. Devlyn had rescued her, now she would rescue his home.

"If I may be so bold, my lady?"

"Yes, of course, Fischer." She smiled at the kindly man.

"I know there's a great deal of work needing to be done here in the keep, but we'll all help to make it what it once was. We love the keep almost as much as his lordship does."

Grateful for the man's support, she leaned forward in her seat. "Thank you, Fischer, for that generous offer of support. I gratefully accept."

"And another thing, my lady, and most likely it's quite forward of me, but his lordship has been in my care since before his father died. I know he can be a bit irascible at times, but he's a good man. You won't find another like him in the whole of England. And from the look of things, I'd say you're just the right woman to bring out the best in him."

The fatherly love in the man's voice endeared Fischer to her, and she stood up to cross the floor. Laying a hand on the man's arm, she gently kissed his cheek. "And I'm certain that's quite forward of me as well, but I'm not an aristocrat, and I'm deeply touched by your kind words. I hope I'm able to live up to your expectations."

Fischer blushed down to his roots, his face a bright red as he shifted his gaze down to his feet. "Thank you, my lady, now I believe I should find you some tea. I'm certain you're parched from all the walking we've done this afternoon."

Thanking him, Sophie watched the older man leave the room then turned to inspect her surroundings. Of all the rooms she'd been in today, this one seemed the most hopeless. The wallpaper wasn't just faded; it was also peeling away from the walls. Overhead the room's one saving grace was the impressive crystal chandelier. It was well cared for and gleamed in the afternoon sunlight that poured through one of the salon's front windows. She walked to the fireplace, her hand caressing the beautiful Italian marble mantle.

Outside the room, she heard loud voices in the main hall. Seconds later the salon doors flew open to reveal her father's rotund body in the doorway. Stiffening at the sight of him, she froze. Rage had turned his face beet red, and as he caught sight of her, his color took on a purple hue.

With a cry of outrage, he crossed the floor and before she could dart away, his hand cracked against the side of her face. "You traitorous bitch."

Sophie staggered under the brute force of the slap, struggling to remain on her feet. Straightening, she suppressed a tremor of fear. She inhaled a quick breath as she met her father's furious gaze.

"I fail to see how I've betrayed you, my lord."

"Don't try to mince words with me, woman. You know damn well how you've betrayed me. Well, if you think I'm going to let this marriage stand, think again."

"I hardly see how you can do anything about it, my lord. The marriage is quite legal, and it's been consummated more than once I can assure you. In fact, I might even be carrying Devlyn's child as we speak."

"You! With child!" Lord Townsend snorted with sarcastic amusement. "You're too old to have a child, Sophie. The only reason that bastard married you was because he wants to get back at me."

The words sliced through her. For the first time, she realized she wanted to give Devlyn a child. A son she could love and cherish when her husband tired of her. Her hands balled into fists as anger welled up inside her at her father's cruel, callous statement.

"That bastard, as you refer to him, is my husband, which makes me the Countess of Devlyn. For once in your life, have the couth to refrain from acting like the bourgeois you are by birth. A true gentleman would never behave in the manner you are presently exhibiting."

Fury darkened her father's face. As he stepped toward her menacingly, she trembled but held her ground. Her hands behind her back, her fingers brushed over the poker. Closing her hand over the tool, she pulled it out from behind her and pointed it at her father.

"Take one more step toward me, and I'll make you wish you had never sired me."

Surprise crossed his face, and he came to a halt. The sudden light of respect in his beady eyes infuriated her. All these years she'd tried to please him, and now that she was standing up to him, he actually seemed pleased.

"Well, Sophie. It seems you have more backbone than I realized. I'm delighted to see you're far from the meek mouse I've always believed you to be."

"I've never been a mouse, my lord. I simply wanted...." She couldn't say it. It was too much like begging. She was the Countess of Devlyn. Not a submissive daughter doing everything she could to earn her father's love. She refused to beg for his love. Never again would she beg anyone for anything.

"I'll ask you to leave, my lord. We have nothing further to say to one another."

"Don't you get uppity with me, Sophie. Get your belongings, you're coming with me."

"I'm not leaving my husband, Father."

"Husband? Husband! That bastard isn't fit to be anything."

"He was good enough for your precious Eleanor," she spat out with pent up bitterness.

"Well, we know what happened there. The bloody bastard got your sister pregnant and then refused to marry her."

"That's a lie, and you know it. Eleanor is a harlot."

If possible, her father's face grew darker with anger. "I ought to beat you within an inch of your life for saying such a thing, but as it is, I'm going to be gracious and take you home."

"Don't make me laugh. You don't even understand the meaning of the word gracious. You simply want an unpaid bookkeeper you can force to conceal your illegal business transactions."

"Damn it, woman. I'm your father, and you'll do as I say."

"Father?" She glared at him. All the pain of his rejections welled up in her as she sneered at him. "You don't know the meaning of the word. I've never had a father. You're simply the man who sired me."

With a wild cry of fury, he knocked aside the poker she held and reached for her. Fear streaked through her and she darted past him. A second later, a beefy hand grabbed her hair to yank her head back. Despite the pain, she refused to cower before a man who'd never spoken one word of love to her throughout her life.

As he dragged her toward the salon door, she caught one of his fingers and bent it back sharply. His cry of pain shrieked through the room, and he released her only to slap her again with enough force to knock her to the floor. The pain in her jaw brought tears to her eyes, but she held them back. She crawled to her feet and heard the sound of running feet. Standing upright, she turned to face her father, expecting him to hit her again. She met his hate-filled gaze as he stepped toward her, but a powerful figure in dark blue followed by two wolfhounds flew between them.

Acting as a protective shield, Beast pressed his large body against hers, his watchful gaze fixed on the scene across the room. Caesar stood a short distance behind Devlyn, his wiry body braced for an attack and his teeth bared as his master dealt with the threat to their mistress.

Devlyn looked like a man possessed as he forced her father backwards until the older man was pinned against the wall, Devlyn's arm pressed against the man's throat. Although he didn't raise his voice, Sophie could hear the raw fury in her husband's voice from where she stood several feet away.

"Where my wife is concerned, this is the only warning I'll ever give you. If you come near her again, I'll kill you. I also want you to know that I'm going to destroy you. I'm going to strip everything from you until you have only one option open to you, and that's to put a gun to your head and pull the trigger."

The suppressed violence in her husband's voice sent a chill down her spine. She'd known him capable of great fury, but not this cold, lethal rage. Her father had paled considerably, and he was gasping for air when Devlyn released him from the chokehold.

As Lord Townsend crossed the floor toward the exit, Sophie held her ground. The hate in her father's eyes made her flinch, but she simply held her head higher. When he was gone, a tremor rocked her body. A gentle hand touched her cheek causing her to jerk with reaction.

"Shhh. Let me have a look."

The dramatic change in him startled her. Tender concern had replaced the deadly expression on his face. His fingers gently probed where her father had last hit her. Over his shoulder, he spoke to Fischer.

"Bring me some ice to stop the swelling." The manservant vanished immediately and Devlyn continued to examine her face. "I'm sorry, Sophie. I should have known he'd come here. Thank God my business with the tenants finished earlier than I expected."

She trembled at the thought of her father and she squeezed her eyes shut to hold back the tears. Crying never solved anything, and she refused to let her father cause her any further pain. Suddenly Devlyn wrapped her in a tight embrace.

"Damn it, Sophie, go ahead and cry." The gruffness in his voice nearly undid her.

"No," she mumbled against his wool coat. "He's not worth it."

"I promise you, Sophie. I'm going to make him pay, and pay dearly."

Pulling back from him, she shook her head. "It doesn't matter anymore. I thought revenge would heal me, make me whole. But it won't do that."

"If you're asking me to forego my plans, I've already told you that won't happen." The steely expression on his dark features reflected his implacable tone of voice.

"No. I'm not asking you to do that. I'm simply saying that revenge won't heal the pain my father and Eleanor have caused me."

Fischer reentered the room with some ice wrapped in a cloth. Taking it from him, Devlyn gently applied it to her jaw. "You're going to have a nasty bruise there, but it will heal. I promise you. If the bastard ever comes near you again, I'll kill him. I protect what's mine."

The fierce possessive note in his words soothed her. Someone finally considered her worthy of protection. A tear slid down her cheek. Gentle fingers brushed it away. Her eyes met his, and her heart skipped a beat at the tenderness she saw in his gaze. Closing her eyes, she leaned into him and rested her head on his shoulder. Devlyn might never offer his heart to her, but he would care for her, protect her, and that was worth more to her than all the gold in the world.

Chapter 8

With a whirr of steel against steel, Sophie clipped a rich, blood-red Beauharnais rose off the bush in front of her. She put the blossom up to her nose and inhaled the deep fragrance of the flower. The rose joined its companions in the basket she held as she reached out to retrieve another blossom off an adjoining bush.

Humming a light tune, she snipped the rose and laid it in her basket. In the past week, Devlyn had shown her how wonderful life could be. He had a zest for living that amazed her, and he was the most attentive, amorous lover she could have ever dreamed of having. She'd even begun to hope he might be coming to care for her some. Despite every bit of her willpower and determination, she couldn't deny the way he made her feel every time he touched her.

He had this power to turn her inside out with a word or touch. The sound of his voice sent ripples of anticipation over her entire body, while just the touch of his hand could make her explode and writhe in a torrid rush of desire. She only wished she had the power to make him feel the same way.

What would he do if she became the aggressor? Would he spurn her, or would he find it arousing? She remembered how much he liked her playing with him, squeezing him. She'd even been daring enough in their lovemaking to kiss his hard length. It had been like rough velvet against her lips, and his groans of delight had rumbled from his throat like those of a fierce lion.

She smiled to herself. The impropriety of her thoughts would have shocked her a week ago. But now? Now, she didn't care about how wicked or risqué her thoughts were. The sight of her husband always aroused a ravenous hunger for the pleasure of his touch. And she wanted him to experience the same with her. She wanted him to beg her for her touch.

Well, perhaps beg was the wrong word. Commanding her to touch him would be more Devlyn's style, but however he did it, in her mind he was fully aroused, besotted with desire that he would never let her go. She sighed. They were fantasies, nothing more.

After all, she was a realist. No matter how much she enjoyed his touch, she was certain it was simply infatuation. What woman wouldn't love to have a man such as Devlyn pursuing her? His reputation simply enhanced the danger he exuded with his masterful behavior and devastating charm. She cut another rose from the bush, and as it fell into her basket, she breathed in the scent of sandalwood. Before she could turn around, a strong arm wrapped around her waist, while a firm pair of lips grazed the nape of her neck.

"Good morning, Countess. You're acting quite cheerful this afternoon."

As always, his touch warmed her skin leaving her with a craving for more. Unwilling to turn into him, lest he think her completely under his spell, she pulled away with a small laugh.

"Would you prefer I act gloomy and dour?" She cast a glance over her shoulder and arched an eyebrow at him.

"God no. Come, put the flowers down and walk with me."

"But they need water. I can't just cut them, and leave them out in the sun."

"There are dozens more you can cut. Leave them."

He extended his hand with his usual air of command. Heaving a sigh, she set the basket in the shade of several bushes and turned to face him.

"There, are you satisfied?"

"Quite." His fingers gestured arrogantly for her to accept his hand. "Come."

She berated herself at the way she willingly acquiesced to his command. Why couldn't she show some backbone and simply ignore him? The answer to that was easy. Devlyn wasn't a man one could ignore. Her hand slipped into his and he smiled with satisfaction.

The smile warmed her. Blast. She really needed to learn some control where he was concerned. He would soon lose interest if she continued this habit of giving in to him without so much as a protest. The idea wasn't a pleasant one. The reality was she didn't want such a thing to happen. It was a sobering thought.

Devlyn tucked her hand in the crook of his arm, pulling her deeper into the garden. In the distance was a small arboretum tucked among tall hedges and surrounded by a small copse of trees. They walked in silence, and unwilling to contemplate the future, Sophie's mind wandered back to the erotic ideas she'd been considering before he'd joined her in the garden.

In her mind, she envisioned him seated naked in front of her. His arousal would be long, hard and thick. He'd recline back in his chair and with that devilish smile of his call her to him. The thought of kneeling in front of him to caress his body with her tongue created a rush of warmth between her legs. She swallowed hard, hoping to banish the thoughts from her head.

"You're preoccupied."

"Wha-what?" She spared him only a quick glance before returning her eyes to the ground in front of them.

"Wherever you were, it was obviously pleasurable. Tell me what you were thinking."

They'd reached the gazebo, and Devlyn stepped into the semi-darkness of the lattice-covered structure pulling her with him. With a deft turn of his hand, he spun her around to face him. Staring down into her eyes, he arched his brow.

"You're looking quite guilty, Sophie. Tell me what you were thinking, or I'll extract a suitable punishment."

"It was of ... of a personal nature."

There, that was the truth without describing her fantasy. That should satisfy him. He eyed her carefully for a long moment before he made to turn away. Relief sagged through her only to become dismay an instant later as he wheeled back in her direction.

"Exactly how do you describe thoughts of a personal nature, Sophie? Surely, you don't think to keep secrets from me."

"No ... of course not ... I was simply ... thinking about...." She bit her lip and turned her head away from him. "Please, it's embarrassing."

"Hmm, now you've definitely piqued my interest. Explain these mortifying thoughts of yours."

"They were ... were about ... pleasing you." She peeked a quick look at him, expecting him to be amused, but saw puzzlement instead.

"Whatever gave you the idea that you don't please me?"

"I didn't actually. I simply ... well... Blast! I meant I was thinking about how I could give you pleasure."

He seemed stunned by her revelation before he turned away from her. Mortified by his obvious rejection, she quickly darted across the gazebo's wooden floor toward the exit. A strong hand halted her flight. With a gentle tug, he pulled her back against him, his hand splayed across her stomach just below her breasts.

"Where the hell do you think you're going?" he growled softly in her ear.

"I have more flowers to cut."

"Running away, Sophie?"

Bristling at the amusement in his voice, she twisted around in his arms and glared up at him. "Don't be absurd."

He nipped her ear with teasing lips before kissing the side of her neck. "Then tell me what you were thinking."

"I told you, I was thinking about pleasing you."

"Tell me *in detail*." This time the gentle mockery in his voice made her narrow her gaze at him. If he thought to embarrass her, it would fail. No, it was time to test her power. Her capabilities as a woman.

She studied him for a long moment, deliberately wetting her lips with the tip of her tongue. When she saw his green eyes flash with desire, she reached up and traced his mouth with her forefinger.

"As you wish, my lord." She smiled slowly. "I was imagining you naked."

"Naked." He inhaled a sharp breath. It pleased her.

"Yes, you were sitting in a chair so that I could see all of you."

"And you. What were you doing Sophie?" His voice throbbed.

"Me? Oh, I was dressed and kneeling at your feet." With a lazy movement, her fingers trailed down his jaw.

"And while you were kneeling, were you doing anything?" His breathing was now rapid and raspy.

"Was I doing anything?" She smiled for a moment and licked her lips once more. "Why yes, I do believe I was."

A low growl reverberated in his throat, as he stood motionless in front of her. As he stared down into eyes, the fire in his gaze heated her blood. God, but she wished they were inside so she could live out her fantasy. From his expression, it was something he wanted too.

"Close your eyes, Sophie."

"Whatever for?" She shook her head in puzzlement.

"Do it," he ordered harshly. "And don't open them until I tell you do so."

Slowly she did as he commanded. As she stood there unable to see him, she heard small sounds that were familiar, but couldn't clearly place. After a long moment, she heard his voice off to one side ordering her to open her eyes.

Turning her head, she gasped with shocked surprise. "Oh dear Lord! Are you mad? Someone might come along!"

"Which makes it all the more exciting, don't you think?" He grinned at her as he lounged back against the railing of the gazebo.

Naked and fully aroused, his beautiful body sent a thread of excitement charging through her. Her mouth went dry and her palms grew damp as she studied him. Her eyes drifted across his body, inciting a desire to taste him. Taste all of him, especially his hard erection, which jutted out from his firm, muscular thighs. He was beautiful, and she was the reason he was so aroused. For just a moment, she glanced over her shoulder afraid someone might stumble across them.

"Haven't you learned not to be timid by now?" His question made her jerk her gaze back to him.

"I hardly think--"

"Adventure is never for those who think." Devlyn crooked his finger at her, an arrogant smile on his face. "Now then, you were saying you were at my feet."

Dazed by his outrageous behavior, and yet thrilled by the daring of it all, she shook her head. "Dear God, Devlyn, what if someone comes out here?"

"We're quite safe from prying eyes, Sophie. Come here."

She stared at him for a long moment, and he arched an eyebrow at her. The challenge in his expression made her remember what she'd started. Determined to regain the power she'd lost at his audacious behavior, she locked her gaze with his and moved forward. Reaching him, she knelt in front of him, her hands on his knees.

"Shall I show you what I was doing on my knees, my lord?"

"Yes," he rasped.

With a firm touch, she slid her hands to the inside of his thighs and pushed his legs apart. He was glorious in his maleness, and his arousal enticed her. Sprawled out in front of her, he was hers for the taking, and she reveled in the knowledge. She slid a hand slowly over his thigh, just past his erection and up his well-muscled chest.

Her fingers brushed over his nipple as she pushed herself forward and leaned into him. His erection jumped as her dress caressed his hard length. It made her want to kiss him right now, but she wanted to make him wild with desire. She pressed her lips to his chest then suckled at his nipple as he often did with her. A deep groan rumbled in his throat, and she gently nipped at his rigid peak.

While her lips were teasing his chest, her hand reached between them and cupped the two large sacs beneath the long, hot length of him. He sucked in a sharp breath. She pulled back from him, cradling him in the palm of her hand. There was a glazed look in his green eyes, and she smiled.

This was what it meant for a woman to be powerful in the bedroom. His expression revealed the heat searing through him--

heat for her. Her gaze still riveted on his face, she stroked him with one finger. He jumped at the touch.

Leaning forward, she pressed her lips to the solid length of him. He growled with pleasure, and her fingers kneaded the inside of his thigh as she feathered light kisses along his erection. In her fantasy, she'd used her tongue to caress his hard staff with long, leisurely strokes. She did so now, delighted with the rumbles of pleasure echoing over her head as her tongue swirled across his hot length. The tip of her tongue edged around the tip of him, and she tasted a salty bead of desire.

The taste of him startled her. He was close to an orgasm. Sweet heaven, only a wicked woman would engage in such behavior in the middle of the lawn, in broad daylight. She rocked back on her heels and stared up at him. The hot need in his face caressed her, flushing her skin with fire. It might be wicked, but dear Lord how she loved making him look ready to explode with passion.

"That's not what you were really thinking of doing, is it?" The hoarse sound of his voice startled her.

"I don't know what you mean."

"You weren't just kissing my cock in your fantasy. You were sucking on me, weren't you?" His language appalled and excited her all at the same time.

"I ... I...."

"I want your lips on me, Sophie. I want you to suck on my cock. Suck on me, now."

The ferocity in his voice was emphasized by the steely touch of his fingers at the nape of her neck. His touch was gentle, but unwavering as he guided her head forward until her lips hovered over the tip of him.

The decadent appeal of taking him into her mouth was wickedly tantalizing, and she flicked out her tongue to swirl around the tip of him. Her hands rested on his thighs, and his muscles tensed beneath her fingers as she stroked the long length of him with her tongue. A dark groan poured out of his throat. When she glanced up at him, she saw his eyes were closed.

As her fingers brushed over the large sacs hanging below his engorged staff, he jumped visibly. She was in control once more. She was the one with the power. He was at her mercy, and the knowledge enthralled her. Once more, she slid her tongue up and across him. His cock jumped at her touch, and she smiled.

"Do you like that, my lord?"

"Christ yes," he growled.

Certain that there was pleasure in the anticipation of the act, she nibbled at the top of him before her tongue glided along the underside of his erection. Another groan accompanied her caresses, and she gently wrapped her lips around the tip of him and slowly took him into her mouth.

Wicked decadence was the only description she could think of for this sinful act. Knowing it gave him pleasure heightened her own sense of excitement. Her fingers circled him at the bottom of his shaft as she slid her mouth down further. The sensation of his hands threading through her pinned up curls surprised her as he guided her to imitate the intimate act they'd performed so many times in recent nights.

He tightened in her mouth and she swept her tongue over the rigid length of him. Another groan rumbled deep in his throat as he gently bucked against her lips. Sweet Lord, she'd never realized how exciting it could be to hear his groans of pleasure. She tightened her lips around him creating a suction that made his fingers tense in her hair.

"Christ Jesus. Faster, go faster."

Obeying the command, she quickly increased the pace of her mouth moving over him. Over her head, she could hear his rapid breathing and commands for her to continue. Beneath her tongue, his erection stiffened and throbbed. Then with a quick movement, he pushed her off him and spilled his seed onto his stomach. Sinking back on her heels, she watched in fascination as he reclined against the bench railing, a satiated look on his face.

Satisfaction sailed through her. She'd pleased the Devil of Devlyn's Keep. A nasty little voice reminded her it was doubtful she was the only woman to please him. She shoved the thought aside. She would live in the present, and at the moment, she and she alone had pleased her husband.

Scrambling to her feet, she retrieved a handkerchief from Devlyn's coat pocket and returned to remove the milky white fluid from his stomach. At her touch, he opened his eyes and his hand slid around to grasp the nape of her neck.

"You, my sweet, are the most devilish wanton I've ever met."

She heard the endearment, but found it difficult to believe he'd spoken it. It was the first time he'd ever spoken with such affection before. Staring down at him, she saw a flash of emotion darken his green eyes before he captured her lips in a hard kiss. Bracing her hands on his warm, sculpted chest, she sighed with pleasure into his mouth. From a distance, she heard a voice calling out, and she stiffened. With a quick shove, she pushed her way out of his arms and straightened. Again, she heard the voice as it drew closer.

"Oh my God, it's Spencer."

A chuckle rippled from Devlyn's throat as he stood and caught her from behind. His lips nuzzled at her shoulder while his hand hugged her breast. "You worry too much."

"Blast it, Devlyn! Will you dress? My brother will think the worst."

"Your brother knows me and my reputation. Then of course there's the fact that we are married."

"Married or not, I'll not have him thinking I lift my skirts for you in a public place."

"Ah, but Countess, you didn't lift your skirts. You simply enjoyed the taste of my cock."

The teasing laughter in his voice appalled and amused her at the same time. Spencer's voice called out for them again from a short distance away. Wheeling around in Devlyn's arms, she kissed him hard.

"If you don't dress now, I swear I'll refuse to taste your cock in the future. Now dress!"

She ignored the stunned delight on his face as she pushed herself out of his arms. Almost at a run, she hurried from the gazebo and down the path toward her brother. As she raced along the pebbled walkway, she prayed Devlyn would hurry. She didn't want Spencer to think badly of him. It wouldn't do for her brother to think ill of the man she loved.

The thought brought her to a halt, her breath stolen away by the revelation. Dear God, how could she have committed such folly? She was mad. She had to be. Only a madwoman would fall in love with the Devil of Devlyn's Keep. Mad or not, she couldn't deny the inevitable. She'd done the one thing she'd sworn not to do. She'd fallen in love with her husband.

Chapter 9

Devlyn grinned as his wife scurried out of the gazebo. God help him, but his wife had a wicked tongue. The memory of it swirling around his cock made him hard again. Damnation, he needed to learn more control.

He heard Sophie greeting her brother, and he moved quickly. It would embarrass her if Spencer Hamilton caught him in such a state. The last thing he wanted to do was hurt her. Hell, he wanted to give her a present.

It was the reason he'd brought her to the gazebo in the first place. Then her deliciously sinful fantasy had distracted him. Everything about Sophie distracted him. She was becoming an addiction, and if he weren't careful, his wife would have him at her mercy. Dressing with speed, he was knotting his tie when he heard her voice calling out to him.

"Devlyn, will you please come out of hiding? Spencer has come for a visit."

Stepping out of the gazebo, he moved several paces down the garden path and around the large hedge encircling the small building. The look of relief on her face tugged a smile to his lips. "I'd hardly call walking through the gardens as hiding, my sweet."

It was the second time he'd spoken so affectionately to her, and he found he liked the sound of it. She was incredibly sweet. Sweet, sensual and passionate. And she was his.

He shook Hamilton's hand before his gaze swept back to his wife. There was a stricken look about her that worried him. Had her brother said something to trouble her? Narrowing his eyes at her, her gaze met his. Immediately, she smiled and he frowned. Had he imagined her expression of dismay?

"I apologize for the intrusion, but I wanted to say good-bye to Phe."

"Good-bye?" Sophie frowned, her eyes flashing with anger. "Did Father throw you out? You know you can always stay here."

She looked at him, silently pleading with him to concur. "She's right, Hamilton. If you need a place to stay, you're welcome here."

The younger man eyed him cautiously for a moment before he nodded an acceptance of the peace between the two of them.

"Thank you, but it's not a drastic situation. The manor was only tolerable when you were there, Phe. Now it's simply a suffocating environment. I informed Father that I wanted to inspect the London properties he awarded me last year. He accepted that excuse."

"Well, at least you know you're always welcome here," Sophie squeezed her brother's hand.

Smiling in return, Hamilton arched an eyebrow. "It seems marriage agrees with you, Phe. I've never seen you look so radiant."

A blush flared in his wife's cheeks, and Devlyn chuckled. "More likely the bloom on her cheeks is from anger. I seem to provoke that reaction in her, among others."

"She can be hotheaded from time to time."

"Indeed. I'm learning how wicked her tongue can be." Beside him, Sophie inhaled a sharp breath at the veiled reference. He grinned at her. "A fact which has prevented me from telling her my news for almost an hour."

"News?"

Their voices chimed in unison. Hamilton straightened with interest, while Sophie looked like she was ready to kill him. He only hoped it would be a sweet death such as the one she'd just given him in the gazebo.

"Yes, my ships reached port two days ago, and I've already recouped my investment and my funds have nearly tripled."

"I say, that's news which warrants a celebration."

He nodded at his brother-in-law's cheerful comment. "I agree. And I've made arrangements for Sophie and me to visit London."

"London," she gasped.

"I've arranged for Devlyn House in Mayfair to be opened, and I've secured a new box at the Alhambra."

"Good God, don't tell me Sophie's convinced you to take her to the opera." Hamilton's exclamation earned him a scathing look from Sophie.

"I'm not all that fond of any theater, but I've yet to give my wife a wedding present, and I believe this is an appropriate one." He smiled at her expression of delight before frowning as her pleasure abruptly turned to dismay.

"But I haven't anything to wear."

"Ah, the proverbial cry of all women. You needn't fret, Countess. I'll see to it you'll have a dozen new frocks." He grinned as he leaned toward her and pressed his lips against her ear. "But I much prefer you naked and between my legs."

Her gasp made him laugh. Releasing her, he clapped his brother-in-law on the shoulder. "Come, Hamilton. Your sister was cutting flowers. Let's leave her to that task. I have some fine brandy we can drink to toast my success, and it's time the two of us got better acquainted."

As he guided the younger man toward the keep, he risked a quick glance back at Sophie. Her embarrassment had given way to outrage and she was glaring at him with daggers in her eyes. Yes, his wanton Countess was as fiery as they came, and it only made him desire her that much more.

* * * *

The noise in the Alhambra's main lobby was deafening. The crush provided him with one more reason to despise the opera. He wanted nothing better than to escape this wild zoo of humanity. An acquaintance caught his eye, and he offered a nod in the direction of the man.

He deliberately looked away to avoid talking with the man. The last thing he wanted to do was add fuel to the gossip mill running rampant since their arrival in London more than two weeks ago. No matter where they went, someone was trying to find out more information about his marriage, and he was damned if it was anyone else's business.

He recognized another individual and he heaved a grunt of exasperation. If Sophie didn't return from the ladies room shortly, he'd create a stir by going in and retrieving her. At least they'd have some privacy in their box.

"Devlyn! Is that you, old man?"

At the sound of his name, he turned his head to see Sir Archibald Millard pushing through the crowd to reach him. Groaning inwardly at the sight of the man, he tightened his lips. Schoolmates at Eton, the man had been a thorn in his side ever since. Millard considered himself a wit, but Devlyn found him nothing short of boring.

Dark hair already thinning on top and his middle section already beginning to sport a paunch, Sir Archibald was the epitome of a man who considered himself a connoisseur of all things, but truly mastered none.

A moment later, Devlyn found his hand grasped by Sir Archibald's beefy one. "I say, Devlyn, you're the talk of the town."

"Am I?" He deliberately drawled his reply to indicate distinct boredom. It didn't have the effect he'd hoped. Sir Archibald plunged on with his babbling.

"Of course you are. Why everyone's talked of nothing else. It's one thing to have an older woman for your mistress, but Good God, man, for a wife?"

"I wasn't aware that age had anything to do with marriage."

"Well of course it does. No respectable man would marry a woman twice his age."

Anger made him grit his teeth. Either the bastard was a complete ass or he was being insulting. It didn't matter. He wasn't going to let someone talk about Sophie in such a disparaging manner. Narrowing his eyes, he leaned into the man.

"My wife is not twice my age and even if she were, it wouldn't be any of your concern. So unless you--" Sir Archibald acted as if he'd not heard a word, his gazed fixed on something over Devlyn's shoulder.

"Good God, who is that ravishing creature?"

Devlyn turned his head to see Sophie heading toward them. She did look ravishing, but he was damned if he wanted Sir Archibald noticing. Her chin was tilted at a stubborn angle, and her cheeks were flushed with color, while her large hazel eyes sparkled with anger. Damnation, something had happened. Had one of his old mistresses taunted her? He should have known better than to bring her here tonight.

Beside him, Sir Archibald elbowed him and laughed. "I should have known better. You might have married, but giving up your light skirts wasn't part of the contract. You've excellent taste as always, Devlyn. She's exquisite. When you tire of her, let me know."

Muscles tightened with raw fury as he restrained himself from pulverizing the man with his fists. As Sophie reached them, he took her hand and raised it to his lips. "Well, Countess. Are you ready to take a seat in our box?"

Beside him, Sir Archibald started violently. Ignoring the man, he wrapped Sophie's arm through the crook of his elbow and pulled her toward the stairs. There was a strained look to her smile, and he noted the stares the two of them were receiving. He turned his head so his mouth was close to her ear.

"Who's upset you?"

She flashed him a quick glance before looking away. "What makes you think I'm upset?"

"It might only be a month since we exchanged our vows, Sophie, but I know you better than you think."

"It's nothing. I knew there would be talk." With a graceful move, she lifted the front of her skirt as they climbed the stairs to the second level of the theater. "It seems we've created quite a stir with our marriage."

"To hell with them. They don't matter. They'll find something else for the rumor mill within a fortnight."

"I know. I just didn't expect people to be quite so vicious." There was a woebegone expression in her eyes as he ushered her into their box. Something else was bothering her as well, but she was unwilling to share it with him. The thought irritated him. As they took their seats, he saw the crowd stir and look toward their box. A tremor shot through Sophie, and he leaned toward her.

"Have I told you how beautiful you look tonight?"

The flush of color in her cheeks pleased him as she laughed. Flicking open her fan in an elegant gesture, she shook her head at him. "That brandy you had before we left home has dulled your senses, Devlyn. However, I appreciate your gallantry."

Annoyed, he grasped her hand and turned it over to examine her wrist displayed in the small, circular opening of her evening glove. Following the edge of the silk circle, he trailed a path across her skin with his forefinger. She trembled at the touch and he smiled. "Haven't you learned by now, that I'm far from gallant? A rake rarely is."

"Very well then, but how do you explain tonight? You hate the opera. You've told me so yourself. How do you explain your presence here tonight?"

Releasing her hand, he leaned closer, his hand pressing against her knee. "I'm here because I'm waiting for the proper moment to seduce my wife in a public place."

Her gasp tugged a smile to his mouth, and her cheeks darkened with color. "You're mad."

"No, Countess, not mad. Simply adventurous. Think about it. You enjoy my fingers sliding through those dark curls between your legs. What if I were to touch you like that, here, once the opera started?"

"You wouldn't," she said in a strangled voice.

"It would be exciting, don't you think? Think about the danger of it."

"I don't wish to think about it."

"Why not? Think about it, Countess. What if I were to make love to you within earshot of all these people."

"It's impossible."

"Ah, so the thought excites you as well." He watched her breasts as they rose and fell at a rapid pace. Her excitement was clearly evident.

"Ye ... no, I simply meant... Blast it, Devlyn. Must you tease me like this?"

"And must you tease me with the thought of sucking on those glorious nipples of yours? Are they hard now, Sophie?" He heard the way her breathing was soft rasps crossing her lips. "Are they hard like I like them?"

The question pulled a low moan from her throat. "Oh God, yes."

Hazel eyes wide in her face, she turned to look at him. Desire glowed in her gaze, and he smiled. "And once I finished with your nipples, I'd find it equally pleasurable to put my mouth against you, drinking that delicious cream of yours."

"For pity's sake, Devlyn, stop." Her fan fluttered frantically in front of her face.

"Tell me, my sweet. Are you wet there now? If I were to stroke that sensitive little nub of yours would you buck against my hand like a wild thing?"

"Damn you, Devlyn." Her voice was hoarse as several shudders shook through her. He smiled with satisfaction.

"No matter how small the orgasm, they're still quite gratifying, wouldn't you say so, Sophie?"

"You're wicked through and through."

He leaned into her, his nostrils picking up her musky scent. "Tell me the truth. You love it when I'm being wicked. You like the danger and excitement of it all."

She opened her mouth quickly in an attempt to deny his statement, but he simply stared her into admitting the truth. "Yes. Yes, I like it when you're being wicked."

Drawing back from her, he reclined back in his chair as the gas lights in the theater dimmed. As the hall filled with music, Sophie leaned toward him.

"And you, my lord," she whispered. "What about your needs?"

"My needs?" He eyed her carefully in the shadows. A slow smile curved her lips as she met his gaze. The minx was up to something.

"But of course, my lord. Surely you have need of something hot and wet around you as well."

He swallowed quickly as her hand slid discreetly up his leg to his crotch. Her touch was light as she stroked her fingers across his cock. It grew solid and firm in an instant. She pretended to watch the opening of the opera as her fingers toyed with his trouser buttons. Bloody hell, he should have known the woman would retaliate. But God, it was a delicious retaliation.

"Are you offering to take me in your mouth, Countess?"

"You'd like that, wouldn't you? I can feel how hard you are. Imagine how much harder you'd be if I took you in my mouth."

Her palm caressed him, and he struggled to suppress the groan waiting to escape his mouth. God but the woman was a temptress hell-bent on repaying him for his earlier teasing.

"Christ, woman. Take care with your words."

"You started this little game, my lord. How could you possibly want to quit now? Especially when my mouth is so willing to assuage your need."

"Bloody hell." His cock tightened with an exquisite pain, and her hand rubbed over him before she squeezed the tip of him with gentle fingers.

"Shall we find a dark corner in which to indulge our sin, my lord? Or perhaps it would be best to simply ponder the idea until we return home. "

Satisfaction curled the corners of her mouth, and he groaned as she turned away to watch the performance on the stage below. Sweet Jesus, but she'd turned the tables on him. A fire burned inside him, and he wanted to pull her down to the floor and rut like a wild animal. How the hell had he come to such a passion?

He'd never had a woman twist his insides like this. Not even Eleanor had driven him toward such a primitive, carnal need. But this woman, his beautiful, wanton Countess, had merely to smile and utter a few well-chosen words and he was jelly in her hands.

A wild thought careened through his head, and he froze. It wasn't possible. No, he was mad to even think it. God, he needed a drink. Rising to his feet, he touched her shoulder as she looked up at him.

"Forgive me. I'd forgotten why I despised the opera so much. This caterwauling has reminded me, so I'm going to take my leave of you."

A mischievous smile curled her mouth. "Shall I come with you?"

"No," he said harshly. "I'll send the carriage back for you."

Puzzlement furrowed her brow, but she nodded quietly and didn't protest. Leaving the theater box, he stood in the quiet hallway, his back pressed against the wall. He refused to believe it. He couldn't believe it. Rakes never fell in love, especially with their wives. No, a rake would walk out of here right now and drink himself into a stupor. That or find a mistress. No. That he couldn't do.

With a violent shove of his arms, he pushed himself away from the wall and strode down the passage. As he entered the vestibule at the top of the stairs, which connected the corridors lining both sides of the theater, he saw Eleanor coming toward him.

How could he have ever thought her beautiful? Even from this short distance, it was impossible to ignore the hardness of her blue eyes or the calculating twist to her finely shaped lips. He turned away and started down the steps. Her voice forced him to stop.

"Devlyn, surely you're not leaving. I've not even had a moment to offer you my congratulations."

He slowly turned his head to meet her gaze. "Forgive me, Lady Shively, but I don't want your congratulations."

"You're being far too cruel, Devlyn. The past is behind us. You're my brother-in-law now. Surely we can at least be civil to each other for Sophie's sake."

With a snort of disgust, he shook his head. "Civility is not for the likes of you and me, Lady Shively. Good night."

Not waiting for her response, he hurried down the stairs and out of the theater. All he wanted to do was to go home and drink himself into oblivion. It took several minutes for his carriage to arrive outside the Alhambra. Without waiting for the new footman to open the vehicle's door, he opened it himself and flung his body onto the soft padded cushions.

Throughout the ride home, he tried to comprehend what course of action he should take, but he still had no answers when the coach rolled up in front of Devlyn Townhouse. Leaving the driver with orders to return to the theater for Sophie, he entered the house and ensconced himself in the library with two bottles of brandy.

It took him little time to deaden his senses with the first decanter of liquor, and by that time, he had removed his jacket and waistcoat, undone his tie and opened his shirt at the throat. He took another deep swig of brandy and stared into the fireplace. Already his head was throbbing and his movements lethargic.

Bloody hell, he'd not be capable of performing tonight. And damn it, he wanted to perform. He wanted to find a way of washing his wife out of his blood. There had to be a way to do so. He simply needed to think. A mirthless chuckle rolled out of his throat. He was in no condition to think. If anything, he was having trouble keeping his eyes open. Sleep, that was a decision that took no effort to make.

Even with his eyes closed, images of Sophie filled his head. She was a vision he couldn't escape even if he tried. And heaven help him, he didn't want to try. She was the best thing that had ever happened to him. No woman had ever touched his heart the way his wife had.

His thoughts crashed together as he sank lower into his drunken haze. Sophie would be home soon, and he needed to have an answer as to why he'd left the theater so abruptly. She'd think it was her fault. Christ, he didn't want to think anymore. It was too much trouble to think.

He jerked his head up. Thinking, that's what he'd been trying to do. God, he was drunk. His head fell back against the leather chair as he closed his eyes. In the foyer, the clock chimed the hour of eleven. Any minute she'd be home. A light touch pierced his stupor as her gentle hands slid across his thighs. He groaned as she brushed her fingers over him. Damnation, he'd gotten drunk to avoid feeling her touch, and now even in his stupor she was still able to torture him. Grasping her hands, he tugged her upward. As he did so, he caught the faint aroma of an exotic scent. He forced his eyes open and stared into Eleanor's hard blue gaze.

"What the hell are you doing--?"

From out in the foyer, he heard Sophie's laughter as she said something to Fischer. The sound of her voice drew near, and in his drunken state, he moved too slowly. Before he could push Eleanor aside, the study door opened and in that small instant, the woman crushed her lips against his. With a growl of fury, he pushed her away from him, and looked toward the doorway where Sophie stood.

"Christ almighty ... Sophie, it's not what you think."

Pale, serene and regal, his wife smiled coldly. "Nothing is ever as it seems, my lord. Forgive me for intruding on you and your slut."

The door closed softly behind her as he staggered to his feet. He nearly fell down as he stumbled over Eleanor who was lying at his feet laughing. For the first time, he clearly saw the state of his sister-in-law's dishabille. Her gown was open to reveal the tops of her breasts and her hair had been artfully disarranged to give the impression she'd been in the heat of passion. The bitch had deliberately set him up, but why?

He wanted to go after Sophie, but first he need to rid himself of this malicious creature. Reaching down, he dragged her to her feet by the hair on her head. She squealed her protest.

"God damn it, Devlyn, let me go."

His fist locked in her hair. He yanked her head back and stared down into her bitter, triumphant gaze. "First you're going to tell me what you're doing here."

"Revenge, Devlyn. Nothing more, nothing less. You refused me. I couldn't allow my older sister to have you unchallenged. Besides, Father and I wanted to give you something special for your wedding present."

His fingers tightened in her hair and he smiled cruelly as she winced. "Always the little whore to please your father. Did it ever occur to you that I despise you?"

"Of course, but it changes nothing. I succeeded in putting a wedge between you and my sister that will never heal. Sophie knows all too well how easily I can usurp her in a gentleman's affections."

The vicious laughter pealing from her lips disgusted him. With a roar, he pulled her toward the main foyer. As he dragged her across the marble floor to the front door, she kept batting at his arms in an effort to make him release her. Throwing open the door he barely controlled his impulse to shove her down the steps. Instead, he made sure she was clear of the door, then slammed it in her face.

Turning back toward the stairs, his blurred gaze traveled up to the second floor landing. Now he needed to convince Sophie that what she'd seen had been staged. His head thundered with pain, and he experienced a short bout of discomfort in his stomach. Bloody hell, he needed some coffee before he could even consider confronting Sophie. He was in no condition to argue with her. Sobriety was the order of the moment.

Chapter 10

Sophie locked her bedroom door behind her. She doubted Devlyn would try to enter her room, but she didn't want to take the chance. Her gaze traveled to the door connecting their room, and she moved to lock that one as well. Protected from unwelcome intrusions, she walked slowly toward the middle of the room. Her listless fingers undid her cloak. It slid to the floor unnoticed. Dazed, a shiver ran through her, and she stumbled toward the fire.

Stretching out her hands, she tried to warm her icy fingers. Another shiver crashed through her, and she sank to her knees, praying for the fire to make her warm again. It was like a bad dream. She should have known something was wrong when Devlyn had left the theater so abruptly. But never in her wildest nightmares had she expected to see what she'd found in the library.

He was more of a rake than she'd ever dreamed him to be. He'd teased her with the intimacy of a lover at the theater only to return home and rut with her sister. She squeezed her eyes shut tightly. Eleanor. Always Eleanor.

The pain of betrayal surged through her with the strength of a wild bull. It gored through her body until tears streamed down her cheeks. God, how could she have been so stupid? She'd been realistic enough to know his attraction for her wouldn't last. She'd expected this, his need for a younger woman, but she'd never contemplated it would be her sister.

She'd thought he possessed honor, but she knew now how wrong she'd been. An honorable man would never have done to her what he had done tonight. Betraying her with another woman might be a forgivable sin, but to betray her with Eleanor was reprehensible. How could he have done this when he knew what her sister had done to her? And Eleanor. What depraved nature made her sister hate her so much that coveting her husband was amusing? For Eleanor had been quite amused. She'd been laughing as Devlyn had stumbled to his feet.

The cruelty of it nauseated her. Her stomach lurched and she pressed the back of her hand to her mouth to keep from retching. What was she going to do? Staring into the flames, she tried to find an answer, but none was forthcoming. She was so cold. Why didn't the warmth of the fire penetrate her body? It was as if she were dead.

Yes, that's what it was. She was dead. She'd made the mistake of falling in love with her husband, a renowned rake, and now she was paying the price. What had made her think that Devlyn would be any different from all the other men she'd met or known?

Every man she'd ever known or loved had failed to see her wants or needs. Even Spencer, as much as she loved him, had never understood how unbearable her life at Townsend Manor was. He had always been able to leave. She couldn't.

So, she'd adapted and persevered in spite of her father's uncaring attitude. When she'd propositioned Devlyn, she'd wanted two things. Escape from her father's house and the experience of a lover's touch. She'd truly believed it possible to keep herself distanced from him while experiencing sexual pleasure in his arms.

Well, she'd experienced what she'd wanted and in doing so had lost her heart. Devlyn had never claimed to be anything else but what he was, a notorious rake with no desire to remain faithful to a wife almost twice his age. It shouldn't surprise her. After all, she'd proposed this mad arrangement to Devlyn. She'd known what would eventually happen.

But then she'd never dreamed of falling in love with him. God, he'd made her feel young again. It was a sensation she'd not experienced in quite some time. Young and beautiful was how he'd made her feel. Now she recognized his attentions for what they were. A rake dallying with the affections of an inexperienced old maid.

Had he laughed to himself at the way she'd responded to his lovemaking? From the beginning, he'd been forthright in claiming his rakish character. But she'd thought him honorable. She'd entered into this devil's bargain of her own accord, fully aware they'd eventually lead separate lives.

Still, there had been moments when she wondered if things might turn out differently for the two of them. Moments where she'd thought she'd seen a look of tenderness in his eyes or face. It wouldn't happen now. They'd part company, but it wouldn't be the quiet, unnoticed parting she'd envisioned.

Tonight's humiliation destroyed that possibility. The matter wouldn't remain private. Eleanor would see to that. The loathsome memory of seeing Eleanor in the ladies room tonight at the Alhambra returned vividly. Her sister's blithe announcement that it wouldn't be a fortnight before a woman would steal Devlyn away had been nothing more than a performance. It had been for the spectators in the ladies room.

The indiscreet whispers had only escalated after Eleanor's little scene. It was impossible to block out the voices expressing shocked outrage about the age difference between her and Devlyn. That people viewed her marriage as scandalous was one thing, now she'd be an object of pity as well. They'd see her as a spinster who'd thought to win the love of a younger man. What a fool. What a lovesick fool. She shivered again.

A soft sound outside her door froze her limbs. Her gaze darted to the main door, and she watched the knob turn slowly until it could go no further then it rolled back into place. Her heart rose in her throat as she waited for a heavy foot to break down the door. The silence stretched on, her nerves taut with trepidation.

When nothing happened, she sagged inward, her chin touching her chest as she realized he wasn't going to break down the door. Another tear forced its way out of her eyes that were squeezed shut. God help her, she'd wanted him to break down the door. She'd wanted him to barrel his way in here and tell her it had all been a mistake. But that wasn't going to happen.

Drained and exhausted, she climbed to her feet. A quiet click behind her forced her to spin around toward the door that connected her room with Devlyn's. As the door opened, her body grew wooden and stiff.

His features implacable, Devlyn entered her room holding up a master key for the door lock in silence. For a long moment, he stared at her, his eyes never leaving her face. Uncomfortable under the penetrating stare, she turned away and watched the blaze burning in the fireplace. The silence between them was almost tangible and she grew tired of the tension it created.

"What do you want, my lord?"

"You."

She wasn't quite certain what she'd expected, but she hadn't expected this particular response. The bold arrogance of it amazed her. Did he really think he could make such a demand after what she'd seen in the library? Her gaze flew to his enigmatic expression. The misery he'd caused her welled up inside her in the form of steely anger.

"Always the rake, amusing and witty no matter what the occasion."

"It wasn't a jest, Sophie."

The fine line of her brow arched upward with disdain. "Then it should be, for I find it quite amusing."

"Damn it. I want to explain." No, he wanted to do more than explain. He wanted to tell her how much he loved her. He wanted to make her understand that there would never be another woman for him.

"Explain what, my lord? I have eyes, and I have no need of details." She forced a laugh past her lips.

"It's not what you think." Stepping forward, he drew up short as her hand snapped at the wrist to halt his forward momentum with her silent gesture.

"Spare me your explanations, my lord. Revenge brought us together, and we enjoyed a pleasant, but brief physical interlude. Now it's time to address the issue of leading separate lives."

"Pleasant interlude?" Bloody hell. He wanted to kill her. Brushing her hand aside, he moved within a foot of her. "You have the audacity to tell me that every moment of passion between us has been *pleasant.*"

"Would you prefer I label our encounters as satisfactory?" A bitter smile twisted her lips.

"And perhaps you'd prefer me to show you how *pleasant* our little encounters have always been."

"You'd like that wouldn't you. Two sisters in one night. I'm surprised you aren't begging me to participate in a *ménage a trois* with you and the slut."

With a quick movement, he pulled her into his arms. "No, Sophie. I prefer my women one at a time so I have total control over their pleasure and mine."

"But I'm not your woman, my lord. I never will be."

"You're mine, Sophie. Shall I prove it?"

"Prove what? That you're stronger than I am? That you can bend my body to your will? Do as you wish. But know this. I despise you. I detest the sight of you. You aren't merely a rake; you're a callous, soulless wretch who isn't fit to touch me."

Each word had the strength of harsh blows pelting his body. God, she couldn't have hurt him more deeply than if she'd driven a stake through his heart. Couldn't she see how much he loved her?

"So you won't even allow me to explain," he rasped.

"Explain what? That revenge against my family included rutting with not only me, but my sister as well?"

"God damn it, Sophie! I was not rutting with your sister. I didn't even touch her."

She stared at him in amazement, speechless. He really expected her to believe him. Believe that he wasn't kissing Eleanor, when she'd seen the two of them together in a state of semi-undress. Suddenly, it occurred to her how amusing it all really was.

After all these years, he was still in love with Eleanor. How ironic, given her sister had stolen her fiancée. A small laugh escaped her. Then a flood of laughter parted her lips. In less than an instant, she was laughing hysterically at the entire situation.

His hands gripped her arms tightly and he shook her roughly. "That's enough. Enough, damn you."

Her laughter died at his furious expression. "You're quite right, my lord. Enough. Enough of this ludicrous conversation. I'll be out of the house tomorrow morning."

"The hell you will. You're my wife, and you'll stay here."

"No, my dear boy, I'm simply the woman you married." A brittle laugh escaped her lips. "You've been a wonderful tutor, but my bedroom education is complete now. You can hardly expect me not to put it to use. I'm sure there are more dissolute rakes in the Set willing to bed me."

"Take care with your words," he growled softly.

She ignored how his eyes were sunken in, his pallor almost white. His scar etched its way vividly down his face, while his mouth was nothing more than a thin, harsh line. He obviously didn't like being crossed. Well, this was one time the Devil of Devlyn's Keep would find his way thwarted.

"Surely you're not going to restrict me from using my education. With my detailed experience in the uses and abuses of a rake it shouldn't be difficult at all to acquire a lover."

"This is your last warning, Sophie."

"Or what? You'll cross the line and reveal yourself for the immoral, dissolute, odious bastard you really are? Forgive me, but I've already paid for and received those services. You performed exceedingly well given you're not much more than a callow youth."

His head jerked as her words lashed out through the air. For a fleeting instant, she believed he was going to hit her. Instead, he released her abruptly. With a sharp bow, he wheeled about and returned to his bedroom.

The door slammed shut behind him. She remained frozen in place for several moments, half expecting him to return, grateful, yet disappointed, when he didn't. Had she misjudged him? Throughout the conversation, he'd maintained his innocence. But there could be no denying what she'd seen. No, she'd not made a mistake. He'd been the one to err in thinking her a fool, willing to accept whatever nonsensical story he concocted.

Tomorrow she would have to visit Spencer and see if he would let her stay with him. She had no wish to remain under the same roof as Devlyn. It would be too painful. She closed her eyes. How was she going to live without him? They'd known each other only a short month, but it hadn't taken her that long to fall in love with him. Now, the depth of her love only intensified her pain and despair. Not even her father had ever cut her as deeply as Devlyn had tonight.

Exhausted, she undressed with lethargic movements before she eventually tumbled into bed. Sleep took its time coming to her, but when the little death overtook her, it was a welcome relief from the agony flowing out of her heart with every painful beat.

* * * *

The quiet rattle of china penetrated Sophie's sleep, and she stirred beneath her covers. Memories of the evening before washed over her. The heartache was still present, but it had numbed her. Sitting up in bed, her gaze settled on Emmie's worried features. A coil of dread tightened like a spring in her stomach. Something terrible had happened to Devlyn.

"What is it, Emmie?"

"My lady?" The girl shifted her gaze away from Sophie.

With nimble actions, Emmie poured a cup of chocolate and brought it to her with a white envelope. She accepted the cup and saucer, nodding for the girl to lay the envelope on the sheets in front of her. Sipping the hot beverage gingerly, she stared at the envelope. Emblazoned across the white parchment in Devlyn's bold, arrogant handwriting were the words Countess of Devlyn.

Was it a note of apology, humbly begging her forgiveness? No, Devlyn would never beg, and he would never ask for forgiveness. It must be a legal matter. Her heart twisted painfully in her breast. Fingers trembling with trepidation, she set aside her chocolate and reached for the envelope. Opening the letter, she perused the dark strokes across the paper.

Countess,

I neither invited nor wanted your sister to visit me last night. I finished with her long ago. When I arrived home last night, I drank myself into a stupor, for reasons I'll not discuss here. I awoke to what I thought was your sweet touch, only to find myself entrapped by your sister's twisted sense of amusement and revenge.

I have made arrangements to stay at the Marlborough club until we settle this matter between us. And settle it we will. I leave you in possession of Devlyn House until such time as you come to your senses with regard to my innocence.

Your husband,
Devlyn

The letter slid from Sophie's fingers. He believed her a fool. For she'd be nothing more than that to believe he'd been craving her touch when Eleanor awoke him. How could he maintain his innocence in the matter? She closed her eyes and forced herself to relive the memory of walking into the library last night.

The images were crisp and clear. Devlyn had been reclined in his favorite reading chair with Eleanor on her knees in front of him. Her sister had appeared somewhat disheveled, but not as badly as one might expect for a woman engaged in a romantic encounter.

Devlyn's appearance had been tousled as well, but upon reflection, he'd not presented the appearance of a man in the throes of passion. She'd memorized the way his scar would tighten and whiten when he was excited. If anything, he'd worn an expression of bewilderment as he pushed Eleanor away from him when he'd seen her standing in the doorway.

She furrowed her brow as she tried to remember his expression at that precise moment. Another emotion had darkened his face besides confusion. It had been a look of pained helplessness. Almost as if he'd lost a treasured item and realized there was little he could do to find it again. It had been a look of intense vulnerability.

Frowning, she scoffed at her nonsensical imaginings. His words were merely trying to trick her into believing his outrageous story. Her fingers caught up his note and crumpled it in a furious noise of anger. No. She refused to let his words sway her. He was a rake.

The behavior of a rake was rarely innocuous. Their protests of innocence were simply a means of achieving another goal. But what goal? What did Devlyn hope to achieve by maintaining his innocence? Whatever it was, she refused to help him accomplish it.

Chapter 11

Leaning against a pillar in the Manchester ballroom, Devlyn watched with increasing fury as one more male swelled the ranks surrounding his wife. For the past two weeks, she'd been quietly attracting the attention of numerous admirers. On the rare occasion when she'd recognized his presence, Sophie's manner was cold and distant.

Her anger was understandable given the way Eleanor had set out to destroy them both, but why did she persist in this ridiculous standoff? He was doing everything possible to prove he was innocent of any wrongdoing. More than a week and a half ago, he'd seen Eleanor at the Beresford soiree. His deliberate cut had been brutal to the point of humiliating the woman.

The gossip over the entire incident had raced through the Marlborough Set with the speed of hounds at the hunt, and Eleanor had removed herself from London the next day. It had been at that point he'd been certain Sophie would come to believe in his innocence. But she'd ignored his letters and turned from him whenever they met in public.

"Devlyn." The sound of Spencer Hamilton's voice made him turn his head. "Do you mind telling me what the hell is going on here?"

"Nice to see you too, Hamilton."

"Damn it, Devlyn. What the hell is going on?"

"If I knew what you were babbling about, perhaps I could oblige you."

"I went to Portsmouth on business a couple of weeks ago, and when I returned today, I find the Set exploding with gossip about you and Phe."

"There's always been gossip about us."

His gaze returned to where his wife stood. It hadn't taken Sir Archibald any time at all to force himself into Sophie's little sphere. Folding his arms across his chest, Devlyn glared at the group paying court to his wife. Bloody hell, she was actually laughing at something Sir Archibald had said.

"And is this gossip true?"

"Gossip is never true."

"Damn it, Devlyn. I overheard a conversation that Phe was going to ask you for a divorce."

He jerked his head around to scowl at his brother-in-law. "I won't give her one. I'm not about to part with her."

"Why not?"

With a snort of disgust, he turned his attention back to Sophie. "Because what's mine, I keep."

"Are you sure there's not another reason?"

"What other reason could there be?"

"You're in love with her."

Stiffening, he remained silent. He wasn't in the mood for games, especially where Sophie was concerned. Hamilton leaned toward him.

"She's in love with you, you know." His brother-in-law's words were confident, but it was the confidence in the younger man's face that made the words all the more powerful.

"How the hell do you know that?"

"Because I've seen the way she looks at you."

"Then you're mistaken. Sophie despises me."

"No, I'm not mistaken. Whatever happened between the two of you must have hurt her deeply to drive this wedge between you."

"I have one word for that wedge. Eleanor."

"What does Eleanor have to do with this?"

"The woman deliberately put me in a compromising situation solely for the purpose of convincing Sophie that I'd betrayed her."

"Sweet Jesus." Hamilton blew out a breath of fury. "What the hell did she do that for?"

"Because your father apparently instructed her to do so."

"The bloody bastard." His brother-in-law grimaced as he looked across the dance floor toward his sister. "And what about Phe?"

"She thinks I'm guilty. You can imagine how she might feel given it was Eleanor who stole Shively away from her."

"What are you doing to get her back?"

Devlyn sent his brother-in-law an arched look. "Doing?"

"Yes doing. What are your plans for convincing her that you're in love with her?"

"You expect me to tell Sophie I'm in love with her?" He stared at Hamilton convinced the man had lost his mind. Telling Sophie he was in love with her would give her the power to destroy him.

"Are you willing to watch her fall into another man's arms?"

"That will never happen."

"No? Take a close look, Devlyn. Those aren't just ordinary men surrounding my sister. They're some of London's wealthiest men, who would think nothing of making Sophie their mistress."

"Damn you, Hamilton," he snarled. "If you think I've not already considered that, you're a fool. Why the hell do you think I'm dogging Sophie's heels? Wherever she goes, I go."

"But will it be enough? How are you going to convince her you're in love with her?"

"I thought cutting Eleanor would ease her anger, make her see I'm innocent. You can see how well that worked. Hell, I've even disposed of the ledgers. Gave them to the local authorities yesterday."

"Ledgers? What ledgers?"

"I'm sorry to say it, Hamilton, but your father's a thief. My brilliant, stubborn wife had been keeping two sets of books of your father's finances. It's why she came to me. She offered me her set of books as a means to destroy him in exchange for my marrying her."

"Good God! I never realized... She never talked about Father's affairs." Stunned disbelief whitened his brother-in-law's face. Devlyn immediately regretted mentioning the nasty business. Hamilton gathered himself and shook his head.

"Have you told her what you did with the books?"

"No." He turned back to study the ballroom, his gaze finding Sophie waltzing around the room in the arms of Sir Archibald. Bloody hell, he was going to choke the man for even looking at her.

"Well, if she doesn't know what you've done with the books, then she's not likely to comprehend your change of heart."

"What the hell do the account ledgers have to do with my love for Sophie?"

"You might love your wife, Devlyn, but you've a lot to learn about how my sister thinks. If she believes you still have those books, that's like saying your revenge is more important than she is."

His jaw tightened as Hamilton's words sank in his brain. The man was right. Sophie would see his humiliating snub of Eleanor as little more than a falsehood. She'd think it was his way of appeasing her. The question was how could he get her alone to explain everything?

"I see you understand your dilemma. Might I make a suggestion where my sister is concerned?" Hamilton paused as Devlyn gave a sharp nod for him to proceed. "Phe invited me to join her at the opera tomorrow night--"

"Bloody hell, she knows I hate the opera."

"Precisely. She indicated in her note that it's the one place she's certain you won't haunt her."

"So she's not completely immune to my presence." Relief sped through him at the knowledge. Could Hamilton be right? Could Sophie actually be in love with him? The idea bolstered his spirits immensely. The sound of his brother-in-law speaking interrupted his thoughts.

"What did you say?"

Hamilton shook his head with amused annoyance. "I said you can use Revelstoke's box at the opera. He's in the country, and he told me to use it whenever I like. His box is directly across from yours. When you see me leave, you'll be free to join Phe."

"If she even lets me into the box."

"When I get done talking to her, I'm certain she won't protest your arrival. Are we agreed?"

"Agreed." Devlyn shook his brother-in-law's hand. Soon he'd have the opportunity to explain everything. And afterward, he'd make sure his lovely wife never thought to live apart from him again.

* * * *

Seated in the Revelstoke opera box, Devlyn waited impatiently for Sophie to appear in the private space across from where he sat. The crowd in the vestibule had been more crowded than he cared for, and he'd decided to take his seat early. The theater was already almost completely full, and still there was no sign of Sophie or her brother.

Irritation seethed just below the surface as he watched the crowd finding their seats. The minutes stretched on, and the orchestra began to warm up their instruments. A moment later, he saw Sophie enter their theater box followed by Hamilton. The relief he experienced was almost palpable.

His gaze slid over her face. She was more beautiful than he'd ever seen her. Her skin glowed and her mouth looked ripe, succulent. The gown she wore was a lush green, almost the color of grass in the springtime.

It molded and highlighted her curves. Curves he knew all too well and wanted to worship again with his mouth and tongue. His cock stirred to life at the image. How he'd missed her. When she was back in his arms, he was taking her home to the keep. Away from all these admirers of hers. He would take his time telling her, showing her, how much he loved her.

Relief was a short-lived experience as he observed Sir Archibald entering the box. His jaw tightened with fury as the man bent over

Sophie's hand before taking up a seat next to her. Tonight was the last time Sir Archibald would ever get near his wife again. That was if he didn't kill the bastard first.

His brother-in-law had taken the seat on the other side of Sophie and he leaned forward to say something. He grimaced as Sophie shook her head firmly, causing her brother to frown. The sight of Hamilton's determined expression gave him hope as he watched the man lean toward Sophie again.

It was obvious from his wife's glare that she was far from receptive to Hamilton's words. It was not going well. Not well at all. Damn the woman, was he going to have to kidnap her and hold her prisoner until she believed him innocent?

Sophie flipped her fan open to stir the air in front of her at a languid pace. Unshakeable in his resolve, Hamilton spoke something in her ear. She immediately stiffened, her fan falling into her lap as she turned to stare at her brother. An expression of satisfaction settled on his brother-in-law's face and Sophie appeared confused. Adorably so.

She shook her head slightly, and he watched Hamilton lean forward to speak again before turning in the direction of the Revelstoke theater box. The orchestra struck up the overture as the lights in the opera house dimmed.

Light from the stage illuminated Sophie's bewildered expression and he watched her slowly turn to look in his direction. His eyes locked with hers, and he stared at her with all the intensity of his being. He could see her wavering, uncertain as to whether she should look away. God, even now, when she might not want him, he still loved her.

It was tangible, this emotion that engulfed him. It made him want to caress her with his hands, but all he could do was to make love to her in his head as he stared into her face from across the chasm of the opera house.

He visualized running his fingers across her skin in a light caress. She'd quiver in that unique way of hers that told him how much his touch was affecting her. It would make her breathing a little erratic. There would be that rapid beat of her pulse fluttering wildly on the side of her neck. Sophie's hand flew to her neck, to the exact spot he was picturing in his head.

Despite the dim light, he saw her mouth part slightly so her tongue could dart out to wet her lips. A low growl reverberated out of him. God, every time she did that he wanted to devour her. Did she have any idea what type of effect that had on him? Her hand came to rest against her skin just above the décolletage of her gown.

Was she imagining his lips against those soft swells? It was torment to be so close to those beautiful nipples and still unable to suckle at them in the manner that made her plead with him so sweetly. Her hand skimmed discreetly over one breast and a surge of triumph sailed through him, tightening his cock until it was hot and hard.

Excited and aroused. It was the only way to describe the sensations cascading over her. They flooded her senses, making it impossible to think straight. Spencer's words had been confusing enough, but to see Devlyn sitting across from her was unbelievable. He despised the opera, but he'd come here willing to sit through it for her. In a way, he was sacrificing himself for her. How could she ignore such a gesture?

She tried to look away from his bold stare, but found it impossible to do so. His eyes were caressing her as if they were his hands. She licked her dry lips. She didn't know what to do. The memory of her sister kissing him was so strong, so powerful. He'd steadfastly proclaimed his innocence, and he'd cut Eleanor in a fashion that was brutal even for him. But was she ready to believe him? To believe what Spencer had told her about the ledgers?

The intensity of Devlyn's stare made it a struggle to breathe normally. Even with his eyes, he could make love to her. Oh, God, her nipples were taut and they ached with that delicious pang only he could stir in her. She slid her hand downward, her fingers barely touching her hardened nipple as she laid her hand in her lap. It was enough to spread the ache down into her nether region.

It was as if his hand was sliding down her waist then across her thigh to touch her intimately. Heat swirled in her belly and rushed downward at the image of his fingers sliding into her, stroking her. She bit her lip as a rush of liquid heat flowed from her.

His expression darkened and she wanted to melt beneath his hot gaze. He knew. Somehow, he knew she was wet and ready for him. Her breasts swelled and grew heavy with desire. His eyelids drooped slightly, just the way they did when they were making love. Oh God, she wanted him. She wanted him inside her now.

Beside her, Sir Archibald leaned close and touched her hand. Uncaring of how it might look, she brushed his hand away. Heat flowed through her and she fanned herself furiously. She had to leave, catch her breath somehow. Snapping her fan closed, she jerked her gaze away from Devlyn's and jumped to her feet.

When she stood, both Sir Archibald and Spencer rose to their feet.

She shook her head at both of them and offered a brief excuse before she hurried out of the box and into the corridor. She needed air. Fresh air. The carpet muffled the sound of her shoes as she ran down the hall. As she turned the corner to enter the second floor vestibule, she came to a halt. Devlyn stood before her. He'd followed her. The passion in his gaze had not diminished and she sucked in a sharp breath at the sight of him.

He'd never looked more handsome or masterful than he did at this moment. Sweet Lord, if only they were home. In the privacy of their own bedroom. His eyes conveyed the same urgency rushing through her. Without a word, he stepped forward and grasped her wrist to hurry her down the stairs. Together they bolted through the front door of the opera house, ignoring the surprised looks of staff.

The cool air brushed over her heated skin, but it didn't dim her ardor. Still he didn't speak, but his expression told her everything. His craving for her was as great as hers was for him. With a gentle tug, he pulled her along the street until they encountered a dark alley.

Darkness enveloped them and his mouth was on hers. The exquisite heat of his lips against hers shot through her and into her blood. God help her, she wanted more. She refused to think, only to feel. There was only this moment in time and her need for him. His mouth left hers to nibble on her ear and then at the side of her neck.

A soft moan escaped her as he trailed his fingers across the tops of her breasts. He followed the hot path with his mouth. When his tongue slid into the valley between her breasts, her fingers entwined themselves in his dark silky hair. She wanted more. She wanted to feel his hand on her. She wanted her hands on him.

Her hands slid across the crisp white linen of his shirt, then his waistcoat and down to his waist. Trembling now with a wild need that could only be assuaged by his possession, her fingers found his rock hard length pressing through the expensive material of his trousers. She had believed once that she would never beg anyone for anything ever again. But now she was beyond pride. She needed him. Needed him now.

"Devlyn, please."

Pulling back from her slightly, he stared into her eyes. The passion glowing there singed her, making her burn with need. She threw caution to the wind. Nothing mattered except the love burning inside her, craving his touch.

"I need you," she whispered with desperation.

"I know."

"For the love of God, Devlyn, *please*." Her hands captured the sides of his face and pulled his mouth down to hers. Just before she kissed him, she murmured, "I want your cock inside me now."

He stiffened against her as she sought his lips. For a moment, she thought she'd shocked him. Then his mouth was plundering hers with a frenzied passion that took her by surprise. It was glorious.

Damn, she tasted good. He'd almost spilled his seed when she'd whispered her need for him. Whenever she used that low, throaty voice in such a lusty fashion, it undid him. She rubbed her hips against his. Hell, she wasn't just ready for him; she was on fire. He didn't have to touch that swollen nub of hers to know she'd cream all over his cock the moment he entered her.

With a quick movement, he guided her backward until she was pressed against the brick wall of the building. His hand gathered a handful of material and lifted one side of her dress. He intended to bind her to him forever. Never again, would there be any doubt in her mind how much he loved her.

His hand grazed the top of her thigh and she jumped at his touch. The touch of her hand against his hardness tugged a groan from him. He had to have her. He needed to embed himself inside her. Quickly, he freed his cock from its restraints and cleared a path through her petticoats.

"Wrap your leg around my waist, my sweet."

The moment she did so, he plunged into her. Sweet Jesus, she was tight. It was incredible the way her snug passage clung to him, rippled over him. She convulsed around him with a torturous pleasure he had only ever experienced with her. Christ, he was about to explode. Without thought, he plunged into her again and again as she whimpered with increasing pleasure.

He could feel the power of his desire flooding through him, and at that moment, she peaked. Her hot, tight passage clenched at him with intense spasms, and his cock throbbed in that ultimate release as he spilled his seed into her.

A small cry parted her lips, and he buried it beneath his mouth as they shuddered in each other's arms. For a long moment, he stayed buried inside her. He didn't want to move, but he wanted to lay against her with nothing between them. They needed to go home.

Warmth seeped through him as he slid out of her, allowing her dress to fall back into place. Quickly he adjusted his clothing and stared at his wife. Her eyes were closed. There was a sated expression on her face, her mouth curled in a slight smile of delight.

"I love you, Sophie."

Her eyes flew open and she simply stared at him. The pounding of his heart filled his ears as he waited for her to answer. When she didn't, he frowned. Christ, he'd just given her the power to destroy him.

"When a man speaks of love, he usually expects a response."

She nodded in a dazed fashion. "I know. I just don't have one at the moment."

"What the hell do you mean you don't have an answer?" He took a step back from her and watched as she bit her lip. Damnation, he was ready to strangle her. He'd just bared his soul to her, and she couldn't respond in kind? She sent him a helpless look, and he expelled a loud noise of anger.

Grasping her wrist, he pulled her toward the end of the alley. They were going home, and he was going to make love to her until she said the words he needed to hear. There would be no more games.

"Where are we going?"

"Home. I'm going to make love to you until you tell me what I want to hear."

"Don't be ridiculous, Devlyn. You can't force people to say what you want them to say."

"Watch me."

He sent her a cold glare as he signaled for the carriage. When it rolled to a halt in front of them, he helped her inside, then entered the vehicle and closed the door behind him. Seated across from him, she realized he had every intention of pleasuring her until she spoke her heart.

There was no doubt she loved him, but while seeing Eleanor with him had been heartbreaking, she knew the issue went deeper than that for her.

In twenty years, he would still be in his prime, but her youth as well as her prime years would be well behind her. How could she ask him to choose such a lifestyle? How could she ask it of herself? The thought of him tied to her, wanting a more youthful wife, knowing that she might have to let him go in the future. She didn't want that, couldn't countenance that. The only thing to do would be to let him go.

While she believed him about Eleanor, what would she do when another woman, younger and prettier than her tried to come between them? What would she do then? No, far better to break the ties now than suffer heartache of the deepest kind in the future. What she'd experienced over the past two weeks would be a pittance compared to the painful price she'd pay later if she allowed this relationship to continue. She couldn't do it.

"Quentin." It was the first time she'd ever used his Christian name, and his eyes narrowed as he met her direct gaze. "Even if I tell you what you want to hear, it won't change anything. The age difference is too great. It's highly doubtful I'll ever bear you a child, and I could never accept you keeping a mistress once you tire of me. It's best that we part company now and go about our individual lives."

"Are you quite finished?" There was a dangerous edge to his voice.

"I don't know what else there is to say."

"Well I have a few things to say, and you're damn well going to listen to them without a word of interruption. Is that understood?"

He waited for her nod of agreement. Satisfied, he eyed her carefully. He could tell she was afraid. She was afraid of the risk involved in loving him. For he was certain now that she loved him, she was simply too frightened to admit it. But by God, before the night was done, she'd declare her love, and he'd see to it there was no more talk about leading separate lives.

"First I want to hear you say what I've already said." She stared at him in surprise for a moment before she glanced away. He refused to let her avoid the task. "Say it, Sophie."

"I love you." She snapped the words at him, the fear poignant in her voice.

"Say it again."

"For God's sake, Quentin. Why are you doing this?"

"Say it."

"I love you." A tear trickled down her cheek.

"And I love you. That's all that matters, nothing else."

"Will you be reasonable?"

"I'm being quite reasonable, Sophie. We love each other, and I'll be damned if I let you toss that away. You're right, we might not be youthful lovers, but by God, I don't want any other woman in my bed but you. We're not old yet, but I want to grow old with you. And while I'd be proud and delighted if you bore me an heir, it doesn't matter to me if that never happens. I'm not giving you up. Not for money, not for an heir, not for age, not for anything."

He inhaled a deep breath, his gaze pinned on her face. Her expression displayed her indecision, and he pushed the point.

"I learned something these past two weeks. Without you, I'm nothing. I need you in my life to make me whole, to make my life worth living."

Tears were streaming down her face now, and she shook her head. "I don't know. What if you--"

"Don't ask questions, don't think. Love me and let me love you."

She stared at him for a long moment, and he held his breath. Had he won? An instant later, she threw herself across the carriage into his arms. Her hands cupped his face as she kissed him with fervent desperation. He pulled her onto his lap, holding her close.

"A wise decision, my love."

"I never stood a chance against you." She laughed and sobbed at the same time.

"Why would you? I knew we were meant for each other the first time I kissed you in Devlyn's Keep."

"Oh, you did, did you?" She pushed away from him and gave him a playful punch in the shoulder as the carriage rolled to a halt.

The door opened and he unceremoniously dumped her on to the carriage seat. Exiting the vehicle, he turned toward her as she stepped down onto the narrow step of the vehicle. With a quick movement, he swept her out of the carriage into his arms.

To the amusement of the coachman, footman and Fischer who'd opened the townhouse door, he kissed her long and hard.

"That, Countess, is just a taste of what to expect now and for the rest of our lives."

"I love you, Quentin."

"And I you," he murmured, his green eyes flashing with emotion. "Now I suggest we retire for the night and you show me just how much you love me."

With that, he carried her up the townhouse steps determined to make her happy until the end of their days.

Epilogue

Devlyn paced the hall corridor as another scream of pain echoed out of Sophie's bedchamber. Damn it, this waiting was the most excruciating thing he'd ever done in his life. The door opened and Mrs. Michaels, the housekeeper Sophie had hired several months ago, came out of the room with a basin and wet towels. Glaring at the woman, he blocked her path.

"Well?"

"She's having a rough go of it, my lord. It's hard to say."

Another scream ripped its way out into the hall. The sound of it chilled his skin with fear. To hell with propriety. The woman he loved was in pain, and he'd be damned if anyone was going to keep him from her.

Skirting the woman in his way, he threw open the door to his wife's room and strode toward the bed. The alarmed protests of the doctor and midwife rose over his head, but he ignored them as he approached Sophie's side. She was pale, and her usually lustrous hair was now damp with sweat. Still, she was the most beautiful creature he'd ever seen.

Her eyes were closed, but as he sat on the bed beside her, she slowly opened them. A brilliant light of happiness lit her from within as he grasped her hand. Leaning forward, he kissed her forehead.

"I think it's high time you delivered our daughter, Sophie."

Her chuckle was weak as she gave a slight shake of her head. "It's not as easy as that, my love."

"Isn't it? If you can tame the Devil of Devlyn's Keep, then you are more than capable of providing young Spencer with a baby sister."

Her eyes closed as another pain rippled through her body, and her hand gripped his with the strength of vise. On the other side of the bed, the doctor leaned toward her.

"Please, my lady. You must push."

"I can't. I simply can't. I'm so tired." Sophie shook her head wearily.

The worried frown on the doctor's face sent another chill through him. He wasn't about to lose his wife to a child. Turning his head back to her, he scowled at the expression of tired defeat on her face. She could rest later, now wasn't the time to quit.

"So that's it. You're giving up." Her eyes fluttered open to stare up at him in surprise. "And I suppose you think I'll raise this child and Spencer on my own?"

"Quentin, you know--"

"No, Sophie, I don't know how to be a mother to our children, which means I'll be forced to marry again."

Her eyes flashed with anger before another cry of pain broke past her lips. Seeing her hurting twisted his gut, but he refused to give in to the desire to console her. She needed to fight if she and the babe were to live. The pain eased and she glared up at him.

"And who would have you as their husband? Your reputation for debauchery still stands."

"Perhaps that young Miss Wilson you invited to dinner a few months ago. I understand her father's seeking a title for the girl."

"You'd grow--" She gasped as another pain twisted through her and she strained to push. "Tired of her in less than a month."

"Then Lady Overton. Widows always possess experience."

Gasping for breath, Sophie scowled at him in fury. "You're doing this on purpose."

"What? Rattling off a list of possibilities to replace you?"

"Ye-yes!"

"So who do you suggest?"

"No ... one. I'm the only woman who'll ... tolerate ... you."

Her body writhed on the bed as another pain ripped through her. Fear struck at the very heart of him. "Well, then push, damn you! Push, Sophie."

With a cry of anger, she lurched upright, her fingernails biting painfully into the palm of his hand. The strain of her efforts was telling on her face and neck, and for a moment he was certain he'd lose her simply from the ferocity of her attempt. Then with a loud cry, she strained once more before an expression of release crossed her exhausted features and she collapsed against her pillows.

Glancing over his shoulder, he saw the doctor bring their second child into the world. A loud smack echoed in the room, and the baby's angry cry filled the bedchamber. The man beamed at him broadly.

"You've a daughter, my lord. A strong, healthy looking daughter."

Shoulders sagging, he leaned forward and rested his forehead against Sophie's shoulder. Tender fingers drifted across the thinly lined scar on his cheek.

"You, my lord, are a brute," she whispered.

He lifted his head to stare down into her hazel eyes. They glowed with love and a tired happiness that sent a bolt of relief through him. "What would you have me do? Lose you?"

"But Lady Overton?"

"I saw no need to eliminate her as a potential replacement. She's quite lovely to look at." Mischief twisted his lips in a small smile.

"You know full well, she's an empty-headed twit."

"Then it's most fortunate my wife decided to survive the birth of our child." His statement made her brush her fingers across his lips. To anyone else the words might have sounded flippant, but she heard the relief beneath the cavalier response.

"Thank you, my love. You always know exactly what to do. I don't know how I existed before that day I entered your study."

"I adore you, Sophie."

His words were so low she barely heard them, but the depth of his love for her gleamed brightly in his green eyes. She sighed softly as his hand captured hers and his mouth caressed the inside of her wrist. Happiness flooded through her at his touch and she bit back the tears of joy threatening to overwhelm her. His eyes met hers, and he smiled.

"Come, my lady, I think it's time you met your daughter."

Rising from the bed, he accepted his daughter from the doctor and carried the child back to her. When he laid the precious bundle in Sophie's arms, he sat beside her his arm around her shoulders. She smiled as the baby yawned and gripped her finger tightly in a small fist. With her husband's arm holding her close, Sophie welcomed the sensation of warmth and security his body gave her.

"So are we to name her Emily?"

"Yes." She chuckled. "I seem to recall that's the name you picked out."

"You know full well, Countess, that if you'd desired a different name, you would have succeeded in changing my mind." The twinkle in his eye made her smile. She looked down at the babe in her arms.

"She looks like you, Quentin. But time will tell if she takes up your rakish behavior." She smiled at him, a laugh parting her lips at his askance look.

"She will toe the line as her mother does." His teasing remark pulled another soft laugh from her.

"If you believe that, then you're doomed to be wrapped around the child's finger."

"If she does wrap me around her finger, it will simply be love's revenge."

Puzzled, she frowned. "Love's revenge?"

"A need for revenge brought us together, my love. But instead, love turned us toward each other. Spencer and Emily are evidence of love's revenge on us."

Looking up at him, she saw his love shining down on her, and she sighed softly. He was right as usual. Love had taken its revenge on them by bringing them together and binding their hearts as one. No matter what else happened in the course of their lives, she would always be grateful for love's revenge.

LOVE'S PORTRAIT

Chapter 1

London, 1892

"It's wicked, Julia. Absolutely wicked!"

Alva's squeal of shock made Julia Westgard smile with delight. Her friend was right, the painting was wickedly shocking. She turned back toward the painting she'd commissioned. Tipping her head to one side, she studied it with a critical eye.

Was that really how Isaac Peebles saw her? The nude painting made her look lush and sensual, almost beautiful. Almost, but not quite. She did like the way he'd captured the color of her hair. Soft golden highlights glistened in the dark red hair that tumbled over her shoulders. It was her best feature. And he'd made her eyes close to the green they got when she was angry. He'd made her gaze far more attractive than the plain hazel one she saw in the mirror everyday.

"I like it." Hands resting on her hips, she smiled. "I like it very much. Do you think I should hang it in the salon or the study?"

"Good Lord, Julia. You cannot possibly be serious!"

Tickled once more to have shocked her friend, Julia turned toward the petite woman, the bustle of her gown whispering softly at her quick turn. The horrified look in Alva's blue eyes made her realize she'd teased her friend enough. One hand pressed against the dove gray taffeta of her dress, she shook her head.

"I'm teasing you. I don't have that much self-confidence."

The relief on her friend's pale features made her grimace. No, of course she didn't have that much confidence. The confident air she put on for family and friends was nothing short of bravado. Everything she did was an act to cover up the inadequacies she felt every day--the shortcomings Oscar had regaled her with the entire time they'd been married. Even though he'd been dead almost two years, she could still feel the sting of his cruel taunts and behavior.

Ever the impeccable husband in public, in private he'd found numerous ways to shame and degrade her. From vicious insults to the occasional slap, Oscar had controlled every aspect of her life. She'd never quite figured out how she'd survived, but she had. And she was all the stronger for it.

Still, she'd yet to succeed in shedding herself of the insecurities her husband had cultivated in her. They were always close at hand, just beneath the surface. It was one of the reasons she'd commissioned the nude portrait. It was her attempt to repair her spirit, to regain the independence she'd lost in her marriage.

"Ah, there you two are." Catherine Dewhurst poked her head into Julia's boudoir. "I thought you two would be in the study discussing the latest review of Lady Windermere's Fan."

Julia stepped forward to embrace her cousin by marriage. Of all her in-laws, Catherine was the only one who could see beyond the false façade. The woman had been her guardian angel on more than one occasion.

"I have something much more exciting than a review of Oscar Wilde's new play. Come see what I have."

"Is it here? Finally?"

Julia nodded and grinned as her cousin moved to look at the front of the painting. Catherine's face went red before laughter parted her lips.

"Oh my word, however did you manage to keep from fainting, Alva?"

Affronted, Alva's pale face took on a pinched look. "I have no idea. It's scandalous, I tell you, scandalous."

"I don't think it's scandalous." Julia shook her head

"Rubbish, it's shocking. Why, the man saw you naked."

Frustrated with her friend's straitlaced tone that sounded so much like Oscar's disapproval, Julia tossed a pleading glance in her cousin's direction. "Do try to explain to her, Catherine."

"Perhaps she has a point, Julia. It is a bit … risqué, even for you."

Disappointed by her cousin's response, she stalked to the painting and replaced the cloth that had covered it earlier. If she'd wanted an unfavorable assessment of her behavior, she only had to listen to Oscar's voice in her head for that. It wasn't as if she'd gone without a chaperone; she'd taken her maid with her to each and every sitting.

Sitting for Isaac Peebles had offered her a freedom she'd never experienced before. The portrait sittings had been a release from the rigors of society. More importantly, they had been a means of freeing herself of the yoke Oscar had settled on her from the day they were married. With a final adjustment to the cloth over the painting, she turned to face her friends.

"There. You don't have to burden your eyes with the subject matter anymore."

Catherine arched her eyebrows at her and shook her head. "I didn't say I didn't like it. I merely pointed out that it was a bit more ... adventurous than most portraits."

"He did manage to get your hair color right, and that's not easy to do. Even in the more…," Alva blushed deeply, "... the more intimate places."

The woman's words hung in the air for a long moment as Julia stared at her friend in stunned silence. Was prudish, little Alva actually teasing her about the portrait? She shot a glance over toward her cousin. Catherine's expression was equally astonished. Indignation tilted Alva's pointed chin upward.

"Well, I can be daring sometimes too," she huffed, sending them both a sheepish glance as the room exploded with laughter. Julia shook her head as amusement continued to bubble out of her.

"If you found the portrait daring, then wait until you hear what I've planned for the Society's next fundraiser." She turned to her cousin. "Shall we tell her, Catherine?"

"Oh, there's no we in this idea at all." Catherine carefully removed the hat from her head, meticulously pushing the hat pin into the back of the peacock feathered plumes that trailed down the back of the accessory. Sweeping the train of her dark green gown to one side, she took a seat next to Alva.

Julia faced the two women seated before her. Her best friends. The only two people she could count on to love her no matter what she said or did. And of late, she'd been quite bold. Securing shares in St. Claire Shipping had been viewed by Oscar's family as not only excessive but foolhardy as well. If they were to discover she was actually reviewing accounting ledgers and conducting business in person with St. Claire, the family would close ranks around her in an attempt to control her just as her husband had. But perhaps they would have good reason in this instance.

Morgan St. Claire. The thought of the man sent a shudder rippling through her. He was an arrogant bastard. One who didn't like anyone questioning his way of doing business--something she'd done quite a bit of over the past few weeks. Even she'd been surprised by her daring, and it was a miracle the man hadn't choked her yet.

Still, as an investor in his company, she'd insisted on reviewing the books. She wasn't about to hand over a small portion of her fortune without solid evidence that the man knew how to run his business. He'd rebelled against the suggestion, but when she wouldn't budge on the issue, he'd begrudgingly agreed to her request.

The fact that he'd conceded defeat in the face of her persistence had amazed her. It had been a small concession, but one that had bolstered her confidence more than anything else she'd done since Oscar's death. It had helped ease the feelings of worthlessness he had fostered in her.

The question now was whether her friends would support her in this new adventure she had devised. It was for a good cause, and she needed to do something daring. Something to break out of the narrow confines of the life she'd lived for far too long.

Even though Oscar was gone, the repressive atmosphere lingered in the house they'd shared. It was as stuffy, stiff and rigid as Queen Victoria herself. That was why she'd chosen to do something foolhardy and daring. She would be the one in control--no one else. It would be one more silent shout against the oppressive life she'd endured for so long. One more protest against Oscar and his hypocrisy. She inhaled and exhaled a deep breath.

"We're--" She paused as Catherine arched a threatening brow at her. "I'm going to acquire a silk handkerchief from Morgan St. Claire and auction it off at the Society for Lost Angels to raise money for the new orphanage."

Alva tipped her head to one side, her expression puzzled. "Well, that doesn't sound all that bold. I'm sure Mr. St. Claire will be happy to part with a piece of silk for the children."

"I don't intend to ask him for the handkerchief. I intend to sneak into his rooms at the Clarendon tomorrow night at the dinner party he's having for his investors." Julia smiled at the notion.

She was feeling quite pleased with herself about this bold plan. To pull one over on Morgan St. Claire would be almost as pleasurable as when she occasionally found errors in his books. More importantly, it would be a blow in support of all the women he'd dallied with before leaving them with simply a monogrammed handkerchief as a token of the affair.

"Oh my! You can't do that, Julia. What if he catches you?" Alva sent her a horrified look.

"I don't intend to get caught. I've already made arrangements for one of the maids on his floor to give me access to his rooms."

"Couldn't you just ask him for the handkerchief? He's such a gentleman, I'm sure he won't refuse your request."

"Oh, don't get her started on Morgan St. Claire." Catherine grimaced at Alva. "We'll be here all day listening to her rail at the man's shortcomings."

"But I've always found Mr. St. Claire quite charming," said Alva in a bewildered tone.

Julia glared at her. "Morgan St. Claire is full of himself and enjoys tempting women into heartbreak. He's a scoundrel of the worst kind."

"Which makes me wonder why you chose to invest in his company?" Catherine sent her a look filled with mockery.

"Business should never be guided by emotions. St. Claire Shipping is a sound investment."

"I see." Catherine's ironic tone earned her a look of puzzlement from Alva and a glare from Julia.

"I still don't see why you're going to sneak into the man's hotel room instead of just asking for a handkerchief." Alva frowned in disapproval.

Closing her eyes, Julia shook her head. "Because it won't have as dramatic an impact if I ask him for one. Sneaking into the man's hotel room and taking a handkerchief without getting caught will cause a stir among the ladies. They'll want details about his hotel room, which I'll be happy to elaborate on as they bid on the blasted thing."

"Surely you're not going to admit to the Society that you entered the man's room." Alva looked askance at the idea and Julia frowned. For once her prudent friend was right.

"I see your point." With a wave of her hand, Julia smiled. "Well, I'll just explain that the woman who took the handkerchief prefers to remain anonymous. I can just share this mysterious woman's adventures as she might herself."

Catherine coughed her disapproval at this change in plans, forcing Julia to send her another glare. She refused to give way on this adventure. It was something she had to do. She wasn't sure why, it was simply that she needed to test the waters and her new found courage. Of course, she wasn't sure how courageous it was to undertake such a foolish adventure. But she'd declared her intentions, and she refused to back down now.

Alva's brow puckered. "How will you prove that it's really Mr. St. Claire's handkerchief?"

"His monogram. I have it on good authority that he always gives a handkerchief to each of his ladies when they part so the woman can dry her tears." Julia grimaced at her words. The arrogance of the man.

"Oh, that sounds so romantic."

"Don't be a ninny, Alva. It's not romantic at all." Catherine turned her glare on Julia. "As for you, cousin, I think you've gone mad. If you're caught, you'll cause a sensation, with the distinct possibility of being ostracized. You know how the Queen is about circumspect behavior. Although as far as Prince Edward is concerned, the man would probably applaud you. Still, polite society won't overlook an outright indiscretion of this sort."

Julia waved her cousin's concerns aside. "I won't get caught. I have it all planned out. Dinner is being served in St. Claire's private dining room at the Clarendon. I'll simply ask to refresh myself then run upstairs and retrieve the handkerchief from the man's room. I'll be back at the dinner party before anyone is the wiser."

"What is that old adage? The best laid plans go astray?" Catherine mouth was tight with disapproval, but there was concern in her gaze too.

"My maid knows the maid on St. Claire's floor. The girl is quite trustworthy. I promise you, nothing will go wrong."

Julia smiled at both of her friends. No, nothing was going to go wrong, and she was going to enjoy auctioning off one of St. Claire's handkerchiefs. She would be the first woman to own one that hadn't been handed out in a moment of pity.

* * * *

With a smile pasted on her face, Julia cast a furtive glance at Morgan St. Claire as he talked quietly with the guest seated across from her. She didn't know why the man unnerved her, but he did. Tonight, he was making her distinctly uneasy, far more than during their occasional interactions at his office.

He'd been nothing but charming since her arrival, but there was a dangerous glint in his eye whenever he looked at her. She couldn't decipher the look, and the truth was she didn't really want to. Her fingers grasped the stem of her wine glass, and she took a sip of her drink.

A king in his castle could not have been more at ease than the man sitting next to her at the head of the table. It nettled her to admit it, but he was handsome. She approved of his clean-shaven look. There was nothing she despised more than whiskers down to the jowls or waxed mustaches. His appearance clearly indicated he was his own man and bowed to no one--not even fashion.

Observing him covertly as she toyed with her food, she could understand why women fell for him. The chestnut colored hair, those dark brown eyes that seemed capable of seeing right through a person, and then there was the man's physique.

She'd heard he was a rower on Viscount Atherby's rowing team. It would explain the muscles that rippled beneath the snug fit of his evening jacket. If she didn't find the man's arrogance so irritating, she would no doubt have found herself among the victims St. Claire always left behind.

Fortune had favored her as he'd left her alone with the account ledgers she'd been poring over for the past few weeks. It would have been much more difficult if he'd hovered over her shoulder. But he hadn't, and for that she was grateful.

Lowering her gaze to her plate, she took a bite of the poached salmon. Still, the man did know how to entertain. The Clarendon was known for exceptional meals, but tonight's meal was beyond her expectations. In fact, the entire dinner party illustrated the man's wealth and power in a subtle fashion, from the selection of foods to the delicate wines served with the meal.

"You seem distracted, Mrs. Westgard."

The deep note of his voice warmed her skin, and she frowned at the tingling sensation skimming over her body. What was she doing reacting to him like this? This was St. Claire. A scoundrel and ladies man to rival any in the Marlborough Set, even Prince Edward himself. She raised her eyes to meet his searching gaze. Heavens, a woman could drown in those dark, mysterious depths. The thought made her tighten her grip on her fork. What on earth was wrong with her?

"No, I was simply enjoying this delicious salmon. The hotel's chef has outdone himself. Do you suppose he would send me the recipe?"

"Actually I have a personal chef who prepares all my meals, and I'm afraid Henri refuses to share his secrets--even with me."

"What a pity." She enjoyed the morsel she popped into her mouth. "This is a dish I could eat quite often."

"Then come back for dinner again, next week."

He'd leaned toward her, his voice dropping a level so that his invitation reached only her ears. Startled, she almost dropped her fork. The expression in his eyes was mesmerizing as she attempted to force a confident smile to her lips.

"I think that would be unwise. One should never mix business with pleasure."

"Perhaps." He pulled away, one shoulder lifted in a shrug. "Although I'm sure it would be quite pleasurable."

She suppressed a shiver at the way he almost purred the words. Dear Lord, the man's reputation was well earned. His gaze was a sensual caress as he scanned her features before moving downward to her bodice. The warmth of a flush filled her cheeks at the blatant stare of interest. No, not interest--insolence, that's what it was. He was being insolent. She'd been a thorn in his side for the past few weeks, and now she was paying the price for daring to question the great St. Claire.

He didn't take his eyes off her as he reached for his wineglass. It was difficult not to swallow the knot in her throat as his fingers stroked the stem of the crystal goblet. Taking his time, he drank from the glass, and all the while she was hypnotized by his actions. A secretive smile curved his mouth and he arched an eyebrow at her.

Flustered and embarrassed that she'd been staring, she jerked her gaze back to her plate and resumed eating. With her head down she didn't see him lean forward, but his presence was a hot sun against her body.

"You blush quite charmingly, madam. However, I do confess to being curious as to what prompted such a becoming color."

Irritated that she was acting like all the other women who'd fallen for St. Claire's charms, she clenched her jaw. Fixing a neutral expression on her face, she met his mocking gaze with her steady one.

"Are you flirting with me, Mr. St. Claire?"

"Would you like me to?" There was a dark note in his voice, and she shivered.

"No."

"As you wish." The enigmatic smile on his lips evolved into one of dry amusement.

She tried to avoid drawing blood as she bit the inside of her mouth. God, he was arrogant. The sooner she secured the item she'd come for the sooner she could leave. Perhaps Catherine was right. Maybe she should sell her interest in St. Claire shipping.

Being in this man's presence was becoming increasingly difficult to manage. He was too sure of himself, which made him dangerous. The man probably thought she was ready to throw herself all over him. Well, he was in for a rude awakening if he thought Julia

Westgard was going to succumb to his sensual charms. She'd had more than her fill of pompous, controlling men.

Without waiting for him to speak again, she turned to the man on her left and started a conversation. Anything to avoid conversing further with Morgan St. Claire. Although she couldn't see him watching her, the blast of heat warming her skin told her the man's gaze was still pinned on her.

The effect of St. Claire's intent look was nerve wracking and she barely managed to focus on her conversation with the man next to her. Being only one of two women investors in the small party of twelve was enough to strain even her own daring. She found herself wishing Lady Falkenhouse was not at the opposite end of the table.

For the first time she wondered why St. Claire had placed her on his left. She frowned at the thought. That would imply he'd deliberately chosen her seat. No, she was reading too much into the seating arrangements.

With the meal almost complete, she excused herself from the table. Aware that the moment of truth had arrived, she left the dining room. The warmth on the back of her neck was a clear indicator that St. Claire's gaze was following her, and she suppressed the butterflies milling in her stomach.

Once she was in the hallway, she quickly made her way up to the fourth floor of the hotel. A young girl waited at one end of the corridor. Without speaking, the girl glanced furtively over her shoulder then quickly opened a nearby door before scurrying away as if hunted. Uneasy at the girl's behavior, Julia peeked into the room the maid had unlocked. The first thing she saw was a painting of the Calcutta, one of St. Claire's prized ships. She smiled to herself. Victory was close at hand.

Sliding into the room, she exhaled the pent-up emotion that had been building inside her since she'd left the dining room. For all her bravado, she realized getting caught was not something she wanted to contemplate. There would be too much explaining to do, and she didn't think Morgan St. Claire would find her explanations amusing. Despite the thought of her intimidating host, she experienced the familiar rush of exhilaration that always flowed through her just before she was about to take a risk. It was still quite a new sensation, and she relished it.

Blood pumped its way madly through her veins as she stared about the masculine room. It was as sensual in nature as the man who slept here. The large canopied bed was draped with heavy curtains. It was difficult to tell if they were navy blue or black. Gold tasseled cords held back the material, and the bed itself was covered with a matching spread. The overall impression was one of elegant decadence.

With a shake of her head, she grimaced. She was wasting time. Dragging her eyes away from the bed, she glanced around for the wardrobe. The large chest was across the room, and with swift steps she crossed the floor to open the doors.

More than a dozen suits filled the massive storage and she shifted her gaze to the drawers that lined one side of the piece of furniture. The first drawer revealed nothing but cuff links and watch fobs. Closing it, she moved on to the next drawer.

When it didn't offer up the treasure she sought, she uttered a noise of frustration. She went through two more drawers before she found the prize she hunted. Triumph sailed through her as she pulled one of Morgan St. Claire's monogrammed handkerchiefs from the drawer.

"It appears you've found one of my handkerchiefs."

A surprised cry flew from her lips. Whirling about she saw her host watching her with a narrowed gaze. Arms folded across his chest he studied her in silence. The quiet echoing through the room heightened the tension brewing inside her, and she swallowed the fear threatening to close her throat. Dear Lord, how was she going to explain what she was doing?

"I … I'm sure this must look terrible to you, sir. But it's not what it seems, I can assure you."

"I'm listening."

He was listening. Of course he was. The question though was what to tell him. The truth. She could tell him the truth. No, he'd never believe her. If she were him, she wouldn't believe her story. Stealing a handkerchief to auction off at the Society for Lost Angels would sound too fantastic, and he would immediately label it a falsehood.

"I … I was curious … I mean I wanted to know … umm … I wanted to have one of your handkerchiefs."

"I see."

When he didn't move, she sucked in a quick breath, suddenly conscious of the fact she was trembling. At least he hadn't asked her to return the silk material she held in her hand. The best thing to do was flee. That is if she could make her feet move. She took only one step before he was blocking her way.

She'd never seen a man move so fast or so silently before. It was disturbing. He not only barred her path, but he was inches away from her. Having him stand so close to her set her pulse pounding even faster than it had when he'd first caught her in his room. She sucked in a sharp breath. What if he took this as a sign she was interested in him? No, she'd made her distrust and dislike of him quite clear.

"Surely, you're not leaving so soon." His voice was as smooth as the silk she held in her hand.

"I ... I've been terribly rude and ungracious in the face of your hospitality, Mr. St. Claire. I am deeply sorry."

"There's no need to apologize, Julia."

"Thank you, now if you'll excuse me, I'll return to the dinner party." It was a struggle, but she managed to avoid sounding as breathless as she felt.

"There's no need to hurry. I came up to retrieve a couple of papers for Jepson, but when we both turn up missing they'll assume you and I had unfinished business to attend to."

There was a glint of amusement in his brown eyes, and she frowned at the slight curl of his sensual mouth. They had no unfinished business--

"You bastard. They're all going to think--"

"I don't care what they think."

"Naturally, it's not your reputation in jeopardy," she snapped.

"Perhaps you should have considered the risks more carefully before visiting my hotel room."

She grimaced at his words. It was incredibly irritating to have to admit that he was right. She'd not sufficiently weighed the risks of her actions. Well, there was little she could do about having been caught. What mattered now was escaping.

"As much as I hate to admit it, you're correct, Mr. St. Claire. I erred in my risk calculation. I apologize for intruding. Now if you'll excuse me, I'll rejoin the others."

In a quick movement, she tried to skirt him, but he was faster. Once more he blocked her way. Heat radiated from his hard, lean body, and it created a frisson across her skin that alarmed her. She swallowed her dismay as she met his penetrating gaze.

"You've yet to explain why you needed one of my handkerchiefs, Julia."

The way he said her name let loose a dozen butterflies in her stomach. There was a possessive sound to it, and she wasn't quite certain what it meant. One thing was perfectly clear to her. The resolute line of his lips said she wouldn't leave the room until she'd given him an explanation for her behavior. She clenched her jaw in frustration.

"If you must know, I wish to auction off the silk at a luncheon for the Society for Lost Angels. We're trying to raise money for a new orphanage."

"And you thought my handkerchief would draw a large sum." Humor sparkled in his eyes as he arched an eyebrow.

"Unfortunately, there are a number of women who think it romantic that you offer an abandoned lover a handkerchief with which to dry their tears."

He studied her with that mesmerizing gaze for a long moment before he smiled. It was a smile of dangerous charm, and she sucked in a sharp breath at the power it held over her.

"And you do not subscribe to that romantic myth."

"No, I do not."

"Interesting, although I'm not convinced any of your Society's members will buy this small trifle."

She trembled as his fingers glided along the side of her forearm before flicking the silk square she held tightly in her hand. Even through her evening gloves his fingertips singed her. The amused skepticism in his eyes infuriated her. The man obviously knew nothing about the women in the Society. The handkerchief she held would bring a tidy sum to the orphanage fund.

"Shall we make a wager on that, Mr. St. Claire?"

His gaze narrowed. "Hmm, an interesting notion. What do you propose we wager?"

A shiver of trepidation skated down the length of her spine. God in heaven, she was as reckless as Catherine said she was. But she was in the pond now. There was nothing for it, but to swim for shore with what little decorum she had left.

"If I sell the handkerchief, you must offer up an equal sum for the orphanage fund."

Folding his arms, he arched an eyebrow. "An intriguing wager. So if you sell this handkerchief to a Society member, I'm to offer up the same amount."

"Correct." For the first time since their conversation began, she relaxed. She would still escape with the means to increase the orphanage finances.

"Very well, since you've laid the foundation for this wager, I think it only fair that I name my terms if I should win."

"Of course." She smiled at him with a touch of self-satisfaction as she waited to hear his condition of the bet.

"I saw a portrait recently, quite lovely in fact. I want to see the model reclined in my bed, a willing participant in a night of passion."

The soft edge in his voice raised the hair on the nape of her neck. Triumph mixed with desire to darken his brown gaze and she swallowed the trepidation squeezing her throat closed.

"I don't understand. What portrait are you referring to?"

"It's quite erotic. Just looking at it made my cock spring to attention."

The shocking words made her gasp, but words of protest failed her. She could only stare into his eyes with a sinking feeling of horror as he offered her a wicked smile.

"Let me see if I can describe the portrait. The woman is quite lovely to look at. Her hips are wide, softly curved and voluptuous. Her mouth is full and parted in a seductive pout. But it's her breasts that I find so entrancing. They're large and full. Quite succulent."

"Oh, my God."

"And her hair--it's a beautiful color. Not quite red, not quite brown, even the nest of curls between her legs is the same delectable color."

He was describing her portrait. How had he seen it? Isaac Peebles had given his word he wouldn't show the painting to anyone. But how else could St. Claire know about the portrait? A shudder shot through her, and she clenched her fists as she struggled to maintain a dignified composure.

She wouldn't go through with it. She'd return the bloody handkerchief and leave his room with at least her reputation intact. No. That was impossible. If she backed out of the bet now, he'd be insufferable.

It would be unbearable dealing with the man when it came to her financial investment. No, she had to see it through. He might have seen the portrait, but it was in her possession. She had nothing to fear in that area. More importantly, he couldn't win this wager. She'd make sure Catherine or Alva would bid on the silk. After all, as long as one of the ladies in the Society of Lost Angels bought the handkerchief, she'd win.

"This woman in the portrait, do I know her?" She tilted her chin at a proud angle, hoping to convince him she didn't understand him.

His hands grasped her arms and he pulled her against his hard body. A small squeak of surprise escaped her. Heat enveloped her and made her heart race with excitement even though she tried to slow the mad pace of its beat.

A strong arm curved around her waist, binding her close. His mouth was so close to hers she could smell the expensive wine on his breath. For a fleeting moment, she wondered what it would be like to taste that liquor on his tongue. Shocked by the traitorous way her body was behaving, she braced her hands on his chest and tried to push away from him.

"Surely you're not going to deny that you have the most delicious looking mocha nipples, Julia. Seeing them in that portrait made me ache to suck on them."

His fingers skimmed her exposed skin at the lower edge of her bodice. The touch made her mouth go dry at the sudden longing that gripped her. What would it be like to be this man's lover? Immediately, her mind careened to a halt. Sweet heaven, she needed to keep her wits about her where this man was concerned. She needed to close this wager and flee with what little dignity she still possessed.

"I don't deny anything, sir. But if you think you can win this wager, I dare you to accept."

"So you agree that if I win you'll recline yourself on my bed." The look of satisfaction sounded alarm bells in her head, but she was in too deep to stop now.

"It is easy to gamble when the outcome is certain to be in one's favor, sir."

"Then let us seal the agreement."

The sudden possession of his mouth took her by surprise. The warmth of his firm lips covering hers made her stomach flip with excitement. It was like being engulfed by fire. As his tongue swept into her mouth, she relaxed into him, unable to prevent the wild reaction of her body. Hands rough with calluses scraped over her sensitive skin as he cupped her face. It was a kiss of seduction, possession and mastery all in one.

Her body reveled in the experience, all the while her head was scrambling for clear thought. Rough fingers trailed down to the base of her neck, where a long finger slid under the edge of her bodice. A wave of sensation swept over her at the touch, and her nipples grew hard as her breasts swelled and tried to push their way out of her corset.

Sweet heaven, no wonder women fell at the man's feet. His touch was like a drug. He captured her mouth again, his kiss drowning out every one of her thoughts. She found herself clinging to him with abandon, while strong, rough fingers undid several buttons at the back of her dress. In protest, she tried to push away, but her gown slipped off one shoulder before she could free herself.

One tapered finger slid its way between her skin and corset, and she gasped as he gently eased her breast up so her nipple popped over the edge of the snug fitting garment.

"Beautiful," he murmured as he lowered his head and flicked his tongue over the taut bud. The action singed her skin and she uttered a soft cry. An instant later, his teeth gently clamped on her and tugged at the nipple in a playful manner. The world shifted beneath her feet.

"Please … please…." Her voice evaporated as he began to suck on her breast. The pleasure singing through her veins was indescribable. Moist heat gathered at the apex of her thighs. A moment later, she wondered what it would feel like for his hand to touch her intimately. The picture shimmering in her head shocked her.

Wrenching herself out of his arms, she backed away from him. He looked completely unfazed by their recent embrace, and she was certain she looked disheveled and disconcerted. In the back of her mind, she knew all too well that the only reason she was free was because he'd been willing to release her.

Embarrassed, she adjusted her clothing with great speed, all the while fully aware of his dark eyes watching her. It was disturbing. Even more so because, deep inside, she liked the way he watched her. The way he'd touched her.

Shaken by the knowledge, she struggled to regain her composure. Her gaze flashed toward him only to see him smiling at her, the glow of desire in his eyes. "I shall enjoy having you in my bed, Julia."

His confidence should have frightened her. Instead it infuriated her. Her senses restored somewhat by his arrogance, she glared in his direction. "I think not, sir. You forget that I hold the upper hand."

Sweeping around him, she raced from the room. She heard his laughter trailing after her. It made her heart lurch with an intense pleasure she didn't want to feel, but the sensation spread its way through her body like a raging river. It made her want to return to his arms and experience the delight she was certain she'd find there. Oh, if only she were that daring.

Chapter 2

Today was the day. Morgan swung his walking stick out in front of him with a quick flick of his wrist as he walked, letting the cane briefly touch the ground before it repeated the outward movement in another clean stroke. He did it with the same smoothness with which he always pulled on the oars of his rowing boat. Today, Julia Westgard would have to admit defeat when she failed to sell that bloody silk handkerchief of his to a woman in her Society.

Agreeing to her investment in St. Claire Shipping had been a serious error in judgment on his part. Even worse was his endorsement of the contingencies she demanded as part of the transaction. He'd never expected her to review the accounts personally.

In the first two weeks, she'd questioned almost every business transaction for the past year. Now she simply asked questions on a weekly basis. Even more irritating was the realization that her inquiries were based on sound logic. She'd even managed to offer some ideas for improving his distribution channels. That, in and of itself, was galling. He frowned and his cane hit the sidewalk with a small crack of noise.

Even his solicitor had been surprised by the addition of Julia Westgard's name to the investor list. Women were rarely allowed to invest in his businesses. And certainly not young, attractive ones. It was a way to ensure peace in his daily life. As a child, he'd learned that women were calculating creatures without emotion and avoiding them was in his best interest.

He'd also come to realize that houses were generally filled with discord, and to escape the bitter memories of his childhood home, he chose to live at the Clarendon Hotel. It suited his needs well, while eliminating the possibility of a mistress thinking there was anything permanent in their relationship.

Marriage was a shackle he had no intention of falling prisoner too. He knew all too well what havoc that institution could wreak. And it was exactly why he'd made it his habit never to do business with a woman unless she was well beyond marrying age. Now he'd broken that unwritten rule, and he was paying for it.

Why the devil had he agreed to let the woman invest in his company? He grimaced. That was an easy question to answer. He could have easily found several other investors to make up for the sizable capital she'd put into the business. But he hadn't, and why? All because of that cursed portrait. It was that blasted painting that had gotten him into this infernal mess.

Ever since his first glimpse of Peebles' canvas, it had kept him and his cock awake more nights than he cared to admit. It had been quite by accident that he'd seen it. While visiting the artist's studio, he'd bumped into the painting with his elbow, dislodging the material over it. The partial view had been so enticing he'd exposed the rest of the portrait despite Peebles' outraged sputtering. Then the man had refused to offer up any information about the subject.

He hadn't even known her name--until she walked into his offices on Beckton Road near the docks. Rarely was he taken by surprise, but Julia Westgard had managed to render him speechless for a moment. The portrait had painted the image of a sensual, sultry woman accustomed to pleasing a man and enjoying the same in return. But Julia in person was vastly different from what he'd imagined. In fact, she was a challenge.

From the moment he'd seen her portrait he'd been determined to find her and bed her. His determination hadn't ebbed. If anything, it had grown out of control because of her demeanor. With her cool exterior and impervious resistance to his flirtations, she was a challenge he couldn't ignore.

She was all the more tempting since he'd discovered her in his bedroom stealing one of his silk handkerchiefs. For once, that ridiculous story circulating among the Marlborough Set had yielded something other than his amusement. It would give him Julia, and he would enjoy every minute of her comeuppance.

Then, of course, there would be the night to enjoy as well. When he was done with her, she'd be begging for a second silk handkerchief. He paused at the stoop of Lady Eldred's town home. Pulling his pocket watch out, he clicked the timepiece open.

Excellent, just in time for the auction. Lady Eldred had taken great care to apprise him of the Society's meeting schedule and had agreed to keep his impending visit a secret. Julia was about to have the surprise of her life. He smiled as he strode up the steps and used the brass knocker.

The door opened immediately, and he handed over his homburg, gloves and cane to the butler. From the partially open salon door, he heard Julia's voice ringing out. It was a melodious sound. But then everything about her was pleasing, right down to the way her pulse throbbed erratically when she was in his arms.

He slid quietly into the room to take a seat in the chair Lady Eldred had told him she would save for him. Julia's attention was focused on one of the Society members, and he was pleased his arrival had gone unnoticed. From his seat in the back of the room, he watched and waited.

"So you see, ladies, this handkerchief is available to the highest bidder today. Think of it, this silk square belonged to the notorious Morgan St. Claire, and it was procured under the most harrowing circumstances."

"Exactly what were these excruciating conditions, Mrs. Westgard?"

"Start the bidding with twenty pounds, Lady Plumton, and I'll tell you."

He watched the woman in question nod her head in agreement. Julia's radiant smile made him suck in a sharp breath and his cock stirred in his trousers. Christ, but the woman was an enticing witch.

"Thank you, my lady. I have twenty pounds--do I hear forty while I share with Lady Plumton as to how I came by this silk square?" Julia turned back to the first bidder, her manner far from the restrained woman he was accustomed to seeing in his shipping office. "First I must tell you that I'm sworn to secrecy not to reveal the identity of the friend who acquired this infamous handkerchief."

"I bid thirty pounds, Mrs. Westgard. How did this friend of yours acquire the handkerchief? Is it from one of St. Claire's discarded lovers?"

"Thank you, Mrs. Fellowes. No, this item was not given freely. It was taken right from underneath the great man's nose itself. My friend, who shall go nameless, entered the lion's den, simply to acquire this handkerchief."

"Good heavens! Do you mean your friend ... oh my word." Mrs. Fellowes went silent.

"I bid fifty pounds if you tell us what lion's den, Mrs. Westgard," said a timid looking young woman on the front row.

Julia, hazel eyes shining with mischief, moved to the other side of the room and smiled at the bidder. Folding his arms across his chest, he bit back a grin. The minx was enjoying keeping these women on tenterhooks.

"Thank you for that bid, Miss Alverton. In fact, the lion's den was no other than," Julia paused for effect, "Morgan St. Claire's very own room at the Clarendon."

The collective gasps in the room merely widened Julia's smile, and it was difficult not to laugh out loud at her mischievous pleasure.

"Oh no, Mrs. Westgard ... surely not." The woman called Miss Alverton shook her head in horror.

"I'm afraid so, although my friend confessed it was a frightening adventure."

He watched her dramatically hold up the handkerchief for inspection. "As you can see, here are the illustrious initials of the man himself. So which of you lovely ladies dares to own a genuine Morgan St. Claire handkerchief? All without having succumbed to the man's licentious charms?"

Her blithely spoken words made his muscles tense with annoyance. Licentious. The woman was about to find out just how unrestrained he could be in the bedroom, and he'd make certain she was begging for more before he finished with her. Relaxing back into his seat, he studied Julia's lush, voluptuous figure.

He knew what hid beneath that modest gray dress of hers. His eyes narrowed as he watched her continue to encourage the bidding for the handkerchief. The snug material of her gown clung with seductive longing to her breasts. The pattern slid downward to a pointed vee, just below her waist, before the material covered her hips in a graceful swag to the bustle behind her.

The image of her portrait entered his mind, and he visualized exactly what that vee was pointing to. A nest of reddish-brown curls lay beneath that meek gown, and he had every intention of exploring the velvety folds those curls covered--and soon.

"Do I have any more bids, ladies? I have a hundred pounds from Lady Plumton, do I hear a hundred twenty?"

"Two hundred pounds." He watched as the sound of his voice reached her. The color drained from her face as she finally caught sight of him in the rear of the room. The entire room had erupted into a bevy of whispers, and he arched his eyebrow as he saw the outrage glittering in her eyes. They'd turned the loveliest color green.

"I ... Mr. St. Claire ... I ... I don't think this auction is open to bidders outside of the Society for Lost Angels."

"I see. Lady Eldred, I was given to understand that my bid would be welcome today, did I misunderstand?" Slowly rising to his feet, his gaze sought and met Lady Eldred's mortified expression.

Her plump face flushed with embarrassment, he watched his hostess rise to her feet. She nodded at him. "Yes, Mr. St. Claire, I did tell you we'd be delighted to have you bid at our auction. I … I failed to mention this to you before the meeting started, Mrs. Westgard. I do apologize, my dear."

The woman turned toward Julia, whose face resembled a statue. Despite her lack of emotion, he could see the tension in her tight smile. He could almost see her brain working on a way to escape the trap into which she'd stumbled.

"Well then, Lady Eldred, Mrs. Westgard, since I'd like to bid on this item, I repeat my bid of two hundred pounds."

"But you--" Her glare made him smile. She was captivating when she was angry. And she wasn't just angry, she was furious. His smile broadened.

"Two hundred pounds, Mrs. Westgard. Do I hear any other bids?" He glanced around the room, enjoying the looks of shock and curiosity on the faces of the women surrounding him.

"I … I bid three hundred pounds." Confidence glowed from her features again as she tilted her head at a stubborn angle. The muscle in his jaw twitched as he gritted his teeth and forced a polite smile to his lips.

"Four hundred."

"Five."

"One thousand." Damn the minx. He'd extract a suitable punishment the moment he had her alone.

"Two."

A stand off. She was hell bent on saving herself from the wager she'd made. She would continue to outbid him until she was penniless. Her anger was almost tangible as he narrowed his eyes to study her. She was definitely far too confident. But he intended to teach her a lesson. No one--no one--ever stole from or cheated Morgan St. Claire.

"Before I make another bid, Mrs. Westgard, I'd like to view the merchandise."

Without waiting for her agreement, he skirted the chairs in front of him, moving along the side of the room until he reached the front row where Julia was standing. As he drew near, her body was no longer supple, but rigid. He extended his hand and waited for her to drop the silk square into his palm. Although her face was serene, he saw her fingers tremble as she gave him the auction item. Bending his head, he pretended to study the handkerchief.

"You seem determined to win our wager, Julia, but I have no intention of losing." He lifted his head to stare into her strained expression as she took in his quietly murmured words. "Shall I continue bidding, or shall I explain how you really came by this handkerchief?"

The sharp inhale of her breath indicated his words had struck home. He turned toward the waiting members of the Society.

"Ladies, I'm thoroughly convinced this is indeed my handkerchief, and I offer up a bid of five thousand pounds."

He turned his head and arched an eyebrow at Julia. The defeat was evident in her eyes. But it was the look of vulnerability in her hazel gaze that tugged at him. It wasn't an unpleasant sensation, but it was most certainly a disturbing one. She drew in a deep breath before forcing a smile to her mouth.

"Sold to Mr. St. Claire for five thousand pounds."

The moment her words faded in the air, the room filled with the loud buzz of conversation. Glancing at Julia, he frowned. He should be feeling elated right now. He'd won. She was going to come to his bed. Then with a sharp twinge of consternation, he realized he wanted her there willingly, not bought and paid for like a whore.

"Bloody hell," he muttered.

Her eyes and face empty of emotion, she nodded at him. "You've won our wager, Mr. St. Claire. What time am I to present myself for your disposal?"

The cool mask of detachment angered him even more. The problem was that he wasn't angry with her. He was furious with himself. When in the hell had he suddenly taken to bedding women who didn't want anything to do with him? And there was no doubt she didn't want anything to do with him.

Teeth clenched in frustration, he studied her in silence for a long moment. Beneath his gaze he saw the veneer of her cool composure crack slightly. No, he refused to bed a woman who was unwilling. But damn it, his body still wanted her. Suddenly, his lips curved upward.

Genuine pleasure filled him as he offered her the most charming smile he possessed. Hazel eyes flashed with first surprise and then a guarded expression. He gave her a slight bow.

"Mrs. Westgard, are you planning on attending the St. Claire Fete next Friday?"

"I … yes ... as an investor, it's my obligation to make an appearance before the company's employees."

"Excellent. I hope you'll save me a dance then. The party can sometimes be a bit rowdy, but I can assure you, I'll not let you come to any harm."

"I am quite capable of taking care of myself, Mr. St. Claire."

"Indeed." His smile broadened at the flush of irritation that tinged her creamy cheeks as her lips tightened into a straight line. "Well, then. I'll take my leave."

"But I--"

"Yes?" He arched an eyebrow at her, fully aware that she was completely bewildered by his actions.

"I … I thought that…."

He nodded and leaned toward her, deliberately keeping his voice low. "Our wager still stands, my sweet. However, I think we should become better acquainted before payment is made."

"Oh."

"I look forward to our next meeting."

Surprise and puzzlement pulled her mouth into a lovely pout. The sight stirred the beast in his trousers. Sweet Jesus, if they were alone--no, he needed to hold a calm and steady course with her. Julia was going to be the most difficult challenge he'd ever faced. But she was a prize he intended to win. With a quick nod, he turned and walked away. Time for a change in plans.

* * * *

Morgan threw his pencil down onto the open ledger in front of him in disgust. Leaning back into the soft leather of his office chair, he closed his eyes in pain. This headache was one of the worst he'd suffered in months. He dragged in a ragged breath as a wave of nausea roiled in his stomach.

He should have gone back to his rooms at the hotel an hour ago. The head housekeeper, Mrs. Welkins, always had some of his special tea ready for brewing and he could use the stuff now. The throbbing in his right temple hammered away at him, increasing the level of his pain. The sound of his office door opening was a banshee's wail as the pins squealed in their hinges.

"Whoever you are, get the hell out of here or I'll cut your heart out," he snarled, refusing to open his eyes as the light made the pain worse.

"I believe you would."

Julia's cool tone caught him by surprise. His eyes flew open to meet her haughty gaze. What the devil was she doing here? Another sharp pain gripped his temple, and he closed his eyes again as he swallowed a groan. God damn it, he didn't want her to see him this way. It made him appear weak, and the last thing he wanted was Julia Westgard thinking that he, Morgan St. Claire, was weak.

"Go home, Julia. I'm not in the mood for any questions today."

"Well, I am. I noticed The Merry Widow's manifest indicated it brought into port a cargo of tea, spice and silk. I was wondering if this was a normal shipment. She's made the same run on other occasions, but in less time."

He didn't give a bloody farthing how fast or slow the Widow was, he just wanted her to get the hell out of his office before he lost the small meal he had eaten at the noon hour. Gripping the arms of his chair he lurched to his feet.

"Get out, Julia." His wounded roar filled the office and accentuated the throb in his temple. With great effort, he barely suppressed the churning in his stomach. "Get out now, or I'm likely to say or do something we'll both regret."

His strength ebbing away, he collapsed into his chair. Eyes closed, he waited to hear the obnoxious sound of the door closing behind her. Instead, he heard the quiet rustle of taffeta rounding the corner of his desk.

"Damn it, Julia. I want you out of here."

"Hush, it's obvious you're not well." The warmth of her hand rested on his forehead for a brief moment as if checking for a fever. "Do you suffer from migraines often?"

"Yes," he growled.

Her fingers gently stroked his throbbing head. The light touch on his skin could have been a feather, but it was enough pressure to ease his pain a small fraction. Inhaling a deep breath, he released it as her fingers slid through his hair to soothe his scalp. Beyond the door, he heard the noisy workings of his staff. He was grateful for the buffer, but he knew he'd have to traverse through the outer office to reach his carriage.

"You should be at home, resting." The gentle whisper made him catch her hand and halt her healing caress.

"I had work to do."

"And now?"

"Now, I'm going home for some peace and quiet."

Forcing himself to stand, he gripped the edge of the desk to keep from swaying as the pain in his temple lashed out with the strength of a hot iron. A quiet noise of disgust flew from her lips, but he was too focused on remaining upright to look at her. A firm hand pressed against his arm as he willed the churning in his stomach to stop.

"Sit down, now. I'll order your carriage and call one of the men to help you outside."

"No," he rasped as loudly as his head could bear. "I'll walk out of this office under my own volition. I'm not some weak fool, unable to handle a minor headache."

She made a sound that was quite close to a snort. It made him want to smile. If he'd not been feeling so miserable, he would have.

"You're a stubborn man, Morgan St. Claire."

"Yes."

"I propose a compromise. I'll order your carriage, and when it arrives, I'll help you reach it safely."

The idea of Julia Westgard escorting him to his carriage struck him as terribly funny. No, more like humiliating. But he didn't have the strength left to argue. God knew it wouldn't be the first time he'd let the woman have her way.

"Fine." Sinking back down into his chair, he closed his eyes and rested his head against the warmth of the burgundy leather.

Taffeta rustled softly as she moved toward the door. He waited for the squeal of the pins in the hinges. When it came, the sound made him flinch. The throbbing pressure in his temple reinforced its message that he remain still. He complied. If he didn't he'd never make it out of the shipping office without showing his staff he was nothing more than a weakling.

Slowing his breathing, he must have drifted off, for it seemed like only seconds had elapsed before Julia was touching his hand.

"Morgan, the carriage is here."

He answered her with a grunt and rose to his feet once more. Using the desk to hold himself steady, he made his way around the furniture at a slow pace.

"Walking stick."

His rough command was hardly a whisper, but an instant later his cane was offered to him in silence. Her hand encircled his waist as he moved toward the door. It was a pleasant sensation. He'd never had a woman he was attracted to aid him in such a manner. Reaching the door, he took a deep breath and gently pushed her away from his side.

"I prefer to walk without help, Julia."

"And you have the audacity to think me obstinate and foolhardy."

Ignoring the irritation in her quiet voice, he braced himself for the noise about to assault his senses. He straightened his shoulders as he opened the office door. "We can discuss my audacity at another time. Right now, I'm waiting on you to lead me out to my carriage.

She sent him a glare as she swept past him and toward the main door of the St. Claire Shipping offices. As he followed her, his head clerk hurried toward him.

"Mr. St. Claire, I need your signature on some documents."

"Not now, Jeremy."

"But sir,–"

"I said not now." Each word resounded in his head with the force of a gunshot. Stomach churning, he brushed past the man and walked as steadily as he could toward the front door. Julia waited for him in the open doorway. The light behind her was blinding. It exacerbated his pain and bile rose up in his throat.

Beyond her voluptuous curves, he could see the open doorway of his carriage. Determined to maintain his composure until he was in private, he continued forward. It seemed like an eternity until he reached the coach door. With what little reserve strength he possessed, he pulled himself up into the vehicle and onto the padded seat.

Surprise broke through the throbbing in his body as Julia climbed in behind him and closed the door. He had no time to speak as the carriage suddenly rocked into motion, which made him lurch forward and retch violently. When he'd finished, he sank back against the leather seat. A softly scented piece of linen dabbed at his mouth. It smelled of lavender.

"You'll be home shortly. It will please you to know that the men simply thought you were in a bad mood. They didn't suspect you were unwell."

He barely nodded before turning away from her. It had been a long time since he'd been this miserable. Of course, he had no one to blame but himself. All the signs of an impending migraine had been there, he'd simply ignored them.

The most puzzling thing was Julia's behavior. She'd either been coolly reserved or antagonistic with him in the past. This gentle, caring demeanor of hers was confusing. And he hated being confused.

Women never confused him. He confused them. It had become an art form with him. His head reverberated with a jolt of pain. He failed to suppress the groan that poured out of him. Christ, would this infernal carriage never stop. As if hearing his internal curse, the coach rolled to a halt, and he steeled himself for another performance just to get to his rooms.

The silk of Julia's glove touched his bare hand. "I instructed the driver to take us to the back of the hotel. I didn't want you to feel it necessary to repeat the heroics you displayed at your offices."

There was no censure in her voice, but there was a distinct thread of humor. If he hadn't been so exhausted, he would have taken the time to make an appropriate retort. Instead he grimaced. Moving his head was too painful. The carriage door opened and Julia exited, then turned and waited for him to climb out of the vehicle.

The fresh air gave him a renewed sense of energy, and he steadied himself against the black lacquered panels of his carriage. A warm body slid up alongside him as she wrapped an arm around his waist to guide him forward. Grateful for her help, he put one foot in front of the other until they reached the hotel's back door. As a bustle of activity exploded around him, he pitched forward into a black hole.

Chapter 3

His room was every bit as decadent as she remembered. A shudder went through her as she watched two footmen lift Morgan St. Claire's tall, sturdy frame onto the bed. She'd lost her bet to him almost a week ago, and the blasted man had yet to send her a note or pay her a call to arrange for the collection of his winnings.

Silently, she cursed her stupidity at having entered into a wager with him. St. Claire's silence in the matter was nerve wracking. She kept waiting for the man to spring some unexpected demand on her. Such a tactic had been one of her late husband's finer skills--it was how Oscar had controlled her. That, along with fear and criticism.

Distancing herself from the painful memory of her repressive marriage, she looked toward the bed where Morgan lay. He stirred something in her she'd thought long dead. She bit her lip at the thought. It alarmed her to know she was attracted to the man. He was a threat to everything she'd fought so hard to achieve since Oscar's death.

With a man like Morgan St. Claire, her independence would be at stake. He was a man used to commanding everything and everyone in his world. She'd already seen his reaction to her inquiries about his business accounts. The man hated being questioned, and he didn't like to be thwarted.

The footmen, having closed the drapes and lit candles, passed the hotel's head housekeeper on their way out of the room. Tall and thin, Mrs. Welkins entered with a tray of rags and lavender water. As she set her burden on the night stand beside Morgan's bed, the woman turned to face her.

"Thank you for agreeing to tend to Mr. St. Claire for a short time, ma'am. I have several other things to attend to before I can return, and he'll be wanting his tea when he wakes up so I must set that out to brew. I promise not be too long."

"You're quite welcome, Mrs. Welkins. My father suffered from migraines so I'm familiar with what needs to be done."

With a grateful smile, the woman left her alone with Morgan. Sighing softly, she removed her hat and snaked the hat pin through the plumes. Carelessly, she dropped it onto a nearby chair along with her gloves before moving to the side of the bed.

Morgan's face had lost some of the harsh lines that emphasized his libertine status. At the moment, he was defenseless. She was certain he wouldn't like anyone seeing him this way. With a gentle touch she pushed a lock of chestnut hair off his forehead. Flustered by her actions, she quickly turned to the bowl of lavender-scented water Mrs. Welkins had left.

Her fingers swished a rag in the water as she seated herself on the edge of the massive bed. She gave the cloth a sharp twist then with a light touch, she laid it across Morgan's forehead. For some reason, it seemed quite natural for her to be here tending to this man.

It wasn't an unpleasant feeling, but it was confusing. Her fingers tingled from the heat of his skin as she adjusted the cloth on his forehead. There was a pinched set to his firm mouth. Even unconscious he appeared to be in pain. She shook her head slightly at the memory of him walking past his shipping clerks as if he was hale and hearty. It had been nothing short of magnificent.

With a frown, she retrieved another rag to soak in the scented water. She didn't want to find Morgan St. Claire magnificent. She didn't want to think or feel anything about him. The man was a rake--a dangerous one at that. With his handsome face and silk-edged compliments, it was understandable why women fell at his feet. But she had no intention of being classified as a St. Claire woman.

The man might have won their wager, but he would never win her mind or heart. She would see to that. Water droplets wet her palm as she gently dampened Morgan's pale features. There was an intimacy to her actions that disconcerted her. Unwillingly her gaze drifted down to a strong, tanned neck showing through the open folds of a white shirt. The footmen had removed his jacket, stock pin, and tie, then undone the top few buttons of his shirt. The vee revealed only a small portion of his throat and chest, but it was enough to make her imagination soar.

She bit her lip as her gaze roved over the length of him. The sight of his large hands on the black bedspread brought to mind the way he had pulled her into his arms the night he'd caught her stealing his handkerchief. His lips had seared hers, and the memory was so vivid her fingers flew up to her burning mouth. She'd never been kissed like that in her life, and she liked it. It had made her feel wicked and daring.

It was the same sensation she'd gotten when she'd posed for her portrait. Swallowing the knot of confusion that tightened her throat, she shook her head slightly. The man was far too attractive for her peace of mind. God only knew what would happen to her when he demanded she pay up on their wager.

She'd gotten herself into such a mess and there was no way out of it. Even more disturbing was the fact she would find it almost impossible to avoid succumbing to his charms. She scowled at the thought. There had to be some way to put an emotional barrier between them.

Her gaze drifted back to his face, noting the tightness at the corners of his mouth had eased somewhat. The cloth on his forehead had lost its coolness so she lifted it from his head and soaked it again. Replacing the damp cloth on his skin, she was pulling away when a strong hand gripped her wrist.

Startled, she froze. The last time someone had held her so fast, she'd been tied to a bed while Oscar rutted on top of her. She suppressed the hideous memory, and focused her gaze on Morgan's face. His eyes were still closed.

"You may leave now, Julia." His voice was husky, almost hoarse.

"And if I go, who will change the cloth on your forehead?"

"I'll manage."

"I told Mrs. Welkins I'd wait for her return." Stubbornness had to be this man's most annoying trait. She glared at him, mentally challenging him to look at her. He didn't. Instead a long finger rubbed against the inside of her wrist. The simple gesture filled her belly with fire. A small smile tipped the corners of his mouth.

"As soft as I've imagined."

"Stop that." She tried to tug herself free, but his grip simply tightened around her wrist.

"I like the feel of your skin beneath my fingers."

"I care little for what you like, St. Claire. Release me this instant."

"Ahh, there it is again, that waspish tone." His fingers relinquished his hold on her, and she stumbled to her feet. She watched him open his eyes carefully to meet her gaze with just a hint of the irreverent mischief she was accustomed to seeing in him.

"Whatever are you referring to?"

"You get defensive whenever you're frightened."

"I do not." She scowled at the way his mouth twisted with amusement. "You're right. I should leave. You no longer have need of me."

With a final glare, she wheeled about and walked stiffly toward the chair that held her hat and gloves. She'd only taken a few steps when a loud crash, mingled with a weary oath of frustration, filled the air behind her. Whirling around, she saw Morgan flop wearily back into the mattress. At the foot of the nightstand, the bowl of lavender water lay in pieces on the floor. Annoyed by his bullheadedness, she returned to the bedside and adjusted his pillows none too gently.

"You, Morgan St. Claire, are the most obstinate man I've ever met. One of these days, that pride of yours is going to cause you to fall flat on your face." Straightening, she glared down at him with her hands on her hips.

"Your confidence is one of the most intriguing things about you, Julia. I like a confident woman in my bed."

The observation stunned her. How on earth could he possibly think she was confident? She was the least self-assured person she knew. "I am not in your bed, St. Claire."

"But you will be, and quite soon, I think."

"Then collect your damned prize and leave me be." She turned away, only to feel the warmth of his hand on her wrist once more.

"You are definitely a prize, my sweet, but I'll collect my treasure at a time of my choosing, not yours."

The possessive gleam in his liquid brown gaze set her heart pounding, and she stood mesmerized, unable to look away from him. She flicked her tongue out to wet her dry lips, and his eyes narrowed. Good Lord. She was far too attracted this man. Heaven help her if she became involved with him. The man would control and manipulate her until he tired of her.

Her gaze fell on his fingers holding her fast. The sudden image of her hands bound in a black necktie made her shudder. She'd lived that hellish existence while Oscar was alive. He'd been a bastard, but he'd taught her one thing. Never let anyone control her. Never again.

Jerking free of Morgan's hand, she knelt to clean up the pieces of broken china, while using the last of the cloths to soak up the spilled water. To hell with the man's headache; he could reuse the cloth he'd been using. He was deliberately tormenting her, keeping her on pins and needles as she waited for him to demand she make good on their wager. But he had no intention of telling her when. He simply enjoyed making her stew and wait until he surprised her with his demand for payment. If there was one thing she hated, it was surprises.

Oscar had always taken great pleasure in surprising her, but they'd always been unpleasant events. Never anything pleasurable.

Using one of the cloths from the nightstand, she swept it across the floor to wipe up the water. The sudden sharp edge of a broken piece of porcelain she'd missed cut into her finger and she yelped. She climbed to her feet so she could examine the wound under the light of the candle.

"Let me see."

His harsh command grated each and every one of her nerve endings. She wouldn't have cut herself if it hadn't been for his pig-headed behavior. With a shake of her head, she tossed him a disdainful glance over her shoulder before studying the small cut in the light of the candle.

"I'm fine. It's a small cut."

"Let me see your finger, Julia." The soft words contained a warning note, and she glared at him again before thrusting her hand toward him.

"As I said, it's an insignificant cut."

He studied her finger for a moment then released her hand. His mouth tightened into a firm line as he turned his head away from her. Glaring at him in frustration, she stalked away from his bedside back to where she'd dropped her gloves. With quick, jerky movements she tugged on first one glove and then the other.

Blast the man and his arrogance. The sooner she escaped this den of decadence, the better. It was disturbing enough to know she would return in the future, and not solely of her own volition, but because of her foolish tongue.

As she reached the door, his voice made her pause. "I shall pay you a call tomorrow afternoon, Julia."

"I'm afraid I have plans." She threw a glance over her shoulder to see him lying still on the bed, his eyes closed.

"Tomorrow afternoon, Julia."

There was no need for him to say anything else. She knew exactly what he meant without any further explanation on his part. If she didn't make herself available to him tomorrow, he would extract a price she would not find pleasant. No, that wasn't the problem. The problem with any punishment Morgan St. Clair levied on her head was not how unpleasant it might be, but how much she'd enjoy it. Not about to answer his autocratic command, she left the room.

* * * *

Head bent over her needlepoint, Julia stiffened as the sound of voices in the foyer drifted up the stairs and into the salon. It was easy to distinguish Morgan's voice from that of her butler, Calvert. A tremor shot through her as she heard heavy footsteps climbing the stairs. What to do? Greet him as though he were expected? No, far better to make it appear that his visit was of little consequence.

Once more she returned her attention to the complex bird of paradise pattern in her hands. She punched the needle through the material just as he entered the parlor. Slowly, she turned her attention toward him in an attempt to illustrate her indifference. There was a smile of amusement on his face, almost as if he could read her mind.

"Good afternoon, Mr. St. Claire. I trust you're feeling better?"

"Exceedingly so."

She returned her attention to her needlework and tied off her thread. The silence filling the room surprised her. She darted a look in his direction to find him studying her through narrowed eyes. He looked every inch the gentleman in his dark blue suit coat with gray vest and trousers. Still, even dressed in the height of fashion, there was a dangerous air about him. Determined not to lose her composure, she arched an eyebrow as she met his gaze.

"Would you care for a cup of tea? My cook was preparing some scones earlier, I'm certain they're done by now."

"I think a cup of tea would suit me well."

Setting her work on the half-oval shaped table next to her wing-backed chair, she rose to her feet. Unnerved by his presence more than she cared to admit, she pressed one hand against the jade silk of her afternoon gown as she moved to ring for tea. The white lace on the sleeve tickled her wrist, reminding her of how he'd stroked her skin yesterday. Disturbed by the memory, she tugged the bell cord a trifle more than she should have.

The sudden movement that flashed just on the edge of her vision made her jump and she turned to face him. He'd moved to stand in front of the brass fire screen, but he wasn't looking at her. His gaze was focused on the small fire burning in the grate and there was tension in his jawline.

She tipped her head to one side. "Is something wrong?"

Immediately his expression changed as he turned to look at her, his smile filled with breathtaking charm. "Not at all. Being in your company is exceptionally pleasant."

"Please save your flattery for someone more susceptible to your charms, St. Claire."

"You seem to enjoy challenging me. The question is, what will you do when I accept?"

"It was not my intent to challenge." She moved toward the center of the room and drew in a sigh of relief at the sight of Calvert entering with a tray of tea and scones. The butler set his burden on the low table in front of the burgundy velvet couch.

"When you rang, Cook thought you would want tea brought up to the salon, madame."

"That was most thoughtful of her. Please thank her for me, Calvert."

The short, stocky servant smiled, then bowed and left the room. To her dismay, he closed the door behind him. Why on earth hadn't she thought to tell him to leave it open? It was bad enough St. Claire was here at all, let alone taking tea with her in such intimate conditions. It might make the servants think the man was courting her. After all, Oscar had been dead for some time and it wasn't unheard of for widows to marry again.

Marriage. No. Ten years of torment was more than enough for a lifetime. Even now she could see Oscar sitting in the chair at the fireplace, berating her for speaking to the wrong person at a social gathering. The first time she'd protested, he'd slapped her. The sting of his abuse tingled its way over her skin once more, and she automatically lifted a hand to her cheek. It infuriated him when she would try to explain. She'd learned to tread carefully from that point forward.

She'd been a puppet he could manipulate at his command. There had been no love or affection. And her worst offense had been her failure to offer him an heir. He'd blamed her for being cold and unresponsive in bed, punishing her by tying her hands to the headboard while he rutted on top of her. She flinched at the memory.

She had fought against believing Oscar's words, fought it desperately. But after ten years, it had been impossible for his comments not to have had some effect on her. Now she was free of him, and she intended to remain free. Never again would any man control her as Oscar had.

She closed her eyes for a brief moment to gather her wits before turning back to face her visitor. He smiled at her as he met her gaze. It was a smile filled with charm, and her heart slammed into her chest as the impact of it affected her senses.

"Your servants are quite efficient," he said with amusement. "One would think you'd been expecting company."

"I always have tea at this time of the day, visitors or not." She sent him a cool look before moving to sit on the sofa. Sitting on the edge of the loveseat, she leaned forward and lifted the dainty rose-covered teapot to pour him a cup of tea. As he sat next to her, the warmth of him engulfed her. With a quick hitch of her breath, she offered him the cup.

It pleased her that her hand remained steady as she handed him the tea, although inside she was shuddering with reaction to his nearness. The man radiated charm, and it was difficult not be affected by his overpowering presence. The size of him was emphasized by the way his hand swallowed the tea cup she'd offered him. What would it be like to have his hands cup her, tease her skin? Heavens, what was the matter with her?

Jerking her gaze away from him, she quickly poured herself a cup of tea and took a sip of the scalding beverage. The heat of the tea burned her tongue and she grimaced. An appropriate punishment for her wicked thoughts. The sudden warmth of Morgan's body sank into hers as he set his cup on the table, then leaned into her side.

His male scent flooded her senses as he pulled her cup from her numb fingers. Sweet heaven, why didn't she even offer up a protest? Instead, she was simply allowing him to do as he pleased with her. A hard hand cupped the back of her neck, while his thumb pressed against the pulse beating rapidly on the side of her neck.

"I can always tell when you're nervous or excited. Your pulse flutters wildly, right here." The pad of his thumb caressed the side of her neck in a sensual movement. It teased her skin, causing her heartbeat to increase its pace. "Ah, you see, it skipped again."

"You're imagining things."

"I don't think so, my sweet."

"You are far too full of yourself, St. Claire."

"You called me Morgan yesterday." She breathed in a trace of sandalwood and spice. It was a fragrant aroma. Almost heady. Her pulse lashed out a frantic beat through her body.

"Did I? I don't recall doing so."

He chuckled. "Perhaps you were too angry with me."

"Only with your stubbornness. I find it quite annoying. In fact, it's the most annoying thing about you."

"So you admit I'm not a hopeless cause after all."

"Everyone has a saving grace, even a man such as you."

"Then tell me what my saving graces are, Julia." His mouth caressed her earlobe as he whispered his command into her ear. A shudder rippled through her.

"I cannot … cannot think of them at the moment."

"Not even one?" The warmth of his mouth grazed the point of her jawline. It shot a volcanic rush of heat through her limbs, leaving behind a languid tranquility in her body.

"No," she breathed. Oh, how she wanted his kiss. She actually craved it. Insane. She had to be insane. It was the only explanation for why she was experiencing these traitorous emotions. The man was a libertine and she didn't want to be labeled his woman.

"You have a lovely mouth."

His soft words made her gasp. Inside her head, an alarm screamed shrilly for her to take care or she'd be a St. Claire woman in no time at all. No, that wouldn't happen. She'd see to that, but would it hurt to indulge her senses just a little? No man had ever made her want to break all the rules the way this one did.

How it happened, she wasn't certain, but she was no longer sitting upright. Instead, she was reclining back into the couch with a warm body hovering over hers. Dark brown eyes glittered in his handsome face as a smile of satisfaction curled his lips. There was another emotion there as well. It was passion, rich and earthy in its honesty. It struck a chord in her. Excited her.

Every part of her body tingled with sensation as her gaze remained locked with his. God, but he was mesmerizing. Wetting her dry lips, she trembled at the low growl that rumbled in his chest. He lowered his head and grazed her cheek with his mouth. It was a feathery caress, but it made her blood sing with fire.

In the next moment, his mouth tasted hers. It was a light touch, but it stole her breath away. Oblivious to anything else but his kiss, she sighed softly as she kissed him back. He pressed his lean, hard body against hers as her fingers splayed across his chest. Lethargic warmth oozed its way into every inch of her body, as she breathed in the delicious heat of his scent.

Her fingers spiked through his hair, the softness of it caressing her skin like silk. He tasted heavenly, hot and male on her tongue as it danced with his. She'd never realized how a woman's breasts could grow so heavy with desire. The room's cool air brushed across her leg before a warm hand caressed her calf.

Starting with surprise, she murmured a protest. He raised his head, and stared down into her face. If she had been cold, his heated gaze would have been enough to warm her. His hand stroked her lightly as he studied her.

"That beautiful mouth can deny it, but your body tells me you're on fire."

The confidence in his voice barely registered as his hand slid up to stroke the skin above her garter. She swallowed hard. This was far more than just an indulgence of her senses. It was a veritable gate to irresistible decadence. She inhaled a sharp breath as his fingers trailed a path over her inner thigh.

"Have you fantasized about me, Julia?"

A fiery heat crested over her cheeks as her gaze darted away from his. While it was true she'd imagined him touching her like this, it had only been in her dreams. She'd not even dared to think of it during the waking hours.

"I have not."

"Such a charming liar," he said with a quiet laugh. "Well, I've had fantasies about you, sweetheart, and in them you're always hot and wet for me."

The wicked words made her look up at him aghast. Speechless, she tried to stop the shiver of anticipation that shimmied down her spine as his hand cupped her mound. Her mouth went dry at the dark emotions flashing in his gaze as his finger parted her folds to trace a light circle over the nub hidden inside.

"You're hot and wet now."

The moment his thumb pressed and circled the sensitive area, she shuddered. Excruciating need shot from her belly into the nether regions of her body. Sweet heaven, she liked him touching her there. A heated rush twisted her insides and she uttered a small cry as his fingers dipped into her.

"Oh, God." She squirmed beneath his heated strokes.

"In your fantasies, Julia, does my touch always make you this hot and creamy?" His voice was raw with desire as he teased her with one tantalizing stroke after another.

She moaned at the explosion of sensation spiraling through her body. Her hips shifted restlessly, writhing beneath his expert touch. Never in her life had she experienced anything like this. Heat engulfed her, and she clutched at his jacket as a small shiver of pleasure spread through her.

"Admit it, you like what I'm doing to you." His mouth nibbled at her ear.

"N-no. I…."

"Admit it." His fingers delved into her in a sinfully delicious thrust and her insides curled with tension.

"Dear Lord, yes. Yes, I like it." The words were a hoarse cry of need. In the deep recesses of her mind she barely recognized the voice as her own. It was as though she was on fire from the inside out. He continued to tease her, his fingers working an incredible magic on her body.

"Soon, very soon, my sweet, I'm going to fill you completely. I'm going to enjoy having this tight cunny of yours squeezing on my hot cock until you make me explode with pleasure."

The erotic image filled her mind with a numbing heat. The words only served to make her hotter and she bucked against his hand. Her body craved more and she moaned low in her throat. His thumb swirled around her sensitive nub nestled in her slick folds.

"Damn, you're going to feel good wrapped around my cock. It's going to be like hot, liquid velvet wrapping around me."

The image tugged the last breath of air from her lungs. With a jerk, her body surged upward against his hand just before she exploded. Intense waves of pleasure rolled over her, and small shudders shook her body.

Dazed she opened her eyes to look at him. Before she knew what she was doing, her hand cupped his cheek. She could see the desire in his eyes, and she knew he wanted her. And she wanted him. Desperately.

But she couldn't say the words. This was a wager to him. There could only be one night between them. Anything more and she realized she might very well be lost. But, oh dear Lord, how she wanted that night now. This very instant.

As if he could read her mind, he quirked an eyebrow upward and smiled. "No, I don't think so. Not yet, even though the thought is quite tempting."

Appalled by her wanton behavior and the desire still curling in her stomach, she shoved her way out of his arms and rose to her feet. She was mortified to know he was toying with her. She didn't want this man to control her, but already his touch was capable of holding her captive to wicked pleasure and delight. The thought frightened and angered her. With shaking hands, she straightened her clothing and tried to regain her composure.

"I think it's time for you to leave, Mr. St. Claire."

"Why? Because I refuse to take you here and now?"

She whirled away and stalked toward the window. Hands pressed against her belly, she tried to still the churning inside her.

"I don't understand you. I have said I will honor my debt, and yet you toy with me like a cat does a mouse. I care little for the sensation."

"It's sensation I want you to feel, Julia. I want the woman I saw in that portrait—lusty, bold and adventurous." Joining her at the window, he turned her to face him. "I want you to come to my bed of your own free will."

"That portrait was not for anyone to see. It's not real. That woman doesn't exist." Fists clenching the fabric of her green silk skirts, she grew stiff as a metal rod as he dipped his head toward her.

"You're wrong, Julia. That woman exists. A good artist always sees beneath the surface. You're simply afraid."

"I am not," she exclaimed with anger. But even as she spoke, she knew he was right. And she didn't like having to admit Morgan St. Claire might be right about something where she was concerned. She watched his eyes narrow with a speculative gleam until cold determination filled his expression.

One hand pressed against the base of her throat, she inhaled a ragged breath. God help her, she didn't know how she was going to fulfill her wager without losing a part of herself. He studied her for a long moment before he shook his head with a gleam of frustration in his dark brown eyes.

"Today was a step in the right direction. We'll see about expanding your horizons tomorrow night at the St. Claire Fete."

His soft voice sent trepidation sliding down her back. No … she needed to throw herself on his mercy and have done with it. If he continued this seduction she would be lost. Not looking at him, she laced her fingers together, trying not to tremble.

"Would not tonight be a better opportunity?" The sooner this was done, the sooner she could regain her sanity.

"No, I have an appointment this evening."

For a fleeting instant, she found herself wondering what woman would be in his bed tonight. It wouldn't be her, and the knowledge nipped at her like an angry puppy. She turned away from him to watch the traffic in the street below. A strong arm wrapped around her waist as he pulled her back into his chest. His mouth nibbled at her ear.

"And no, my sweet, it's not another woman."

Appalled that he'd been able to read her thoughts, she jerked away from him and put several feet between them. "I care little as to whom you entertain, St. Claire."

"So you say, but your face is quite expressive, Julia. Even more so when you climax beneath my touch."

With a wicked grin on his lips he strode from the salon, leaving her to sputter with indignation as the door closed behind him. The man was insufferable and far too arrogant. Climax indeed. The thought made her cheeks burn with mortification. When a woman had sexual relations with her husband or lover, it was supposed to be about the man's pleasure. Oscar had made that very clear.

The memory chilled her. Pleasure had been the farthest thing from her husband's mind when he'd come to her bed. He'd been a rutting boar, spilling his seed in her without one thought for her comfort or pleasure.

Her husband had disgusted her. She'd been grateful when after nearly two years of marriage he'd stopped coming to her bed. Her inability to have a child had earned her nothing but his contempt, but she had gladly accepted it in place of his sexual attentions.

A tremor wracked her body as she remembered how differently Morgan made her feel. She had experienced no disgust at his touch. In truth, it had been far too exciting. It had been exhilarating, and the thought made her heart skip. She did not want to let the man excite or exhilarate her. She simply wanted to fulfill her debt and be done with him.

Of course what she wanted and what Morgan St. Claire wanted were two different things. The man wouldn't disappear from her life until it suited him. And that was what worried her.

Chapter 4

Standing in the loft overlooking the warehouse floor, Morgan watched the spirited party below. The building had been emptied for the annual St. Claire Fete, and at one end of the large storage facility, the band he'd hired was playing a lively jig. On the makeshift dance floor, his employees and their guests danced with an exuberance that pleased him. There was an unrestrained freedom in the boisterous antics of the dancers as they cavorted to the music.

Like the partygoers he wore no jacket, and the sleeves of his shirt were rolled up past his elbows. He wanted his guests to feel comfortable. Dressing in the same manner they did removed the barrier of wealth that usually existed between them. His parents were no doubt rolling in their graves. A grim smile of satisfaction tilted one corner of his mouth.

His shoe tapped lightly against the planks of the loft floor as his gaze scanned the activities below. Across the dance floor from the band, temporary tables made out of sawhorses and planks lined the wall. Covered with bright, blue-checked tablecloths, the tables sagged with a bountiful assortment of meats, vegetables, breads and the Clarendon's famous cranberry scones.

It was a sight that had never been seen in his father's time, but then his father had never been one to coddle the workers. Neither of his parents had thought of anything other than themselves, least of all the child they'd both had a part in bringing into the world. He frowned.

Living with parents who hated each other had made for a miserable childhood. His father's indifference had been bad enough, but his mother had found the sight of him unbearable simply because he was a reminder of the man she hated. His jaw tightened at the unpleasant memory.

On the floor below, he saw an older couple enjoying the party from the sidelines. The man had an arm around his wife as he spoke into her ear. It amazed him how many of his employees were happily married despite their harsh lives. On occasion he'd visited their homes to check on sick employees. Despite their woes, there'd been a warmth in their homes he'd never experienced during his childhood.

As a boy, he'd believed a home of his own would be someplace he could escape to, but when he was old enough, he realized it wasn't possible. A house symbolized marriage and all the discord that went with it. And marriage was an institution to be avoided at any cost. Shrugging off the morose images, he folded his arms across his chest and studied the party goers.

From this height, he could easily see the comings and goings of everyone in the building. Several of his investors stood around the large keg of ale he'd brought in for the occasion. His most important investor had yet to arrive, and he shrugged his shoulders in an impatient gesture. He didn't like the fact that he was so eager to see Julia Westgard.

The woman was occupying his thoughts far too much for his comfort. He simply needed to bed her and get this lust out of his system. In the same instant, he knew that wasn't possible. If he forced her into his bed before he'd wooed her sufficiently, the result wouldn't be to his liking.

He needed to take his time with her. Julia was a complex creature, but he was certain of one thing. Fear kept her wrapped up in that mantle of repression she wore with such vigor. But she'd not been able to completely suppress her curiosity. It was there in her eyes, in the way she responded to his kisses. Even more intriguing was that she didn't seem to fear society's judgment. If that were true, she never would have dared to invest her money in St. Claire Shipping or any other business venture, let alone involve herself so actively in her investments.

No, she wasn't frightened by society's opinion. If anything, she demonstrated her determination to flaunt the restrictive rules of present day mores. Something else frightened her. The key to unlocking Julia so she became the woman in Peebles' painting was finding out what really frightened her.

Out of the corner of his eye, he saw one of his younger clerks bow to a partner before sweeping her into his arms and out onto the floor. Again, his gaze swept over the crowd below him searching for some sign of Julia. Where was she? The muscle in his jaw tightened at the thought she might not have any intention of coming, despite her words to the contrary. His fingers bit into his arms as he glared down at the dancers. Christ, one would think he'd lost his senses when it came to the woman.

He caught sight of his clerk spinning his partner around the dance floor and frowned. There was something familiar about the woman's dark hair. The way the light caught the golden highlights in the dark red... Bloody hell. With a grunt of exasperation, he wheeled on the back of his heel and strode along the loft's landing to the stairs leading to the floor.

She'd lost her mind. It was the only explanation. Why else would she dress like one of his employees and dance with Bentley? The woman obviously didn't realize how easily her presence could stir up trouble with men who'd been drinking. Not to mention the potential for jealousy where the womenfolk were concerned. The music came to a halt as he reached the dance floor.

Weaving his way through the crowd, he saw the clerk bow once more in front of Julia. Flushed from the exertion of the dance, she was radiant. Hell, she wasn't just radiant. She looked exactly like Peebles had painted her. His groin immediately tightened. She was laughing at something the boy had said when he came to a halt in front of them.

From the way Bentley blanched as their eyes met, Morgan knew his expression was forbidding. The woman was twisting him in knots. He didn't like it one bit. The boy didn't deserve his anger. Determined to put the clerk at ease, he forced a smile to his lips. "I see you managed to persuade Mrs. Westgard to take to the floor, Bentley."

"Yes … yes, sir, Mr. St. Claire. I didn't like seeing her standing on the sidelines. Wasn't socially polite."

The firm resolve in Bentley's voice made him grin. The lad would go far in the company. It wasn't often one of his employees had the gumption to politely tell him to go hang himself.

"I like a man who does the right thing, Bentley. Now off you go to get something to drink. I'll see to Mrs. Westgard." Jerking his head in the direction of the keg of ale, he sent the clerk on his way.

As the young man disappeared from view, the band launched into a new song. Without asking her permission, he pulled Julia into his arms. Her gasp of surprise made her mouth form a soft moue, and he grinned as he whirled her about in several quick turns. She wasn't wearing gloves, and he liked the way her fingers clung to his arms. He half expected her to protest angrily, but she didn't.

Instead she tipped her head back and smiled. He inhaled a sharp breath. When she smiled like that, he was close to offering her the world. Whirling her around in another dizzy circle, he dipped his head toward her.

"Perhaps you would care to explain your manner of dress for this evening."

"My dress?" She frowned in puzzlement before understanding cleared her furrowed brow. "Oh, you mean my borrowed clothing. I didn't want the women comparing their own dresses to anything I wore. No one should ever be made to feel inadequate. It's not a pleasant experience."

He was stunned. He couldn't find any other word for it. No other woman of his acquaintance would have ever thought of doing such a thing. For some reason, her actions pleased him enormously. His arms tightened around her as he pressed his body into hers. She was warm and soft against him. His gaze fell to her mouth as desire stiffened his cock. Feeling hot and needy, he looked deep into her eyes.

"You're an extraordinary woman, Julia."

"You've been in the ale already." She averted her gaze, her voice stiff and cool. "There's nothing special about me at all."

"Ah, but you're wrong. I've seen the woman beneath that shroud of repressed emotions you wear."

"I don't know what you mean." Her haughty tone challenged him.

He wasn't about to let that go. "Then perhaps it's time I showed you."

"Tonight?" She gasped. Her cool demeanor gone, she met his gaze with an anxious look.

Damn it, he hadn't meant to make her stare at him like a frightened rabbit. The woman was a conundrum. He should abandon the matter entirely, but something inside him refused to let her go. The woman made him feel out of control, and he didn't like that sensation one bit. With the last note of the music, he swung her off the dance floor. Uncertainty paled her face, and with a quick move, she left his arms. He let her go. Hazel eyes, wide in her oval face, stared up at him. Fear glowed in her gaze, but a hint of excitement was there too.

In silence, he studied her for a long moment before making up his mind. Whatever fear kept her enshrined in that cloak of virtue, he intended to strip it away. That tiny glimmer of anticipation in her gaze was all the invitation he needed. He might not bed her tonight, but he was damn well going to give her a taste of what to expect. Igniting her desire might even take the painful edge off his lust. Besides, the thought of hearing her plead for more was a pleasurable one.

Music swelled around them again as he grabbed her hand and tugged her toward the warehouse door. When she hesitated, he pulled her into his side and propelled her out into the night. The crisp spring air nipped at his skin as Julia suddenly regained her senses.

"What do you think you're doing, St. Claire?"

"Taking you to a place where we'll not be interrupted." He tightened his grip on her as she almost managed to slip away from him.

Crossing the street, he reached awkwardly in his vest pocket for his office key. The cool metal warmed in his hand as they stopped in front of his shipping offices. The door opened and he forced her through it.

"We must go back to the party, St. Claire. Everyone is going to notice that we've left."

"Let them."

Moonlight drifted through the glass windows of the main office, enough to light the way to the door that opened up into his personal domain. The door gave way with a loud crack, and his body absorbed the tense jerk she made at the sound. Inside the spacious room, he ushered her to the chair in front of his desk and forced her to sit down.

In quick succession, he locked the door, drew the window shade, and turned up the gas light sconce on the wall. Turning around to face her, he narrowed his eyes. She had defied him by rising from her chair. She stood with her back to his desk and wore a prim and proper expression as she glared at him. Defiance in a woman was something he wasn't used to. Another challenge. He would enjoy turning that look into one of desire.

"I do not appreciate your high-handed behavior, St. Claire. I have a distinct dislike for surprises." She glared at him. Even though her lips were tight with anger, they invited him to kiss away her annoyance.

"Unbutton your dress, Julia."

"What?" Aghast, she stared at him with her mouth half open.

Folding his arms across his chest, he arched an eyebrow. "Shall I do it for you?"

The fury in her gaze made him smile as she tossed her head angrily. Expelling a noise of disgusted fury, her fingers flew to the neck of her dress and she quickly undid the buttons down to the base of her throat. Defiance glittered in her eyes as she tilted her head and dared him to do his worst.

His cock swelled as he studied her. She was radiant and fiery in her anger. God help him when she exploded with passion in his arms. His groin tightened at the image and he moved toward her.

There was only a trace of trepidation in her face as she gamely stood her ground. When less than a foot separated them he reached out and trailed his finger from the side of her neck to the base of her throat. She trembled at the touch.

"Your skin is soft as silk, my sweet."

"What game are you playing, St. Claire? This is not part of the wager." There was a breathless quality to her voice, and it shot an arrow of excitement through him.

"Yes it is. I want the woman in that portrait. I'll do whatever it takes to pull her out from under that prim and proper façade you wear."

"I've told you before, the woman you saw doesn't exist. She's a figment of Peebles' imagination."

Not answering her, he began to slowly unbutton his shirt. Her eyes widened as she watched him with stunned fascination. The tip of her pink tongue dampened her lips, and the enticing sight made his cock jump to attention with a sharp tug. His fingers found the last button and with a shrug of his shoulders he removed his shirt, then tossed it onto his desk.

"I want you to touch me."

"Touch you?"

"Yes. Touch me."

"I most certainly will not." She tried to slip past him, but he blocked her escape. He blew out a harsh breath as he lifted her hand and rested it against his chest.

The palm of her hand was hot against his skin, and his body tensed with desire. Christ, the woman only had to touch him and his cock was aching for release. Dampening his need, he met her gaze as she stared up at him in bewilderment.

"Why can't you just take your winnings and leave me be?" The plea in her voice was unmistakable.

"Stop talking and just touch me," he growled as he struggled to keep from tugging her into his arms and kissing her into submission.

Hesitating, she could only stare at his chest. A fraction of a second later he caught her other hand and pressed it against his flesh. Fire heated her skin, and she shuddered. She wasn't ready for this assault on her senses. Desire, mixed with fear, skimmed through her veins. The conflicting emotions made her tremble as he gently forced her hands to explore him.

She remembered how he'd touched her yesterday. The intimacy of his caresses had set her on fire. More than that, his touch had broken down one of her barriers. It had created a longing inside her for something more. The same need was spiraling through her again. She swallowed hard, trying to fight the desire curling inside her belly.

Beneath her fingertips, the hard line of his chest was hot, flexible steel. A tremor sailed through her, but she didn't resist as he continued to make her trace the hard line of his muscular chest. Only in her innermost thoughts had she wondered what it would be like to touch him like this. He was hot beneath her hands. Hot and hard.

A thin line of hair trailed its way from the middle of his chest downward until it disappeared into his trousers. Just touching him was a heady experience, but it was the unexpected sight of his arousal that made her inhale a sharp breath of surprise. Her gaze jerked upward to meet the dark heat in his eyes.

Beneath her fingers his chest rose and fell with a steady, but quick rhythm. Lowering her gaze, she stared at the sight of her hands splayed across his bare chest. She should be outraged by his actions tonight, but she wasn't. The need that had been building inside her made her head swim with wicked thoughts and sinful images.

Without thinking, she leaned into him and pressed her mouth against his bare skin. He tasted warm with a hint of woody spice. Above her head she heard him drag in a sharp breath. In an abrupt move, he grabbed her at the waist and sat her on his desk. Startled, she stared up at him.

The dangerous glint in his deep brown eyes sent a shiver of delicious expectation across her skin. He leaned into her until his mouth was just a hairsbreadth from hers. The faintest trace of whiskey feathered its way past her nostrils. It blended with his scent to tantalize her senses as she realized how badly she wanted to lose her self-control with him.

"That's a start," he whispered. "But I intend to make you hotter. So hot that you're going to think you're on fire."

His mouth slanted over hers in a deep kiss. It assailed every one of her senses and heat spread through her limbs as his tongue swept into her mouth. In the pit of her belly, familiar sensations stirred. They hardened her nipples. Her breasts swelled and pushed against her corset with an exquisite pain.

Beneath her hands, the hard muscles of his chest flexed as she caressed and explored him of her own accord. He was hot under her fingertips, his body moving like supple metal against her hands. Sweet heaven, but she wanted more. She wanted to feel his hands on her again, touching her the way she was touching him. Touching her intimately.

As if reading her mind, his warm hands lifted her gown and underskirt up to her waist. Fingers stroking the inside of her thighs, he bent over to press his lips on her skin where his fingers had been.

Shocked, she tried to push her dress down, but he straightened to send her a wicked smile. "Lay back, Julia."

"What?"

"Lay back." His finger stroked the outer rim of her sex.

"Oh, God."

A whimper broke past her lips as her body melted. Slowly she found herself reclining back against the unyielding desktop. He towered over her, an expression of raw desire on his face. In a move that surprised her, he spread her legs apart so she was completely exposed to his view.

His eyes darkened as he studied her. "We talked about fantasies yesterday, my sweet, and I've had several about you. Now I intend to experience one."

She tensed as his hands stroked her inner thighs and moved toward her curls. She wanted his touch. Needed to feel his fingers stroking her, pleasuring her. A small moan of delight escaped her. Her gaze met his and he smiled.

"Let me tell you about one particular fantasy, sweetheart."

The thought of how his words could ignite an unquenchable thirst for his touch made her nod helplessly. She licked her dry lips and his smile dissolved into that of a wicked rake's expression.

"In my fantasy, I get to dip my tongue into your hot cream. I lick every bit of it off these soft folds of yours."

"Oh, dear Lord." She could only stare at him in shock as he knelt between her legs. His gaze did not leave hers.

"I'm going to enjoy licking and sucking on you until you gush that thick cream of yours all over my tongue."

Speechless, she watched as he lowered his head and the sudden fire of his tongue swirling around the rim of her sex tugged a cry of wild delight from her. She tensed at the pleasure filling her belly. An instant later, his tongue stroked along her inner folds, and she melted beneath the temptations of his sinful mouth and his hot-tongued strokes.

The wickedness of it was exhilarating, enthralling. Need cascaded downward from the spiraling sensations in her belly. It tensed her muscles until it created an ache she could not put into words. Her body seemed completely out of control, willing to do his bidding with the slightest touch. But she was beyond caring, beyond anything but the wild sensations quivering through her body.

"Jesus, you taste good." His voice was husky with passion. "You're dripping with hot honey."

His tongue pressed into her slick folds once more. Gently, he nibbled on her sensitive nub of flesh and she uttered a low cry of intense pleasure. She'd never been this aroused before. Was this what sex was really supposed to be like? She wanted to explode. Pressure etched its way down to where his tongue was licking and sucking on her so intimately.

"Oh please, Morgan," she puffed in short breaths. "Please."

"That's it, sweetheart. You're on fire now. You're hot and aching to explode."

"Oh … yesss." She shuddered as he stroked her deeply with his tongue. Her muscles clenched at the intimate contact. Sensation after sensation washed over her as he continued to caress her with his mouth. Never had she experienced anything so erotically satisfying.

He controlled her every thought, her every reaction, but she didn't care. If giving up control could give this much pleasure, it was worth the price of making herself vulnerable for this short period of time. Her body was his to command, and the pressure building inside her exploded in a splinter of tiny shards of sinful delight. With a thrust of her hips, she arched upward and released a cry of exhilaration.

"Oh God, yes!"

A second later she shattered beneath his touch. Oblivious to anything but the heat coating her body, she barely registered the fact that Morgan had picked her up in his arms. It wasn't until he sat in his chair with her in his lap that she realized she was no longer on his desk.

Through the thin layers of her clothes, his hard length pressed against her thigh. Startled, she realized he was still aroused and yet his only thought seemed centered around her pleasure. The knowledge stunned her. Never in her marriage had she ever been shown such sensitivity or consideration.

She swallowed hard at the unexpected emotion his actions evoked inside her. If the man continued to seduce her so patiently, there would be no hope of resisting him or his seductive charms. The man already held too much sway over her. With a glance up into his eyes, she grew stiff with tension.

Satisfaction glimmered in his gaze. He believed he had won. Well, hadn't he? For all intents and purposes, she was a St. Claire woman. He'd branded her in the most intimate way just a moment ago. And while he had pleasured her beyond her wildest imaginings, their association was becoming far too dangerous.

She could not allow it to continue. Never again would she submit to any man's control. Once had been enough, and where Morgan St. Claire was concerned, control was everything. He lived and breathed control.

Even their wager had been an issue of control for him. He'd seen to it that she would lose and he'd have his way. Any involvement with him could mean only one thing. She would be his to command, at his disposal until she was cast aside with only a handkerchief as a memento of their association.

Glancing away from him, she tensed as a warm finger stroked the side of her neck. The musky warm scent of her body drifted near her nose. "Next time, I intend to come inside you, sweetheart, and I promise you'll melt."

Her heart skipped a beat. Oh, how she wanted to accept that offer. But if she did, she'd be lost. What was she going to do? How was she going to keep her heart and soul safe from this man's powerful charms? She had to keep him at bay somehow. He'd already demolished her physical resistance. If she didn't take care it would be her heart next.

Clarity struck at that precise moment. He wanted her in his bed willingly, and if she went to him of her own volition, then she would be free. There would be one blissful night, and then he could make no further demands of her. It was the only way she could protect herself. The longer she put off the payment of the wager, the darker her prospects became for escaping with her heart intact. There could be no other choice.

"Morgan."

He brushed her hair with his mouth. "Hmm."

"I ... I would like ... would you take me to your room tonight?"

She tensed as he grew still and silent against her. There was something disturbing about his tautness that increased her tension. Fearful that he might have found her request insincere, she trailed her forefinger down the middle of his chest until her fingers were at the top of his trousers.

The warmth of his hand covered hers. Meeting his gaze, she saw a hunger in his eyes that alarmed her. It hypnotized her. Convinced her that no matter how far she might run, he would always be in her thoughts.

Even in spite of her fear, the dark passion in his expression excited her, and as her hand slid down further, he abruptly set her on her feet and rose to tower over her.

"No, not tonight." He shook his head as he cupped her face and kissed her gently. "I said willingly, Julia. At the moment your body wants me, but I'm not so sure of your head. Tomorrow night if you still feel the same, then come to me. I want no regrets."

She flinched at the words. There would always be regrets. He wanted her in his bed emotionally as well as physically, unfettered by the past. But that wasn't something she could do. When she went to him, it would be for one glorious night and then never again. There was no other way. With a nod of her head, she moved away from him.

In a gesture of frustration, he shoved a hand through his hair before reaching for his clothing. He shrugged into his shirt, wanting to grant her request. Hell, his cock was harder than an iron hitching post, and he ached with the need to bury himself inside her.

Watching her button her dress, he noted how her movements echoed with a stark vulnerability. Something about her request had troubled him. Her eyes had darkened when he'd insisted they wait until tomorrow night, but his gut told him it wasn't with passion.

She was still holding back. Hell, had he really broken through her shell or was it an illusion? Watching her now, he wasn't sure what to make of her current frame of mind. He'd pleased her sexually. That had been more than evident and he relished the thought. His own satisfaction could wait. The thought made his cock tighten in retaliation and he winced.

But he wanted to do more than please her in bed. He wanted to sweep away the darkness that always seemed to shadow her whenever they were together. There was a warm, vibrant woman beneath that reserved façade of hers, and he intended to draw her out. The most frustrating thing was not being able to recognize the enemy holding her hostage.

It was damn frustrating. How could he fight something he couldn't see? Discovering what terrified her so much was the key. The woman was an enigma. She had more secrets than a spy, and he intended to discover each and every one. But something told him that it would take longer than he expected. Much longer. And he wasn't sure what to make of that at all.

Tucking his shirt into his pants, he frowned as she finished restoring her appearance. He noted how she'd retreated behind a composed look of serenity. With quick strides he crossed the floor. She didn't retreat, and although he saw a brief shudder race through her, she met his gaze steadily.

The fullness of her mouth caught his eye, and he kissed her. Lifting his head, he sent her a determined look. "Tonight I broke through that icy shell of yours. Tomorrow night I intend to see that shell shattered completely."

Indescribable emotion flickered in her gaze before she smiled. "And I shall see if the great St. Claire's reputation is all that it is said to be."

The cheeky words caught him by surprise and his jaw sagged. She laughed with genuine amusement and more than a hint of triumph. The relaxed expression on her face warmed him thoroughly. With a grin, he tugged her into his arms.

"I promise you, my sweet," he growled. "Tomorrow night you won't think about anything else except the St. Claire reputation."

Chapter 5

The sweet smell of new grass teased her senses as Julia trotted along the riding track in Hyde Park. It was early yet. Far too early for society to be out riding or walking in the park. She'd not slept well and instead of continuing to toss in her bed, she'd decided to go for a ride.

Usually the fresh air was enough to clear her head so she could think straight. But it was not the case this morning. If anything, her head was more clouded than when she'd been staring at her bed canopy at dawn's first light. Tonight she would go to Morgan's bed willingly. While she knew it would be for only one night--something told her that wouldn't satisfy Morgan. So the question begging to be answered was whether he would realize she had no intention of continuing their relationship afterwards.

There was no doubt the man thrilled her. Heavens, he did more than thrill her. Her body tingled every time he was near. He was a master at making her feel things no man had ever made her feel. With each touch, she wanted to melt into his arms and forget everything except the fact that he was making love to her.

Now, in the light of day, her decision to go to him was not as clear cut as she'd thought. The heated passion of last night had given way to the cold shadows of the morning. And fear was the primary shadow. Fear of giving herself over to his complete control.

But even more frightening was the notion that she might not mind giving up her control. That traitorous thought had shaken her deeply. She heaved a sigh. There was no other choice really. Tonight she would go to Morgan's bed willingly. And there would be no doubt in his mind, or hers, that it was of her own volition. But would she have the strength to leave him before morning came?

With a nudge of her heel, she urged Solomon into a canter. A short time later she reached the end of the narrow track and turned about to return in the direction she'd come. As she did so, she caught sight of Morgan riding toward her.

He cut a fine figure on his gray mount--so fine that he stole her breath away. She tried to check the desire that abruptly soared through her. But the moment she did so, a small voice reminded her that there was no reason she couldn't enjoy the time she had left in Morgan's company.

After tonight, they would go their separate ways, and his touch would only be a memory. Would it be so bad for her to savor the pleasure of his company, if even for just these few short hours? Her mouth went dry as he pulled along side of her, a wickedly charming smile on his sensual lips.

"Good morning, Julia."

"St. Claire." She nodded in greeting.

"I think we're beyond such formality, don't you? Especially given the fact that I can still taste you on my tongue."

The audacious words made her gasp as she glared at him. "How can you mention something so … so … hedonistic in the light of day?"

"If I'm epicurean so be it, but I confess that the taste of your delicious hot honey on my tongue has pleased me more than anything in recent memory."

Unable to respond, she stared at him in horror. There was a look of wicked amusement on his face, and he grinned with almost boyish delight at her appalled expression. Without a suitable answer to his decadent words, Julia prodded Solomon into a walk. She should be furious at him, but his words, as wicked as they were, had pleased her. Had he really liked tasting her as much as she'd enjoyed the pleasure he'd given her? He appeared at her side again, his expression unrepentant.

"Come now, my sweet. I thought we had disposed of that prim and proper shell of yours last night."

"What occurred last night is not a subject for discussion here."

"I see. Then I shall call on you later this morning to further elaborate on the finer qualities of your honey pot, and the plans I have for filling it completely."

"Morgan." She shot him a scandalized look while she struggled to maintain control of her growing arousal.

"Say that again."

"What?"

"Say my name as if I'd just made your honey flow hot and sweet."

"Will you please stop?" Fingers tightening on the reins, she swallowed hard. Morgan's hot words warmed her blood, and the muscles below her stomach clenched then shuddered with a tiny spasm. She shot him a glance, and when his dark brown gaze met hers, she could see the passion glowing in his eyes. With a quick movement, he reached over and pulled her horse to a halt.

"Sweet Jesus. You're hot and slick for me right now. Aren't you?"

She swallowed hard at the desire tightening his jaw into a harsh line. Glancing away from him, she tried not to squirm in the saddle. Already her nether regions were screaming for his touch. If only she could make him ache in the way he was tormenting her.

With a daring she didn't know she possessed, she slowly turned her head to look at him. Deliberately, she wet her lips with her tongue, her eyes meeting his boldly. His jaw went rigid at the action.

"Yes." She saw him swallow his tension. "Isn't that how you like me? Hot and wet on your tongue?"

He stared at her in amazement. She bit back her smile. It wasn't often one could silence Morgan St. Claire twice in less than twenty-four hours. His eyes narrowed on her as he shifted uncomfortably in his saddle.

"Take care, Julia. There are plenty of places here in the park for more than just a slight tryst." The hoarse sound of his voice pleased her. He was as painfully aroused as she was.

"Indeed. Then I must guard my honey well until we meet again tonight."

Not waiting for his response, she flicked Solomon's hindquarters with her crop and cantered away from him. She'd actually matched wits with the man and bested him. Or at least not allowed him to think of a rebuttal. Invigorated by her daring, she smiled.

For once she had gained the upper hand with Morgan St. Claire. She liked the way it made her feel. Powerful, witty and more womanly than she'd ever felt in her life. She'd shared control of the conversation with him and even managed to arouse him with her words.

Tonight, no doubt, he'd make her pay dearly for her behavior. The thought excited her almost as much as it surprised her.

* * * *

Morgan surveyed his room. Everything was ready--all that was missing was the beautiful, seductive Julia. Earlier in the day, he'd sent her a note inviting her to dinner at seven. While she'd not replied, the memory of their conversation in Hyde Park eased some of his misgivings.

The memory of her words from earlier that morning made him inhale sharply. Damn, if the woman hadn't made him rock hard with just a few choice words. He grinned. Tonight he'd extract a delicious punishment from her, but he'd ensure that it was just as pleasurable for her as it was for him. Tonight was the night he'd been waiting for since he'd first set eyes on her nude portrait.

It had been a long time since any woman had captured his interest the way Julia had. Despite everything he did to push her out of his thoughts, she was always there. He was certain it was only lust talking, but it was becoming more difficult to think of her just in terms of his bed. Too often he'd visualized her waiting for him when he came home from a long day at the office.

Home and hearth was something he'd avoided like the plague. It was why he lived in the hotel. Homes simply condoned the state of marriage. That trap wasn't for him. The hellish existence of his childhood had taught him better. The life he led now was simple and enjoyable. No screaming matches, vile accusations or displays of affection that couldn't even warm an iceberg.

Here at the Clarendon, he could enjoy himself without the worry of his latest mistress thinking he might be persuaded into that state most women wanted to enter. But with Julia, his thoughts had wandered far enough off course to think about what it would be like to wake up with her each morning. He grunted with exasperation. He was becoming far too enamored with Julia Westgard. The sooner he expended his lust for her, the better.

The clock began to chime the seven o'clock hour and he glanced toward the door. As the timepiece sounded off a note for each hour, an unfamiliar jolt of apprehension made him tighten his mouth. Well, if she didn't come, he'd go to her. The thought had no sooner popped into his head than a quiet knock sounded on the door.

Eagerly he crossed the floor to let her into the room. She stood in the corridor wearing a long evening cape, and the veil she wore deftly hid her features. Realizing she didn't wish to be recognized, he frowned.

It was the first time he'd ever regretted not having private lodgings. Because of him, she'd been forced to cross the hotel lobby under censorious eyes. As she entered the room, he closed the door behind her. He was relieved he'd ordered a cold buffet. It would eliminate the possibility of any of the hotel staff recognizing her. She would be spared that trial.

Her gloved hands unfastened the cape at her throat, and he helped her slide the garment off her bare shoulders. Unable to help himself, his fingertips brushed across her soft, smooth skin. Dressed in a deep blue evening gown, the silk garment hugged her body as though she'd been sewn into it. The neckline plunged downward into a vee, revealing the cleft between her breasts. The fact that she was still veiled was all the more seductive and arousing. Clearing his throat, he waited quietly as she slowly folded up her veil to reveal her lovely features.

His cock swelled in his trousers as she stared up at him. The sultry expression in her hazel eyes intensified the craving in his body. Watching her remove her gloves, his mouth went dry. Her movements were unhurried and the simple act was one of erotic seduction. Bloody hell, he wanted to tumble her to the floor at this precise moment. No seduction, no teasing, just raw need and passion.

A small smile tilted the corners of her mouth. "Something smells delicious."

He couldn't help himself as he leaned into her and caught a whiff of her soft, tart scent. "You smell delicious."

"Said the lion to the lamb," she said with a quiet laugh.

Although she displayed no outward signs of hesitation, there was just a glimmer of trepidation in her hazel eyes as she met his gaze without flinching. Wanting to put her at ease, he turned toward the buffet servers the hotel staff had brought upstairs.

"Come and satisfy your taste for whatever food you like."

As she moved to stand at his side, his body tensed at her nearness. Lifting one of the silver dish covers, she gasped with delight at the poached salmon arranged on the platter.

"You remembered," she exclaimed as she sent him a glance of surprise.

"I make it a point to remember everything about you." He smiled, while congratulating himself at making her happy with such a simple gesture.

With a laugh, she shook her head. "I think you remember what will serve you in some form or fashion at a later time."

Although her tone wasn't critical, it surprised her to see his eyes flicker with an injured look. Without answering, he filled his plate and moved to the small table he'd arranged near the fireplace. Puzzled, she followed his example and joined him as he was pouring their wine. When she reached his side, he held her chair in a polite gesture as she sat.

The warmth of his body enveloped hers, and she tried to control her breathing as his fingertips trailed across the nape of her neck, then along the top of her shoulder. Looking up at him, the full force of his charm rained down on her as he offered her a wicked smile.

He'd scorned a jacket this evening, and the shirt he wore was open at the neck. There was a relaxed air about him that spelled danger. But it was a danger she wanted to explore--if only for one night.

His muscles rippled beneath his white linen shirt as he moved to take his seat. A comfortable silence fell between them as they ate, and she relished the poached salmon he'd ordered for her. He finished his meal first and reclined back in his chair to study her. The assessment in his eyes might have intimidated her weeks ago, but no longer. Although a wager had brought her to this point, she couldn't deny that she really wanted to be here.

The thought worried her slightly. Her attraction for him was beginning to spiral out of control, making her all the more vulnerable to him. Shoving the thought aside, she reminded herself that it was for one night only. She had no intention of continuing this relationship beyond this evening. For one night she would enjoy the pleasure Morgan St. Claire's touch gave her, while doing her best to tempt him as well.

Arching an eyebrow, she sent him a half-smile as she stretched out her hand toward the plate of fruit sitting in the center of the table. She picked up a fat, luscious strawberry and dipped it into the small bowl of honey that sat next to the plate. The honey slowly edged its way down to the tip of the fruit, and she tilted her head back to catch the first drop in her mouth.

She saw Morgan's enthralled look, and the desire blazing in his eyes pleased her. Tempting him gave her a sense of power--of control. The natural sweetener dripped onto her tongue. It was warm and sweet. Enjoying the taste of it, she swirled her tongue around the tip of the strawberry for more of the smooth, sticky treat. Then with a neat nip of her teeth she bit off the bottom portion of the fruit.

The low sound he made was part growl, part curse. His gaze bored into hers as he rose to his feet with all the swift power of a lion. Her heart slammed against her breast bone as her pulse rate doubled in speed. At first she thought it was fear pounding its way through her veins, but as he stretched out his hand to her, she recognized it for what it was. Excitement.

Mesmerized by the raw passion in his riveting brown eyes, she laid her hand in his. His fingers closed over hers in a strong, but gentle grip as he pulled her to her feet and into his arms. "You have a wicked streak in you, Julia."

She smiled at the gruffness in his voice. The sound confirmed that her attempt to tease and tempt had borne fruit. "As usual, you exaggerate."

"This is hardly an exaggeration." If possible, he pulled her closer to him then guided her hand down to where his erection was hard as iron beneath his trousers. Startled by the feel of him beneath her palm, she met his intent gaze. "My cock is hard for you, Julia. It won't be satisfied until it's buried deep inside you."

The earthy rawness of his language only increased her excitement. There was something in his expression that ignited a flame of need inside her belly. As he encouraged her to rub over his hard length with her palm, her skin tingled with the desire to hold him naked and unrestrained in her hand. Her mouth went dry at the thought of what was to come, and fear tried to crowd its way into the forefront of her emotions. The suddenness of his kiss crushed her fear as she gave herself up to the pleasure of his caress. It was a demanding kiss, but playful too. His teeth gently nipped at her bottom lip.

Hot and needy, his tongue swept into her mouth. Claret tantalized her taste buds as his tongue swirled around hers until her knees wobbled. A strong hand warmed the skin of her shoulder as his kiss deepened. It tugged at her, demanding a response, and she gave it willingly.

Her hands unbuttoned the front of his shirt, and tiny frissons slid across her skin as she touched the solid muscles of his chest. When her dress slid to the floor, followed by her corset, it barely registered in her mind. Cool air brushed her mouth as his lips danced across her cheek in search of first her earlobe and then her neck.

Heat engulfed her as a large hand cupped her and a thumb flicked across one nipple. With a low moan of pleasure, her head fell backward, giving him free access to her throat. His teeth gently nipped at her skin as his thumb continued to circle round the stiff peak of her breast. It was heaven and penitence all in the same instant. Heaven to be succumbing to his wicked touch, while the intense hunger enveloping her body was penance for every moment she'd resisted the pleasure of his caresses.

The moment his mouth captured her sensitive nipple, another moan poured out of her. The wet heat of him suckling her through her thin silk chemise ignited a wild need inside her body. Without hesitation, she pressed herself closer into him. A sigh of bliss whispered past her lips as he massaged her other breast while his mouth devoured her stiff peak. Nothing she'd ever read or heard could have prepared her for the deliciously sinful feelings and sensations he was arousing in her. Desire streaked through her veins, and the moment his teeth clamped gently down on the nipple, her insides grew slick with desire.

On fire, she instinctively reached for him, eager to satisfy the increasing ache below her belly. Fingers flying over the waistband of his trousers, she freed his hard erection and grasped him firmly. Her touch pulled a growl of delight from him, and he moved his body so that his staff thrust in and out of her grasp. The friction from his action burned pleasurably against her palm. He was long and hard beneath her fingers. The thought of him sliding into her made her shiver with a mixture of trepidation and excitement.

Not once had her husband ever incited her to such strong desires, to cravings for a possession she was certain would be a pleasure of deliriously wicked proportions. Her heart pounded in her breast, and she wanted to feel his skin against hers. With shaky fingers, she tugged at her chemise, almost frantic to remove all barriers between them.

Releasing her, he stepped back and swiftly removed the rest of his clothing as she discarded what little she still wore. Naked before him, she sucked in a sharp breath as his hand cupped her chin.

"God, but you're beautiful." The palm of his hand caressed her throat before moving down across her breasts. When he reached her belly, a tremor went through her. "Are you hot and wet for me, my sweet?"

For a moment she didn't answer. Then with a sigh of passion and excitement she nodded. Triumph surged through him as he kissed her again, lusting after the honey-sweet taste of her tongue against his. She was more luscious than he'd ever thought possible.

With an eagerness that pleased him, she pressed her hips into him and her damp curls teased the tip of his cock. Her fingers slid across his back, her fingernails lightly razing his skin as she murmured his name in an achy plea. Christ, he'd never expected her to react with such wanton abandon. He wanted to bury himself in her silky core until they were both satiated.

Eager to assuage their need for each other, he guided her backward until she half-plopped, half-sat on the edge of the bed. Gently, he forced her to lie back on the mattress. The desire glowing in the depths of her eyes as she stared up at him took his breath away. His gaze drifted down to her soft folds and his mouth went dry. Cream slathered her nest of curls and he bent slightly to slide his hands under her buttocks.

The fleshy underside of her was soft and full against his fingers as he shifted her body upward at an angle. Surprise swept over her face as he grabbed a pillow and situated it beneath her. Not waiting for her to protest, he wrapped her legs around his waist and pressed his cock at the entrance to her cunny before filling her to the hilt.

The astonishment on her face disappeared as a sharp cry of intense pleasure broke from her. "Oh God, Morgan. Yes."

Gratified to see the expression of ecstasy on her face, his own desire escalated. The throbbing of his cock intensified as he slid in and out of her with increasing speed. Slick and hot, her insides shuddered and clutched at his rock hard rod. God almighty, but the woman was going to make him come faster than any woman he'd ever been with.

Another cry broke from her lips and her soft, creamy folds contracted around him with spiked spasms of pleasure. The frissons of sensation tantalizing his cock tugged a response from him as well and with a guttural cry he gave one last thrust into her before spilling his seed deep inside her.

Lodged inside her, his body enjoyed the ebbing waves of their climaxes. He knew his body wasn't ready, but he wanted to take her again and again. What was happening to him? He'd never been this infatuated with a woman. Luminous hazel eyes fluttered open to look up at him, and he swallowed hard. When the hell had the tables been switched?

* * * *

Lying on top of the mattress with a silk sheet entwined between her legs, Julia watched Morgan cross the room to the table. From the bed, she admired his sleek, muscular legs and hard flanks. He was the epitome of male beauty, and she recognized a familiar ache between her thighs. It wasn't even the midnight hour and yet they'd made love several times.

With each joining, her body was becoming more in tune to each throb and thrust of his hard body against hers. Soon there wouldn't be a way to determine where she stopped and he began. The haunting thought whispered through her head, but she crushed it. Tonight she intended to relish being in Morgan's arms. Tomorrow would come soon enough, but she refused to let that gloomy fact intrude on her idyllic state.

As he returned to the bed, he carried a plate of fruit. He flopped down beside her like an excited youth, and she laughed as his actions made her elbow shift out from under her. With a wide grin, he offered her the fruit, but she waved it away. She had eaten her fill the last time they'd finished making love. Her gaze drifted around the room, searching for some deeper sense of him.

The night she'd stolen his handkerchief, her impression of his room had been one of decadence and debauchery. Looking at his lodgings now, she realized her opinions about Morgan and who he was had influenced the initial observation of his room. True, the coverlet and sheets were a mixture of bold colors and materials. The red silk sheets caressing her skin were contrasted by the black coverlet that was crumpled at the foot of the bed.

Aside from the bed and its bold coverings, the remainder of the room was stark and masculine. Paintings of several ships from his line hung on the walls, and aside from a few trinkets on the mantelpiece, the room was devoid of any items that reflected the man himself.

"Come now, why such a serious look?" Morgan leaned toward her, the male scent of him pungent and warm.

"I didn't realize I was wearing such a look." She glanced around the room once more. "Morgan?"

She watched him pop a grape into his mouth and he tilted his head at her. At the silent query in his expression, she plunged forward. "Do you really like living in the hotel?"

The question made the immediate tension in him visible. Forearms taut and stiff, he didn't look at her as he swallowed his fruit.

"I'm sorry. I didn't mean to pry," she said gently.

Not looking at her, he stared at the fire in the hearth. "I have no need for a house. The hotel suits my needs, since I'm hardly here except to eat and sleep." The moment his words filled the air, he frowned.

Was there never going to be anything more to his life than work? A sudden longing for a family swept through him. Beside him, he watched Julia roll over onto her stomach. The creamy complexion of her skin made his fingertips tingle to touch her again. An image of waking up next to her for years to come flashed through his head.

Ridiculous, he just needed to rid himself of this lust he felt for her. She was a tempting creature and all evening long he'd been amazed at the response she'd given him. He was certain they would enjoy each other's company for months before they finally parted ways.

Smiling as he contemplated future evenings such as this, his hand reached out to stroke her back. Her eyes were closed, and she smiled.

"That feels nice."

Immediately setting the plate of fruit on the nightstand, he set about massaging her back. Soft sighs of pleasure echoed from her, and he enjoyed her response to his touch. Giving her pleasure filled him with quiet satisfaction. His hands slid down to the rounded globes of her buttocks. She tensed as his finger traced the line of her cleft then skated down the inside of her thigh.

She lifted her head and glanced back over her shoulder at him. Trepidation glowed in her hazel eyes, and he leaned forward to kiss her lips. Retreating, he picked up the bowl of honey off the plate beside the bed. He grinned at the puzzled look on her face.

"Something to make you sweeter." Brushing her hair off her back, he drizzled a thin stream of the natural sweetener over her back and across her round buttocks. Her gasp of surprise made him laugh. "Don't move or you'll make everything sticky."

"St. Claire, what are you up to?" She inhaled another sharp breath as his tongue lapped up a small section of honey from her skin.

"I'm enjoying a rare delicacy. Honey-laced Julia. It's quite delicious."

Laughter rolled past her lips at the wicked amusement in his voice. The man was truly a rake, but a deliciously sinful one. The teasing play of his lovemaking simply reinforced the reason why so many women had fallen for him. What woman could resist such a man? She closed her eyes, enjoying the sensation of his tongue licking the honey off her skin.

Massaging fingertips slowly forced her legs further apart, as he continued to eat the honey off her buttocks. With the slightest touch, his finger skimmed the rim of her sex and her body gave a twitch of pleasure at the caress. His teeth razed against one buttock before he gently nipped at her flesh while his finger slid into her in a smooth stroke.

The pleasure of his caresses tugged a moan from her. God, but the man knew how to please a woman. His fingers slipped between her folds as he increased his attention to her bottom with gentle love bites and strokes of his tongue.

It was a seduction unlike anything she'd ever imagined. The need for more sent her rear arching upward as she pressed back against the stroke of his fingers. The familiar desire skidded wildly through her veins. For a brief moment, she wondered how she was ever going to walk away from this pleasure--from him. Desire and need flung the thought aside and she started to roll over in bed, but a firm hand held her in place.

"Not yet, my sweet."

"Morgan, please. I want to feel you inside me," she whimpered.

"And so you shall."

His finger increased its plunges into her hot folds, alternating with quick flicks to her swollen nub. Unable to help herself, her buttocks arched up higher, pushing against his hand in a silent cry for fulfillment. His hand caressed her belly then helped to ease her up onto her knees, all the while continuing to stroke her with his heated caress. Her insides ached with need, and another whimper broke from her lips.

"Shall I fill you now, my sweet?"

"Oh, God, yes." Was that hoarse cry really hers? Her body was on fire and the torment of desire crashing through her made her cry out again. "Please, oh now, please."

He entered her from behind, and filled her completely. The suddenness of his possession pulled a cry of passion and surprise from her. She wanted to weep from the intensity of pleasure sweeping over her. Stretched and full with him, it was the most hedonistic and rapturous thing she'd ever experienced. He started to retreat and her muscles tried to clamp down on him, keep him inside of her. No, she wanted him to stay inside her like this for a little while longer.

She opened her mouth to protest, but when he pressed back into her hard and deep, her protest became a scream of delight. Once again he retreated, but this time the delay was shorter. In moments he was slamming into her with pulsating thrusts, driving her mad with decadent need and fulfillment. Hot lava rolled through her limbs toward her belly as she met his thrusts with heated passion. As the lava reached her nether region, it erupted into the rapid ripples of her climax.

The way her hot velvet folds clutched at him made him groan. The woman was incredible. Her body gripped his cock, tightening on it, squeezing it until he had no choice but to explode inside her. With a shout, he drove into her one last time and spilled his seed.

Still embedded inside her, he shuddered as the ripples of her climax continued to cascade over his cock. Weak from the intensity of his orgasm, Morgan braced himself against the beautiful roundness of her buttocks, kneading them with tenderness.

Withdrawing from her, he sank back on his heels. As he watched, she fell forward, then slowly rolled onto her back in a sensuous and lethargic move. She looked luscious and inviting. He ached for his cock to grow hard again. Christ, not even that incredible moment of sex had doused his desire for her. The droopy look to her eyes made him smile as he stretched out beside her.

"Sleep." He pushed a stray lock of hair behind her ear as he issued his order.

"I don't want to go to sleep. I want to make love all night."

"Insatiable minx." Chuckling, he kissed her brow. "I promise to wake you as soon as my body will allow."

"I'll hold you..." she yawned widely as her eyes closed, "... to that, St. Claire."

Wrapping her in his arms, he held her close and enjoyed the sensation of her cheek burrowing into his chest. With his foot, he kicked the sheet up into the air and caught it with his hand. Finished tucking the silk covering around them, he stroked her cheek. She was the woman in the portrait, and she had exceeded his wildest expectations.

Tired, he closed his eyes and listened to the soft steadiness of her breathing. Tonight was the start of many such nights of pleasure. The image of a future with Julia in his bed made him smile as he fell asleep.

* * * *

Hours later, a warm body shifted against him as he stared up at the ceiling. He glanced down at Julia's sleeping form beside him. The sight sent a wave of inexplicable emotion coursing through him. For the first time in years he actually felt happy. It was a strange sensation.

Lightly he stroked one finger down her cheek causing her to murmur something unintelligible. With great care, he slipped from her arms and slid out of bed. Retrieving his robe, he crossed the floor to the window. The sky still wore her sparkling jewels as if the dawn was hours away, but he knew better from the clock on the mantle.

Julia had given herself to him tonight with an exquisite abandon that had thrilled and delighted him. When they'd fallen asleep the first time, he'd promised to awaken her. But she was the one to wake first, and she'd massaged his cock until he hardened enough for her to mount him. She'd ridden him with passion and exuberance until each of them climaxed together.

Afterward, they had relaxed amidst the tousled sheets, finishing the remnants off the fruit plate. For the first time since they'd met, she had appeared at ease in his company. Her quick wit and sharp mind combined with her voluptuous body made her a temptation he had succumbed to over and over again.

The memory of their lovemaking made his cock swell. He grunted with irritation. He was hotter than hell for her just thinking about it. He swallowed hard as he struggled to keep from returning to bed and waking her. Bloody hell, he needed to control himself. This entire situation was spiraling out of control. If he wasn't careful, he'd wind up married to her.

He froze.

Married. He had no desire to marry. Did he?

The fact that he was questioning himself made him swallow hard. He turned his head to look at the woman in his bed. He'd set out to bed her, only to discover he wanted something more. But marriage? Wouldn't it just be simpler to keep her as his mistress? No. She deserved better than that.

His shoulder pressed into wood as he leaned against the window jamb. Crossing his arms, he studied her intently from where he stood. A long time ago, he'd learned that the words marriage and happiness were completely incompatible. And yet, she made him think he was wrong. Was he? Closing his eyes, he visualized his life before Julia.

Long days would merge into night as he toiled away at the shipping offices. He owned a successful business and was a wealthy man. But what good was it if he had no one to share it with? It was a cold, lonely existence with the occasional heat of a mistress here and there. Seldom was there any true joy in his life. All of that had changed since first setting eyes on Julia.

How was it possible to have fallen in love with her so quickly, so easily? The moment the insight flashed through his head he jerked upright to stand rigid at the window. Love. It wasn't possible. Morgan St. Claire never fell in love with the women he bedded.

His gaze fell on Julia again as she stirred in her sleep. Closing his eyes, he could see every curve and sweet dimple of her body. And he loved her. The raw simplicity of it floored him. The portrait had merely intrigued him, but the woman had captured his heart. Never in a thousand years had he ever imagined he would fall in love. That he would want to marry and have someone to come home to.

No doubt the Set would find it amusing that he'd finally succumbed to the wiles of a woman. Then again, Julia wasn't just any woman. She was his. Tonight she'd come to him willingly and of her own free will. Not only had she come to him without coercion, she'd offered herself to him with a sweetness and passion that convinced him she had feelings for him.

Quietly, he returned to the bed. Slipping beneath the covers, he kissed her forehead with tenderness. The touch made her stir, and her eyes fluttered open.

"Morgan?"

"Shh, go back to sleep," he whispered.

"But I'm not sleepy, anymore." Her mouth parted in a wide yawn. Chuckling, he flicked her nose with his forefinger.

"Well, I am, and I want to wake up with you in my arms."

With another sleepy nod, she closed her eyes and burrowed into him like a sleek cat. He relished the sensation. Sleep was a relentless conqueror, and as he sank into the peaceful dream realm, he smiled. Tomorrow he'd propose to Julia.

Chapter 6

Pink and orange trails of color glimmered outside the window as Julia quietly finished dressing. She would need to hurry or Morgan might awake. It would be disastrous if she were still here and that happened. He would no doubt try to stop her from leaving, and it would be difficult to resist him. He had a way of bending her to his will, and she couldn't afford to let him change her mind about ending their affair.

Glancing back toward the bed where he slept, she studied him for a long moment. She could have stood there for hours just watching him sleep, watching the way his chest quietly rose and fell from his steady breathing. In sleep, the harsh planes of his face had softened.

He looked almost boyish. The lean hardness of his body was tangled in the red bed sheet and had fallen to his waist. Her gaze caressed the hard curves of his chest displayed so handsomely in the still muted light of the room. Last night she'd adorned that steely torso with loving kisses. It was a memory she would cherish forever.

He stirred in his slumber, and a long, muscular leg thrust its way out from under the sheet to reveal the limb from foot to hip. The line of his thigh was beautiful. No artist could have created a shape so perfectly male. And there was nothing more dangerous than Morgan St. Claire and the unbelievable maleness of him.

Pain wrapped an icy band around her heart. She had not realized how difficult it would be to leave him. To simply walk away. Swallowing the anguish swelling her throat shut, she pulled a piece of white silk from her beaded bag and laid it by his pillow. What would he do when he awoke? Would he be angry?

Of course he would. He'd be furious. The thought frightened her. Oscar had always made her pay dearly whenever she'd made him angry. She frowned. Morgan wasn't anything like her late husband. He'd not said or done anything to make her think she should fear him. It didn't matter. The sooner she left, the easier it would make things. There was no telling what he would do if she were still here when he awoke.

The thought of it made her quickly gather the last of her things. With one last look at him, she pulled her veil over her face. She wasn't just leaving Morgan--she was leaving her heart as well. It was something she'd not planned for. A soft sob whispered past her lips as she raced from the room.

* * * *

Outside his window, the sounds of the city awakening pulled Morgan from a deep sleep. Rolling over, he reached for Julia to pull her into his side. When his hands didn't find her softness, he shot up in bed. A quick glance around the room confirmed his fear. She was gone.

Damn the woman. He'd told her last night how he'd wanted to wake up with her in his arms. When was she going to learn he didn't like to be thwarted? He grinned. It was something he needed to get used to. Julia wasn't likely to become a meek and mild wife once they were married. But then he didn't want her any other way.

Tossing back the covers, he scrambled out of bed. As he did so, a white square of silk fluttered to the floor. A frown furrowed his brow as he bent to retrieve the material. The softly scented handkerchief bore the initials J.W.

Stunned, he stared at the monogram. It wasn't possible. Cold air wrapped around him as he sank down onto the bed. Numb to all sensation but the silk square he held, he rubbed the handkerchief between his fingers. The softness of it disgusted him. It symbolized the view a large sector of society mistakenly held of him. A man whose affairs rivaled even Prince Edward's. He didn't give a damn about society, but he cared deeply about what Julia thought of him.

She must think him a true scoundrel if she actually believed him so callous as to leave a handkerchief with a discarded lover. But then he'd allowed her to believe that ridiculous myth society had created. Otherwise she wouldn't have taken the opportunity to silently declare their relationship null and void in such a calculated fashion. He'd always been entertained by the fictitious stories about his monogrammed handkerchiefs. The legend of how he ended all of his affairs by offering one of them to his lover to dry her eyes had been amusing--until this moment.

Anger barreled through him as he snatched up his robe and threw it on over his shoulders. Cinching the sash around his waist with a sharp tug, he paced the floor of his room. She'd crept out like a thief in the night. But she sure as hell had left her damnable calling card. He crumpled the silk square in his fist.

It had been a long time since he'd been snubbed. He didn't like it one bit. Especially since he had every intention of marrying the woman. She was mad if she thought she could end things between them. She'd felt something last night. He was certain of it.

Her response to him throughout the night had been no act. Everything about her had been passionate, giving and above all, genuine. Julia cared for him.

She had to.

Roughly shoving a hand through his hair, he halted his pacing. He didn't want to consider the possibility that last night had meant nothing to her. If she'd come to him simply to fulfill the wager, it would make what they shared sullied. Their lovemaking had aroused him not just because of her body, but because of who she was.

He wanted more than just a night of passion from her. He wanted a lifetime of them. Then there were the quieter moments he craved. Those times when she wasn't aware of his gaze. When he could simply study her and be thankful he was near her.

Bloody hell. He'd made a mess of things. He'd done everything he could to win her desire, but he'd done nothing to win her heart. What if that weren't possible? Every muscle in his body ached with tension at the very real possibility that she would not want him. He immediately rejected the notion.

No. He would find a way to win her heart. The alternative was unthinkable.

* * * *

Morgan's thumb pressed the doorbell outside Julia's house for a prolonged moment. As he eased up on the pressure, the door opened to reveal her butler. Almost immediately dismay settled on the man's face.

"I'm sorry, sir. Mrs. Westgard is not receiving visitors."

"She'll see me."

"I am sorry, sir, but she made a specific point of instructing me not to let you into the house."

For a moment, he wasn't sure he'd understood the man, but one look at the uneasy expression on Calvert's face told him he'd heard correctly. Damn the woman. If she thought to sway him from seeing her, she was quite mistaken.

"Calvert, I'm a reasonable man. I understand you're following instructions. However, if you don't step out of my way, I doubt you'll be answering this door any time in the near future."

He sent the man a look of grim determination. Threats were not to his liking, but no one was going to keep him from seeing Julia. Not even the woman herself. Calvert took a hasty step backwards.

Nodding his approval, Morgan stepped into the small foyer and handed the other man his hat and cane. With sharp movements he tugged his gray gloves off and dropped them into the soft felt homburg.

"Where is she?"

"The salon, sir."

In two strides he was charging up the stairs and into the salon. Quietly, he closed the door behind him. She sat with her back to him at her desk, writing a letter.

"Who was at the door, Calvert?" She asked in a frazzled tone of voice.

"Good morning, Julia."

With a cry of surprise she sprang up from her chair and wheeled about to face him with an expression of dismay. He studied her for a moment. The yellow silk of her dress hugged her figure just as his hand had done last night. She looked alluring and tempting despite the fact that her lovely body was completely hidden from his eyes.

He would remedy that problem soon enough. Once they settled this small matter of her handkerchief they were going to spend the day in bed. And perhaps tomorrow and the day after that as well. Until he convinced her of the sincerity of his feelings. The pleasant thought twisted his mouth into a small smile.

Her eyes narrowed as she found her voice. "How did you get in here?"

"I'm afraid I resorted to threats. Not a pleasant chore, but necessary given the rather unpleasant calling card I received this morning." Reaching into his coat pocket, he pulled out her silk handkerchief and dangled it in the air.

"Apparently you failed to understand the message. I've paid my wager in full. There will be nothing further between us."

His jaw tensed at her cold tone. Frowning, he studied her carefully. Her mouth was tight with tension, and despite her relatively calm demeanor, the fluttering pulse at the side of her neck belied her serene state. He cleared his throat as he took a step toward her.

"That's where you're wrong, Julia."

Despite the furious glare she directed at him, her face paled considerably. One hand gripping the edge of the desk behind her, she squared her shoulders. "You can't stand it, can you? You can't stand the fact that a woman had the audacity to reject you."

"Damn it, that's not the issue at all. You left me without an explanation."

"I don't owe you any explanation."

"I think you do," he said quietly. "What we shared last night was incredible. I have no intention of letting that go."

"I refuse to join the St. Claire league of mistresses."

"Then marry me."

She stared at him in stunned silence as ice sluiced through her veins. Mad, the man was stark raving mad. What on earth had possessed him to offer her marriage? The way he stood there so calm, so confident. Her heart wanted to break at the sight of him. Part of her wanted nothing more than to fly into his arms and let him hold her.

Immediately she snuffed out the image. Last night had been a beautiful dream. It had made it easy to leave him while he was asleep. Her resolution to end their affair had been much easier to maintain.

Now, having that penetrating gaze riveted on her, her resolve was becoming shaky. And he'd proposed marriage. What possible reason could he have for doing such a thing? Flinching, she pressed her hands against her stomach in a vain effort to stop the wild emotions churning through her. His reasons were irrelevant. She had no intention of marrying Morgan St. Claire.

She would never marry again. Oscar had destroyed all her illusions about marriage with his cruelty and vile behavior. Marriage was nothing more than a prison. The thought had no sooner entered her head than her eyes focused on Morgan's face.

The firm set of his jaw showed how determined, how confident he was. It frightened her. He had a look about him that said he wasn't about to take no for an answer. It was cowardly, but all she wanted to do was escape. She couldn't help it.

She was terrified he might convince her to marry him despite all the reasons she shouldn't and couldn't do so. It would be even worse if he realized she cared for him. Slamming down every barrier around her heart that she possibly could, she steeled herself for the battle to come. The stubbornness in his dark gaze made her quiver as a muscle in his cheek twitched.

"Usually when a man proposes, the woman responds."

"You're delusional," she exclaimed.

"That was not the answer I was looking for."

"It's the only one you'll get," she said as she swept past him on her way to the door. "Now if you'll forgive me, I've matters to attend to. Please see yourself out."

The safety of the salon door was almost within her reach when a strong hand captured her wrist and pulled her to a halt. The heat sliding up her arm from his touch spread its way through her body with the speed of lightning. Whipping around to face him, she stared down at his hand.

Sweet heaven, she didn't want to pull away from him. She fought to suppress the mist of desire threatening to blind her to everything but him and his touch. With a jerk she tugged free of his hold and glared at him. There was an implacable gleam in his dark brown eyes as he met her gaze steadily.

"So you're willing to forget everything that's passed between us. Forget last night?"

Her throat tightened at the gruff note in his voice. If she didn't know better, it could almost be mistaken for tenderness. Glancing away from him, she clutched at the yellow silk of her gown. Why must he make it so difficult? She'd given him her answer and yet he persisted in hounding her.

"Last night meant nothing to me," she said in a tight voice.

The silence in the room was deafening. Rigid with fury, Morgan grasped her chin and roughly turned her head toward him.

"Look me in the eye and say that," he snarled.

"No. I don't have to answer to you."

"The hell you don't. You're afraid."

"I am not." The pulse at the side of her neck had grown even more erratic, a definite lie to her verbal denial.

He bent his head toward her and she hastily stepped backward until she was braced against the wall. Pressing his advantage, he grasped her by the shoulders and gave her a slight shake.

"You're frightened that I made you feel something last night."

"No. I felt nothing. You didn't make me feel anything."

Furious, he wanted to shake her until her teeth rattled. She was lying to him as well as herself. She'd felt something last night. He knew it with such certainty that he would stake his life on it. What had happened between them had touched something deep inside her. Only a woman made of stone could deny it. And he knew first hand that Julia was a woman of deep passion, hardly cut from stone.

"Then let me refresh your memory as to how much I can make you feel."

He bent his head and slanted his mouth over hers. Determined to make her shudder with desire as she had last night, he teased her lips apart until his tongue could sweep into her mouth. She tasted even sweeter this morning than she had last night.

The scent of her was maddening. Fresh, sweet and clean. He wanted to bury himself in the heat of her. Last night she'd driven him over the edge with passion, and he realized now it would never change. There would always be this need, this craving for more where she was concerned. His cock grew hard and heavy in his trousers. Christ Jesus, he wanted to drive into her until she cried out his name with the same intensity she had last night.

His mouth nipped at hers until a soft moan rippled from her throat. Almost immediately she softened beneath his touch. Her willpower eroding, she tried to not feel anything, but it was impossible. His touch set her on fire until her body was crying with a need that surpassed what she'd experienced in his arms last night. Another moan broke past her lips as he caressed the side of her neck with his mouth.

"I want you, Julia. I want to feel your fiery heat clutching at my cock as I slam into you over and over. I'm never going to get enough of you."

The seductive words escalated the desire unfolding inside her. Sweet Lord. When he talked like that it excited her. Despite every logical reason not to, she relished his masterly behavior, the way he commanded her to kiss him or touch him.

He did so in a way that convinced her he was also thinking of her pleasure, not just his. Tiny frissons skated over every inch of her as his hands undid the front of her dress. Warm fingers stroked her skin, and she shuddered beneath the touch. She didn't want to feel this desire, this craving, but it was impossible to shut her feelings off where he was concerned.

A familiar, wet need heated the apex of her thighs, and her belly tightened with desire. As he unbuttoned her dress almost to her waist, she whimpered at the way her breasts ached for his touch, for his mouth against her nipples. He nibbled at her skin where the tops of her breasts mounded up at the edge of her corset.

"God, you feel good. But you're going to feel even better when I'm deep inside you."

There was a note of confidence in his voice that broke through the haze of passion clouding her head. She wanted him. She wanted him as badly as she had last night. No. The need was far more intense this morning.

Her arousal was blinding, and a tiny voice of reason whispered through the fog of desire. If she didn't stop him now, there would be no turning back. She would not have the strength to live without him. The struggle to give in to her passion tore at her heart. If only she could give herself to him once more. If only she had the courage to take that risk. To do as he asked.

But she didn't. It would take far more courage than she possessed to give in to her emotions and let him make love to her. She had to stop him. Stop this mind-numbing passion from consuming her entirely. If it continued she'd be lost for certain. She would lose the small wedge of independence she'd achieved since Oscar's death. That she could not give up.

Desperately she tried to push her way up out of the depths of the passion engulfing her. His hands moved against her skirts and a cool brush of air blew across her calves. Frantic to stop him and end this blissful but dangerous interlude, she tried to push his hands away from her.

Her resistance simply resulted in him pressing her against the wall with his body. With ease, he caught her hands and pinned them over her head. It was a position of complete control. Utter domination. Just like her husband had enjoyed tying her up before--

Her mind went numb.

Desire fled in a heart beat. Morgan's action revealed him for the man he was. He was no different. Oh, God. How could he? For the first time she understood just how much trust she'd placed in him. It was why she'd been able to be with him as she had last night. Somehow he'd made her feel safe, but now she knew she'd been wrong.

Frantic to escape, she tried to pull her hands free of his strong hold. The futility of it struck her like a cold bucket of water dashed in her face. It was happening all over again. The pain, the humiliation, the degradation. The emotions ate away at her and whirled a chaotic path through her body. She'd thought Oscar's death had meant she would never feel this sickening humiliation again, but here it was, welling up inside her like a flood.

Tears she never thought to cry again threatened to run down her cheeks. She squeezed her eyes shut. She would not shed tears over him. How foolish she'd been to think he wasn't like Oscar. She had actually thought him different. When they'd made love last night... No, she didn't want to think about last night. It had been nothing more than a dream.

Revulsion and fear gnawed at her as she froze beneath his touch. His mouth sought hers, but she didn't respond to his kiss. He could dominate her physically, but he would never rule her thoughts. Helpless to stop him, she knew the only way to shut out the pain and humiliation was to close her mind off to everything around her.

Self-preservation forced her to wrap an all too familiar cloak of indifference around her heart and soul to wait until the storm had passed. It was a form of mental survival she'd practiced far too many times with Oscar. She didn't protest. Protesting only increased the pain and cruel torment. She simply went limp in his arms. Turning her face away from him, she waited. It would be over soon enough.

Nibbling at her ear, he rubbed his hips against her bared thigh. The hard length of him throbbed his desire through his trousers. Damn, he was ready to spill his seed any minute. The faint scent of lavender teased his senses. He would never be able to smell lavender again without thinking of her. If he could only make her see how much she meant to him. How the sight of her made him want to forget the world completely.

His mouth sought hers, but she didn't turn her head to meet his kiss. A thread of surprise wove through him. With his free hand he caressed her throat down to her shoulder and paused. The tension in her neck and shoulders relayed the impression she had been etched from a block of granite. He frowned at the way her profile resembled a piece of marble.

Puzzlement rapidly suppressed his desire as he realized how icy her skin was beneath his fingers. Pulling back slightly he captured her chin and turned her face toward him. Her gaze was glassy, devoid of emotion.

She'd retreated from him. Emotionally and physically.

"Julia?"

"Do what you like then release me." There was an inhuman vacancy to her voice that made his blood run cold.

"What? I'm not going to take you against your will, Julia."

"Aren't you? You pin me against the wall. Confine my hands. What else am I to think?"

The glacial words chilled him. He quickly released her and put several feet between them. How could she think all he wanted to do was rut? He'd been excited and eager to touch her. Eager to assuage his desire, and hers. It would always be like that for him. He'd never be able to get enough of her. Whether in bed or just being near her, she was everything to him.

"For God's sake, I--I'd never hurt you."

With narrowed eyes, he studied her as she lowered her hands from over her head. She avoided his gaze and clutched at her wrist, rubbing it slightly. The expression on her face was one of shock, and his body ached as if he'd taken a punch to his midsection. What the hell had Westgard done to her?

"How did he hurt you?"

Flinching at the question, her gaze scanned the room looking anywhere but directly at him. Tension had made her cold and immobile. "It doesn't matter. He's dead now."

"The hell it doesn't." He lowered his voice as he saw her recoil at his fierce tone. "Tell me what that bastard did to you."

Not looking at him, she inhaled a deep breath. "He liked to tie me to the bed, while he--"

"Christ Jesus."

Unable to bear the look of torment on her face, he turned away. He'd always known there was something else driving her to hide behind her cool exterior, but he'd never imagined this. And by his actions he'd reminded her of that painful memory. He shoved a hand through his hair at the thought. She'd associated him with that bastard of a husband.

The knowledge twisted his gut with excruciating precision. It was little wonder she'd fought him every step of the way. He would have to tread carefully. Making her understand that he wasn't like Westgard would take every bit of diplomacy he possessed.

Turning to face her again, he ached to go to her, pull her in his arms and simply hold her. But the tension holding her rigid told him not to try touching her. It was clear she was near a breaking point. He had no wish to cause her further pain.

"Julia, I'm not like Westgard." She didn't answer, her gaze focused on the floor. He tried again. "I want to marry you. I want to make you happy."

"No." The harsh rejection made him wince.

"Listen to me. I will never do anything to hurt you. I swear it."

"I … I can't do it. Please don't ask it of me." The hint of indecision in her tone gave him hope. Perhaps he could persuade her. It was enough hesitation for him to risk everything.

"Would it make a difference if I told you--if I--" he cleared his throat, "... if I said I loved you?"

For a moment, he didn't think she was even going to look at him. Silently, he willed her to do so as his taut muscles ached from the tension flowing through him. She lifted her head slowly to meet his gaze, and his mouth went dry with fear. The hazel eyes looking at him were dull and vacant.

"I will never marry again."

"Julia, you can't--" Even to his ears he could hear the desperation in his voice as she lifted a hand to stay his protests.

"I want you to go now. I don't want to see you any more."

The flat, emotionless words lashed out at him like a bull whip. He wished they had been the whip. The sting would have been far less painful. What the hell was he going to do? How was he going to make her understand that he wasn't like Westgard? That he'd never harm her? Dazed, he shook his head.

"I'll go, for now, but I've not given up on us."

"I'm sorry, Morgan. I won't change my mind."

He flinched at the finality of her words. The resolve on her face was just as unalterable. He flexed his jaw with frustration. This wasn't over as far as he was concerned. She needed time. He'd give her that. But in the end, he'd make her see that they were meant for each other.

Chapter 7

The Lyceum Theater was hot and noisy as Julia took her seat next to Catherine in the Westgard box. Mrs. Langtry was performing in Antony and Cleopatra tonight, and the theater was more crowded than usual.

With a flick of her wrist, she opened her fan and stirred the air in front of her. Peacock feathers brushed across her nose as she leaned forward to see if Prince Edward was in the Royal Box. She chided herself. It wasn't the Prince she was hoping to see. She knew Morgan had a box at the theater, but she wasn't certain where. Sinking back into her chair she sighed softly.

"You've been quite the hermit this past week." Catherine sent her a look of curiosity. "Is there something wrong?"

"Not at all." She forced a serene smile to her lips.

"I see. Then perhaps you could explain why St. Claire is watching you from across the way with such pained hunger."

Startled, she stared at her cousin for a moment before her gaze shifted to the boxes on the opposite wall of the theatre. Morgan sat almost directly across from her, his eyes studying her every move. Her heart skipped a beat at the sight of his handsome face. Even from this distance, she saw the tension in his body. He looked tired. Sweet heaven, had he had another migraine episode? She hated the thought of him suffering.

Her gaze met his, and the intensity of his look warmed her body in a brief second. A flood of emotion surged through her, and she hastily turned her head away. How she wanted to give in to impulse and go to him.

"Well?" Catherine's eyes were filled with a gentle concern. "Are you going to tell me what's going on between the two of you?"

"There's nothing between St. Claire and me. I'm simply an investor in his company."

"Really, my dear, you can try convincing yourself of that fact, but I saw the look you just gave him. You're in love with the man."

Stunned, she jerked her gaze toward Catherine, her head spinning. If her cousin could see she was in love with Morgan, could he? A layer of ice skimmed over her skin. It had been difficult enough to send him away, but if he knew she loved him, he would be relentless in his pursuit.

"You're mistaken. I am not in love with Morgan St. Claire." Even to her ears, the words sounded hollow.

Catherine studied her for a long moment, her eyes sympathetic. "He's not Oscar, dearest."

"I don't know what you're talking about." She turned her head away and fanned herself.

"Morgan St. Claire is a good, honorable man, Julia. He's far and away a better man than your husband ever was."

"That may be true, but I refuse to let him, or any man, dominate me again. The humiliation of it…." She closed her eyes at the painful memories swirling in her head.

"Oh, Julia, you cannot allow Oscar's beastly behavior to deny you the chance for some happiness. That monster turned a young, vibrant girl into a reserved woman who's afraid to live, but I've seen glimpses of the girl I first met since his death."

"I am not afraid to live. I've been quite adventurous of late--scandalous, in fact." There was a note of bravado in her words that made her cousin send her an arch look.

"Having an affair is not the same thing as living," Catherine said quietly.

Silence filled the theatre box as she met her cousin's sympathetic gaze. She swallowed her embarrassment as she tried to find her voice. "How did … who else knows?"

"There's been a small amount of talk, speculation really. I wasn't even certain myself until just a few moments ago when I saw the way the two of you looked at each other."

"It's over," she said tersely.

"Is it?" Catherine reached over and touched her arm. "From your reaction, I'd say it was far from over."

"I cannot and will not allow myself to be dependent on any man. The price is too high." She bit her lip at the thought of giving herself up to Morgan's control, his masterful lovemaking, the safety of his arms. He was different from Oscar, logic told her that. But emotionally, she did not want to face the prospect of giving up control over her own destiny.

"Is that what really frightens you or are you afraid to risk trusting him--and yourself?"

Turning her head toward Catherine, she shook her head in disbelief. "Are you suggesting that I open myself up to such a risk?"

"What I'm suggesting is that you trust yourself to be with him simply because he makes you happy.

"It's … it's impossible." She snapped her feathered fan closed with an abrupt movement.

"Happiness is never impossible once you choose to accept it." Catherine smiled at her gently as the house lights dimmed. "It's the trusting that's difficult."

The soft words whispered through her head as the curtain rose and she tried to focus on the performance. Catherine had no idea how difficult it was for her to trust. Once she had been able to trust herself and others, but Oscar had changed all that. She wanted to trust Morgan. It was something she wanted desperately. But trusting him meant believing he would never hurt her. She wasn't certain she had that much trust within her to give.

If that were true, then how had she been able to trust him each time he touched her? In her heart, she knew he would never force her to do anything she didn't want to do. He was first and foremost a gentleman. Last week, he could have easily taken her by force, but he'd stopped.

A lesser man would have seen her submissive behavior as a signal to do as he liked. Not Morgan, he'd known something was wrong by her meek response. Time and again he'd proven how considerate he could be toward her. Although it had taken several days to recover from the shock of that last encounter, his respect for her feelings had been clearly demonstrated by his refusal to force her into something she didn't want.

Morgan didn't want her submissive. He'd said he wanted the woman in the portrait Peebles had painted. But did she have the ability to be that woman? Did she have the courage to open herself up to him in such a manner? Perhaps Catherine was right. Could it be she needed to choose happiness? Was it as simple as choosing to love him--to be with him? They didn't need to be married to be happy. And she cared little what society thought of her behavior.

Torn with indecision, her gaze drifted across the width of the theater to find Morgan watching her still. Instantly, the entire world slipped away as they stared at each other. There was nothing but the two of them. He leaned forward just a bit as if he hoped to reach out across the void and touch her. Then he stiffened and reclined back into his seat.

Bloody hell, he'd never experienced this type of torment. This all-consuming need for a woman who didn't want him. Could he blame her? He'd been a brute. The memory of how she'd retreated from him in her salon last week churned at his gut.

In his eagerness to convince her they were meant for each other, he'd dredged up unpleasant memories instead. All the signs had been there, he'd just been too blinded by his own lust. He should have realized Westgard had mistreated her.

Christ, to think that bastard had tied her up. He was afraid to think what else the son of a bitch had done to her. The expression on her face that morning was one he would never forget. Vacant and detached, she had presented the picture of a woman completely disembodied from her physical body.

Even now the thought of it sickened him. She had to be one of the most courageous people he'd ever met. Hell, it was amazing she'd even had the courage to give herself to him. Their lovemaking had built a fragile bridge of trust between them, and then he'd unwittingly broken that bond.

He needed to do something that would reassure her, rebuild that tenuous bond between them. But what? Closing his eyes, he suppressed a groan of despair. He needed to do something. Anything. He looked across the theater again.

To his amazement she was watching him. As their eyes met across the distance, she abruptly jerked her head back toward the stage. She looked beautiful tonight, but she also looked vulnerable. Was that his doing? Had he truly broken through that ice shell of hers?

His fingers dug into his thighs as he struggled to remain seated. All he wanted to do was charge over to her box, scoop her up into his arms and take her home with him. The image of his hotel room filtered its way into his head. It was all wrong for her.

Julia needed a place where she could feel safe--in control. His hotel room was the last place she would be able to do that. No, she needed something more stable, more tangible. For the first time he wished he had a house.

Until now, the hotel had served his needs more than adequately. It had also been a suitable deterrent to any mistress attempting to put her own stamp on any house he owned. His childhood had taught him that a home was a place of bitter discord. It was the primary reason why he'd chosen not to own a house.

But if he could give Julia all the safety, comfort and warmth only a true home could offer, perhaps that would show her how much he loved her. The question was whether or not she'd be willing to share it with him.

Applause sounded in his ears, and as the lights went up in the theater, he realized it was intermission. In the box opposite him, he watched as Julia leaned toward the woman beside her. He had to see her. Hear her voice.

Impulse drove him to his feet and out of his box. Despite the crowd surging out into the lobby in search of refreshments, he was able to reach Julia's box in just a few moments. Pushing the curtain aside, he found her alone. Uncertain as to what his reception would be like, he cleared his throat. The moment he did so, she turned her head toward him.

Pleasure flashed in her eyes before her expression became guarded. She didn't say anything, and clearing his throat again, he bowed. "Good evening, Julia."

"St. Claire." There was a breathless quality to her voice that stirred the desire he'd been holding in check for days.

"May I?" He gestured toward the empty chair opposite her.

When she nodded, he took a seat and studied her. The expression on her face was serene, but the frantic flutter at the side of her neck revealed her nervousness. Her gown was the color of the sea and made her look like a lush water nymph. It hugged her full curves seductively, and his hands ached to caress her roundness.

"Must you stare?"

"Would you have me do something else?" he asked softly.

Pink color tinged her cheeks as she blew out an exasperated breath. Opening her fan, she waved the feathers in front of her in an agitated fashion. "I . . . you should not be talking to me like that."

"Perhaps, but it gives me great pleasure to see you're not indifferent to me." He bit back a smile as she slapped her fan closed with an annoyed twist of her lips.

"I don't know what you mean."

Leaning forward, he slowly stroked the top of her knuckles with his forefinger. She trembled beneath his light touch. "Tell me you feel nothing when I touch you."

"I . . . I cannot." She paled slightly and turned her head away.

"Do you want to know what I feel when I touch you like this?" A rush of exhilaration sailed through him as she jerked her gaze back to his. She didn't speak, but the slight nod of her head pleased him. "I'm on fire for you."

A tiny gasp parted her lips and there was a longing in her eyes that gave him hope. Capturing her hand, he turned it over so he could stroke her bare skin through the opening of her evening glove. "I ache to be inside you, stroking you until you flow hot and sweet over my hard cock."

"Oh, God." Her whisper was almost inaudible, but it was clear his words excited her. He lifted his gaze to meet hers and he drew in a sharp breath. The same hot need burning inside him was glowing in her beautiful eyes. She wanted him. Raising her wrist to his mouth, he pressed his lips to her bare skin.

"Let me take you home." He watched her struggle to make a decision, her expressive face conveying all too clearly the battle raging inside her.

"I ... I--"

"Let me show you we're meant for each other."

She gave a quick shake of her head. "No, I ... you're confusing me."

"Bloody hell," he growled.

Frustration slammed into his muscles as he released her hand and reclined back into his seat with a grunt of anger. He'd never met a woman more adorable or stubborn in his entire life. But at least she'd not rejected him outright. That was a good sign. With a sharp jerk of his head, he agreed to her request.

"Very well. But be forewarned, Julia. This is not the last you've heard in this matter."

Her lips parted as if she were about to say something, when the sudden swish of the curtain behind him stopped her. Rising to his feet he turned and bowed as Julia introduced him to her cousin. With the introductions complete, he bowed over her hand.

"Remember what I said, Julia," he whispered against her fingers. With that, he excused himself and left the box. Despite his irritation at having lost this particular battle, something told him he might well win the war.

* * * *

Julia frowned at the figures in front her. This was the second time she'd found something amiss with the Sea Witch's logs. Nothing added up correctly, and it concerned her enough to bring it to Morgan's attention. With a frown, she worried her lip with her teeth. It had been a week now since she'd seen him at the Lyceum Theatre.

No, that wasn't quite true. She had seen him. He'd passed her several times here at the shipping offices either in the main workroom or in passing as one of them arrived or departed. Each time he'd greeted her with a courteous nod and nothing more. He was doing exactly what she'd wanted him to do since the beginning of their relationship.

She frowned. So why did the fact irritate her so much? For a man who professed to care for her, he was certainly not working very hard to change her mind. Dismayed by the notion, she pulled in a sharp breath.

Had she gone mad? Every time the man was near, her self-control hovered on the edge of total collapse. With one silk-edged word, Morgan could have her eating from the palm of his hand. But the most terrifying thought was that she wanted to do just that. She wanted to give herself over to him completely.

The traitorous thought made her slam the ledger closed. Glaring at the accounting book, she pressed her fingers into its cloth binding. She would have to face him. Prepared or not, she needed to prove to herself that she could control her emotions where he was concerned. Despite what Catherine had said about seeking happiness, she knew her present course of action was the best one.

With a quick step, she left the small office Morgan had given her to use. A moment later she was standing in front of his office door. Hesitation stayed her hand briefly before she rapped on the wood.

Hearing his command to enter, she inhaled a deep breath, and stepped into the lion's den with the ledger clutched tightly to her breast. Morgan was standing at the window as she entered his office. A look of surprise darkened his brown eyes when he turned his head toward her. Abruptly, he wheeled about and strode to his desk. Picking up a sheaf of papers, he sorted through them.

"What can I do for you, Julia?" The cold note in his voice made her wince.

The sharpness of his words cut at her heart. Had he actually given up on her? The question made her swallow a knot of fear in her throat. She had to stop thinking like this. If she wasn't careful she'd be throwing herself into his arms.

Assuming a businesslike manner, she rounded the large piece of furniture and laid the ledger she carried on the desktop. Immediately, a frisson slid over her skin as the warmth of his body heated hers simply by standing next to him. To her dismay, his entire body went rigid. It was as if the man found her presence detestable.

The thought squeezed at her heart, and she opened the ledger with an abrupt movement. When she found the appropriate page, she pointed to the account lines she'd been working on for most of the morning. Her finger pressed against the paper, she uttered a noise of frustration.

"These figures aren't adding up correctly."

He didn't answer for a moment as he leaned over the book and trailed his finger over the numbers. Trembling, she pulled her hand away to guard against his touch. She breathed in the warm spicy scent of him. When she'd first met him, she'd thought that it was indecent for a man to smell so wonderful.

Nothing had changed. He smelled as deliciously dangerous then as he did today. Her heart skipped a beat as she studied his hand. A light dusting of dark hair covered the back of his hand, while a tapered finger tapped restlessly against the ledger page. He had beautiful hands. The memory of what those hands could do stirred her senses as a familiar heat curled in her stomach.

"Everything appears to be in order."

Jerked out of her reverie, she shook her head with frustration. "You don't understand. The Sea Witch was supposed to have a hundred more barrels of Madagascar oil than what she had when she arrived in port."

"That's because I had the captain stop at Gibraltar and hand over those barrels to the Bluebell for delivery to America."

"Oh." She frowned in puzzlement before turning to the Bluebell ledger page where the transaction had been noted. Feeling foolish, she shook her head. "I apologize."

"It was an efficient measure recommended by one of my investors." There was a slight trace of amusement in his voice.

The words took a moment to sink in before she realized she was the investor he'd referred to. Shortly after she'd invested her money with St. Claire Shipping, she'd suggested he should consider using foreign ports-of-call as a means of transferring cargo more efficiently. The thought that he might actually listen to her suggestions had never crossed her mind.

Startled by the fact, she looked up at him. For the first time she realized how close they were to each other. The heat of him encircled her, while her heart crashed into her chest at a frantic pace. She missed his touch, and standing so close to him created the pulsating need to reach out and touch him. It took every ounce of willpower she possessed to keep from reaching out and pressing her hand against his chest. Was his heart racing with excitement just like hers?

Hunger burned in his eyes as he watched her. They devoured her, made her tense with expectation. The muscle in his jaw flexed and the tension in him was almost palpable. If she were to touch him, his body would be hard as a rock. Would all of him be hard? The erotic thought shocked her, and her breathing immediately became shallow. It was a scandalous thought, but it excited her.

She wanted him to be hard with desire for her. Beneath his steady gaze her insides melted and she swayed into him. His gaze didn't flicker as she saw his head start to descend. Dear Lord, yes. He was going to kiss her. She wanted him to quite badly.

She wanted him to kiss her until she couldn't think. It had been so long since the last time she'd been in his arms. Her eyes fluttered shut as she tipped her head back and eagerly awaited his lips to sear hers. When the heat of his body left her, her eyes flew open to see him watching her from several feet away.

"Is there anything else?"

The formality was back in his voice and she suppressed a scream of frustration. Why did he insist on addressing her with such polite civility? He'd held nothing back at other times, and especially not while they'd been in the throes of passion. Once again her thoughts shocked her. She couldn't understand why he'd not kissed her. Disconcerted by his actions, she frowned.

"I noticed you've been out of the office several days this week. Did you have another migraine attack?"

"Your concern is touching, but unnecessary," he said tersely without giving her a reason for his absence.

This was not going well at all. Nibbling at her lip, she sent him a wary look. "Colonel Beresford indicated there was an investor dinner next week. I've not received my invitation and thought perhaps I'd misunderstood him."

"You weren't invited."

His curt response sliced through her as she watched him stride to the window and look out at the docks. Not invited. He'd deliberately excluded her from a dinner party where business would be discussed. Irritated, she glared at his back.

"So because I reject you personally, you feel it necessary to exclude me from business meetings."

"I do not base my business decisions on my personal affairs, Julia. You were not invited simply because your presence would be a hindrance."

He winced at the harsh words. Damn Beresford for organizing this dinner party in the first place. When he'd mentioned the need to apprise the investors of several issues, Beresford had insisted on hosting the dinner.

It wasn't until a few days ago that the man had indicated Madame Evelyn's establishment would provide the evening's entertainment. There wasn't a chance in hell he was going to let Julia attend that dinner. Most of the men would wind up drunk and the whole setting was ripe for an orgy.

"What do you mean I'll be a hindrance?"

"Some of the men find it ... uncomfortable with you in the same room." Keeping his eyes focused on the busy docks outside his window, he swallowed hard. Hell, he was uncomfortable now. Being so close to her was driving him mad with desire. If he couldn't convince her to leave his office soon, there'd be no telling what he'd do.

"Uncomfortable? But you're the owner of the company. Surely you have the final say in matters such as these."

"I don't want you there."

The icy emphasis on each of his words was almost a physical blow. He didn't want her at the dinner meeting. His rejection was more painful than she could ever have expected.

"You don't--" Furious, she swept toward him. With one hand she forced him to face her. "I'm one of your biggest investors. I'm entitled to be privy to any business discussions. You cannot exclude me like this."

"I can and will, Julia."

"It's unacceptable, and you know it. I should have expected this. It's perfectly acceptable to bed me, but accepting me as an equal in our business dealings is unthinkable."

"Take care with your words, Julia." There was a deadly note in his voice.

"Don't you dare threaten me, St. Claire."

In a lightning move, he jerked her into his arms. Startled by the action, a rush of excitement coursed its way through her and her anger disappeared in a flash of heat. Already the warmth from his body was sinking into hers. The familiar sensation ignited a fire in the pit of her stomach.

A sigh of pleasure escaped her. This is what she'd wanted since she came into his office. She trembled against him. His mouth brushed past her forehead, almost as if he were breathing in the scent of her hair. In the next instant, his mouth brushed over her earlobe.

"Hear me, and hear me well, Julia. If you continue to push me in this matter, I'll not be responsible for my actions. Is that clear?"

There was an edge to his voice she'd not heard before. It sounded as if he were ready to throttle her. But she didn't want him to do anything but kiss her. Kiss her until they were both so wrapped up in each other they could blot out the world and the past. Need for him, for his touch, spiraled through her until she ached all over.

Uncertain how to answer him, she tilted her head to look up at him. Dark hunger glowed in his eyes, and it thrilled her. She knew it was ill-advised to be excited, but she was beginning to realize how lonely life was going to be without him. Her hand lifted to touch his cheek. With a jerk of his head, he shoved her out of his arms.

"Get out, Julia. I've work to do." Returning to his desk, he picked up her ledger and offered it to her. "I believe this is yours."

Fury mixed with disappointment as she raced forward and tugged the book out of his hands. The man was being obstinate and loathsome. But even more frustrating was the way she'd been literally throwing herself at him. She wanted him to hold her, kiss her, make love to her again. The thought frightened her almost as much as it thrilled her. Whirling away from him, she marched toward the door. Her hand on the brass knob, she threw him a furious glance over her shoulder.

"You're a bastard, St. Claire," she hissed.

"So I've been told, madame. So I've been told." The nonchalance in the man's voice and demeanor was outrageous.

With a jerk of the doorknob, she opened the door and left the office, slamming it behind her. The loud bang echoed through the office and Morgan slowly sat down. His head resting back against the leather of his office chair, he closed his eyes.

"Bloody hell," he muttered as he rubbed his throbbing temples.

For the past week it had been difficult as hell to keep his distance from her. With the exception of passing her in the office, he'd not seen her since the theater. Her presence in his office just now had pushed the reserves of his willpower to the edge.

It was only by a miracle that he'd been able to walk away from her when she closed her eyes and literally begged him in silence to kiss her. His cock twisted angrily in his trousers as he groaned. God, he wanted her. Needed her. Loved her.

But it didn't matter. If there was to be any real happiness for them, she would have to come to him freely and of her own accord. He should have explained about the dinner with Beresford. He intended to stay through the meal, excusing himself before the debauchery launched into full swing. Clearly he'd botched the explanation, but finding the right way to explain it to her had escaped him.

He wasn't sure he'd made the right choice though, given how furious she was. But her anger had disappeared just as quickly when he'd pulled her into his arms. The only explanation he could think of was that she was more upset over the idea of him not kissing her than a business meeting she'd not been invited to.

Keeping his distance for the past week had been born out of self-preservation. That night at the Lyceum he'd wanted to carry her out of the theater despite her protests. Held in the grip of such powerful emotions, he knew he needed to stay away from her to prevent himself from doing something rash.

He'd never even considered the idea that avoiding her might have the positive outcome of making her to come to him of her own free will. But it seemed to have had the desired effect. It was the only explanation for her behavior a few moments ago.

She was only just beginning to realize she wanted him. But was she willing to act on that impulse? Her behavior suggested she might, but if she didn't do it soon, he was going to go mad. When he'd pulled her into his arms, she'd smelled fresh. Delicious enough to devour. Pushing her away and acting insouciant about it had been a supreme effort he wouldn't be able to repeat on a regular basis. He wanted her in his arms too much.

His desire and need were born of the love he had for her. But did she simply desire him or was there more to her feelings? For his sanity, he had to believe she loved him, but she was too frightened to act on it. It was her love he wanted, but he was willing to accept whatever she gave him. All that mattered was that she at least give them a chance.

Chapter 8

Morgan strolled through the empty parlor. The fireplace was cold and empty, but it was easy to see how it would warm the room when there was a fire burning merrily in the hearth. More importantly, the room itself was bright and airy. He moved across the floor into the hallway.

"You'll find the house reasonably priced, Mr. St. Claire, a veritable bargain. The last owner outgrew the place, but there are plenty of bedrooms and a nursery as well. Not to mention the servants' quarters on the third floor."

The solicitor gestured with his hand toward the flight of stairs leading upward. Nodding, Morgan climbed the steps. The master bedroom was quite large, and he was pleased to find a dressing room adjoining it. Small and dimly lit, the room would make an excellent place for him to retreat during a migraine attack.

Leaving the bedroom, he took his time viewing the rest of the floor. The last room he came to was the nursery. Warm and cozy, it spoke of a childhood he had always wished for, but had never known. The happy ambiance of the room was in direct opposition to what he'd known as a child.

He turned to the man waiting at the door. "Draw up the papers for the sale and send them to me at the Clarendon. I'd like to take ownership by the end of the week."

"Certainly, sir. And will you require assistance securing furniture?"

"Yes, but only the necessities for the time being." He glanced around the nursery. He wanted Julia to have the pleasure of decorating the house. It would be one more way of showing her how much her happiness meant to him, showing her he had no wish to crush her spirit or her sense of self.

Satisfied with his purchase, he left the house and strode down the steps to his carriage. Instructing his driver to return to the office, he climbed into the vehicle to settle back into the leather seat. Despite his pleasure at having found the ideal house to buy, it had been an unsettling experience. Never having had the responsibility of a household, the notion of a permanent residence had proven more disturbing than he'd expected. Now that it was a fait accompli, he acknowledged the process had been a cleansing in some respects.

While it wasn't a home yet, it was a start. All that was required now was to explain to Julia why he'd bought the house. He had to make her understand he only wanted to offer her a place where she would feel safe and loved. Making her believe his intentions were good would be easy compared to the challenge of convincing her to marry him.

Her resistance to the idea wouldn't be easy to overcome. After the incident in his office yesterday, he wasn't certain what to expect when he saw her next. The first thing he needed to do was explain about Beresford and the dinner party. He'd been a fool not to explain things to her. Being focused on keeping his hands off her wasn't a valid excuse.

The carriage rocked to a halt, and he stepped out of the vehicle. About to enter the shipping office, a firm hand settled on his shoulder.

"St. Claire."

Turning his head, a wide smile of pleasure curved his mouth. "Devlyn! What are you doing here?"

"Looking for you actually," the other man said as he shook Morgan's hand. "I've an investment opportunity I thought might interest you."

"If it's one of your ideas, I'm certain it will. That deal we brokered in America almost ten years ago is still generating revenue."

Morgan opened the door to St. Claire Shipping and ushered his friend through the hustle and bustle of the clerks. Once they were situated in his private office, he sat in his desk chair to study the man seated opposite him. "Marriage agrees with you."

A grin of satisfaction on his face, Devlyn nodded. "Quite. Sophie is the best thing that ever happened to me."

"And where is the Countess?" Morgan reached out and offered his friend a cigar from the box sitting on his desk.

"No, not for me." Devlyn dismissed the tobacco with a wave of his hand. "Actually, Sophie and the children are getting settled in our new home over on Curzon Street. It's another reason why I called on you. We want you to come for dinner Friday evening."

"I wouldn't miss it. What time--?" A sharp rap on his office door made him tense. Only one person knocked at his door like that. Rising to his feet, he sent Devlyn an apologetic glance. "Come in."

Julia entered the room with a determined look in her eyes. "St. Claire, we need to talk about this business dinner."

"Yes, we do," he said smoothly. "However, now isn't the time to do so."

She opened her mouth to argue, but as Devlyn rose to his feet, she frowned. "I'm sorry. I didn't realize you were occupied. I can come back at a later time."

"It's quite all right. Let me introduce you to my friend, Lord Devlyn. Devlyn, this is Mrs. Westgard."

Frustrated, she struggled to control her anger at Morgan. The man had avoided her all afternoon yesterday. Confound it, she wanted this matter resolved, and the last thing she wanted to do was make pleasant with some stranger. With a sharp nod of greeting, she extended her hand and the man brushed his mouth across her fingertips. The smile the man sent her was filled with charm.

"Your husband is a fortunate man, Mrs. Westgard."

The man's devilish smile set her on edge. Another rake set on charming her as Morgan had done. Arching her eyebrows, she sent him a cool look. "Actually, I'm the fortunate one, my Lord. He's dead."

The response made Lord Devlyn cough as he choked out his apology. "Forgive me."

"Damn it, Julia. That was uncalled for," Morgan growled in protest.

Glaring at him, she grimaced. Blast the man, he was right. Lord Devlyn had simply been paying her a compliment. It wasn't his fault she was ready to crown Morgan for his stubborn attitude about the business dinner. She pushed her fury aside and turned back to Devlyn.

"As much as it pains me to admit it, my Lord, St. Claire is right. I was extremely rude, please forgive me."

Recovered from his coughing fit, the man eyed her intently. Too intently for her liking. It was as if he understood why she was behaving so badly. "There is nothing to forgive, madame. It's obvious something is troubling you. Is there anything I can do to help?"

The question was a sincere offer, and it took her by surprise considering her behavior. "Thank you, my Lord, but it's a business matter."

Her gaze flew to Morgan's face, which was dark with annoyance. The look of suppressed anger he directed at her made her tilt her chin in defiance. No doubt, he intended to take her to task at a later time. Well, two could play that game. The man needed to understand he could not shut her out of St. Claire Shipping's business discussions if he expected to continue using her money. She met his warning gaze without flinching until he turned back to his friend.

"Julia is irritated with a decision I made yesterday."

"Irritated is not quite the word I would use." She glowered at him then directed her attention to Lord Devlyn. "But I do appreciate your offer of assistance, my Lord. Your thoughtfulness is an example others should follow."

"What the hell is that supposed to mean?" Morgan snapped.

He wanted to wring her neck. He'd actually allowed her to provoke him. Damn her. She was the only woman who'd ever managed to do that.

"Why nothing at all, St. Claire. Nothing at all."

She glared back at him as he sent her a hard look. Then to his amazement, Devlyn burst out into laughter. The unexpected sound reverberated in the office, and Morgan saw Julia start with surprise. Still laughing, Devlyn shook his head.

"I think the two of you need to declare a truce before blood is drawn."

Morgan gritted his teeth and the tension in his body made his muscles ache. Drawing blood wasn't exactly what he had in mind for Julia. At the first opportunity, he was going to kiss the woman senseless. She was testing his patience beyond measure. Once her anger was gone, he'd explain about the dinner. Then he'd make love to her until she agreed to marry him. To hell with his vow to give her time and not push her into a decision.

A strained smile on her lips, Julia nodded at Devlyn. "I think I'll leave the two of you to continue your discussion."

With a nod toward Devlyn, she turned and headed toward the door. Her hand was on the doorknob when Morgan saw his friend suddenly stride after her.

"Mrs. Westgard, one moment if you please." Devlyn took her hand in his. "I wonder if you might do me a favor."

"A favor?" Although she hid it well, there was cool suspicion in her voice. Devlyn seemed oblivious to it, but Morgan heard crackling as she surrounded herself with an icy layer of reserve.

"You see, my wife doesn't have many friends in London, and I think you and she would get along quite well." The smile Devlyn sent her made Morgan's stomach clench as Julia smiled back, a distinct expression of relief flitting across her face.

"Oh … why of course. If you'll give me your address, I'd be happy to call on her."

"Actually, I was thinking perhaps you might join us for dinner this Friday night. I know Sophie would be delighted to have you come."

"Dinner? Oh, well--"

"Then you'll come." He paused as he waited expectantly for Julia's nod. "Excellent. Shall we say seven-thirty? We're at twelve Curzon Street."

The confusion on Julia's face made it clear she wasn't certain how she'd agreed to a dinner engagement. His anger subsiding, Morgan bit back a smile as Devlyn kissed her hand, then held the door open for her. Julia hesitated for a brief moment as if she was going to say something then with a slight shake of her head she left the office.

As the door closed behind her, Devlyn turned around and grinned. "I believe you're expected at our house for dinner this Friday night as well."

Returning his friend's smile, he nodded. "I wouldn't miss it."

* * * *

The hackney cab rolled to a halt in front of twelve Curzon Street. Exiting the small carriage, Julia climbed the steps of the house and pushed the door bell. A moment later a short, elderly man opened the door and invited her inside, closing the door behind her.

The man took her shawl and beaded bag from her just as a toddler charged across the hall with a loud laugh. A woman followed him at half a run.

"Master Spencer Blackwell, come back here this instant." Although her words were stern, the laughter in the woman's voice only made the youngster giggle louder. With a quick maneuver, the woman caught up with the boy and scooped him up into her arms. As she pecked his cheek in a quick kiss, she ordered him to be still.

The woman turned as if suddenly realizing there was a guest in her foyer. A frazzled smile wreathing her handsome features, she sent the butler a beseeching look. "I'm terribly sorry. Fischer, would you mind taking Spencer up to Nanny? I'll take care of Mrs. Westgard."

The butler nodded and smiled as he took the boy into his arms and headed up the stairway. Their conversation was indiscernible, but it was obvious the boy adored the older man. Turning toward her, the woman smiled and stretched out her hand to Julia. "Please forgive me. It is Mrs. Westgard, isn't it?"

Julia nodded as the woman shook her hand then drew her into a large salon. "I'm afraid perhaps I'm a little early, Lady Devlyn."

"Oh, not at all, and please, we're quite informal here. Do call me Sophie."

The welcoming expression on Lady Devlyn's face made Julia warm to the other woman. With a smile she nodded. "All right, but you must agree to call me Julia."

"Julia. What a lovely name."

"Yes, it is." The deep, seductive sound of Morgan's voice made her go rigid. Slowly she turned her head and met his enigmatic gaze. Why the sight of him was so unexpected, she really didn't know.

"St. Claire." With a nod in his direction, she managed to keep her voice steady as she greeted him, barely noticing that Lord Devlyn had entered the salon behind Morgan.

Tension and heat tightened the muscles below her belly as she studied him for a brief moment before looking away. Blast it, but just looking at the man was a dangerous pastime. It was impossible not to find him sinfully handsome, and her body responded to his raw power even from across the room.

Every time she saw him, her need for him slowly eroded the slippery slope she stood on. Soon she'd have to come to a decision where he was concerned. Not only did she want his kiss and touch, she wanted one more chance to experience the ecstasy of that single night they'd spent in each other's arms. The knowledge didn't really surprise her, but the intensity of her craving for him did.

Determined not to let him see how vulnerable she was to his presence, she turned back to Lady Devlyn.

"My la--" She stopped at the pleasant look of discouragement on Sophie's face. "Sophie. How old is your little boy?"

"Spencer will be four in about six months, although he seems far older than that sometimes."

A deep laugh poured out of Lord Devlyn's throat as he moved to his wife's side. Pressing a kiss to her cheek, he grinned. "He's his mother's son, impudent and well aware that he has the entire staff wrapped around his finger."

With a gesture toward the two couches that faced each other across an oval coffee table, Sophie moved to take a seat. "Why don't we sit down until supper is ready?"

Julia followed her hostess and sat across from her. An instant later, her skin grew hot as Morgan joined her on the love seat. Inhaling a deep breath, she trembled as he stretched his arm out along the back of the sofa. Perched on the edge of her seat, her mouth tightened with annoyance as she heard his quiet chuckle.

Determined to ignore him, she watched Lord Devlyn take his wife's hand and hold it in his in a tender gesture. They were the image of a happily married couple. A streak of envy flashed through her. Quickly she killed the emotion. Marriage was out of the question for her. Leaning forward slightly, she smiled. "Lord Devlyn tells me you've only recently moved into this house."

"Yes, it's been a little more than two months now. We haven't been frequent visitors to town, but with this new venture Quentin is starting, we needed a place to stay and entertain."

Devlyn leaned toward his wife with a wicked grin. "Admit it, my love, you simply want to drag me to the blasted opera. Although I confess there is one opera I have quite pleasurable memories of."

A delicate blush crept over Sophie's cheeks, and once more, Julia found herself envying the affectionate rapport between the couple. Is this what the words happily married meant? This give and take between a husband and wife? She darted a glance at the man beside her. Morgan's eyes met hers in a quiet look of assessment. The sudden hunger darkening his gaze sent a shudder of longing through her. What would life be like if she were to marry him? The thought made her tug her gaze away from him as she struggled to cope with the sharp desire to consider his proposal.

From the salon doorway, a young maid announced dinner, and Julia allowed a soft sigh of relief to part her lips as she quickly stood. Seconds later, another wave of heat cascaded over her as Morgan rose to stand next to her. His nearness was a searing reminder of the passion that still echoed across her skin.

Unwilling to let him see how unsettling his presence was, she forced a smile to her lips as he offered his arm to escort her into dinner. Her hand curved lightly around the crook of his arm as they followed Lord and Lady Devlyn into the dining room.

The tension flowing between them was taut with unspoken words, and Morgan's muscles hardened beneath her touch. God help him, but the woman was driving him mad. She wanted him. Every time she looked at him, the need and love she was struggling to suppress revealed itself in her beautiful eyes. Then just when it seemed she might open up to him, her fear drove another wedge between them.

He'd hoped seeing Devlyn and Sophie together might persuade Julia to reconsider her refusal to marry him. His friends' happy marriage was the perfect example of what he was certain he and Julia could have. Watching her in the salon as she'd studied the other couple had given him hope. He'd always envied Devlyn and Sophie's happiness, but it wasn't until Julia entered his life that he'd realized marriage might bring him happiness as well.

As he held her chair for her, impulse made him graze the back of her neck with his fingertips. The silky warmth of her skin made his entire body ache with desire. At his touch, he saw her stiffen. She refused to look at him as he sat across from her. Damnation, he needed to find some way to convince her they were meant for one another.

Seated opposite him, she was a luscious vision of temptation. No matter how old they grew, he'd never lose this need to be near her. She was as important to him as the air he breathed. Although she seemed determined not to look at him, there were moments when she couldn't avoid doing so. In those brief instances, he glimpsed the woman he knew was hiding behind a wall of fear.

Toward the end of the meal, the sound of running feet made him turn his head as Spencer rushed into the dining room. Following close behind was a young woman carrying a little girl. As the children entered the room, Sophie quickly scooted her chair back and accepted the baby from the nanny's arms, while Spencer raced toward the end of the table to fling himself into his father's lap.

Laughing Sophie smiled as she looked at him and Julia. "Please forgive us, but the children are always allowed to come say goodnight to us, even during an informal dinner party."

"I didn't realize you had a little girl," Julia said with a forgiving smile. "She's beautiful."

"Emily takes after her mother, doesn't she Spencer?" Devlyn grinned across the table at his wife as the boy nodded vigorously.

Regret lingered on the curve of Julia's mouth as he watched her looking at the children. From where he sat, her sadness for what she'd miss was plain to see. Watching the goodnight hugs and kisses between his friends and their children, he realized how much the idea of a family appealed to him.

Looking across the table at Julia, he imagined her round with his child. She would be even more exquisite than she was already. As if aware of his thoughts, her gaze met his, and he saw her study him with a wary expression before looking away.

If only he could make her understand that happiness was hers for the taking if she would just gather up her courage and reach out to him. With a frown, he watched her expression melt as Emily reached out her plump little arms to Julia. Whether the woman liked it or not, he was going to see her home. No matter how difficult she might be, he wasn't ready to give up on their happiness.

* * * *

The silence in the carriage was thick with raw tension. Ever since seeing Julia holding little Emily in her arms, his need for her had escalated to the point of an exquisite pain. Studying her profile as she looked out the window, it was difficult to tell what she was thinking. She'd seemed to enjoy their evening with Sophie and Devlyn, but whether it had made her consider his marriage proposal in a positive light was impossible to tell.

"Did you enjoy yourself this evening?"

"Yes," she said coolly. "I like Sophie a great deal."

"I could tell she liked you as well."

When she didn't respond, his jaw muscles tightened with frustration. Obstinate as always, she refused to make things easy between them. "Their marriage is a happy one. I've always thought them well suited for one another."

Her head slowly turned as she looked him in the eye. "They are well suited, unlike others."

"If you're referring to us, then you're wrong. We're very well suited for one another. You're just too stubborn to see it." Narrowing his eyes, he folded his arms across his chest to keep from reaching out and shaking her.

"I might be stubborn, but I'm not arrogant enough to make use of an investor's money while excluding them from business discussions." The disdain on her face as she arched her brow changed his annoyance to anger.

"Damn it, Julia. I'm perfectly willing to explain about that dinner meeting, but I've simply not found the right opportunity to do so."

"In other words, you've not been able to come up with a credible excuse."

The scorn in her voice sent his teeth grinding against each other. If the woman wanted an explanation, he'd bloody well give her one she'd never forget. Seething with anger, he leaned across the seat and dragged her roughly onto his lap. A small cry parted her lips, and she pushed against his chest as he glared down into her shocked expression.

"Let me show you why you're not going to that business dinner, Mrs. Westgard," he rasped as desire mixed with his fury.

In a swift move, he covered her mouth with his in a passionate kiss. He cupped the back of her neck as he pressed her close against him. Beneath his caress, her mouth parted and she grazed his lips with the tip of her tongue. The erotic touch pulled a deep groan from him, and he swept his tongue into her mouth.

God, he wanted to shut out the world until she surrendered to him
completely. The taste of sweet wine on her tongue blended with the
peaches they'd had for dessert, filling his mouth with delicious
nectar. His thumb found the pulse beating frantically at the side of
her neck. It throbbed like an erotic tattoo against the pad of his
finger.

In his trousers, his erection jutted up toward his stomach in a
painful cry of desire. A soft mewl escaped her throat, and his cock
lunged at the sound. It nearly undid him completely. Christ Jesus,
but the woman had him wrapped around a barrel. She could ask
him for anything at the moment and he'd give it to her.

Deepening their kiss, he struggled to keep from lifting her dress
and stroking her with his fingers. There was no doubt she'd be wet
with liquid heat. His cock jumped at the thought as his ballocks
drew up tight against his groin. A groan rumbled in his chest. He
didn't want her like this. He wanted her to come to him of her own
choosing. But God help him, he didn't think he had the strength to
refuse what she was willing to give him right now.

His hands slid across her bare skin to where her gown hugged the
edge of her shoulder. Beneath his caress she trembled, her mouth
dancing with his tongue for a moment longer as she broke away
from his kiss. Agitation marked her movements as she hastily
unbuttoned his shirt and pulled it out of his trousers with a sharp tug.

The moment her hands touched his hot flesh, the tension that had
been building in her belly rushed to the apex of her thighs in a taut
explosion of fiery desire. His head fell back to rest against the
carriage wall, and she pressed her lips against the tangy skin of his
throat. From there she lowered her head until her mouth was on the
rippling muscles of his chest. Her tongue flicked out to circle his
nipple, and a low growl rumbled out of his throat.

Sweet heaven, she'd missed him. Missed this. It had been too long
since she'd been able to touch him like this and she needed him.
Wanted him inside her, filling her, throbbing against her tautness
until they both caught fire and exploded at the same instant. Her
senses swimming with heat and need, she nipped at the side of his
neck with her teeth as her hand slid down to stroke the hard length
of him pressing into her thigh.

He jumped as she stroked the hardness of his erection with her
hand. Under her palm, he was hot and harder than she remembered.
He wanted her. Jubilant at the knowledge, she applied a gentle
pressure to him that made him groan deeply. Tonight she was

willing to give in to her passion and tomorrow she'd deal with the consequences of her actions.

Strong fingers captured her chin and he took her mouth again in a mind-searing kiss. Lost to the sensations flooding her senses, her fingers spiked through his hair as she returned his kiss with all the heat exploding inside her. Warm fingers stroked her bare throat down to the valley between her breasts.

A shudder sped through her as his hand glided down over her breast. Her rigid nipples scraped with agonizing sensitivity against her undergarments at the touch. Whimpering with the need for more, her fingers sought the buttons of his trousers as her hunger for him spiraled out of control. Desire engulfed her body and touching him was all that mattered.

With a suddenness that pierced her aroused state, a large hand encircled her wrist like a vise and pushed her hand away from him. Small pants escaped her lips as she looked up into his eyes in bewilderment. What was wrong with him? He'd provoked this intense encounter and now he thought to end it? The dark hunger in his eyes made her reach up to touch his cheek. He ignored the touch as he lifted her off his lap and back into the seat opposite him.

"Not like this, Julia," he said in a low, firm voice as he buttoned his shirt in a hurried fashion.

Bemused by his abrupt rejection, she shook her head. "I … I don't understand. You kissed me. I … thought you…."

Shoving his shirt tails back into his trousers, he grimaced. "I do want you, Julia. I want you more than you know. But you have to come to me of your own free will."

"Blast you, St. Claire, I just offered myself to you, and you have the audacity to reject me with the condition that I come to you." She wanted to hit him. The man was demanding an absolute surrender. One she wasn't willing to give.

"I've been patient with you Julia. I've given you time, but I'm through playing games. If you care for me, you'll come to me at a time of your choosing. Completely free of any enticement from me." His voice was implacable as he watched her through narrowed eyes.

"What you mean is that I have to sacrifice myself on the St. Claire altar."

"No. Our relationship will be one of mutual independence. I know how important that is to you. But I want to know you're going to be there when I come home at night."

"But you don't have a home, you have rooms in a hotel," she said with a sniff of derision.

"Not any longer. I've bought a house. A house that needs a woman's touch. I want that woman to be you."

The words were like unexpected gunfire. She wasn't quite certain she'd heard him correctly, and yet she knew she had. For a long moment, she simply absorbed his news. He'd bought a house. Morgan St. Claire--confirmed bachelor, unmitigated rake and notorious womanizer--had bought a house.

He was up to something. She didn't know what, but he was scheming to get his own way. There was some ulterior motive for this behavior. There had to be. Meeting his dark gaze from across the carriage, a tremor went through her. It was the honest hunger in his eyes that frightened and confused her. Dear God, could the man possibly be telling her the truth? No. She refused to believe it. There had to be something else motivating him. This was a game to him.

The carriage rolled to a stop. In silence they exited the vehicle and Morgan escorted her up the three steps to her front door. As her hand grasped the doorknob, a large hand covered hers.

"If you choose not to come to me, Julia, we'll not see each other again." There was a grim tilt to his mouth. "Come to me. Don't let that bastard win."

Without waiting for a response, he spun around on his heel and returned to his carriage. The finality in his voice made her throat close in fear. Would he really not see her again? Inside a voice cried out to stop him, but she crushed the protest. No. She couldn't agree to his terms. She would have to live without Morgan St. Claire--no matter how painful and difficult that would be.

Chapter 9

Julia passed through the main door of St. Claire Shipping, her gaze automatically flitting toward Morgan's office door. Just as it had been for the past three days, the door stood open. It was a declaration that Morgan had not yet arrived.

Worrying her lip with her teeth, she walked slowly toward the small office she used. There was little need for her to even be here today. She'd finished reviewing all of Morgan's accounting ledgers and there wasn't much else for her to review at the moment. If she were honest with herself, the only reason she was in the shipping office was because she wanted to see Morgan.

Since escorting her to her doorstep three nights ago, she'd not seen him. When he'd left her, there had been such finality in his demeanor. Her hand grasped the cool brass of the office doorknob, but she didn't turn it. She stood there for a moment as if suspended in time.

Morgan was a good businessman. Surely he wouldn't stay away from his business for such a long time simply because he wanted to avoid her. Even if he were ill, she would have seen him here in the office. What if he had gone out of town on business? That would make sense. She whirled around and hurried over to Morgan's head clerk, Jeremy Crane.

"Mr. Crane, I was wondering if you could tell me where Mr. St. Claire is?"

The clerk frowned slightly. "I'm not all that certain, Mrs. Westgard. He left here a couple of days ago with a terrible scowl on his face, and I haven't seen him since."

The man's response made her grow cold. If Morgan were away on business, she was certain he would have informed Mr. Crane. The man knew almost as much about St. Claire Shipping as Morgan did. What would keep him away from his office for so long? A woman?

The idea made her stomach flutter. Shoving the thought aside, she swallowed hard. With a firm grip on her beaded handbag, she reassured herself. He wasn't with another woman. She refused to believe such a thing. Noting Mr. Crane's curiosity, she frowned.

"He didn't tell you where he was going?"

"No, ma'am. But he did send word that if I required his signature, I was to send the paperwork to this address." The clerk pushed a piece of paper toward her.

Morgan's strong, elegant penmanship filled the sheet. Memorizing the Mayfair address, she met Crane's curious expression with a small smile. "Thank you, Mr. Crane. If by chance Mr. St. Claire does come into the office today, would you please let him know that I'd like to speak with him?"

"Of course, Mrs. Westgard, of course."

Nodding her head toward the clerk, she turned and left the shipping offices. The address Crane had shown her rolled about in her head. It was in the fashionable residential district. Could this be the house he'd bought?

She should check on him. Make certain he was all right. After all, his absence was quite unusual for him, and he might be ill. There was nothing wrong with paying a courtesy call on someone. If anything it was the polite thing to do. Outside, she signaled for her carriage and gave her driver Morgan's address before settling back into the plump seat of the vehicle.

As the carriage rolled through the city, she closed her eyes. She was lying to herself if she thought she was simply visiting him out of polite concern. She needed to know why he'd not been at the office. Most of all, she needed to know he wasn't with another woman.

Even though she had no intention of marrying him, the idea of another woman in his arms twisted and clawed at her insides with devastating force. Biting her lip, the salty taste of blood spread across her tongue. She didn't want to contemplate the possibility of such a betrayal.

Whatever the reason for his absence, it didn't matter anymore. A moth singeing its wings on a flame was more capable of flight than she was of fleeing the love that bound her to Morgan. Over the past three days, she thought she could crush the love she had for him. She'd been mistaken. Not only mistaken, but miserable too.

Miserable without the sound of his voice or the sight of his face to brighten her day. Every time she'd tried to push him out of her thoughts, something happened to ensure the image of him didn't leave her head. Love wasn't something one could control, and with each passing day, her love for Morgan had only grown stronger.

A sigh parted her lips as she leaned forward to look out the window. He'd warned her that she would have to come to him on her own. Now she was doing just that. Wincing at the thought, she frowned as the carriage rolled to a stop in front of a lovely white stone façade. Larger than the usual town home, the dwelling was impressive and yet inviting at the same time. If this was the house he'd purchased, it was larger than she'd envisioned.

She exited the vehicle and quickly climbed the steps and rang the bell. A moment later the door opened without a squeak, and relief swept through her as she met Mrs. Welkin's pleasant gaze. This had to be Morgan's new residence, and he'd apparently convinced the hotel housekeeper to come manage his home. It relieved her to know he was being looked after by someone used to his migraines.

"Mrs. Westgard, how lovely to see you. Won't you come inside?"

Now that she was here, she didn't know what to do. With a silent nod, she stepped into a large, empty foyer. As she closed the door, Mrs. Welkins gestured toward a closed door. "Go right on in, ma'am. Mr. St. Claire thought you might be stopping by today."

The remark made Julia's muscles tighten with irritation. The arrogance of the man. She ought to leave right now. Impossible. She needed to see him, hear his voice. With another nod, she moved through the door into a study. Candles lit the room, while navy blue curtains covered the windows and blocked out the sunshine.

"Come in and shut the door."

The deep notes of his voice wrapped around her, caressing her with instant warmth. Her eyes quickly adjusting to the dim light, she turned her head to see him sitting in a large library chair a small distance from where she stood. The door behind her clicked closed as she obeyed his command.

Long legs stretched out in front of him, and crossed at the ankles, he was the epitome of a nonchalant rake. He didn't wear a jacket, and the white of his shirt was a sharp contrast to the deep wine leather of the chair. Swallowing her nervousness, she searched his shadowed features. There was just enough light to reveal his profile, but his eyes were unreadable in the dark. A tremor shot through her. "I . . . I came by because I thought you were ill."

"As you can see, I'm quite well." There was no hint of emotion in his words at all. He merely stated facts, nothing more.

She frowned. The man wasn't even going to stand up to greet her. Would he not give one quarter? She'd come to him, just as he'd demanded. Worry had prompted her to come, but she would have come even if she'd known he was hale and hearty. Annoyed by his silence, she ventured deeper into the room.

"If you're well, why do you have the drapes pulled and all the candles lit? Why aren't you at the shipping office?

"Because I've been waiting for you." There was a rough edge to his voice as he watched her from his seat. He didn't move, but she could see the tension in his body.

"Arrogant as always."

"No, Julia. Far from it." She watched him uncurl from his chair with unbelievable speed. "In fact, I'd just about given up hope."

"I simply came to see if you were ill." Her body tensed as he drew near, his head bending toward her. A moment later his mouth brushed lightly against her ear.

"Liar."

The heat from his body was an inferno across her skin. Tilting her head back, she looked up into his eyes. His expression was open and blazing with hunger. She swallowed hard as she tried to speak, but her throat was dry. She wanted him to touch her, but he didn't move. Being so close to him created a knot of tension in her stomach that settled in the sensitive spot beneath her belly.

"Tell me why you're really here, Julia."

The words formed in her head, but it was too difficult to speak them. He was asking for complete surrender, and it wasn't something she was ready to give him. "I already told you. I wanted to ensure that you were in good health."

A split second later, Morgan wheeled away from her and threw himself down into his chair. "Now that you've seen I'm well, there's no need for you to stay."

Surprised by his reaction, she frowned. The man was impossible. Hadn't she done as he asked? She'd come to him. Perhaps under the guise of ensuring his health was satisfactory, but she was here nonetheless. Why did he have to be so stubborn? Why did she have surrender to him completely? Frustrated, she clenched her hands and one balled fist burrowed its way through the silk swags draping her hips to press into her leg.

"Blast you St. Claire. I came as you asked--no--demanded. What more do you want from me?"

Silence filled the room, and she tried to read his expression as she glared at him. Why was she standing here, allowing him to control her like this? But was he really controlling her? The thought took her breath away. No. He wasn't the one controlling, she was. She was allowing his actions to control her own. She could easily leave, but she was choosing not to. All she had to do was leave, but she knew she didn't want to walk away from him. Her love held her here.

"Undress for me." The soft command pierced her turbulent thoughts. She stared at him in amazement.

"Wha … What?"

"Stand in front of me and remove your clothes. Slowly."

"You're mad," she snapped.

"I've seen to it that no one will interrupt us."

"But … I…."

"Afraid?" He asked with a smile.

The arrogant smile held a dash of playfulness, and it was the only reason why she didn't reach for a nearby vase to hurl at him. As he reclined back into the massive armchair, he arched an eyebrow at her. Tension threaded its way through her as she narrowed her gaze and watched him closely.

He looked as amused now as he had the night she'd stolen his handkerchief. She gritted her teeth at the thought. It infuriated her how well he could control his need. He'd not hidden his desire, but he kept it so firmly in check. It had been maddening to have him so close just a moment ago and know that she'd not been able to tempt him into losing control. And now … now he wanted her to undress for him while he watched.

Just once she'd like to turn the tables on the man. Tease him, tempt him. Drive him to distraction until he… Her thoughts crashed into one another. Morgan had always been the one pleasuring her. What if she pleasured him? The idea made her suck in a sharp breath.

Could she be that daring? Was this what Morgan had been trying to show her all along? That she could be as powerful as he in their lovemaking if she only had the courage to try. She stiffened her spine, then whirled around and hurried toward the door before she changed her mind.

Turning the key in the lock, she glanced over her shoulder. He was standing as if ready to prevent her leaving. Perhaps he wasn't as sure of himself as he led her to believe. The thought made her smile. Today, Morgan St. Claire was going to get exactly what he wanted and more.

Facing him, she pressed her hand against her throat, her eyes locking with his. The stillness in the room was so intense their breaths were audible. They stood there, staring at each other in a battle of silent wills until he sank back down into his chair. He'd never seen her like this before. There was a sultry confidence in her gaze that made his cock stir in his trousers.

Enthralled, he watched her hand glide over her breast and down to her stomach. There was an uninhibited air about her that amazed him, excited him. It made him hard. Made him crave the heat he knew resided between her thighs. Mesmerized, he could only watch in mute fascination as she slowly undid a button on her dress and then another.

The candlelight shimmered across her skin, giving her a luminescent quality. The woman from the portrait met his gaze boldly and without shame. Her eyes never left his as she slipped her dress off a creamy shoulder. God, she was making him hot. Hotter than he'd been the night she'd come to his bed.

She pushed the dress to one side as she continued to disrobe. His mouth went dry as her corset came off and he saw the light mocha color of her nipples through her thin chemise. The sight made his cock jump with a cry for action. But he didn't move. He couldn't. It might break the spell she was casting on him, and he didn't want that to happen. Not yet.

Moments later she stood in front of him completely exposed. With a half smile curving her lips, she reached up to undo her hair. The movement lifted her breasts higher, and he ached to flick his tongue across her hard nipples. Silky, burnt sienna tresses tumbled down onto her shoulders and dipped to brush across the stiff peaks.

"Is this what you wanted me to do, Morgan?" The husky tone of her voice made his cock jump with anticipation.

"Yes," he growled.

She moved toward him and knelt at his feet. He smelled the lemony scent of her hair. There was also the scent of her passion. It was a hot musk, and it teased his senses until he was rigid with longing.

Not once did her gaze waver from his face. His cock rubbed against his clothing in a demanding cry for release. In silence, she rested her hand on his hard length. The moment she did so, he sucked in a deep breath. God almighty, she was a siren. She'd bewitched him. He didn't move as her fingers undid his trousers. As his cock sprang out in eager anticipation of plunging into her heated depths, he struggled to control his ragged breathing. No other woman had ever wrapped him in knots like this.

One elegant finger traced a line from the tip of him down to his ballocks. It was a light touch, but it generated an excruciating need for more. The warmth of her hand encircled him, and he released a groan of pleasure. Candlelight threw one side of her face into the shadows, but the gleam in her hazel eyes warned him she knew exactly what she was doing.

It was a confidence he'd not seen in her eyes before. It was clear she knew how she was making him feel, and she was reveling in the knowledge. He watched her head descend toward his cock. Was she--?

"Christ Jesus," he rasped as her tongue stroked up the length of him and swirled around the tip of his cock. The seductive caress made his erection strain to its longest length. Barely able to control his need, he slid his hands through her hair, massaging her scalp as she blew a hot, yet cool breeze across his bare skin.

Her tongue slid over him once more before her beautiful mouth wrapped around him in a tight grip. The flick of her tongue over the ridge of him pulled another groan from him as he watched her sliding her mouth up and down his cock. He couldn't help but watch, his body shuddering at her touch as she sucked on him. It was the most erotic thing he'd ever witnessed.

Hell, if he were honest, no woman had ever given him this much pleasure. He'd had the best suck on his cock, and not one of them had come close to making him want to explode the way she did. She slid her mouth up and down his hard length faster now, the friction creating an exquisite pain that needed an outlet. Closing his eyes, he rocked his hips against her mouth, his cock sliding deeper into her throat. She took it willingly.

"Oh, God, that feels good. Oh, yes. Sweet Jesus, yes."

The hoarse words echoed above her head, and she grew elated with his reaction. He liked what she was doing to him. This was what he'd meant when he'd told her he wanted the bold woman in the portrait.

Another groan rumbled out of his chest, and she tightened her mouth around him. She hadn't expected to enjoy pleasing him this way, but she did. It was a powerful sensation to know she was responsible for his raspy breaths and growls of excitement. Then there was the spicy male scent of him, the salty taste at the very tip of him.

Her tongue swirled around the cap of his erection as she took delight in tugging another cry of pleasure from him. For the first time in her life, she was in control. But it was a consensual control. His hands threaded through her hair as he guided her, encouraged her to take in more of his hard length.

Excited by her new-found power, she wanted to hear him say how much she liked what she was doing to him. With a lingering stroke of her tongue, she retreated, her fingers brushing against the sacs beneath his rigid length.

The touch of her fingers on his ballocks made him jump and then cool air swept over his hot cock. His eyes flew open to watch her rise to her feet and stand in front of him, the reddish-brown curls at the apex of her thighs so close and yet so far away.

He struggled not to lose control of his faculties as she trailed her fingers over her breasts and caressed her nipples. In disbelief, he watched one hand trail down over her stomach to part her velvety folds and stroke herself.

"Do you like watching me like this, Morgan?"

The husky sound of her voice tantalized him, while the sultry twist of her lips teased him as he watched her play with herself. His eyes caught a glimpse of cream on her fingers, and he growled. It was time to end this tempting display and take what his body demanded. Christ, his body wasn't just demanding satisfaction it screamed for it.

He reached out for her, but she took a quick step back. A small smile curved her mouth, as she trailed her fingers across her rigid nipples again. The look of astonishment on his face pleased her. For once, she was in control, and she liked it.

Cupping her breasts, she rolled her thumbs over the stiff peaks, her fingertips skating over her dimpled areoles. He didn't take his eyes off of her, and the desire in his expression thrilled her. "You didn't answer me, Morgan, do you like watching me?"

"Yes,." His voice was hoarse as he rose to his feet and stepped toward her. She retreated again.

"Do you want me?" Heart pounding, she waited for his reply.

"Damn it, you know I do. I want you now."

The growled response made her smile as he stepped forward. She reached out her hand and pressed it against his chest, stopping him in his tracks. Beneath the palm of her hand his heart beat a fast pace. His breathing was rough as if he'd run a great distance. "How badly do you want me?"

His gaze narrowed and she wet her lips as he stared down into her eyes. "What game are you playing at, Julia?"

"This is not a game. I simply need to know how badly you want me." She deliberately reached out to delve her hand into his open trousers and grasped him in a tight grip. "Tell me."

"God in heaven, woman, do you want me to beg?" He groaned.

"Would you?" She held her breath as she watched his jaw flex with tension.

"Yes," he rasped as he caught her shoulders in a rough grip. "I'd move heaven and earth for you. I'll give you anything you ask, just let me love you."

Her hand slid off his erection and she pressed her body against him. The tip of his phallus pressed into her curls as she pulled his head down toward hers. Brushing her mouth against his, she laced her tongue over his lips. "That's all I wanted to hear."

The groan rumbling from deep in his chest reverberated over her skin, and she melted into him as his mouth seared hers in a hot kiss. Beneath her hands, the soft fabric of his shirt interfered with her need to touch him. As his tongue swept into her mouth, her fingers rushed to undo the buttons of his shirt.

Eager to feel his hard muscles beneath her hands, she tugged his shirt open and glided her fingertips across the hard ridges of his chest. The heat of his kiss stirred a hot need in her belly and it sped through her limbs until she was consumed by it. As he discarded his shirt in a rough movement, he pulled her closer. Her nipples tingled from the sensation of brushing against his chest.

His mouth slanted off hers and blazed a path of heat down her throat to one breast. A hot tongue swirled around her nipple and the erotic touch made her legs wobble underneath her. The masculine, spicy scent of him filled her senses as her body cried out for his possession. A moan parted her mouth as her fingertips dug into his shoulders in an effort to remain standing.

"Oh, God, Morgan. I want you. I want to feel you inside me."

Lifting his head, his thumb continued to stroke the sharp peak of her breast. He shuddered at the way her skin glowed from the heat of desire, and her eyes were partially closed in a sultry look that made his blood boil with need. She'd come to him. He'd almost despaired of her doing so. But he needed to hear the words from her.

"Say it, Julia." He watched her eyes open wide to meet his as hesitation flitted over her lovely features. "It's only three words, my love."

She swallowed hard as she shook her head. "Morgan, please…."

He pressed his forehead against hers. "I need to hear you say it, sweetheart."

"I … I love … you," she stuttered.

The moment the words were spoken, a sense of relief flooded through her. She'd done it. She'd actually admitted her feelings for him. There was a sense of freedom in having done so. As he exhaled a deep breath, she realized he'd been unsure of her. The knowledge surprised her.

He'd always presented such a sure and confident façade. To think that Morgan St. Claire, renowned womanizer, might be uncertain of her was astonishing. In the next moment, his hard kiss against her mouth drove all thought from her head. The taste of him on her lips made the flame in her nether regions spread to every nerve ending in her body.

Heat covered her, as they sank down to the large Brussels carpet. As he removed the rest of his clothing, she pressed feverish kisses along the line of his jaw and down to the base of his throat. With a low, throaty growl, he cupped her face and slid his tongue past her lips to explore the warmth of her mouth.

Their tongues mated in a hot duel of desire as he pulled her downward until they were entwined in each other's arms on the floor. With each thrust of his tongue, his cock grew harder and it throbbed for the heat of her.

Unable to wait any more, he rolled onto his back, pulling her with him. Silky skin caressed the pads of his fingers as he grasped her round hips, then with a sharp tug he settled her slick velvet folds over his hardness. As her honeyed sweetness slid over him, coating him with heat, he surged up into her with a guttural cry of pleasure.

Christ, she felt good wrapped around his cock. Her muscles clutched and squeezed him with intense pleasure, and for the first time in his life he knew he wasn't going to be able to prolong the experience. He'd craved her for too long. It would be fast this time, but there would be plenty of time later to indulge in each other.

The spasms rippling over his hard length came fast and furious as she shuddered with need and love over top of him. Arching her back, she pressed her hands into the top of his thighs meeting his thrusts with equal measure. Desire curled tight in her belly as she instinctively increased the pace of their joining. Her senses flooded with sensation, she cried out as he drove up into her one final time.

Wrapped in an exquisite mist of decadent pleasure, she heard him utter a low cry before he throbbed inside her. For several long moments she didn't move. Instead, she let the shudders cascading through her subside before she relaxed. Spent from the intensity of their union, she fell forward as he pulled her close against him, nestling her against his chest. The keen emotions coursing through her veins frightened her and yet convinced her that she belonged in this man's arms. Warm lips pressed against her forehead as a soft laugh rumbled out of him.

"You continue to amaze me, my sweet. I always knew you had a bold streak in you, but you've surpassed anything I'd imagined."

The tenderness in his voice tugged at her heart strings, her love for him opening her heart completely. Raising herself up on her hands, she smiled down at him.

"Does that mean you like it when I'm naughty?"

Another laugh parted his lips and he nodded. "Absolutely. And when we're married, I'll teach you how to be naughtier still."

His words laced her muscles with tension, and with a quick movement, she slid off him and climbed to her feet. How could she make him understand that she was more than willing to be his mistress? Eager in fact. But marriage? No, that she couldn't do. Without looking at him, she found her undergarments and proceeded to dress.

"Out with it, Julia. Tell me what's going on in that complex brain of yours."

With a glance over her shoulder, she saw him sit up and arch his brow at her. One leg bent, his arm rested on top of his knee. She'd never seen a more resplendent picture of male beauty. Strong, muscular and seductive, he stole her breath away. His gaze narrowed when she didn't answer. Scrambling to his feet, he caught her arm and turned her to face him.

"Something's wrong."

"No. Not really." She grimaced. What was she supposed to say to make him understand how she felt? She'd come here because she loved him, but that didn't change her feelings about marriage. The matrimonial state would strip her of her rights, her independence. Being his mistress would empower her. It would give her the wherewithal to leave him if he ever betrayed her. "A few moments ago, you told me you'd do anything for me."

Relief eased the lines of tension in his face. "Is that what this is all about? You want me to do something for you."

"Yes. I want to be your mistress."

"What?" Disbelief stiffened his features, and his fingers bit painfully into her shoulders making her wince.

"It's the best solution." She bit her lip as she watched anger storm over his face.

"Best for whom?" He pushed her away from him then turned to snatch up his clothing from the floor. "Christ Jesus, you came here knowing full well you had no intention of marrying me."

"No, that's not true," she cried out. The bitter accusation sliced into her heart with the sharpness of a blade. "I didn't plan any of this."

"What do you take me for, Julia? A fool? You said you loved me, what else was I supposed to think?" The icy note in his voice frightened her as she watched him jerk on his trousers with unrestrained violence.

"I do love you," she said quietly. Sick at heart, she continued to dress while her gaze kept track of his angry movements. She should have known he would react this way. As he shrugged into his shirt, he whipped around to face her.

"Tell me why you refuse to marry me."

"I … it's just that … I just can't be with you in that way, Morgan."

"That's not an answer and you know it," he ground out through clenched teeth.

"I told you I loved you, what more do you want? I will not give up my independence." Her tone defiant in the face of his anger, she tugged viciously at the laces of her corset. The man was just being stubborn. Why couldn't he be satisfied with the fact that she was willing to be with him? Admitting that she loved him had been difficult enough. She grabbed her dress up off the floor and threw it on over her head.

"I'll tell you what I want," he said in a tight voice. "I want you to love me with all your heart, not just a part of it."

"I do love you," she said once more, her voice filled with frustration.

"If you did, you'd marry me. You'd trust me not to hurt you. Love involves trust, Julia ... you can't have one without the other." The quiet resignation in his voice told her she was losing the battle to make him understand why she couldn't marry him. It shot a bolt of panic through her.

"Please, Morgan, I can't. Don't you understand? I can't take that sort of risk."

"Life's a risk, Julia, without it there's no reward. I want all of your love, not just a piece of it. You're my passion, and if I can't have all of you, then God help me, but I'll find a way to live without you." Without looking at her, he strode toward the study door and turned the key. A white knuckled hand gripped the doorknob as he yanked the door open. "I think you know the way out."

Stunned, she watched him leave the room, taking her heart and soul with him.

Chapter 10

Storming up the stairs, Morgan reached the second floor landing and strode down the hall to the master bedroom. His anger boiled inside him with the force of a steam engine over its limit. The door to his room flew back from his violent rage to crack loudly against the wall. Damn her.

He paced the room, his body tense with frustration. Halting his frenzied stride he slammed the bottom of his fist into the window frame. In the street below, he saw Julia hesitate in front of her carriage. For a split second, he held his breath as she turned back toward the front door. An instant later, she whirled about and climbed into the vehicle.

It had never occurred to him that she might have the audacity to offer herself up as his mistress. He didn't want a mistress, he wanted a wife. Someone to love him in spite of his faults. Someone to grow old with.

There had been no hesitation in her when she'd strutted for him in that dance of seduction she'd performed. She hadn't wavered in tantalizing his cock with her mouth or her honey pot. And yet afterward, she'd blatantly refused to commit herself. She'd been unwilling to trust him.

Hell, she'd even admitted she was in love with him, but she'd stopped short at making the commitment he wanted her to make. What was it going to take to convince her that he could be trusted?

Once again his fist thudded against the window jamb, and he strode to the middle of the room. Why was he letting her get to him this way? He needed to let her go. There wasn't anything he could do to change her mind.

He'd fought the best fight possible, and yet he'd lost. He shoved his hand through his hair before rubbing the back of his neck. He'd go to her. No. It would be a pointless action. Julia was stubborn. When she made up her mind about something, there was little point in trying to alter her opinion. But if he thought for one moment that it would make a difference, he would gladly humble himself again.

God, the irony of it all. How many times had he had women beg him to stay with them? Beg him to love them. He'd never been cruel when breaking off an affair, but now he fully understood the pain those women had experienced. Now he was the one willing to beg. Willing to give up his precious pride and beg her to marry him.

What the hell was he going to do? Worse yet, what was he to do with this monstrosity of a house? The empty silence of it tugged at him with a wrenching ache. The sound of her laughter echoing in this room--this house--wasn't to be. Both hands clutched the back of his head as he stared down at the floor.

Living without her was going to be harder than anything he'd ever done before in his life. Not even his mother's cold rejection during his boyhood or his father's disinterest in him could equal the pain of losing Julia. And he'd lost her. The moment she'd refused to marry him, he'd known deep in his heart that he'd lost.

When she'd come through his study door, it had taken every inch of will power he possessed not to pull her into his arms and overwhelm her senses with lovemaking. But he'd promised himself to let her choose. He'd just never contemplated the notion that he could lose her.

His gut tightened with emotion, and he knew the only remedy for dealing with his pain was work. He'd work until he'd driven her out of his head, out of his blood. He'd work until he was numb from everything. The numbness would take away this ache inside him. With a grunt, he strode out of the bedroom to go to the office. There at least he could keep his mind focused on something other than Julia.

* * * *

The woman in the portrait smiled at her. A self-satisfied, confident smile. Glaring at the painting, she turned away from the artwork and started to pace the floor of her bedroom. Why couldn't she be like that woman? She wanted to, but she didn't know how. No, that wasn't true. How wasn't the problem, what she lacked was the courage to be that woman.

It had been more than two weeks since Morgan had stormed out of his study, leaving her to find her own way out of his house. She was a fool. Her refusal to marry him was the worst decision she'd ever made. Choice hadn't been an issue when she married Oscar. Her mother had seen to that. But Morgan was different. She could have agreed to his marriage proposal if she'd only had the fortitude to do so.

The sound of the door bell echoed softly through her room. Unable to help herself, she raced out into the upstairs hall. When she reached the top of the steps, she struggled to keep her disappointment from showing as she met Catherine's arched look.

"Well, that's a fine look to greet me with," her cousin said with a bite of humor. "I take it you were hoping to see someone else."

Leading the way into the upstairs salon, she shook her head. "No, not exactly ... I just thought--oh it's not important."

"You thought I was Morgan St. Claire."

The statement made her jerk her head around to eye her cousin. "I did not."

Ignoring the protest, Catherine swept across the room to the fireplace. As she tugged off her gloves in precise movements she gave Julia a stern look. "Do not treat me like I'm an addle-brained halfwit. You were hoping St. Claire was charging up those stairs to whisk you away."

"Now you're being ridiculous." Julia flipped her hand at her cousin in a dismissive gesture.

"No, that would be your forte, my dear." Catherine shook her finger at her. "I thought you had more backbone than this."

Julia turned away from the disappointment in her cousin's eyes. "Even if I found the courage to do something, it's too late now. He doesn't want me any more."

"How do you know that?"

"I just do. Our last parting was far from amicable." She flinched at the memory of Morgan's cold anger as he stood at the door of his study telling her to see herself out. The claw marks on her heart still lay open and bleeding from that moment.

"Well, it would seem St. Claire has forgotten about that little misunderstanding." Catherine sent her a triumphant look. "I saw the man this morning on Rotten Row, and what do you think the first thing out of his mouth was? It was to ask about you."

The declaration made her heart leap and she turned away from Catherine to hide the hope she knew had to be lighting her face. He'd asked about her. Even despite his anger, he'd inquired as to how she was. Alarm shot through her. Oh, God. Catherine was not known for her discretion, but rather for her blunt speech. What had she told him?

Whirling back around, she scowled at her cousin. "What did you tell him? If you told him I was pining away for him, Catherine, I shall ... I shall make certain Lord Blakemore finds out about that little tryst you had with Lord Dunham last year."

"Rubbish," Catherine half snorted with disgust, "It was hardly a tryst, and I could care less what Lord Blakemore thinks."

Julia frowned in puzzlement at the blithe statement. Of course Catherine cared what Blakemore thought of her. There was a long history between the two, and her cousin's cavalier response surprised her. Had something happened between the couple?

"But I thought you and he--"

"Don't you dare try to change the subject." Consternation flashed in the other woman's eyes but she didn't give Julia time to interrupt. "This conversation is about you and how you're going to resolve this matter. It's high time you go after the man."

"That's impossible," Julia snapped.

"Nothing's impossible. Go to him."

"I can't." She turned away from her cousin with a vehement shake of her head. Catherine crossed the room and wrapped an arm around Julia's shoulders.

"What is it you're afraid of, dearest?"

The gentle quiet of her relative's voice made her swallow a hot knot inside her throat. Closing her eyes, she stifled the tears threatening to spill down her cheeks. "I'm afraid of loving him so much that I'll lose myself--the person who I am."

"Is your life now--without him--better than loving him so much you forget where he ends and you begin?" Catherine's softly worded question tightened the vise around her heart.

For more than two weeks she'd suffered more torment and pain than anything Oscar had ever inflicted on her. Her body, mind and soul cried out for Morgan every waking minute. Life had become bleak and dark. It was as bad, if not worse, than when she was suffering the bedevilment of her late husband. And now Catherine had reminded her of Morgan's words. Life was a risk. Without it there was no reward.

Those words were the key to her happiness. Convincing Morgan she trusted him could be accomplished only one way. Words would no longer work. He would always question her decision. Maybe not openly, but it would always be between them. She had to show him how much she trusted him, and there was only one way to do that. The question was whether or not she had the courage to go through with it. Could she make him understand that no matter what the risk, she was willing to do anything just to be with him? There was only one way to find out.

Turning her head, she saw the empathy in Catherine's eyes. It reassured her. "Did Morgan say what his plans were over the next few days?"

With a conspiratorial smile, her cousin nodded. "I believe he did. Shall we formulate your plan of attack?"

Filled with fear and yet a delicious anticipation, Julia nodded. Soon she would know whether or not her gamble would reap the love and happiness with Morgan she so desperately wanted.

* * * *

Morgan wearily entered his darkened house, closing the front door behind him. Rolling his head in a half circle, he attempted to relieve some of the tension in his neck. Before entering his study, he turned up the gaslight in the foyer. Embers glowing in the hearth were the only light illuminating the room. The liquor cabinet enticed him as it had for almost three weeks now. Opening the door on the piece of furniture, he pulled out a decanter of whiskey. Why he ever thought work would push Julia out of his head was beyond his comprehension.

Despite his best efforts to bury himself in work, thoughts of her continuously filled his head. He found himself listening for the sound of her voice or a glimpse of her as she darted back into the office she'd been using. But she'd not been in the shipping office since that day in his study.

He should have agreed to keep her as his mistress. At least she'd be with him now. But that hadn't satisfied him. Instead he'd pigheadedly demanded more, asking for more than she could give. Even now the memory of her touch, her scent, made him ache. His cock grew hard and pressed against his stomach.

"Bloody hell," he muttered as he splashed a generous portion of liquor into a glass. The decanter top rattled as he dropped the stopper back into the container's neck. With a jerk, he tossed the whiskey down his throat in one deep gulp. He welcomed the fire that burned its way to his stomach. It was a reflection of the pain ripping him apart inside.

Eager to occupy his head with something other than thoughts of Julia, he took the decanter and glass over to his desk. With a flick of his wrist he turned up the flame on the gaslight lamp sitting at one corner of the workspace. Shrugging out of his jacket, he tugged his tie off his neck and undid the first few buttons of his shirt.

He grunted with weariness as he threw himself into his chair.

From his seat, he stared at the messages stacked neatly on the desktop. On top of the stack he recognized a note from Mrs. Welkins. Listlessly, he lifted the folded missive off the top of the stack and opened it.

Mr. St. Claire,

A courier delivered a package for you just before I left. The instructions were to place it in your bedroom, and I have left it there for you. I also left a cold supper for you in the kitchen.

Regards, M. Welkins

He tossed the note to one side and leaned forward to pull the whiskey decanter toward him. Another liberal bout of liquor filled his glass. This time though he only drank half of what he poured. What sort of package was upstairs in his room? He couldn't remember ordering anything that required delivery to this mausoleum. Picking up the note again, he studied his housekeeper's writing as he took another drink from his glass. With a frown, he got to his feet. If the woman had wanted to pique his interest, she'd done so. He was curious to find out what was in this mysterious package. His glass thudded softly against the top of the desk as he set it down. With quick strides he moved out into the foyer and climbed the stairs. Walking down the hall toward his room, he snorted in disgust. He should have brought the whiskey decanter and his glass with him. It was just as easy to get drunk in his room as the study. At least he could have wound up in bed instead of the uncomfortable... He froze as he opened the door to his bedroom.

Christ Jesus.

He was dreaming. It had to be his imagination. Nothing else could explain this exquisite picture. She was the portrait come to life. Reclined against a bed of navy blue pillows trimmed in gold, Julia was a feast for his eyes. The first and only time he'd seen the painting, he'd memorized every little nuance, every colorful detail, but none of what he remembered matched this erotic picture.

Candles filled the room, and their light reflected the auburn tints in her hair. Just like the painting, her hair was swept around to drape over one shoulder. It splayed across the navy coverlet she lay on top of. She was incredible. In the candlelight her skin possessed a golden hue and it beckoned him like a siren.

The nipples on her firm breasts were already rigid, ready for his mouth to tease. Her hand rested on her softly rounded belly. It made him want to touch her there. No, he wanted to touch her everywhere. He wanted to rut with her until he was exhausted, and then he wanted to do it with her again.

Even from where he stood he could smell the tart lemony scent of her. His gaze slid downward to the triangle of wiry curls just below her hand. He suddenly realized it was impossible to swallow when one's mouth was dry. What the hell was she doing here? Was this another way to torture him? If she thought to come in here and tease him simply for her own pleasure, then she could leave before he even touched her.

But, God, he wanted to touch her. His cock hardened and throbbed a desperate signal to him. He ignored it. Folding his arms across his chest, his fingers gripped his biceps. It was a struggle to keep his aroused state under control as he cleared his throat and fought to find his voice.

"What are you doing here, Julia?" Hell, his voice sounded like he was suffering from a sore throat. The small smile curling her mouth upward on one side said she knew just how the sight of her was affecting him.

"You told me once that you wanted to see the woman in the portrait in your bed."

She stretched out her hand to him as she spoke. With great difficulty he suppressed the urge to go to her, and his fingers dug deeper into his arm. Damn it, he wanted to know what game she was playing. She'd done this to him once before, and he wasn't willing to go through that hell again.

"I seem to recall you telling me the woman in that painting didn't exist."

The smile on her lips disappeared and a shadow darkened her gaze until the hazel color blended into a mossy green. Her expression grew troubled as she sat up straight. The movement sent a lock of hair tumbling down over a shoulder to curl around one nipple. He suppressed an achy groan at the sight.

"I didn't think she existed either, but you showed me how to be the woman you want."

"That still doesn't explain why you're here." The harsh statement made her flinch, but she didn't retreat.

"I'm here because I love you, Morgan. I'll be your mistress, I'll marry you, I'll do whatever you want, but I can't live without you."

There, she'd said the words. Made her declaration. What would he do? She sucked in a sharp breath as she watched the emotions playing across his features. He stood still as a statue as he studied her. It was impossible to read his thoughts, and she trembled as she realized he might very well reject her.

His eyes narrowed as he arched an eyebrow. "If you think to make a fool of me, Julia, you're mistaken."

"I'm the one who's been the fool. I don't blame you for not trusting me, but would you at least give me a chance to prove my sincerity?" She searched his expression for some inkling as to his thoughts, but he was closed off from her. Each and every one of her nerve endings was screaming with tension.

"If all I wanted was for you to satisfy my unruly cock, Julia, I would never have proposed marriage. You didn't trust me to love you, so tell me why I should trust you now?" The bitterness in his voice tore at her heart. She'd hurt him. Badly. It was evident from the harsh twist of his lips.

"I knew you might think that. I knew there was only one way to prove that I trust you implicitly." Swallowing the tiny ball of fear in her throat, she reminded herself that this was Morgan. The man she loved. A man who'd declared his love for her time and time again. Slowly, she reclined back onto the bed and reached for the black silk tie she'd knotted to the headboard earlier.

The implacable expression on his face disappeared as she slid her hands into the noose she'd created and grasping the end of the tie with her teeth she pulled it snug around her wrists. The horror in his gaze reassured her that she had made the right choice. He loved her and didn't want to cause her pain.

In three long strides he was at the side of the bed, his hands reaching for the silk strap that bound her to his bed. With a vehement shake of her head she stopped him.

"Morgan, no!"

Staring up at him, she saw the rapid rise and fall of his chest as his eyes fixated on her bound wrists. The tension in him was visible to the naked eye. She saw a muscle flex in his cheek as he swallowed hard. Her gaze drifted downward to where his erection was stiff and hard, his trousers stretched tight across his arousal. He was hot and excited. She could tell by the way he held himself rigid. She looked up at him, but he averted his gaze in a manner that told her he was appalled at being so aroused by the sight of her bound to the bed.

"You don't have to do this, sweetheart," he rasped. She heard the desire and heat in his voice that he was trying so hard to suppress.

"Yes, I do." She swallowed again, but this time with something akin to anticipation. "I need to prove how much I trust you. Not just to you, but to myself as well."

"Bloody hell, Julia." He shoved a hand through his hair, the movement taut with mixed emotions. "You're asking me to make you relive--"

"No! No, I'm asking you to make love to me, Morgan."

What her husband had done to her had nothing to do with love. But when Morgan touched her, there was no pain, only tenderness and passion. She met his eyes with a steady look. A look she hoped showed him how much she trusted him.

Inside her chest, her heart raced with a bevy of emotions she couldn't separate. Desire, fear and love mingled together in one consuming blaze that sped through her veins until her body was hot with need.

Silently protesting with a sharp shake of his head, he stared down at her for a long tense moment. Raw passion and hot desire burned in his eyes as she watched him struggle to control his aroused state. His reluctance told her everything she needed to know. This wonderful, passionate man loved her. He'd never hurt her. Because of his love she could vanquish all the demons Oscar had tortured her with over the years.

"Just this once, my love," she pleaded softly. "Do this for me. For us. I don't want anything between us."

"Christ Jesus…." His voice faded into nothing as his hot gaze swept over the length of her. He looked as if he could devour her from where he stood.

"It excites you?" The breathy sound of her voice surprised her. She realized she was excited too.

"God, yes. You've no idea how much."

"Then show me," she whispered as her eyes locked with his.

A dark groan broke from him as he pressed one knee into the bed and bent over her to capture her lips with his. The fiery hunger in his kiss echoed the craving pulling at her insides. Without the use of her hands she couldn't pull him closer so she lifted her head to return his kiss with equal passion.

Her mouth parted beneath his and she teased her tongue across his lips. His sharp intake of breath allowed her tongue to dance with his as he deepened their kiss. There was the sharp taste of whiskey in his mouth, and she breathed in the faint scent of bergamot. God, she wanted him. Never before had her need for him been this intense, this compelling.

Slowly, he sank down onto the mattress beside her, his hands sliding across her skin in gentle exploration. The soft lawn of his shirt tickled her breasts as he pressed her into the bed. Hovering over her, he teased her mouth with his teeth. Gently he tugged on her lower lip as he brushed the lower half of his body across her stomach in a suggestive act.

She was melting. It was the only way she could describe it. Desire circulated in her blood like a raging fever. Without thinking, she tried to reach for him, but the tie holding her hands didn't give way.

This was what she'd wanted. A way to prove to him how much she loved him. Trusted him. But it was also maddening being unable to touch him.

His hard phallus rubbed over the top of her thigh and a pleasurable ache settled in her nether region. Writhing beneath him, she whimpered at the need growing inside her. His mouth feathered kisses across the ridge of her shoulder, and she gasped when the rough pad of his thumb rubbed over one nipple.

The heated touch made her back arch, pressing her breast into the cup of his hand. Her submissive movement drew a sharp hiss of excitement from him, as his mouth streaked across her skin to find the hard peak. The moment his lips clamped down on her nipple, she moaned with pleasure. While he suckled her, a strong hand roamed down until his palm pressed against the apex of her thighs.

Desire streaked its way across her skin and another moan escaped her as she moved her hips in an attempt to have him touch her more intimately. Dear Lord, in all the moments they'd been together this one was the most potent yet. Bound to the bed, she knew she was completely at his mercy and she loved it. She loved it because she knew he wouldn't hurt her. It was the most freeing experience she'd ever known.

His fingers stroked the inside of her thigh, teasing her with a feather light caress over her curls before drawing back. It made her body taut with need and she shifted her hips again in an effort to make him touch her.

"Oh please, Morgan … please, I need you to touch me."

"How do you want me to touch you, sweetheart?" His finger parted her slick folds and rubbed over the sensitive nub of flesh inside. She immediately bucked against his touch, and his voice grew raspy. "Like this? Is this what you want?"

"Oh yes. God yes," she cried out with pleasure as he slid his finger in and out of her. Numb to everything but the pleasure of his touch, she thrust her hips upward to match his erotic strokes. A moment later, she was suddenly deprived of his touch. She moaned her protest as he slid off the bed and removed his clothing.

With deliberate slowness he undressed in front of her. Naked before her, he grabbed his rock hard staff and stroked himself. "Is this what you want, sweetheart? Do you want to feel me filling you, driving into you until you come all over this hard cock of mine?"

She gasped in shock, but he saw the flicker of excitement in her eyes. Mute, she nodded as her gaze watched him stroking himself in a languid fashion. Laying on the bed before him, tied in such a submissive position had to be the most erotic thing he'd ever seen. It made him hotter than he'd ever been for any woman in his life.

There was no fear in her gaze, only desire. God, he needed to feel her wrapped around him, her muscles squeezing him with exquisite tightness. He reached out to run his hand over a long, silky leg. A soft sound escaped her at his touch and he smiled down at her.

Returning to the bed, he hovered over her for a moment, the tip of him pressing against her curls. Agitated, she squirmed beneath him in an effort to make him penetrate her. He resisted, but barely. Her eyes were closed, and he swallowed hard. He wanted her to see the love in his eyes as he took her this way.

"Look at me," he growled.

As her eyes flew open to meet his, he plunged into her slick heated depths completely. God, but she was tight. Desire and love glowed in her gaze as he repeated his thrust. It was like having a velvet vise wrapped around him. With ever increasing rhythm he stroked his cock against the hot friction of her cunny.

Seconds later, the glow of ecstasy warmed her face as his name flew from her lips and she shattered around his cock. The intensity of her rippling contractions tugged at him with increasing pressure until with one last thrust he exploded inside her. Still shuddering in her hot depths, he reached out with one hand and released her from the bindings holding her hostage.

The moment her hands were free, he rolled onto his side and pulled her with him. A tremor lanced through her and she buried her face into his chest. The silence between them was warm and drowsy as she breathed in the hot earthy scent of him.

Happiness and love swelled inside her. He'd given her not only his heart, but her freedom as well. Without Morgan's love, she would never have been able to escape the demons of self-doubt that Oscar had instilled in her. More than that, she'd overcome her deepest fears to show Morgan how much she loved him.

His lips pressed against her forehead and she tilted her head back to smile at him. The somber expression on his face stifled her happiness. Something was wrong. Had she failed to make him understand why she'd chosen to do what she'd done?

"Morgan, I--"

A warm finger pressed against her lips. "Shhh. It's all right. I was simply thinking how precious a gift you've just given me. Why?"

Her hand came up to hold his, and she kissed his palm. "I needed to make sure you understood that I trust you implicitly."

"Your coming here of your own accord was more than enough, sweetheart." His arm tightened around her in a protective manner. It made her feel safe.

"No," she murmured as she looked away from him. "I needed to destroy the demons Oscar left behind. I did it for me as much as I did it for you."

"And are they gone?" Despite the nonchalance of the question, she could hear the concern in his voice.

"Yes." Her gaze returned to his face as she smiled. "I should have listened when you told me that there were no rewards without risk."

"And you've realized the error of your ways." There was a light teasing note to his voice, and she tapped him playfully on his chest.

"You're far too arrogant, Morgan St. Claire."

"Perhaps, but I'm deeply in love, which brings us to the subject of our marriage." His gaze was intent as her searched her features. "Tomorrow, we're going to find someone to marry us, and until we do, you're not leaving my sight."

"I promise I won't run this time."

I know that sweetheart, but I'm not willing to give you the chance to have second thoughts. Besides, I can't think of anything more pleasurable than spending the rest of the night and early morning, making love to you."

Sighing gently, she nestled her cheek against his shoulder, content to remain there forever. The thought of the portrait flitted into her head. Had she really succeeded in becoming the woman Morgan had seen in the portrait? Was she only a figment of his imagination or did she really exist? With a quick movement, she forced Morgan onto his back and straddled him. Her hands braced on the bed above his shoulders, she leaned toward him.

"Tell me, St. Claire. This portrait you saw several weeks ago. Does the woman really exist or is she a figment of your imagination?"

Flames flickered in his beautiful brown eyes as a seductive smile curled his lips. "Yes, she's quite real. In fact, I'm certain I can retire my handkerchiefs for good."

"An excellent idea. Because I'm the last affair you're ever going to have, Morgan St. Claire."

Lowering her head she brushed her lips lightly over his as his erection jumped against her thigh. Warm hands cupped her and breathing a sigh into his mouth, she proceeded to show him exactly why Morgan St. Claire would never buy another monogrammed handkerchief for distribution.

Printed in the United States
67675LVS00002B/64-93